THE HUNT FOR TRUTH

THE HUNT FOR TRUTH

SURY PATRU VISWAM

NAVA WAVES
PUBLISHERS

Published by Nava Waves Publishers LLC, U.S.A.

The publisher is not responsible for websites (or their content) that are not owned by the publisher.

Cover design by Nava Waves Publishers.

First edition

ISBN – 978-1-952906-00-8 (eBook)

ISBN – 978-1-952906-01-5 (Paperback)

ISBN – 978-1-952906-02-2 (Hardcover)

For Indu and Akash
From the luckiest person in the world

September 11, 2001
1:30 AM
Delaware

THE DARKNESS of the night was flooded with a blinding flash as lightning pierced through the sky. It was then followed by an explosive thunder that shattered the stillness of the night. Within a few seconds, the sky opened up, and rain came crashing down from the heavens.

In the dark hours of the night, the off-road which takes you to New Castle County, the northernmost county of the state of Delaware, can always be counted to be deserted. It was precisely what the young couple, Chris and Anna Hendrix, hoped for when they took the exit leading to this secluded road. Both of them were pretty hammered as they left the sports bar, and they did not want to get pulled over by a cop. They were out late celebrating Chris getting an offer to join one of the top firms in the state. Getting a DUI is the last thing you need if you want to stay and grow in any prestigious firm.

Anna leaned over to turn up the volume as the song, "*With or Without You*," came on the radio.

"Do you remember?" Anna, visibly drunk, started to mouth the lyrics of one of the most romantic songs.

"Baby, how can I not!" Chris leaned over and kissed Anna on her full lips.

"What? What? Say it," Anna began to slurp her words.

"You are crazy to even think that I would forget," Chris placed his right hand on Anna's legs.

"Say it. Say it." Anna's voice began to quiver as Chris's hand began to slowly caress her upper thighs.

Chris stole a moment away from the meandering road to kiss Anna deeply and said, "Our song. The song we danced in our prom, before I …" Before Chris could complete his thought, Anna was on top of him; removing her top; kissing and full-on making out with him.

"Anna…." Chris moaned as Anna placed his hand on her breasts and helped him fondle.

"Let me pull over." As Chris began to pull over, Anna said, "No. Keep going. This reminds me of so much of our first road trip in college." Anna, sitting on top of Chris, twisted her body and hit the control to open the convertible top.

"Now, let us go back in time," Anna provocatively said, and ramped up the sexual temperature.

Chris, now barely able to keep his eyes on the curvy road, began to kiss on her breasts. The car started to swerve on the meandering path, and somehow Chris managed to miraculously keep it on the road and not crash into the woods.

Anna raised herself from Chris's lap and unzipped him. "Mr. Big Shot," Anna whispered in a sexually charged way and began to reach down.

Chris closed his eyes, surrendering his senses as Anna began to go down on him.

Thud. There was a sudden burst of loud sound as the car struck something, and it went flying over the top of the car, banging the windshield on its way.

"What the hell happened!" Chris screamed, trying to regain control of the vehicle as it began to swerve from the collision's impact. The impact threw Anna backward, and her head coiled backward, hitting the dashboard.

"Oh no, oh no… I am bleeding, what the …." Anna cursed, seeing the bloody cut on her forehead.

"Stop. Stop. This is so bad. I think I hit…." Chris struggled to say the words, looking back at the road.

"What, silly. Have you never hit a deer? Trust me; it happens to people."

Chris opened the door in a hurry and sprinted twenty yards before kneeling on the road.

Anna could hear Chris sobbing but couldn't see what made him cry.

Anna quickly slid her top over her head and rushed towards Chris.

"Honey, what…?" Anna stopped her question mid-way as her eyes landed on the body lying on the road. They didn't kill a deer; they killed a man. They killed a human being. He was lying on the asphalt in a pool of blood, and he certainly was not moving.

"Oh god, he is dead," Anna shouted hysterically. "What should we do…"

Chris placed his hand over his head and bawled, "I am screwed. This is all over."

In the meantime, Anna moved a few yards in either direction, examining the place for any activity.

"We should go," Anna said coldly.

"What?"

"Let's go." Anna began to walk towards the car.

"We can't just leave the body here. We have to call the police."

"You stupid! If we do that, we are doomed."

"But…" Chris stopped talking when he heard a loud gasp. The night was dark and silent, and even a mumbled gasp echoed loudly to Chris and Anna's ears.

Chris and Anna rushed towards the sound and noticed the man lying on the road was coughing up blood.

"He is not dead!" Anna screamed.

Before she finished her sentence, the man's eyes closed, and he seemed to be drifting away.

"Hey, don't die on us." Chris checked his pulse and began to do CPR.

"We have to call 911. He is not going to last long." Chris drew his Nokia phone.

Anna abruptly pulled the phone from Chris's hand before he could dial 911.

"What are you doing?"

"Saving your life before you flush it down the drain."

Seeing Chris' 'I don't understand' look, Anna continued, "If you make this call, our life as we know it is over. We both are drunk, and we can't claim that he came out of nowhere. Most certainly, you will end up going to jail."

"We can't leave him here to die. Now knowing he is still alive, we can't do that." Chris slowly uttered the words.

"I know. I am not saying we should do that."

"What do you propose?"

"Do you remember the emergency phone near the…"

"Mile 24 marker," Chris finished her thought.

"Exactly. We should call from that phone. Anonymously."

"That will take at least ten minutes to call. He might die."

"I don't see any other option that would not land you in jail."

Chris glanced at the man lying on the road, one last time, before walking away.

2

September 12, 2001
Germantown, Philadelphia

A WOMAN, who was visibly pregnant, gingerly entered a police precinct in Germantown, a suburb in northern Philadelphia. She was feeling nervous and looked visibly worried as she slowly made her way towards the desk officer. This was her first time to a police precinct, not just in this town, but in her life.

"Hello, Officer," she said with an anxious voice.

The desk officer, who seemed occupied with papers in front of him, motioned his hand for her to wait. She obliged the command of the male police officer without any hesitation. For all of her life, her parents preached that she should obey the police without any questions or attitude. If not, they said you will end up beaten, or worse, you will disappear.

"What can I do for you, Ms...." The officer looked up at

the young woman, who was patiently standing behind the booth.

"Sania Tariq – my name," the young woman replied.

"Ms. Tariq, what can I do for you?" the officer asked as he answered a call on his phone.

Sania did not want to disturb the officer while he attended the call and waited patiently. The main area of the precinct looked odd; it was frantic. It resembled more of a marketplace in her hometown in India than a police precinct.

What do I know? Maybe it is always buzzing, Sania thought to herself.

"Ms…," the desk officer's voice interrupted the swirling thoughts in her head.

"Sania Tariq," Sania replied.

"Yes, Ms. Tariq, what can I do for you?" the desk officer asked.

Sania's heart was thumping hard as the words, "My husband is missing. I am here to find out about him," escaped her mouth.

"Has the case been filed?"

Sania nodded anxiously.

"When?"

"Yesterday. 9/11," Sania's voice trembled.

The officer's demeanor changed instantly when he heard the date – 9/11.

"Sorry to hear that," the officer said with a concerned tone.

Sania nodded to appreciate the officer's concern.

"Was he working in the towers?" the officer questioned.

"No," Sania shook her head.

"Was he working in New York?"

Sania shook her head.

"Was he visiting …."

Sania was getting tired of the questions, and she interrupted the officer. "He was not in New York."

"What do you mean? You said it is related to 9/11." The officer gave her a quizzing look.

"No, no." She shook her head vigorously, which she seemed to do a lot whenever she got nervous. It was often a gesture that was ridiculed by her friends in the past.

"I meant he disappeared on 9/11. It is not related to 9/11…." She searched for the words.

"Terrorist attacks," the officer completed her sentence.

"Yes, yes. He went missing on that day, but not in New York."

"Do you want to file a case?" The officer's tone changed; it was still warm but not emotionally invested.

"I already did." Sania went on to explain that she called 911 the previous night and filed a missing person report over the phone.

"On the phone, the 911 operator mentioned that an officer would call or stop by to gather pictures and additional information about my husband." Sania raised the folder she had in her left hand.

"I see. I can take it from you and make sure it gets to the detective in charge." The officer motioned his hand to request for the folder.

Sania hesitated for a moment before handing the file to the officer. "Officer, can I talk to the detective?"

"You mean to the detective assigned?"

Sania nodded.

"Let me see." The officer's fingers danced on the keyboard. "Hmm. He is not here at this moment."

"I can wait," Sania said, almost in a pleading tone.

"Sorry, it would take a while. You know, with what happened yesterday, the whole unit is at an emergency meeting. I can't tell how long it would be."

Sania understood the situation. It was not just her; the whole country was on edge. She had lived through horrible terrorist attacks in her home country, the 1993 bomb blasts in Mumbai, India. But she had never imagined that she would revisit the same kind of barbaric senseless attacks in her adopted country. Her heart stopped when she saw the towers come down yesterday. It was not just her, but the whole country felt the same.

IT HAD BEEN over forty-five minutes since Sania decided to wait to meet with the detective assigned to her husband's case. Sania was feeling tired, anxious, and exhausted. She hadn't slept well for the last two days, and, given her condition, being eight months pregnant, it was not ideal to abandon sleep. She was also feeling hungry.

Is it proper to feel hungry and sleepy when your husband is missing? Sania battled with her thoughts, but biology doesn't take a backseat to emotions.

"Ms. Tariq." Sania glanced sideways towards the direction of the sound.

"Sorry to inform you that ..." The desk officer was interrupted by a female voice who called out Sania by her first name.

"Sania, is that you?" a female detective said, approaching Sania and the desk officer.

"Arya ...?" Sania said, struggling to stand up to meet the young female detective.

Arya Martins is a police detective in the Philadelphia Police Department. When she got promoted to the rank of detective a few years before, it became a news story, and she got interviewed in the local evening news. The news interest was not because she was a celebrity kid; it was because she was a trailblazer. Arya was the youngest woman to wear a detective badge in the city of Philadelphia.

Arya's smile beamed when Sania rose from her chair, and her large pregnant tummy showed. "What? You are pregnant!" Arya went past the standing desk officer and gave a very friendly embrace to Sania.

"Sit, sit." Arya held Sania's hands and helped her to her chair.

"I can't believe I just ran into you after all these years, and that too in here." Arya raised her hands to gesture how odd it is to run into Sania in a police precinct.

Sania smiled, but her eyes were filling up with tears.

"What happened? Why are you crying?" Arya leaned closer to give another hug to Sania.

"Must be the pregnancy," Sania wiped her tears.

"How many months? Nine?" Arya placed her right hand on Sania's large belly.

"Eight."

"Wow! Look at you; you are glowing!" Arya exclaimed.

"Who knocked you up, and where is he?" Arya joked.

Sania's eyes started to fill up, and she shifted her eyes from Arya towards the desk officer.

"Ms. Tariq is here to follow up on a case involving her husband," the desk officer chimed in.

"What? Did he do something to you?" Arya asked with genuine concern for her friend.

"No, no…. He is missing." Sania teared up as the words escaped her mouth, and the tears started to roll down her cheeks.

Sania's sudden outburst created a scene in the precinct, and multiple officers' gaze shifted towards Arya. Sania was now visibly shaking and weeping audibly, resting her head across Arya's shoulders.

Arya, taken aback by the sudden revelation, took a moment to process the information.

"Okay. It's okay," Arya mouthed inaudibly to let the other officers in the precinct know that she had it covered.

It took almost a minute before Sania got hold of herself and regained composure.

"Sorry I got your nice shirt wet," Sania said, seeing her tears on Arya's white shirt made of silk.

"Nah. Don't be silly." Arya waved her right hand, quickly dismissing the silliness of Sania's worry.

"Detective Martins." A voice rang out from across the long room.

Arya turned immediately and spotted her lieutenant, Mike Cooper, standing across the room. It does not seem to matter where LT Cooper stood; no one could miss spotting him. He was tall, well over six feet, had broad shoulders and was built like a middle linebacker. The legend has it that he got drafted by the Giants after his third year in college, but something happened in his personal life that made him join the force.

Arya turned around to meet LT's gaze, who gestured for Arya to come into his office right away.

Arya motioned her hand to gesture that she was on her way.

As LT Cooper closed his doors, Arya turned towards Sania and said, "Give me five minutes. I want to talk to you."

Sania nodded, "Sure."

"Do you know the Starbucks that is across the street?"

Sania nodded again.

"Get a table and wait there. I will be there in a jiffy."

"Sure," Sania said, sounding like she was whispering.

Arya embraced Sania one more time, said, "See you in five," and rushed towards the LT's office, leaving Sania standing with hope.

3

OUT OF NOWHERE, the clouds rolled in and masked the sun, which was shining brightly a few minutes before. Sania made her way to the corner table in Starbucks with a raspberry mango iced tea in her hand. The sky above grumbled, threatening to open up. Sania peered through the glass wall, looking for her friend, Arya.

Sania felt weird and happy running into Arya under these circumstances. It had been many years since she saw Arya. As a flash of lightning split the sky, Sania reminisced about the last time she saw Arya.

She remembered the day as it was yesterday. The day was seared into her memory for a well-founded reason. It was the day that her life changed forever.

June 22, 1992

"CHUG, CHUG, CHUG...." The chants from Sania's friends filled the Goose, a bar in Queens, NY. The girl on the front lines leading the chants was her best friend, Arya.

"I can't... I... I am going to throw up," Sania slurred after downing one of the many tequila shots.

"C'mon Sania, don't be silly. The night is just getting started, isn't it, ladies?" Arya egged everyone on.

"Chug! Chug! Chug!" The chants continued as a hot bartender topped Sania's empty shot glass with another round of Crouching Tiger.

As Sania hesitated to down the latest shot, Arya jumped on the table and began to dance.

If the chants didn't turn everyone's attention towards them, Arya's sexy moves on the table did the trick. Before you know it, all of Sania's friends joined the dance party.

"Are you Ms. Aziz?" Sania turned around to find a police officer staring at her. The officer was young, must be in his early twenties, and looked like an Abercrombie model; blonde hair, blue eyes, delicate skin, and a body to die for.

Sania nodded hesitantly, feeling confused. The many shots she downed didn't help with her thinking, and she had a clueless look, staring at the officer.

The chants came to an abrupt halt, and all the eyes landed on Sania.

Arya stopped dancing and jumped down from the table. Sania's gaze shifted to Arya and noticed something weird. Arya had a silly smile on her face.

Before Sania could figure out what the hell was happening, the police officer pulled his handcuffs from the belt buckle and approached Sania.

"Ms. Aziz, you been nothing but trouble," he said in a husky voice, leaning weirdly a lot closer to Sania's body.

"What?" Sania's voice quivered.

"We need to go downtown, bad girl," the officer said,

ripping his shirt open. The music erupted in the bar, and the officer started grinding behind Sania.

"What the …?" Sania mouthed, feeling stunned as Arya and the girls joined the dance party.

"Happy bachelorette night, bad girl," Arya screamed, planting a kiss on Sania.

Arya and the girls had hired one of the bartenders to pretend as a cop for the bachelorette night. The night turned raucous as the girls cut loose, and they partied like there was no tomorrow.

As the clock edged closer to 4 AM, the music died down, and the bar began to empty out — including their friends.

"Girls, last call." The bartender smiled at them.

"I am done… I drank enough for weeks," Sania smiled.

"How about one for the road?" Arya insisted, gesturing the bartender for another round.

After downing the last shot, Arya remarked, "Baby, you know, Reza is one lucky guy to land you."

Sania smiled shyly, "Have you seen him? I am the lucky one."

"Don't sell yourself short; you are quite a catch."

As Sania waved dismissively, the door burst open, and Reza darted into the bar. Reza's eyes swept the room hurriedly, trying to find Sania. The same moment his eyes landed on the far corner table where Sania was sitting, she looked up. Their eyes met only for a brief moment, but that was enough for Sania to realize that something was wrong. People say that eyes don't lie, and, at this moment, it was very much true. Reza's eyes had tears welled up, and, the moment both of their eyes met, tears started streaming down his face.

Seeing her love in distress, Sania jumped from the table and rushed towards Reza.

"Baby, what happened?" Sania put both her arms around Reza's back and tightly embraced him.

Sania's voice and the warmth of her body broke the wall that held his tears. Reza began to convulse as he sobbed against Sania's shoulders.

"My family is dead," he said in almost a whisper.

"What are you saying? Who?" Sania said in a shocked tone.

Reza slowly raised his head and said, "Everyone."

4

September 12, 2001
Germantown, Philadelphia
Starbucks Coffee

Sania jerked back to the present when she heard a voice sounding her name, piercing through her consciousness. Sania turned her head towards the sound and found Arya leaning towards her to give her a friendly hug.

"So sorry, Sania, it took longer than I thought," Arya said, embracing Sania for a long moment before making herself comfortable in the chair across from Sania.

"We are all going crazy with what happened yesterday," Arya explained the state of everyone's mindset after what the terrorists did to the homeland.

"Fucking Bin Laden… and fuck the jihadis…," Arya continued with her heartfelt rant.

"So many people lost their lives yesterday, all because these fuckers thought that they will go to paradise to fuck the virgins…." Arya stopped her sentence mid-way as she realized there was a family with two small kids in a nearby table.

"Sorry about the language." Arya raised her hand as a gesture to apologize for being foul-mouthed.

The father in the nearby table, seeing the detective badge that was clipped on Arya's belt, waved his hand to dismiss the apology. "No need, Detective. Thanks for doing what you do."

Arya smiled while the local barista bought her a cup of coffee to the table. The pleasantry exchange between Arya and the barista indicated that she was a regular in this joint, and the barista knew exactly what she wants.

Arya, after taking a sip of her hot coffee, looked up towards Sania.

"Sorry for the outburst. We are all on edge, walking a tight rope - not knowing which shoe is going to drop next."

Sania stayed silent, feeling lost in her own situation.

Arya realizing Sania's predicament placed her hand on top of Sania's hand, and both made eye contact for a prolonged moment.

"Don't worry, Sania. Reza will be okay."

Sania's head dropped, and she just shook her head.

"Trust me. Reza might have got stuck somewhere with what happened yesterday, and before you know it, he will call you."

Sania pulled her hands from under Arya's palms and said, "It is not about Reza."

Arya gasped in surprise, raising both her hands to cover her mouth. "Are you saying what I think you are saying?"

Sania nodded slowly.

"You didn't marry Reza Tariq!" Arya said in a raised voice.

"Shhh…." Sania motioned her hand for Arya to keep her voice down. She felt a dozen eyes in the coffee shop landing on her, thanks to Arya.

"But, I heard the officer address you as Ms. Tariq?" Arya asked, whispering.

"Yeah. My husband's name is Sam Tariq."

"You married someone with the same last name as Reza?" Arya asked, feeling surprised.

"Yes. Sam's last name is Tariq," Sania answered flatly.

"His first name is Sam?" Arya asked with a puzzled look. Sam and Tariq didn't seem like a name that goes together. Sam sounded more like a Christian name.

"Samir Tariq. He goes by Sam here in the States," Sania clarified.

Arya sat back, thrown off by the surprise that her friend ended up not marrying the love of her life. They seemed so much in love in college, and she definitely thought they were going to end up together, especially with the history they had.

Sania, realizing a myriad of questions would be hurled at her by Arya, said, "Arya, I know you wanted to know what happened after that night in the bar, but...." She paused to look straight into Arya's eyes and said, "I am not ready to talk about the past — Reza. Right now, Sam is missing...." Sania could not complete her sentence as she got choked up, trying to hold back her tears.

Arya realized that she had gone off on the wrong track. The curiosity about the past has blinded her from treating Sania as a victim. Sania had just reported her husband as missing. Arya's behavior was unbecoming as a detective or a friend, and it was time for her to act accordingly.

"I am sorry, Sania." Arya crossed over to Sania and gave her a hug.

"No... I didn't mean to make you feel bad," Sania choked up.

"I know.... Let us start from the beginning; tell me how

long it has been since Samir is missing," Arya asked, sitting back in her chair.

"I don't know…. I can't say when Sam went missing," Sania struggled with her response.

"I meant to ask, when did you realize Sam was missing?" Arya rephrased her question.

"After the towers came down."

5

ARYA SHUDDERED, and her facial muscles constricted in shock when she heard her friend utter those dreaded words. The images of the tower coming down flooded her thoughts, and left her speechless. It took her a moment to regain her senses to imagine what her friend must be going through.

"I am so sorry, Sania. I didn't realize Samir worked in the towers." Arya's voice trailed off as her gaze met Sania's.

"What are you talking about?" Sania said, raising her eyebrows. "Samir was not in the towers." She felt surprised that Arya had thought Samir was in the towers.

"Oh, I thought you said...." Arya stopped her sentence mid-way when a barista stopped by their table to drop off Arya's macchiato. After thanking the barista, a young blonde woman who looked like a college kid, Arya gazed back at Sania and apologized, "I misconnected the dots."

Sania nodded in understanding and said, "I must have called him at least ten times after the towers came down, and he never answered."

Arya listened with concern. "Is that why you think he is missing?"

Sania nodded, biting her lower lip to control her emotions.

"You know, Sania, phone lines have been jammed from yesterday. It is quite possible that he tried and couldn't reach you."

"I know deep down that is not the case," Sania said firmly.

"Okay... I know you said Sam was not in the towers; was he in New York?"

Sania quietly shook her head.

"He had business in New York, but he didn't go there yesterday. He went to Los Angeles." Sania went on to explain that Samir took the evening flight on September 10th to Los Angeles.

"How did he go to the airport? Did he take a cab?"

Sania shook her head and said, "No, I drove him to the airport."

"You did?" Arya asked rhetorically. Sania driving Samir to the airport crosses off one of the questions Arya had. *Can anyone confirm Samir went to the airport?*

"I know this might be odd, but it is something routine that I have to ask...," Arya hesitated with her question.

"What?" Sania gave her a quizzing look.

"Has he ever been on a trip where he didn't call you for an entire day?"

"Yes. But this is different." Sania leaned forward on the table and asked Arya, "I forgot to ask you. Are you married?"

"No," Arya answered, feeling slightly taken aback by Sania's tangential question.

"Boyfriend?"

"Not anyone I cuddle every night; you know what I mean." Arya sat back in her chair and said, "What's with these weird questions? If you want to catch up and chat about my love life, I am game for it. But...." She stretched the 'but' word and continued, "Do you seriously want to do that now?"

"Did you call your parents after the towers came down?" Sania asked with a stoned face, not reacting to Arya's questions.

"Yes. Why?"

"Exactly," Sania thumped her index finger on the table.

"What?" Arya looked flabbergasted.

"I don't know anyone who didn't call their loved ones yesterday after the towers came down. Husband, wife, boyfriend, girlfriend, parents, sisters, and brothers…," Sania said, holding her gaze at Arya.

"You got me." Arya pointed her index finger at Sania and, with a smile, said, "Like the old days."

Sania's lips slightly parted for a smile and said, "You still owe me."

"Whaaatttt?"

"From all the bets you lost in our sorority games. You still owe me." Sania smiled.

"Whatever." Arya laughed, waving her hand dismissively.

"Thanks," Sania said, extending her hand across the table to hold Arya's. "It is comforting to have you, my best friend, to help me with this awful situation."

"Don't worry, Sania. We will find him," Arya said, holding Sania's hand.

After a moment, Sania lifted her gaze and asked Arya, "Can you promise me you will find him?"

Arya knew nothing about the case assignment and if it was already assigned to a different detective. But, at that moment, she knew Samir Tariq's case was going to be hers. There was no way she was going to let her friend down.

"Yes," Arya firmly said, holding Sania's hands.

6

A FLOOD of memories burst into Sania's head upon meeting Arya. As with anyone's past, not all of them were good. There were plenty of good memories, but a slice of terrible memories came along with it that she preferred to remain buried.

A loud honk jolted her back to the present. At the nick of time, Sania swerved her car back to the lane and avoided hitting the car to her left.

"Sorry," she mouthed to a pissed-off driver, who hastily gave her the middle finger before pulling ahead of her.

Sania made sure the rest of the drive to her house was uneventful. The last thing she needed was an accident and getting her baby hurt.

Just as Sania was getting out of her Toyota Highlander, she heard her name being called out. Sania turned around to spot her neighbor, Kate Halladay, waving at her. Sania responded back, but not with the same enthusiasm.

Kate motioned for Sania to wait as she hurried towards her.

"Any news about Sam?" Kate asked, breathing hard like she had just run a hundred-meter dash.

Sania shook her head. "No, Kate," she mouthed.

"What about the cops?"

"They haven't started the investigation yet," Sania replied flatly.

"Unbelievable!" Kate shook her head before adding, "The first 24-48 hours are the most crucial in the missing person case, and I can't believe they haven't started to look into it."

"I don't know Kate; this is all new to me. I never thought I will be in this position," Sania said despondently.

"Don't worry, Sania. It will all be okay," Kate said in a low voice and hugged Sania.

"You know, I can look into it," Kate continued, rubbing Sania's back gently.

"You can?" Sania asked as she slowly withdrew from Kate's arms.

Kate nodded enthusiastically. "Definitely."

Sania's expression changed in a moment from optimism to uncertainty. "Kate, you have been a good friend, and I don't want to ruin it by taking advantage of your goodwill."

"Don't be silly…." Kate waved dismissively before continuing, "If not for a moment of need, what is a friend for…?"

Sania became overwhelmed with emotions and hugged Kate. "Thanks. Will Tom be okay with it?"

Tom Halladay is Kate's husband, and they both work as partners in running their private security firm, Dark Shadow.

"Of course, this is as much his idea as mine. We both love you, and you know we will do anything for you."

Sania knew in her heart that Kate and Tom feel that they owe an enormous debt to her. She also knew why; her past actions seemed to be paying forward when she really needed it. The day that started with complete despair has now transformed into a day with hope. First, she ran into Arya – her best friend, who happened to be a detective, who promised her that she will find Sam. And now, Kate and Tom have offered to use their private security resources to look into Sam's disappearance.

It seemed almighty Allah is looking out for her.

"Sam will be okay. Don't worry; we will find him." Kate's words breathed more optimism to Sania.

"Inshallah," Sania mouthed silently.

7

SANIA HURRIED inside her house as fast as she could upon hearing the phone inside her house ring. As she rushed towards the phone, her heart was thumping hard with the eager anticipation that the person calling was Sam.

"Sam," she answered, breathing hard, "Sam, is it you?" She continued her hopeful cry as she heard silence on the other side of the call, and, just before Sania called out Sam's name again, the connection went dead.

Sania hurriedly pressed the switch hook on the phone's cradle with the faint hope of reconnecting the call, but her efforts ended up futile. All she heard was a dial tone.

As she placed the phone on its cradle, Sania couldn't help remembering the stupid fight she had with Sam a few months before. It was on the morning of May 13, 2001. There was no way she could forget the date as it was their wedding anniversary. Sania had wished for a cell phone as her surprise gift from Sam. She was extremely confident that Sam would have picked the latest mobile from Sony as her gift, given the number of breadcrumbs she dropped in spring. Oh boy, was she in for a surprise when she opened the gift. It turned out to be a phone, but not the phone she had wished; it was a rotary phone from the '60s.

Sania was perplexed. *Who in their right mind would get a phone from the '60s?*

She ended up arguing and fighting with Sam about it. Sam's excuse for this inexplicable gift was that he wanted it to be unique. He said that anyone can gift a cell phone, but no one will think of gifting a rotary phone in 2001.

The whiff of nostalgic memories washed over her, reminding her how unique and different Sam was. She might have known him only for four years, but every day with him had been a joyful ride. When she married him four years ago, it was not her choice. Instead, she was forced to marry him out of tremendous debt her family owed.

There is an old Yiddish adage, "Mann Tracht, Un Gott Lacht," meaning, "Man plans, and God laughs." Despite our careful planning, the road to life is unpredictable. Sania felt the Yiddish adage was tailored just for her.

In the summer of 1992, her plans were all coming together beautifully. Her wedding with Reza was set, and the plans were well underway for a beautiful wedding in NY. Both their parents agreed to the marriage, despite their religious differences; Reza was a Sunni Muslim, and Sania was a Shia. The difference to outsiders might sound small, but in the Muslim world, the rift between them was vast. The history was filled with countless wars between these two sects.

Sania and Reza couldn't have been happier when both their religious parents agreed and gave their blessings. Sania planned to get married to Reza, with or without her parents' blessings. But for Reza, the approval of his pious parents mattered.

However, all their plans came to a standstill when Reza got the fateful call on her bachelorette night. It was the night she learned that Reza's entire family in Yemen got killed. It left both of them devastated, and the life she had dreamed was never the same from that moment onwards.

SANIA WAS LOST in her memories, and she was jolted back to the present when the sound waves of the chiming clock reached her ears. The antique clock was one of the possessions she kept when she moved from New York to Philly. It reminded her of one of the secrets that she had kept hidden from Sam. 'One of the secrets' is the operative phrase to keep in mind. At that time, Sania thought that it would be her only secret, but fate had other plans for her.

For reasons her heart would know, the clock chiming sounded ominous. It was 7:00 PM, and, in her heart, she knew something horrible has happened. Just as the worrying thoughts entered her mind, the phone rang loudly.

"It is about time," Sania thought to herself and rushed towards the phone.

"Hello, hello," Sania answered hurriedly.

There was no response on the other side of the line. It was just silence.

Sania breathed raggedly, repeating her hellos. For a moment, she wondered if the line got disconnected, and that thought soon went out the window when she heard breaths on the phone line.

"Sam...?" Sania said hesitantly.

"Is it you?" Sania held the phone tighter and pressed it closer to her ears.

There was no response.

"Are you okay?" Sania's voice began to tremble.

Still, there was no response from the other end of the line.

"Please…. Please say something if you hear me. I am distraught," Sania pleaded.

All she heard was a click, followed by a dial-tone.

Sania's heart was beating hard, her palms were sweating profusely, and her head felt like it was bashed with a baseball bat. She was a wreck.

She gazed at the clock and began to mumble, "7:10. Something has gone wrong." It didn't matter how many times she rubbed her temples; the worries in her head continued to spread like wildfire.

The lack of rest didn't seem to suit her or the baby. Sania stopped her nervous pacing and took a deep sigh, feeling the unusually strong kick of her baby. Sania reflexively acted by gently rubbing her belly to comfort and console the baby. Reflexes are evolutionary traits that we, as humans, have developed over millions of years ago. They are involuntary and automatic, designed as a protection mechanism. We don't have to think to blink when something flies towards your eyes or something bright flashes. We do it without even thinking about it; we have been hard-wired to act. Sania's wiring screamed for her to slow down, rub her belly and make sure her baby was well.

As much as she wanted to slow down, her anxious mind didn't allow her to do so. After the baby settled down and there were no more kicks, Sania's mind pushed her to do something that she would repent in the future. Sania picked up the car keys from the coffee table and walked out of her front door.

8

As Sania sat in her car and inserted the ignition key, she hesitated to start it. A debate was waging in her own head; should she go, or should she stay in her house? After a moment's hesitation, she turned the key as the compulsion to do that was so much stronger than the prudent decision to stay put in the house.

The neighborhood streets were dead; no one was playing on the streets or going for a stroll. It seemed like everyone was glued to their television sets, watching the news. Sania imagined that to be the case across the city and across the country. Quite understandably, there had been wall-to-wall coverage about the 9/11 attacks on the television. Everyone wanted to know how this happened on American soil — multiple coordinated attacks across various cities, resulting in over three thousand casualties. It was unfathomable. Everyone was on edge, and they desperately wanted to know if these attacks could happen again in the next few days. People across the nation were angry and terrified at the same time.

Sania stopped the car in the four-way stop sign before

exiting her neighborhood to enter Midvale Avenue. Sania was pre-occupied with her own thoughts to notice a silver-colored Honda following her from the moment she had left the house.

Sania was perturbed about the repeated blank calls. Everyone at some time in their life must have received blank calls, but how many would have received it from their missing husband's phone? That threw Sania off. When Sania saw the caller ID, she knew it was from Sam's phone. *Why did he not speak? Was it a weak connection?* Sania imagined it was a weak connection until she heard the deep breaths on the other end of the line. The person on the other end definitely heard Sania call out Sam's name and listened to her outcry. However, the line remained silent. *Why?*

Sania's head was splitting; she had a pounding headache – the lack of sleep and the stress had started to weigh her down. Running into Arya was unexpected, and finding out that she was a cop could be useful in her current situation. Sania, now crossing the intersection of Henry Avenue, gazed at the speedometer to ensure she was driving within the speed limit. The last thing she need was to get a ticket; she didn't want anyone to know where she was headed, including Arya.

The Honda continued to keep pace with the Highlander, always trailing by a hundred yards. Whoever was driving the Honda knew what they were doing; this was not their first rodeo. Sania did not suspect that she was being followed, and why would she? Maybe in hindsight, she should have been careful and should have expected being followed. Especially given what she had done in the previous few months, from the moment her past collided with the present.

Sania gazed at the sky as she turned into Kelly Drive; it was pitch-black and was devoid of any stars. It almost felt

like the sky was in mourning, reflecting the nation's sentiment, with what just happened in the country.

Just as she had imagined, Kelly Drive was isolated. There
were no runners or cyclists; it was just Sania and the curvy
road. Sania drove past the Temple Boathouse with her eyes
glancing at the Schuylkill River on her right. The images of
her rowing for the first time with Sam flooded her mind.
Rowing was not something she was into; it was indeed her
least favorite activity to do. It was more of Sam's thing, and,
if you ask Sania, he treated rowing as a religion. When they
got married, his fascination with rowing used to upset Sania
tremendously. He used to disappear for hours with his boat;
sculling was his favorite. Once, he even forgot that they had
planned to go for a Friday night movie, and Sania ended up
being stranded in front of the theater. She fumed; he apologized and said he would change, but, in the end, nothing
happened. He continued to disappear for hours with his
boat. After a while, Sania understood his passion and gave up
pushing him. She tried joining him on a few of his trips to
the river and tried sculling, which instead ended disastrously.
Sania was clumsy with the oar, and, even after repeated
attempts, she never got the hang of it. In the end, she saw the
light and realized rowing was not for her and gave up on it.

Sania glanced at the rear-view mirror as she made the
steep curve past the Columbia Bridge, and there was no one
behind her. It was five minutes to 8:00 PM, and she wanted
to make it to her destination before the top of the hour. She
hoped to find answers.

Sania slowed down to under twenty miles-per-hour
when she got closer to the Strawberry Mansion Bridge. She
swept her eyes from the rear-view mirror to both sides of the
car, nervously looking for signs of life, but she couldn't spot
a soul. She brushed the hair that fell across her face back and
took a deep breath as she pulled her car to the parking lot

next to the Temple Boathouse. The clock on her car dashboard showed 8:06 PM.

She was late, but not by much. She was hopeful that she could find answers that eluded her. She should know what happened last night soon.

Sania killed the engine, sending the parking lot back to darkness, and slowly stepped out of her car. Her heart was thumping hard, her mouth felt thirsty, and the adrenaline was rushing through her body. In other words, she was a walking bowl of anxiety.

This parking lot nor the boathouse was new to her. Over the last four years, she has been here a few times with Sam. However, the frequency of her visits to this place significantly increased during the previous three months.

From the paved parking lot, Sania turned left at the marker for the Schuylkill River Trail and entered the secluded river trail. The trail was quite uneven and slippery; the overnight rain certainly didn't help with the conditions. To add to her misery, there were no lights on the trail. Low visibility and slippery conditions were not an ideal recipe for a pregnant woman to take this trail at night.

Sania knew she was not that far from her destination. With every step, she felt not only getting closer to her destination but also to the truth. With that hope, Sania labored on.

It took her another five minutes to take the meandering path, which led her to a secluded wooden bench by the Schuylkill River. When Sania found the bench to be empty, her mind raced in diametrically opposite directions. Was she late or early? She was a few minutes late to the meeting spot if she had to go by her watch. However, she was not terribly late.

Sania found the five long minutes of waiting to be painful. With every minute, the amount of self-doubt in her head began to spread, making her a nervous wreck. The rippling sounds of the Schuylkill River as it flowed along its bed made Sania feel fretful. The other sounds of nature – buzzing insects, chirping birds, and croaking frogs created a nervous effect on Sania. She started to question herself if she had made a terrible mistake by coming here. Little did she know that her fears were not unfounded.

As Sania nervously waited on the bench by the river trail, a man hiding behind a thick tree was taking pictures of her using a telephoto lens. He was the same man who followed Sania on a silver Honda from the moment she left her house tonight. The moment Sania made the turn on Midvale, he knew where Sania was headed. It was not the first time he had followed Sania to this secluded bench on the river trail. It was his fourth time.

If it was any other day with the usual traffic on Kelly Drive, he would have just stayed a few cars behind and followed Sania. But he knew today was nothing but typical, and this part of Kelly Drive would be deserted. The years of experience on the job informed him that the best way not to get made by Sania would be to take an alternate route. He followed his instinct and took Ridge Avenue, which ran parallel to Kelly Drive, and got to the river trail by choosing one of the narrow streets. He was reasonably confident of Sania's destination — the secluded bench on the river trail. He was optimistic that he would be able to get there to catch her with his long-range lens.

As he had expected, there she was, sitting on the bench and gazing at the river. The image he saw through his lens was the same as the other four times, except for one vital difference. She was all alone. No one was sitting by her side, holding her hand or rubbing her back.

9

SANIA FELT restless as minutes started to add up, and she began to nervously pace around the bench. Whatever hope she had coming here started to wither. After waiting for another twenty minutes, she knew the time was up. There would be no answers today. It was time for her to go back to her house and wait for the phone to ring. Hopefully, this time she would get to hear him.

A hundred yards away, the man lowered his Nikon D7200 camera and watched Sania pace nervously.

"What did you do?" the man muttered to himself. "Where is he?" He twisted his hand to glance at his Timex and thought, "He has never been this late; something is up."

Even though Sania had been to this place many times, she felt uncomfortable walking back to her car. The terrain was slippery and uneven, and she felt unsteady, probably due to the stress of the situation.

As she neared the paved portion of the trail, Sania's heart skipped a beat and stopped still. She heard what sounded like a ringtone of a phone. Her heart was beating so hard that anyone nearby could have heard it. Her mouth turned dry;

she felt parched. She swiftly turned around and stared at the bench. She swung her glance from one side to another, and she couldn't spot anyone.

"Hello, anyone there?" she called, clearing her throat. All she heard was silence, except the natural sounds of the river. It was incredibly silent, and that didn't help with her jittery heart.

Did she hear what she thought she heard — a phone ring? Or is it just her imagination running wild? She began to doubt herself.

Her mind got sprayed with a myriad of questions, and, at this moment, she had no definitive answers.

At the same time, the man behind the tree took a crouching position to avoid detection from Sania's sweeping eyes. His phone rang, and he cursed himself for being so careless not to turn the ringer off. From his vantage point, he still had eyes on Sania and hoped that she wouldn't walk towards his position. If she did, he had two options. One was to attack her, and the other was to run away. The presented choices were just a mirage; he knew that he really had only one option. He had to run and avoid being spotted. If he got spotted, his cover would be blown, and he won't be able to catch her in the act. More importantly, he would lose a fortune.

He sighed a big relief when he saw Sania started to walk towards the paved trail. She didn't suspect being followed. He stayed behind for few more minutes, just in case Sania changed her mind. When he saw the coast was clear, he slowly raised himself from the uncomfortable position. After a quick sweep of the place, he was convinced that it was now safe for him to move.

From his past visits, he knew where to go next. He moved swiftly towards a nearby slope and used his hands like a claw to climb up. He was glad that he was wearing his hiking boots. One thing that he learned from years of experience was to always be prepared. That mindset has saved his life many times on the streets.

"There you are," he whispered, viewing Sania opening her Highlander door through his Bushnell Equinox Night Vision binoculars. He couldn't count the number of times this beauty had come to his aid in the past. Those specific binoculars could help him see targets a thousand feet away, whether it was day or night. It might not be as good as the night vision goggles that he used during his service, but it is more than enough for his current civilian needs.

He waited for Sania to pull her SUV from the parking lot before scurrying towards his silver Honda. He lost her once a couple of nights before, and he didn't want that to happen again.

10

It was the third time Arya rang Sania's doorbell, and the result was the same as the previous times; no one answered.

Arya glanced at her watch, feeling disappointed. It showed 9:30 PM. Arya wondered if Sania had already gone to sleep. She knew that it was late, but given the circumstance, she thought Sania would still be awake.

After waiting for another minute, Arya walked back to her car that was parked in front of Sania's house. She decided it would be best to try Sania in the morning. If Sania managed to sleep, it was probably for the best.

As Arya roared the Crown Vic to life, she saw a white SUV in the rear-view mirror pull up. She narrowed her eyes to get a better look at the driver, and when the image became more evident, she parted her mouth slightly and grinned.

"Hi, here you are," Arya said, getting down from her Crown Vic after killing the engine.

"Arya, is it you?" Sania asked, feeling surprised to see Arya show up at this time of the night.

Before Arya could reply, Sania hastily asked, "Is everything alright? Any news about Sam?"

"Oh no, everything is alright," Arya said, realizing her showing up at this late hour gave a wrong impression — false hope to Sania.

"Alright? You mean…," Sania asked with hope.

"I am sorry…." Arya was crossed with herself for digging a bigger hole. "I meant to say that no new worrying news about Sam."

Sania slowly nodded her head, but Arya could clearly see the disappointment all over Sania's face.

"I should have called; showing up unannounced is clearly a bad idea." Arya raised her shoulders, which she tends to do when she felt awkward.

"Don't be silly, Arya." Sania waved dismissively and leaned closer to embrace her.

"Ouch!" Sania gasped, as Arya's service gun poked slightly at Sania's belly.

"So sorry," Arya hurriedly said, withdrawing. "So sorry, I forgot about this…," she said, pointing at her Glock 22 clipped to her waist.

"It's alright. It was just a poke; I overreacted." Sania gave a welcoming smile.

They both stood still, staring at each other for a moment. A slight breeze was blowing from north to south, and along with it came old memories from up north. It almost felt unreal to Arya.

"You know, I looked for you."

"Where? Did you wait too long?"

"No, no," Arya said, shaking her head. "Not now. I meant after that night. What happened? Where did you go?"

"It is a long story," Sania said, holding her gaze firmly at Arya.

As Arya started with her next question, Sania gestured with her hands for Arya to pause. "I know you have a hundred questions, but let us not do that here." Sania pointed at the road. "Also, I really got to pee."

"Uh-oh," Arya reacted apologetically.

"Don't be…. It is not your fault, this little one," Sania paused to point at her belly, "makes me pee all the time. The baby makes me pee like I swigged a lot of beers — like how we did in college."

They both burst out laughing, remembering their wild nights in college.

Laughing heartily, they began to walk towards the front door. The pace was slow, given Sania's house stood raised a few feet above the ground level.

As they gingerly walked towards Sania's front door, a man observed the whole exchange from the confines of his silver Honda. As they disappeared through the doors, the man pulled a Marlboro Red from his cigarette case and brought it to life.

"It's going to be a long night," he muttered to himself, blowing smoke through his mouth.

11

"Now I can talk," Sania smilingly said, coming back from the bathroom.

"Is it your first?" Arya asked affectionately.

Sania nodded. "Our first."

Arya smiled, meeting Sania's eyes.

"I was reluctant to get pregnant so fast after we got married, but Sam wanted a baby." Sania paused for a moment before continuing with a wistful tone, "He loves kids. He wanted to be a father from the moment we got married." Sania's voice cracked, reminiscing her past with Sam.

Arya reached over to comfort Sania by placing her hands over Sania's.

"You know he loved the baby." Sania gently caressed her belly. "We even picked a name." Her eyes started to well up with tears.

Arya nodded, holding her emotions in check, listening to her emotional friend.

"Sara." There was no stopping the tears then; it rolled down Sania's face. "We named her Sara." The dam was broken, the tears started to flow, and Sania began to cry profusely, shuddering.

Arya rushed to her friend's side, leaned over, and gave her a loving hug.

"I will give you my word; I will find Sam," Arya said with conviction, hugging her long-lost best friend. At that moment, Arya knew she has a new mission in life – to find Samir Tariq.

The moment lasted a minute, but it seemed to Arya like an hour. Finally, when they parted with their embrace, Sania asked, "Do you have any?"

"Any?" Arya asked, quizzingly.

"Kids, any kids?"

"Nah, Nah…." Arya shook her head vehemently like she was being accused.

"I didn't even ask if you were married; how selfish of me," Sania said disapprovingly of herself.

"You did," Arya said, pointing Sania to the conversation they had in the coffee shop.

"So sorry! I somehow forgot the whole exchange," Sania apologized.

"Don't be silly." Arya waved her hand dismissively.

"Okay. Let me ask you again; are you married?" Sania smiled.

"Me? Noooo…." Arya shook her head again, quite vehemently.

"What is it with you? You are acting like I asked something unimaginable," Sania frowned.

"No. Nothing like that; it is just," Arya paused to search for the right word, "it is just so far-fetched now."

"What? What happened with Carl?" Sania asked, referring to Arya's boyfriend at NYU.

"Carl! That is a name I almost forgot. We split right after."

"Really? I thought you guys were perfect," Sania quipped.

"Not funny; you seriously thought he was my prince charming!" Arya stared at Sania, making a face.

"Jokes apart; what happened?" Sania hugged a throw pillow.

"He cheated; that is what happened."

"What? He cheated?" Sania raised her brows in surprise.

"That guy is a douchebag. Not one, he cheated with two people. He cheated the person who he cheated me with."

"What!" Sania began to laugh.

"You are laughing, great." Arya acted like she was offended for a moment. It didn't last long, and they both began to laugh.

Sania couldn't live in her past when her present was clouded.

"Did you talk to your supervisor?" Sania asked, bringing the conversation back to Sam.

Arya nodded, holding her gaze at Sania.

"And?" Sania asked eagerly.

Arya lowered the glass of water from her mouth and said, "It is going to be me."

"What? That is awesome." Sania genuinely felt excited knowing that her best friend, Arya, was now assigned to the case.

"You know, this is probably the first good news I have got in the last few days." Sania started to well up.

"Sania...." Arya reached out to Sania affectionately and rubbed her shoulders.

"This must be the hormones. I am not usually this much of a crybaby," Sania half-laughed, making fun of herself.

"I am not sure if I agree with that; you were always a kind of a crybaby," Arya cracked.

Arya's joke landed the way she had intended, and both of them started to crack up.

After the laughter died off, Sania asked, "Who was assigned before? What did they find?"

"No one," Arya told the truth.

"What? How could they do that? It has been close to forty-eight hours, and how is that even possible?"

"Under normal circumstances, you are correct – they would have had someone assigned. But after what happened yesterday – the 9/11 attacks – everything is different."

"Sorry if I sound ignorant or selfish, but isn't 9/11 more of an NYPD situation? Are you guys affected?" Sania slowly asked.

"True. NYPD and mainly the Feds are running the show, but it is going to be so much more. Law enforcement across the country, in all forms, are affected. We all got to unite and share our information to get those fanatics," Arya said in a raised tone, visibly upset and angry.

Arya's furious reaction was the norm that day across every law enforcement agency. Everyone felt united with a common purpose, to hunt and kill the terrorists who cowardly attacked and killed thousands of their fellow citizens. The inter-agency politics and territory squabbles seemed to feel very trivial then.

Sania felt the temperature of the room raise, following the real and emotional outburst from Arya. "I couldn't believe it. It is so sad," Sania said in a lowered voice, reflecting the enormity of the events that have gripped the country from yesterday.

"I know that fu…." Arya blurted out a few expletives and then paused for a moment to form her thoughts. "You know what beats me? Those terrorists had families – parents, wives, kids. How did they all not know?" Arya asked rhetorically.

Sania remained silent, allowing Arya to vent.

After a moment, Arya realized that she hijacked the

discussion on a different path. "Sorry, I went off on a tangent away from Sam's case."

Reading Sania's face, Arya realized that Sania might be concerned if Sam's case would be ignored, given the situation. Arya chided herself for putting those thoughts in Sania's head and said, "Given all I said; still, Sam's case is going to be a priority."

Sania looked up at Arya with suspicion.

"It is a priority for me; you got to believe me." Arya firmly looked into Sania's eyes.

Sania nodded. "I believe you."

As Sania's gaze met Arya's, they both nodded to show they understood each other.

"Can I ask you something? Isn't the first 24 to 48 hours the most crucial in a missing person case? Sam has been missing for almost 48 hours now, isn't that a problem?"

"You are watching too much of Law and Order on TV; that is not always the case," Arya countered.

"How so? So that timeline is just fiction?" Sania was now pretty worked up.

"I won't completely rule it out. It is often true in the case of missing children, but Sam here being an adult makes it different."

"Oh, I didn't know that. So, what is the timeline?"

"Sania," Arya met Sania's eyes, "there is no specific timeline. Each case is different. I just want you to trust me; we will find him." Arya held Sania's hands in hers, trying to calm Sania down.

"Okay, okay. This is all new to me," Sania stuttered.

"I know, that is why you got to trust me. We will find Sam."

Sania composing herself slightly nodded and said, "It makes me so happy that I have you in this situation."

Arya smiled. "Me too."

After allowing the calming moment to settle in, Arya said, "Now, I need something from you. I need you to slowly and methodically answer all my questions."

Sania briskly said, "Anything. What do you want to know?"

"WHEN WAS the last time you spoke to Sam?" Arya asked, flipping her pocket notebook open.

"Around 5:00 in the evening, when I dropped him at the airport." Sania eyed Arya taking notes.

Realizing that Sania's quizzing eyes were on her, Arya asked, "Are you okay with me taking notes?"

Sania nodded immediately.

"Thanks, it helps me remember. You know, with all the tequila I consume, I can't seem to remember the movie I saw last week," Arya made a lame attempt at a joke.

"September 10th? Philly airport?" After the failed joke, Arya brought the conversation back to the case.

"Yes, Philly airport and September 10th," Sania confirmed the date she dropped Sam at Philadelphia International Airport.

"Do you know the flight number?" Arya asked, without looking up.

"No, I don't remember. But I know the flight was scheduled to depart at 7:10 in the evening." Sania went on to confirm that it was a direct flight to Los Angeles.

"This is useful." Arya explained that she could now quickly pinpoint the flight Sam took to LA. She felt confident that there would be only one direct flight to LA at that specific time, 7:10 PM.

"What about the hotel?" Arya continued.

"I don't know. Sam's office would have made the bookings."

"You didn't ask?" Arya looked up, resting her pen between her lips.

"No," Sania said with slight hesitation on her face, like there was more to that story.

"Uh-oh, I know that face. What are you not saying?" Arya eyed Sania.

"I was least interested in his trip because we had a terrible fight," Sania confessed.

Arya eyed Sania to go on.

"When I got pregnant, Sam promised that he would cut down on his travel. At first, he did," Sania said.

"What happened after?" Arya invited Sania to open up.

"Then it increased quite drastically. In the last few months, Sam traveled constantly."

"That caused a rift?" Arya asked questions that would open up Sania further.

"Yes, yes, it did. We started constantly arguing before each of his trips. Then he stopped. He didn't travel for almost two weeks, and then this happened."

"This flight to Los Angeles?"

"Yes. Sam mentioned to me about the trip on the day of his flight. When he said it was a crucial trip, and a lot was riding on it, I became enraged. I just lost it and went off at him." Sania shook her head in disbelief and said, "I can't believe that I fought with him the day he disappeared. It must be the hormones we never fought before." Tears started to form around her eyes.

"Don't be so hard on yourself, Sania. I would have done the same." Arya tried to console Sania.

"That is not such a relief," Sania took a dig at Arya.

"Ouch! That hurts," Arya made a face.

Sania and Arya both half-laughed.

After a moment, Sania continued, "But we made up before he left."

"Oh good," Arya said with a tone that raised Sania's curiosity.

"What?" Sania asked, trying to find the cause for Arya's awkward tone.

"Nothing, just trying to find out about Sam's state of mind when he left that day," Arya said, looking away from Sania.

"Are you saying that Sam disappeared intentionally because of the fight?" Sania asked, feeling upset with Arya.

"No, no," Arya replied quickly, defusing the tension. "This is just routine psychological questions. Nothing more to read."

"Okay, but Sam would never disappear on me intentionally," Sania said confidently. "He loved me and," she pointed at her belly and continued, "And more than anything, he loved this little girl very much. Sam couldn't wait to become a daddy. He would never disappear on us," Sania said emotionally with tears in her eyes.

Arya's experience on the job taught her the number one reason the adults go missing is that they don't want to be found. Forget the histrionics and fallacy shown on TV; the truth is that adults rarely get kidnapped in this country.

Arya knew she had to tread carefully with Sania. The training has molded her to act with empathy in these situations. Arya allowed the moment to settle and for Sania to regain her emotional stability. Once Sania got her footing,

Arya continued, "Based on what you said, you didn't talk to Sam after he landed in Los Angeles?"

Sania shook her head and gently moved her hands across her eyes to wipe drops of tears.

"Okay, got it; the last you heard from him was in the Philly airport," Arya jotted down in her pocketbook.

"No," Sania flatly said, stopping Arya cold.

"What do you mean? You just said that you last spoke to him at the airport," Arya asked, feeling confused.

"Yes, that was the last time we spoke. But Sam called me later that night and left a voicemail."

Arya leaned forward; the new development got her interest piqued. "What did he say?"

"He said that he was sorry, and he kind of cried."

"What? He cried? What exactly did he say?"

"Do you want to know word by word?" Sania asked, gazing at Arya.

"Yes, if you remember." Arya paused and rephrased it. "Whatever you remember," she added, knowing it would be hard for anyone to remember the exact words.

"Would it help if I play the message?" Sania asked, pointing to the answering machine in the corner of the room.

"Definitely," Arya nodded with a hint of surprise in her face.

Sania gingerly got up from the couch and moved towards the answering machine. Arya followed her closely.

"Okay, here it is." Sania then proceeded to play Sam's last message.

"Sania, are you there? If you hear me, please pick up the phone. I am so sorry. Believe me, I feel devastated, leaving for the trip with the fight hanging on in my mind. I am so sorry, that was the last thing I wanted. I didn't want to fight you; I love you, and you know how much I love Sara. I love you, girls', a lot. If I had a choice,

under any other situation, I wouldn't have left you. But this trip... I wish I could tell you more about it, but I can't. You will soon know about it. This is bigger than anything I had imagined for my life. I pray to Allah that you will forgive me. Please forgive me; I love you and Sara a lot."

Those were the last words from Sam.

13

"CAN YOU PLAY IT AGAIN?" Arya asked, closing her eyes to keenly listen and register every word spoken in the message.

As Sania replayed the message, Arya keenly listened, paying close attention to Sam's tone and his choice of words. Her training has taught her to listen to the hidden meaning behind words.

The replay of the voicemail ended, but Arya's eyes remained closed. She kept replaying the message in her head; both the tone and the message's content seemed to unnerve her.

"What is it?" Sania's voice interrupted Arya's stream of thoughts. Arya opened her eyes, and when her gaze landed on Sania, she quickly glanced away from her.

"What?" Sania repeated her question.

"Nothing," Arya said, avoiding eye contact with Sania.

Sania knew something was bothering Arya when she noticed her restlessly fidgeting with the bracelet on her right arm.

"Come on, Arya, I know what that means," Sania frowned,

pointing towards the bracelet that was getting restlessly twisted.

"You remember," Arya raised one of her brows, feeling surprised.

"Of course, you are always an open book to me."

"Now, I remember where all my trauma stemmed from." Arya made a frowning face before breaking out into a silly smile.

After a brief smile, Sania went back to her question, "What is bothering you?"

Arya glanced towards the answering machine.

"Sam's message?" Sania asked, following Arya's gaze.

Arya nodded and, in a low voice, said, "The apology seemed to be quite elaborate for a trivial argument."

"What are you implying?" Sania held her gaze on Arya, searching for the hidden question.

"Are you saying – he ran away?" Sania frowned, feeling exasperated.

Realizing she ruffled Sania's sentiments, Arya motioned both her hands up to surrender. "My bad, my bad."

"You know, if you knew him, you wouldn't have even entertained that question. He loved me." Sania shifted her eyes from Arya towards her belly and said, "More than that, he loved this little girl."

"You are right; I don't know him. Can we forget that I broached that possibility?" Arya pleaded with her eyes, making a sad face.

"For old times' sake, I am calling that your mulligan." Sania relaxed her stiff shoulders and took a deep breath. "This whole thing has me wound up pretty tight; I shouldn't have gone after you like that." Sania appeared to understand that Arya was just trying to do her job.

Sania took Arya's hands and asked, "What were you about to ask before I went off on you? Was it about the voicemail?"

Arya nodded. "Did you call back?"

"Yes, but not right away. I must have turned down the volume on the phone upstairs; I didn't hear the call. I noticed it only in the morning," Sania paused, her eyes looking up as she tried to recollect the timing. "I think I called him around 3:15 in the morning when I woke up to pee."

"3:15," Arya repeated, as she wrote down on her pocket notebook.

"I am certain as I stared at the wall clock in the master bathroom," Sania said confidently.

"Does it help?" Sania asked, eyeing Arya.

"Yes. Every little detail helps in cases like this," Arya said reassuringly. From training, Arya knew that it is essential to encourage and reassure family members. Only when they feel comfortable and helping with the progress, they would remember little details – information that invariably cracks open the case. Only on TV shows would you invariably have an 'aha' moment in the first thirty minutes. But in real situations, it is always a slog, and, most commonly, information considered minutia or minor mistakes committed by perpetrators lead to arrests.

"Wait, how did you know where to call him?" Arya asked suddenly, realizing Sania had earlier mentioned that she didn't know the hotel Sam stayed in Los Angeles.

"Sam's phone," Sania said flatly before adding, "Sam had a mobile phone."

"Oh, that makes sense." Arya couldn't believe that she didn't think of it before. Nowadays, almost everyone of importance carries one. Given Sam's job, it would be imperative for him to have a mobile.

Sania went on to share further details about Sam's mobile: phone number, model, color, and for how long Sam had that same mobile device and number.

"Did he call you back after that?" Arya asked.

"No. He never did," Sania said glumly.

"Did you call later?"

"Yes, many times."

"Do you remember the times, even if it is just an approximate?" Arya wanted to collect as much information as possible when it was fresh in Sania's mind.

"Hmm. I must have called at least 10 times. I am not sure if I remember the exact time; I became panicked when I saw the towers come down," Sania responded, expressing sorrow.

"I understand this could be overwhelming. Just think and answer what you remember," Arya said calmly, trying to reassure and guide Sania towards that fateful day.

Sania closed her eyes, trying to walk herself back to that morning. "Sometime before 8:30. I remember because it was before the first tower got hit. He didn't answer, and I left him a voicemail asking him to call me back."

Arya noted down the time and motioned for Sania to continue.

"When the second tower got hit, I got scared. I went nuts. I knew Sam had some friends in that building, and I started worrying about them. Sam being in LA, I knew he would be sleeping, so I tried him again. I wanted to let him know before he sees it on the news."

"So... Did Sam answer?"

Sania shook her head. "No, it was voicemail again. I was glued to the TV, just like everyone on the coast, trying to understand what the hell was happening. And then it happened. The South Tower went down." Sania sounded jittery - scared and astonished. She was pulling those memories from her head and reliving them again.

"I just couldn't believe it," Sania said in a high-pitched tone. "One minute, I stood frozen, and the next minute, I was scrambling around like a maniac. I just couldn't believe my eyes."

Sania's experience was not foreign to Arya or to millions of other people. The whole country was in shock and couldn't believe their eyes when they saw the towers go down. That moment would forever be etched in everyone's memory.

"He didn't answer again. As I was cursing on his voicemail, the unimaginable happened again: The North Tower collapsed. I gasped; all those poor people. I just couldn't believe it." Sania explained the roller coaster of emotions she had felt; shock, desperation, deep sorrow, anger, vengeance, anxiety, fear…. Again, those feelings were not unique to Sania; it was felt by every American across the great nation.

The tears started to well up in Arya's eyes. As Sania narrated her experience, it transported Arya to that ill-fated day. The day started just like any other day for Arya. Living single, she had picked up the luxury of experimenting pleasures with different people. On that doomsday, she woke up next to a loser whose name she didn't even know. She met him at a bar downtown, playing a game of pool. The downside or upside of alcohol, depending on how you look at it, was that she ended up sleeping with him. As the sun leaked into her bedroom, she realized that she not only slept with the loser but also brought him to her home. Just like how she had dealt with situations like this before, she woke him with a firm nudge and kicked him out before her partner, Edgar James, knocked on her door. The plan almost worked; the loser found his clothes, she hurried him to the door and pushed him towards the stairs, and, when it all seemed to work, it went awry. Edgar was leaning by his car, calmly sipping his morning joe and glancing towards the stairs as the loser rushed down. It would have been awkward if it was the first time, but, given that they had both lost count of similar encounters, they ended up exchanging looks and broke out laughing.

She wished the day would have stayed the same, silly and humorous. However, it didn't.

Edgar was driving, and Arya was riding shotgun, when it all happened. They listened to the first tower being hit on the radio, and she thought immediately, "What a screwup – the pilot must be wasted to pull such an accident." However, the feeling didn't last long. When the second plane hit the south tower, they both knew instinctively the country was under attack. It was a calculated and deliberate hit on the nation. At that point, Arya didn't know who, but she knew in the gut that it was not over. They pulled next to a deli that had a television on and watched the whole tragedy go down. Towers were on fire, the Pentagon was filled with smoke, people were jumping off the towers, and finally, the unthinkable – the towers crumbling.

The whole place went silent; it almost felt that everyone was in a dream. No one could believe what had just happened. How could this happen? This was not the 60's; the Cold War was over, the good guys triumphed, and the Red Army lost. The whole generation knew nothing about the fear of being hit by an enemy on their soil. This was not supposed to happen. Everyone was in shock; their mouths dropped, heads shook in disbelief, and tears were streaming down on their faces. It was a moment that everyone would replay in their head for years to come.

"And I called again, again, and again. But Sam never picked up." Sania's voice hauled Arya back to the present.

Arya rubbed her temples and narrowed her eyes as a way to regain focus. "So, he never called you after the night he left Philly?" Arya asked, pulling the conversation back to the night in question.

Sania nodded slowly, "Yes."

"Did you leave a voicemail?"

Sania nodded.

"Every time?"

"No, not every time. I think only the first couple of times and then once after the towers collapsed."

"When was the last time you called him?"

"When I got back from the station today," Sania answered immediately.

"Did you leave a voicemail?"

"No, it said it was full," Sania responded in a low voice.

"Okay, do you remember when was the last time that it didn't give a voicemail full message?" Arya wanted to confirm the timeline. It might be useful later to determine if Sam was checking his voicemail in Los Angeles and just didn't respond to any of Sania's calls.

Sania lowered her head and placed both her hands on top of the head as she tried to focus hard. After a moment, she shook her head. "Sorry. I don't know the exact time. Is it important for finding Sam?"

Arya reassuringly shook her head. "It's okay; don't fret about it. We have other ways to find out about Sam's call logs, and we will find the answers we need. So, don't worry about it."

Sania half-smiled, feeling reassured.

"You earlier said that he often traveled for work. Where does Sam work?"

"Aries Financials," Sania said flatly.

Arya silently mouthed the company's name as she wrote it down on her notebook.

"Do you know them?" Sania asked, eyeing Arya.

"Yes, I do." Arya glanced up towards Sania and said, "CNBC is my guilty pleasure. I watch them sometimes to keep me updated."

"Updated? Oh, I almost forgot that you are a trust fund baby," Sania exclaimed.

"Don't say that. I hate that term – trust fund baby," Arya mouthed the term mockingly.

"I forgot we used to call you Ms. Richie," Sania laughed.

"I hate that name too." Arya scowled.

"Seriously, why the heck are you working this job? If I am you, I would be sipping mojitos in the Caribbean or one of those exotic Greek islands."

"Trust me, I tried, and it gets boring so fast," Arya expressed dramatically.

"Boring!" Sania raised her brows, "You know who says that? Only people who are filthy rich. For commoners like me, that sounds like paradise." Sania closed her eyes, imagining herself tanning on a white sand beach with rum in her hand.

"You know what? If I did that, I wouldn't have met you now."

"You know I am so glad. I can't think of anyone better to help me under these circumstances," Sania said, expressing her genuine feelings.

Arya nodded with an acknowledging smile before asking, "What exactly did he do in Aries Financials?"

"Trading desk."

"Wow, that should have been exciting," Arya remarked.

"Sure, for him. If you ask me, I hated it."

Arya raised her brows.

"The late hours and the constant trips, crisscrossing the country. Sam was gone a lot, and it put a strain on our marriage."

Arya nodded, understanding the situation. Given her line of work, she has seen similar stress being placed on many of her fellow officers. When you work as a cop, you become a cop — it becomes your identity. The work consumes you — the evil you hunt has a way to haunt you, irrespective of whether you are on the clock or not.

Arya wanted to prod more about the 'strain on the marriage' that Sania just revealed. However, she knew the timing might not be right. Sania earlier blew her casket when that possibility was discussed, and Arya thought it would be prudent to park that discussion for later.

An uncomfortable silence fell between them as Arya contemplated her next question.

"Did you call them yesterday?" Arya broke the silence.

"Aries?" Sania asked rhetorically before answering, "Yes, I did, but I didn't get much. I was not able to reach Sam's supervisor or HR because of what happened yesterday."

"You mean the attacks?"

Sania nodded. "They have an office in New York – the south tower. I can't imagine the loss of life," Sania said solemnly.

Arya shook her head, expressing her dismay.

"Omar Raqqa. He is Sam's supervisor on the trading division," Sania chimed.

Arya mouthed 'Omar Raqqa' as she jotted down his name on her pocketbook.

"Do you have his number?" Arya asked. From experience, she knew people who handle money like to throw lavish parties where families get to socialize. Just like she expected, Sania knew Omar Raqqa's number.

"I called; he hasn't been picking up," Sania said, as she provided the phone number.

"I am sure it was a lot to take," Arya said, referring to the loss Omar's firm must have suffered when the south tower came down.

"I will give it till tomorrow and try calling him," Arya said, writing down the phone number.

"Oh, God!" Sania exclaimed suddenly, covering her mouth with both her hands.

"What happened?" Arya was taken aback by the sudden outburst by Sania.

"Poor Omar. Oh no. I can't believe that I forgot," Sania said dramatically. "His wife works in New York."

"South tower?" Arya quickly asked.

"No, no. Thank God, no. She works in the Stock Exchange."

"Wall Street?" Arya asked, referring to the NYSE.

"Yes. I hope she is okay," Sania said silently.

"She should be. Wall Street was not impacted by the attacks."

"I hope so," Arya closed her eyes; it looked almost like she was praying.

"Do you know them? I mean personally," Arya asked, seeing the concerned expression on Sania's face.

Sania nodded. "I met them a few times; they are good people."

Arya paused her questions about Sam's work when she noticed Sania's eyes battling to stay open. Sania had been running on fumes; it had been close to forty-eight hours since she slept. Arya understood it was time for her to stop, especially given Sania was into her thirty-sixth week. The rest of the questions could wait until tomorrow. Anyway, she had enough information to start her investigation. Her first stop – Aries Financials.

Arya reassured Sania one more time about finding Sam before leaving Sania's house.

When Arya roared her Crown Vic to life, disturbing the stillness of the neighborhood, the time on her dashboard read 11:25.

A few feet away, a man sitting in darkness in a parked silver Honda watched Arya drive away. He pulled a cigarette from the silver stainless steel case, and thoughtfully tapped the case with the cigarette in his hand as he glanced towards Sania's house. In Sania's house, the lights downstairs were turned off, and he waited for a few more minutes to see the lights go out upstairs. He then took a long drag, filling his lungs with toxins from the cigarette, and slowly exhaled, closing his eyes, filling the car with smoke. No one needs to tell the man; he knew smoking was not good for him. He and his buddies always considered the warnings on the box as a joke. When a man doesn't change to his daughter's tearful plea, there was no way a sign on the box would change the man's behavior. The days like this – waiting endlessly in a car, surveilling the subject, had made cigarette his friend. It was not just him; most of his buddies on the job have the same vice – Red's and Jack's – two benefits that you got as part of your job.

His eyes were closing in as the time stuck midnight. The lights remaining turned off, and it seemed like Sania was not going anywhere. He finished the cigarette in his hand – he lost count of how many he had smoked tonight – before calling it a night and driving away into the darkness.

14

ARYA NARROWED HER EYES, squinting to adjust to the bright sun shining bright and early in the morning. Arya reached inside her car to get her shades – a classic Ray-Ban Aviator; her preferred glasses for the fall. She loved them so much that she has fifteen of them, one in almost every color it was made. She ruffled through the collection and picked the flash green one that goes with her light green top.

"Now we are talking," Arya said to herself with a smile as she gazed at the Aries Financials building without squinting her eyes.

As Arya approached the front door of the Aries Financials building, she heard her phone buzz. She pulled the phone resting on her belt, and her expression changed to familiarity when she noticed the caller ID on the phone.

"What's up? You are bright and early," Arya said on her phone, addressing her partner, Edgar James, on the other end.

"Where are you?" Edgar answered abruptly.

"Wow, wow. Slow down. No greetings for me. Are you a boss man now?" Arya teased Edgar.

Edgar and Arya go way back; they were both at the Academy at the same time and graduated together. Looking in from the outside, Arya and Edgar were as different as chalk and cheese. Edgar loved football, and Arya hated football. Edgar is a hard-core carnivore who loves to eat meat every day, and Arya is a vegetarian. Edgar grew up in a low-income neighborhood, and having money was as foreign as a Greek island, and Arya was affluent - born rich. Edgar is a card-carrying Republican, and Arya is a liberal. Overall the odds were stacked against them to not like each other, but lo and behold! They became best friends.

"Where are you?" Edgar asked.

"Center City; Market and 18th," Arya announced her location.

"What the hell are you doing in the financial district?" Edgar asked with a surprise.

"Buying a bank," Arya teased.

"Aries Financials?" Edgar pulled up Arya's location using the GPS locator tagged to Arya's Crown Vic.

"Yup, that's it. Do you want in on the buy?" Arya asked playfully.

"Arya, today is not a time to goof around." Edgar paused before adding in a hushed tone, "LT is asking for you."

"Why?"

"We have a briefing in thirty minutes."

"From whom?" Arya asked, entering the swiveling front doors of Aries Financials.

"Not sure, but the rumor on the floor is FBI," Edgar said, stressing each syllable.

"Is it about 9/11?" Arya said, motioning her hand towards the Aries Financials' security guard to hold on for a minute.

"No clue. LT just popped into the squad room and asked us to get our asses in the conference room."

"I think it should be about the 9/11 investigation. Why

would the Feds come to our meager grounds?" Arya wondered out aloud.

"You might be right. You better come here. LT specifically asked about your whereabouts."

"What did you say?"

"You stepped out for a coffee run."

"Good cover; he knows I hate that shitty squad room coffee."

"He asked me to haul you in; get your ass here," Edgar said with urgency.

"I am on my way."

Before Edgar could breathe a sigh of relief, Arya added, "This pit stop shouldn't take more than fifteen minutes. Cover me, I might be slightly late." Arya ended the call, leaving Edgar stunned.

Given Arya's current location, Edgar knew it would be difficult for her to make it to the station on time, even if she left straightaway. With whatever she was doing in Center City, it would be impossible for her to make it to the station before the briefing started. He wasn't surprised Arya asked him to cover for her; it has become quite frequent nowadays. All officers do it for their partners; it is an unwritten code among the brethren. However, the surprising element was how Arya asked; there was no hint of nervousness in her voice.

"It is good to be rich," Edgar said, shaking his head with a smile on his face.

"PHILLY PD," Arya announced, holding her badge.

The Aries Financials security personnel nodded approvingly and asked, "What can I do for you, Detective?"

"I am here to talk to Omar Raqqa; he works in the trading desk," Arya said authoritatively.

"One-minute Detective, let me get him." The security personnel addressed Arya with respect and asked her to wait in the spacious lounge as he went inside to get Omar.

In a rush this morning, Arya uncharacteristically skipped her second coffee before leaving her home. Arya eyed the waiting lounge on her right and decided to take advantage of the opportunity to fuel up with coffee to get her through the morning. It had been a standing bet between Arya and her partner, Edgar James, on who could hold out longer without going over the five-a-day coffee limit. The score then stood lopsided in favor of Edgar.

When Arya stepped into the expansive lounge and did a 360-degree survey of the place, the memories from her past flooded her mind – specifically, the visits to her dad's office building in Manhattan. The lounge was modern in style and luxurious in substance. The walls were adorned with artwork depicting the historical progression of the marketplace from Greeks to Wall Street bankers. The historic artwork was in contrast with the room design: furniture in the room and the amenities provided in the place. Arya was a person who usually doesn't get impressed that easily. However, when she spotted a futuristic coffee maker that could make every type of coffee anyone had ever desired, a smile washed over her face. After a moment of deliberation, she decided to pour herself a cup of Kopi Luwak coffee. Kopi Luwak was not only one of the most exotic coffees in the world, but it was also one of the most expensive coffees. The word on the street is that a couple of pounds of Kopi Luwak retails at a whopping seven hundred dollars on the market.

Arya glanced at the morning edition of the Wall Street Journal, Philadelphia Inquirer, and The New York Times as she sipped her morning juice. All the articles on the front page had coverage related to one news story, the 9/11 attacks; After the Attacks: The Investigation; Bin Laden cited. The word 'Investigation' spiked Arya's curiosity, and she flipped open the Times to devour the frontpage article.

The article reported that the hijackers who commandeered the jetliners into the World Trade Center and Pentagon were followers of Osama Bin Laden, an Islamic militant who headed a jihadi terrorist group named 'Al-Qaeda.' It explained that Bin Laden had attacked American interests before, in Yemen and in Africa, but this was the first time he was able to carry the attacks on the mainland. The article cited unconfirmed sources while reporting that four to six hijackers might have participated in hijacking the four planes. It was also reported that most of the hijackers entered the country through student or tourist visas, and some might have overstayed their stay. The investigators have executed warrants in Massachusetts, New Jersey, and Florida, and they are now in the process of executing more warrants across the eastern seaboard.

Arya raised her brows when she read the line regarding cities across the eastern seaboard. *Is Philly going to be one of them? Was the briefing this morning related to these warrants?*

"Detective Martins." Arya was hauled back to the present when she heard her name being called.

Arya turned around, and her gaze landed on a man dressed in a black suit.

"Jonathan Ashton." The man extended his hand and introduced himself to Arya.

Arya reached forward and took the man's hand. "Arya Martins, Philly PD."

"What can we do for you?" Ashton asked formally and respectfully.

"It is about Omar Raqqa," Arya said, holding her gaze at him.

"Oh, I see. Let us step into that room that would give us some privacy," Ashton said, motioning his hand to point to a room that was adjacent to the coffeemaker.

Arya nodded and followed him to a long room, which looked like a visitor's room. As they entered the room, the overhead lights in the room came to life.

"Can I offer you anything to drink?" Ashton politely asked.

"I am fine," Arya replied, taking a seat opposite Ashton.

"Did you find out what happened to Omar Raqqa?" The question from Ashton surprised Arya.

Arya narrowed her eyes and asked, "What do you mean? Did something happen to Raqqa?"

Ashton's expression changed to confusion. "I thought you said it was about Omar."

Arya nodded, "Yes, it is. I wanted to talk to him."

"I guess that is not possible," Ashton said, leaning back in his chair. "He is missing."

"Missing?" Arya asked rhetorically. "From when?"

"About three months back. I thought you were here about Raqqa's case," Ashton said with a puzzled expression on his face.

Arya ignored his remark and asked, "Did you report him missing?"

"Yes, we did, around the time he went missing."

Arya queried more and learned that Aries Financials reported Omar Raqqa missing in the Norristown precinct in May. However, Ashton didn't know the name of the investigating officer. He offered to find out from HR and share it with Arya by tomorrow.

"Who reported to HR that Mr. Raqqa was missing?"

"It was the VP of the trading desk – Mr. Trey Landon."

Arya noted down the VP's name and asked, "What made Landon suspect Raqqa was missing?"

"Raqqa missed reporting to work for a couple of days."

"Is that it? I have missed work a couple of days, and my boss didn't report me missing." Arya probed to gather more details.

"True. You are not Raqqa; he has never missed work without calling it in." Ashton paused for a moment and added, "And also the letter." Ashton stressed the word 'letter.'

"What letter?"

"Mr. Landon got a letter from Raqqa – it was a resignation letter. In that letter, Raqqa cited the reason he was resigning was that he was feeling burnt-out, and he needed a break desperately. He mentioned that he was planning to travel and clear his head."

"Oh! Why is that suspicious? It seems Raqqa clearly spelled out his reasons."

"It could be, but Mr. Landon thought something was amiss."

"What?"

"I don't know; I was not privy to that. You have to speak to Mr. Landon?"

"Is he here?"

"No, he is in Dubai. He should be here today, but his flight got canceled because of," Ashton hesitated, and, in an emotional tone, said, "because of 9/11."

A brief silence ensued between them; the room's mood turned somber with the mention of 9/11.

Arya cleared her throat and said, "Can you ask him to give me a call when he gets here?" She then proceeded to give her phone number to Ashton.

"Sure, will do."

"Is there anything else, Detective?" Ashton asked.

"Yes. Can you tell me where Samir Tariq stayed on his trip to Los Angeles on September 10th?"

"Samir Tariq...." Ashton slowly repeated the name, like a

person trying to jog his memory. "Hmm…. Sorry, I can't place his name," Ashton said apologetically. "Should I know him? Is this related to Raqqa?" Ashton asked, wondering about the nature of the question.

If Arya's reaction was of a surprise, she didn't show it. "Samir Tariq works here," she said evenly.

"Here, you mean with us – Aries Financials?" Ashton sounded surprised.

"Yes. Samir Tariq works in the Trading Desk, and his boss is…," Arya paused momentarily to correct her choice of tense, "His boss was Omar Raqqa."

"That is not possible," Ashton said confidently, leaning back in his chair.

The definitive words of Ashton bothered and surprised Arya. Arya raised her brows and asked, "How so?"

"Do you remember the timeline I mentioned regarding Raqqa's disappearance?" Ashton asked rhetorically and continued without waiting for Arya's reply. "That was three months back."

Arya nodded. "So?"

"Do you know who took Raqqa's position?" Ashton showed off his bombastic attitude with his rhetorical questions.

"Ashton, can we stop these show-and-tell games and cut to the chase?" Arya became frustrated with Ashton's showy attitude.

"Sorry, Detective Martins." Ashton raised both of his hands to his shoulders to gesture an apology. "Don't take it the wrong way; I behave the same way with everyone."

Arya thought that only in a jerk's mind that statement could be construed as an apology. "What a jerk?" she thought to herself.

"Was it you who took Raqqa's position?" Arya asked, connecting the puzzle.

"Bingo! That is why you are a detective," Ashton said, making a recoil motion with his hand as if to suggest it was a bullseye shot.

Arya ignored Ashton's dramatics and proceeded with her inquiry. "I presume you don't have a Samir Tariq in your group?"

"Yes."

"Is it possible he switched to a different group when you joined?"

"Yes, it is very much possible. I moved from the London division just after Raqqa disappeared. He might have switched."

"Is there a way to confirm it?"

"Sure, I can do that easily." Ashton flipped open a laptop resting on the table.

Arya's eyes shifted towards the large white screen as it came to life. The laptop seemed to be hooked to a small white rectangular device, a projector, which displayed the details on the hundred-inch white screen.

Ashton pulled up a webpage and typed 'Samir Tariq' in the search box. The page in design looked very similar to Google's search page, which Arya was quite familiar with. With every passing day, Google was becoming her go-to site, which she frequently depends on to find general information. She liked Google's simplistic design way better than Yahoo's design, which she considered to be cluttered.

"Okay, here it is...," Ashton muttered as the screen refreshed to spit out two entries with the name 'Samir Tariq.'

"Wow, that is strange. I thought the name was unique enough that we would get a single hit," Ashton remarked.

"Can we click on the hyperlink?" Arya pushed Ashton to keep it moving.

"Wow! Hyperlink. Someone here is a techie," Ashton said in a patronizing way.

Ashton's obnoxious behavior was getting to Arya. "Ashton, I think anyone with a brain would know what a hyperlink is," Arya snapped.

"I don't think so. Trust me, I know some people who have no clue. Hello mother-in-law," Ashton cackled, boisterously.

Arya felt sorry for Ashton's wife. "It must be a pain to live with this asshole," Arya thought to herself.

When Ashton clicked on the first 'Samir Tariq' entry, a new page appeared on the screen that looked like a Wikipedia page. It contained detailed information about the employee: biographical, work history, education, and comprehensive history about their time in Aries Financials.

Arya's gaze immediately landed on the picture to the right, and she leaned forward to take a closer look. The image was a typical profile photo that we see every day in driving licenses or other forms of IDs. It showed a middle-aged man with a thinning hairline, smiling broadly, and he had facial features typical to people from the Middle East.

"Realty Funds," Ashton read Samir's group in Aries Financials aloud as he continued to swift through his employment history in Aries. "Oh, I see, you are right. He did work for Raqqa before…." He paused as he clicked on another hyperlink that showed more details. "It seems he switched from Trading to Realty the week before Raqqa disappeared."

"That's not him," Arya said flatly, looking at the picture on the screen. "This is not the Samir I am looking for."

"Can you click on the other one?" Arya asked.

"Wait… this sucks," Ashton said, showing emotion for the first time.

"What?"

"This guy is dead. He committed suicide; he cut his hand and was found dead in his bathtub." Ashton slowly shook his head, showing empathy.

"When?"

Ashton went back to the screen to read through the timeline. "Hmm. It looks like June 5th. A week after Raqqa disappeared."

Even though it was not the 'Samir' Arya was looking for, something felt odd to her. The close proximity between this Samir's death and Omar's disappearance troubled her. *What are the odds of something terrible happening to three people in the same group in a short time?* First, it was Omar's disappearance, and then tragedy stuck both the Samir Tariqs – one by suicide, and the other disappearing into thin air. Also, how odd was it that there were two Samir Tariqs in that group. It was not like his name was Jason or John or James. The name Samir Tariq is as exotic as they come.

"This is odd," Ashton said, gazing at his laptop screen.

Arya turned her attention to the projected screen, and her mouth dropped in shock.

Ashton had clicked on the second Samir Tariq from the search results, and the profile picture displayed on the screen was of Sania's Samir. No doubt about that. However, that was not the cause of Arya's shock. Instead, it was due to the employee status shown next to his name, Samir Tariq – Resigned on June 1st, 2001.

Ashton turned towards Arya and exchanged a puzzled glance. "Is this the Samir Tariq you were looking for?"

Arya nodded. "Yes."

"Hmm... I thought you said his wife reported that he was still working here?" Ashton asked with a quizzical expression.

"Yes. I guess Samir must have kept Sania in the dark about his resignation. But why?" Arya thought in her mind.

At this moment, Arya had no clue. Even if she did, she had no interest sharing that with Ashton. "Sorry, I can't get into it. Active investigation," Arya said flatly.

"Hmm… This is bonkers," Ashton said, gazing fixedly at this laptop screen.

Arya shifted her eyes back to the large screen and found Ashton had navigated to Samir's work history with Aries Financials. If Samir's resignation caused her jaw to drop, then what she had just learned about his work history felt like a tremor. Samir had never worked in the Trading Division under Omar Raqqa. Instead, he worked as a service technician in the Environment Division.

"A class liar! I got to give it to this guy," Ashton said, laughing as he read the file.

"This guy is a blue-collar guy. He came as close to the trading stocks like me qualifying for Augusta," Ashton laughed at his own joke.

"How long did he work here?" Arya asked, still trying to make sense of what she just learned.

"Just four months, it looks like he started only in February of 2001."

That was another lie. Based on her discussion with Sania, Samir had been working here since 1999. *If not here, where did he work?*

"Can you tell where he worked before Aries?"

Ashton's fingers danced on the keyboard. "Yes, just one. He has listed a name – Rashid Al Iqbal – as his reference in SAEWA."

"SAEWA?" Arya asked, as she had no clue what the abbreviation 'SAEWA' represented.

"Saudi Arabia Electrical and Water Authority. It states that he was working there from 1996 till the beginning of this year," Ashton said evenly.

The surprises started to mount up for Arya. Samir had not only kept his resignation as a secret from Sania, but he also had blatantly lied about his overall work experience. From what she had gathered from Sania, Samir had been in the U.S. for the last two years working for Aries Financials. How could he have continued to work for SAEWA from the U.S. as a maintenance technician?

"If Samir had kept Sania in the dark about his work, what else did he lie about?" Arya wondered.

She made a mental note to find out about Samir's life before he got married to Sania. One thing has become clear to Arya; Samir had been living a double life for at least two years. But the question is, why? What need did Samir have to lead a secret life? Arya knew that would be the answer to find out what really happened to Samir on September 11th.

"Can you email me both their pictures?" Arya asked Ashton, referring to Omar and the other Samir.

"Sure." Ashton collected Arya's email address. It had been only a couple of years since everyone in her department was assigned an email address. It was optional before. She had always been comfortable with technical gadgets, but the same could not be said for her partner. To her, Edgar was a hunter-gatherer in the digital world.

"Thanks." Arya extended her hands and thanked Ashton for his help in the investigation.

As she walked out of the building, she had more questions than answers. The information she had learned about Samir was soul-crushing. The last thing she wanted to tell her friend was that her husband was a liar and lived a life of deceit.

15

IT WAS five minutes to eleven when Arya finally made it to her precinct.

She stopped her stride as she crossed the cafeteria; it was surprisingly empty. She turned to her right and peeked inside; the coffee machines were enjoying their time off, and there was no commotion around the foosball table. Forget the commotion; there were only two people in the entire cafeteria.

"Hey," Arya signaled towards a Uni who was sitting closer to the refrigerator, enjoying his donut and getting his sports update from the Philadelphia Inquirer.

As the Uni turned towards her, Arya asked, "Where is everyone?"

"Upstairs. They are all huddled in the conference room," he answered.

"Damn it," Arya reproached herself. She couldn't believe that she had forgotten about her conversation with Edgar this morning.

"FBI," she silently whispered to herself as she hurried upstairs.

As Arya reached the top of the stairs, she could see the squad room to her right. There was a reason why the squad room was often called the 'Long Room.' Yes, it was atypically long, but that was not the reason why they started calling it the 'Long Room.' When she first joined here, she met an old copper who was turning in his badge after forty years of service. In his retirement party at Joe's dive bar down the street, he had one too many Jack's. As everyone in the force knows, one of the side effects of Jack's is nostalgia. He began to spin tales about his German ancestry and how his family played a crucial role in establishing this German settlement. He claimed that his great-great-great-great-grandfather chaired the history slavery meeting among the Quakers to discuss their opposition to slavery. He went on to say that the meeting took place in the same room where he had worked for the last forty years. The folklore was that the room was referred to as 'Long Room' because of the shape of the room. No one knew if the old copper's story was true, but the term 'Long Room' stayed on. Everyone in the squad just referred to it as the 'Long Room.'

Arya's gaze shifted towards the far-right corner, where she noticed her fellow officers sprinkling out of the meeting room. She saw her partner, Edgar James, walking towards his desk. As usual, he was dressed impeccably. He had a classic navy suit tailored to fit him perfectly that showed off his muscular physique.

Arya walked across the room and sat across the table from Edgar. The Long Room is arranged like most of the other precincts with tables arranged orderly like in a school. A table is shared by two detectives who are partners.

Edgar glanced at his watch and slowly lifted his gaze towards Arya. "Well, what do I owe to be graced with your presence," he said sarcastically with a smile.

"Thank your good looks," Arya said playfully.

"Jeez! You never change," Edgar chuckled, leaning forward to high five Arya.

The relationship between fellow officers is always a special type of bond. The camaraderie is ripe with elements like respect, trust, and friendship. With the amount of time the partners end up spending together, they become family to each other.

Given Edgar and Arya's friendship blossomed right from the Academy, their friendship has an added dimension to it. The training period for the Academy was quite long. It was thirty weeks, and, somewhere during those thirty weeks, they had become partners, not just professionally at the Academy, but also at the bars. They became each other's wingman, helping each other out with the dating scene. In fact, Arya was the reason Edgar got married to his wife, Simone James. Back in the day, Arya was known for the fanciest parties she threw, and, for one of those parties, Arya invited her friends from the country club. Simone was one of them. As the night went on, the party got thinner, and, by two in the morning, there were only three people – Arya, Simone, and Edgar. They ended up playing truth or dare, and one thing led to another, and Edgar ended up kissing Simone. The kiss lingered longer than the game warranted. The next day, Edgar and Simone ended up going on a proper date, and the rest was history.

"Okay, coming back to you. What the heck where you doing in Center City? A late-night date or an early morning booty call?" Edgar playfully smiled.

"I wish!" Arya let out a deep breath as she rolled her eyes in a jovial way and said, "I do really need it."

Both of them cracked up, enjoying their playful banter.

"Okay, in all seriousness, what the heck were you doing that was so important you missed the briefing?" Edgar brought the conversation back to Arya's morning.

"Do you remember the name Sania?" Arya asked.

"Hmmm…." Edgar shifted his gaze upwards, trying to place the name 'Sania.'

"Is this Sania, the one you were close with in college?"

Arya nodded approvingly. "Yup, from high school onwards. The same Sania."

"What's up with her? Did you meet her this morning?"

Arya slightly shook her head. "I saw her yesterday." Arya paused briefly and pointed her fingers downwards and gently tapped at the table as she said, "In fact, I ran into her right here – in our building."

"That must be a nice surprise. I know how much you liked Sania." Edgar and Arya, being close, got to know about each other's past well. In Arya's past, Sania featured prominently, and she had shared many stories about her friend.

"How did she find you?"

"She didn't." Arya held her gaze at Edgar and continued, "Sania was here to file a complaint, and we kind of bumped into each other."

Edgar leaned forward, expressing interest in hearing more. "What complaint?"

"About her husband, Samir Tariq. He has been missing."

"What?" Edgar expressed surprise.

"Yes. He has been missing from 9/11," Arya said evenly.

"9/11!" Edgar looked dismayed. "Was he in the towers?"

Arya shook her head.

"New York?"

"Nope. He left for Los Angeles from Philly the previous night, and no one has heard from him since then."

"Oh. For business or pleasure?" Edgar asked, getting into the case.

"That is where it gets tricky," Arya said, leaning back in her chair. "As per Sania, he went to LA for business."

"I see a but coming," Edgar chimed in.

Arya slightly shook her head. "He didn't; I checked with his employer."

"I guess that's where you went this morning." Edgar connected the dots between the story and Arya being in Center City this morning.

"Yes and no," Arya said.

Edgar's eyes widened, expressing confusion with Arya's answer. "I get the yes, but not the no."

"Yes, I went to Center City to confirm Samir's business trip to LA, and Aries Financials confirmed that he didn't go there for business."

"I assume Aries Financials is Samir's employer?"

Arya nodded and continued, "That is where it gets trickier. Sania, last night, told me that her husband is working for Aries Financials."

"Don't tell me that Samir is not working for them?" Edgar realized that was the curveball.

Arya sighed as she said, "Samir did work for Aries, but he resigned in June."

"So, he didn't tell his wife. Sneaky," Edgar thought aloud.

"Not just that. Sania told me that Samir has been working for Aries for the last two to three years." Arya paused, raising Edgar's anticipation before continuing, "But I found out that was not the case. Samir joined only in February of this year. He hardly worked there for six months."

"Shit. That is some lying," Edgar said. "I know husbands lie, but this is in a whole different stratosphere."

"No kidding," Arya said, agreeing with Edgar.

"Did you tell your friend?"

"Not yet. I came here right after with the hope of making the briefing."

"They moved it up." Edgar went on to explain that the suits rolled into the office and pushed the briefing earlier.

"What did the FBI say?" Everyone in the force knows

'suits' stand for the FBI, even though detectives across the country also wear suits.

"JTTF," Edgar corrected. JTTF stood for Joint Terrorism Task Force and was first set up in 1980 by the FBI in conjunction with New York state authorities to combat terrorism in the country. FBI's JTTF was formed to build a real partnership between many federal, state, and local law enforcement agencies. The goal was to cut through turf warfare between the agencies by having representation from all of them work hand-in-hand. By 2001, the number of JTTFs grew to a total of thirty-six across the nation. After 9/11, the importance and number of JTTFs grew tremendously.

"We had people from the FBI, Secret Service, USCIS, CBP, and our top brass."

"Here?" Arya was stunned, learning the level of presence that descended on her precinct that day.

"There seems to be some unconfirmed intelligence that some of the hijackers visited our town in July."

"What? Here?" Arya was stunned.

"I couldn't believe it too." Edgar leaned in.

"What did they say?" Arya was eager to hear more about this shocking revelation.

"They didn't really share much about the source or overall investigation. The suits were playing it close to their vest. However, they did say that they will be sharing pictures of those two hijackers who might have visited our town."

"They want us to knock on doors and find out more about them?"

"Mosques…." Edgar stopped his sentence abruptly when he heard Lieutenant Cooper's voice boom across the room.

"Arya." Arya turned in the direction of the voice and found LT Cooper standing at the doorstep of his office with the firm gaze directed towards her.

The stern gaze and firm tone meant only thing; LT Cooper was not in a good mood. Given Arya missed the critical briefing, she knew immediately that she would be getting her ass handed out to her.

"Pray for me," Arya whispered to Edgar as she walked towards LT Cooper's office.

16

ARYA HESITANTLY WALKED through the open doors to find LT Cooper sitting on his desk, peering at a report. Without looking up, he motioned his hand to signal Arya to close the door.

"LT…." Arya didn't get far with her opening as LT Cooper motioned his hand to signal her to hold her thoughts.

An uncomfortable silence descended on Arya. LT Cooper had his gaze firmly on the report, studying and marking notes on it.

Based on her experience, Arya knew that LT was known to ice difficult situations with uncomfortable silence. It was kind of similar to the interrogative techniques they employ with suspects. When a suspect gets to the can or is brought in for questioning, seasoned interrogators typically ice them for hours. The studies have shown that suspects eventually break down and confess to things which they might not have admitted to if they were confronted without the prickly wait. From a psychological perspective, humans are social animals, and nothing makes them more uncomfortable than excruciating silence, especially when they are hiding something or have done something wrong.

Arya shifted her gaze from LT to his desk; it was squeaky clean except the report in front of LT and a framed picture of his family. In the photo, he was standing next to his wife and his son in front of Harvard University. Arya remembers the day very well. It was one of the rare moments when LT had tears in his eyes; his only son was graduating from Harvard. The entire squad later had gone out to Terry's dive to celebrate the moment.

The silence continued to grow with no end in sight. Arya cleared her throat with the hope of catching LT's attention, but it bared no success. LT continued to ice Arya.

Arya pulled a chair and made herself comfortable across from LT. There was no reason why she had to fight the inevitable. LT was going to break the silence when he intended to do it. Arya started to drum her fingers on the table, which made LT look up to give a staredown. Arya caught herself in the act and stopped drumming.

"LT," Arya began, but LT shifted his gaze back down at the report.

LT Mike Cooper is a large man; he weighs around 250 pounds and stood tall at an inch over six feet. His family could be described as a modern American family. It is inter-racial - he is black, his wife is white, and their son is multi-racial. LT Cooper had a deep voice to go with his imposing figure, and that made everyone around him take him seriously, even before he held any title.

It was time to fess up.

"I know I messed up. It's my bad." Arya dragged the difficult words from her mouth.

LT Cooper slowly raised his head. "Go on."

"I should have been here for the briefing. I screwed up.

No two ways about it." Arya raised her hands, gesturing her apology.

"Why didn't you come?" LT glared.

"I was doing a favor for an old friend," Arya started.

"Would that friend be Sania, your old college mate?"

"Jeez. How the fuck did you find out?" Arya lost her language in a moment of surprise.

"Language, kiddo." LT expressed his displeasure with Arya's foul-mouthed language in both an authoritative and paternal manner.

"Did the blabbermouth Edgar rat me out?"

LT shook his head. "He tried to cover for you."

"What did he say?" Arya asked inquisitively, knowing Edgar must be the one who messed it.

"Your papa had a fall, and you had to take him to the hospital."

"Shithead!" Arya cursed loudly at Edgar for royally screwing the pooch.

LT Cooper and Arya's dad, James Martins, go way back; they have been drinking buddies for almost thirty years. When Cooper met Arya's dad, he was a young copper, and James was an ambitious broker in one of the finest NY investment firms. The night they met was August 12th, 1971, a day that Arya or her family would never forget. It was Arya's birthday, literally the day and year she was born.

Arya's dad, James Martins, had just moved to the Big Apple the previous year. Like most young stockbrokers, he was hungry, ambitious, and wanted to make a name for himself. He literally worked day and night, crunching the numbers, reading the charts, following the trades, and literally anything under the sun that would give him a leg up. He strived hard to make himself visible to one of the partners. On the evening of August 12th, James finally got a break, a chance that he had been sweating for the last year. He had foreseen a merger between two airlines, which ended up making a massive windfall for the firm and their big-money clients. This gave him a lucky break, a dinner meeting with managing partners of the firm. Arya's mom, Angela Martins, knew that very well. That evening, when James had called to say about the dinner meeting with the big shots, Angela's water just broke. But, knowing how much her husband craved the meeting, she didn't want him to miss it. Like a wife who loved her husband to death, Angela just wished him well from her heart and hid her condition from him. After she hung up with him, she hurried to her car and tried to drive herself to the nearby hospital. But fate had other plans.

Just as she took an exit from Grand Central Parkway, she felt a painful cramp that made her lose control of the car. A young copper, Mike Cooper, was watching the tail end of the exit for speeding cars when he noticed a car weaving out of control on the street. Cooper rushed with his sirens flashing to the side of the out-of-control vehicle. When he saw the driver was a young woman struggling with unbearable pain and losing control of the car. He tried to desperately signal the young woman to stop the vehicle. Angela, catching the cop's signal, on her side view, tried with all her might and pressed the brakes to bring the car to a stop.

When Cooper hurried to Angela's side, it was then he realized Angela was pregnant. Angela was screaming with unbearable pain, and there was significant water discharge around her. At that point, Cooper knew there was no time to get to the hospital, and the baby was coming out anytime soon. Every cop in the force undergoes training to deliver a baby in case of an emergency. However, in reality, most of them never had to put that training to use in their lifetime. Cooper had no reason to believe he would be any different. However, at that moment, he didn't panic, and the training kicked in. He rushed back from his car with a pair of latex gloves and a sterile blanket. From that moment on, it was a haze for both Angela and Cooper for the next five minutes. At the end of five minutes, Cooper was holding a beautiful girl in his hands. The whole moment was surreal for Cooper. It would be another nine years before he would hold his own baby. In a way, Arya was his first.

When James heard the news, he rushed to the Queens Hospital to see Angela nursing an angel. James had tears in his eyes, and when he later learned about Cooper, he rushed to Cooper's precinct and found him. From that point on, they remained best friends. They might not agree on politics or social causes, but they always remained close.

In the corner of his heart, James even knew Arya decided to be a cop because of Cooper. A lesser man might have been bothered that his angel didn't follow in his footsteps to take over the family business. Instead, she followed his friend's footsteps and became a cop. But James was not a lesser man. He was proud of Arya, and with all his heart, he supported her decision.

"DON'T BLAME EDGAR. He doesn't know James and I are close."

"Did you call him?"

"What do you think?" Cooper narrowed his eyes.

"Shit."

"I am going to kill him," Arya murmured, fuming at Edgar.

"It is not going to help you here. Now spill your guts. When did Sania come back into your life?"

"Yesterday. Sania was here yesterday to file a case; her husband is missing," Arya said, holding her gaze at Cooper.

"Who? The kid from NYU?" Cooper asked. "What's his name? I forgot…." Cooper was searching in his head to recollect the name of the guy Arya's friend was dating.

"Reza Tariq," Arya offered.

"Yup," Cooper nodded, recognizing the name from the past.

"Arya did not marry Reza Tariq; she married a different person," Arya said, drumming her fingers on the table.

"Interesting. What happened to Reza?"

"I don't know." Arya shrugged her shoulders.

"What do you mean you don't know? You didn't ask your friend?"

"I did. But Sania was not ready to talk about him," Arya said and went on to explain that Sania was pretty shaken up with the situation. She didn't want to dig up the past. She had presumed it might have ended up painfully, given Sania and Reza were madly in love when she last saw them in that NY bar.

"I assume you were out this morning because you were on a little expedition for your friend?" Cooper asked, bringing the conversation back to the case.

Arya nodded. "Yes. Last night, Sania mentioned that Samir went on a business trip to LA, and he hasn't returned any calls from her."

"What did you find out?" Cooper asked, raising a glass of water to drink.

"He was no longer working there."

Cooper's raised glass stopped near his lips; Arya's response clearly surprised him.

"Not just that, it seems Samir resigned in June."

"So, he has been lying for a little over three months to his wife," Cooper analyzed the situation.

"Yes. But that was not the surprising part," Arya teased, setting up her big reveal.

"Sania had mentioned that Samir worked in their trading desk, but instead, I found out that he worked as a service technician in their Environment Division. He lied about the type of work he did there."

"Why? Is this some kind of pride thing in that culture? Service technician vs. bigshot broker?" Cooper speculated.

"It was just not that," Arya said, before going over all the details she found out from Ashton.

When Arya filled in about the other Samir Tariq, who worked in the trading desk, Cooper jumped in. "Are you sure it was not your friend's husband?"

Arya nodded. "I saw the pictures they had on file; it was not."

"Jeez, how many Tariqs we got here. Is that a common Muslim name?" Cooper asked, wondering if that explains why there were two Samir Tariqs in one office.

"No. I am not an expert, but I am fairly certain it is not a common name like John or Smith."

"One more thing," Arya started, before sharing details about what she found out about Omar Raqqa.

Upon hearing everything Arya found out so far, Cooper became highly intrigued. "There seems to be a lot of coincidences. Multiple identities, missing people, suicide, and a whole lot of lies."

Arya nodded. "It is more complex than I thought."

"Where did you say Samir go on his business trip? Is it NY?"

Arya shook her head. "I thought the same; that could

explain him not being reachable. But no, he went to LA, the other coast."

"Interesting. What do you think? Cheating husband, having someone on the side?"

"That is a possibility; it could explain some of the lies. But there are other holes which don't fit, at least for now." Arya quickly highlighted a couple of inconsistencies with the case.

"Okay, what do you need? I guess you already assigned this case to you," Cooper asked, showing dissatisfaction with Arya's approach.

"Sorry, I was not trying to take advantage of the situation. I was planning on reaching out to you, but yesterday you were in the headquarters," Arya tried to explain.

Cooper nodded. "9/11, it changes everything. I was in a meeting with JTTF, and we heard all kinds of stuff. Everyone is scared; we don't know when the next thing is going to blow up. Everyone is wound up pretty tight."

Arya interjected, "I heard that one of the hijackers was in Philly."

"That is the prelim info. We are going to get more details shortly. We are going to fucking canvas the area; turn every source we got and see if we can confirm that." Cooper sounded angry and determined at the same time.

"These fucking jihadis chose the wrong kind of people to fuck with," Arya echoed Cooper's anger.

"I know you got your friend's case in your mind, but let me tell you straight," Cooper stared at her and said, "The 9/11 investigation is the absolutely the top priority here."

"Understood. It goes without saying," Arya replied, gazing at Cooper.

"I will let you run your friend's case until we hear more from JTTF. We are going to start with the Unis; they are going to canvas the area. We then need the seasoned detectives hit the sensitive areas – like mosques, restaurants, and stores frequented by Arabs."

"Can't wait," Arya expressed her feelings.

"You can pull Edgar and chase the leads on your friend's case. But...."

"No need to say, 9/11 is the top priority," Arya completed Cooper's thoughts.

1 7

"HERE, THIS IS FOR YOU." Edgar pushed an icepack towards Arya as she neared her desk.

Arya catches the icepack as it was about to fall off from the edge of the desk. "How thoughtful," Arya said sarcastically.

"Was it bad?" Edgar changed his demeanor and now expressed concern.

"At first, LT ripped me apart." Arya made a gesture to let Edgar know that she got a real beating. "But then he came around once he saw my ways." Arya blinked her eye playfully and smiled.

"What does it mean?"

"It means you got to get off your ass and do some real police work," Arya engaged in playful banter.

"Don't tell me he assigned the case to you?"

"No, not to me. To us." Arya punched him playfully on his shoulders.

Edgar pretended like the punch hurt him. "What about the canvasing?" Edgar asked, wondering about the 9/11 canvasing to be done in the neighborhood.

"You got to learn to walk and chew the gum," Arya said, pulling his hands to get him off the chair.

"Where are we going?" Edgar asked, standing tall next to Arya.

"To your momma's house. Let's go," Arya said, as she already started walking towards the door.

"WHAT DO YOU THINK?" Arya asked, as their cruiser turned right on to Ridge Pike, heading north. As usual, Edgar was on the wheel, and Arya was the spotter. Typically, among partners, one has more seniority than the other, and the decision who gets to drive resolves naturally. The person who has more years under their belt gets to decide. However, that was not the case with Edgar and Arya. Their situation was slightly unusual. You rarely see two people who got out of the Academy at the same time get paired up. There were murmurs earlier on that Arya pulled some strings with LT Cooper to make it happen. It was not entirely unfounded; Arya did nudge his favorite uncle – LT Cooper – to get her the pairing she wished. Cooper reluctantly accepted with the condition that he would be watching like an eagle. If things seemed to go sideways, he wouldn't hesitate a moment to break it off. Arya took the deal, and the rest was history. It couldn't have gone any better.

"You know what I think," Edgar said, not looking away from the traffic.

"For the first time in my life, I feel happy to see the Pike clogged with traffic," Edgar said, turning slightly towards Arya.

Arya nodded, expressing her understanding of Edgar's sentiment. It was good to see the people of Philadelphia living their everyday lives and not feeling arrested in their own confines with fear. It was a way that everyone could make their statement to the terrorists who attacked the country; you can attack us, but you cannot frighten us. The country is strong, and the American spirit will prevail over evil.

"Samir is probably shacking up with his mistress."

Edgar's words hauled Arya back to the present. "You mean Samir ran away," Arya asked, clearing her throat.

"What do I always say? There is always an affair when a husband goes missing, or a wife gets murdered."

"How original!" Arya rolled her eyes.

"I didn't claim it to be, but that doesn't mean it is not true. Check the stats," Edgar pronounced.

"I am not sure," Arya hesitantly said, gently tucking a flock of her hair behind her ear.

"You are not thinking straight," Edgar alluded that her personal relationship with Sania was clouding her judgment. "If I take your friendship with Sania out of the equation, you would see it from a different angle."

"I know," Arya conceded to Edgar's argument. "But you didn't see the way Sania talked about her relationship with Sam."

"Sam?" Edgar asked, hearing Samir's nickname for the first time. "You mean Samir?"

Arya nodded. "Sam was his nickname. It seems everyone around here called him Sam," Arya recounted what she had heard earlier from Sania and Ashton.

"You know Sania wouldn't be the first wife who swears that her missing husband was not having an affair." Edgar turned sideways towards Arya. "You know I am right. The wife would typically be the last person to know about the man's affair."

"Check the stats." Both of their voices echoed that sentiment at the same time. Arya knew that Edgar would turn to the stats to bolster his stance.

"Finally, you are starting to see through the maze." Edgar playfully punched Arya on her shoulders, and both of them smiled.

"Do you think your stats would hold up if the wife is pregnant?" Arya asked evenly.

"What? Are you saying Sania is pregnant now?" Edgar exclaimed.

"Why are you shouting?" Arya was taken back by Edgar's abrupt reaction and reacted by closing her ears. "Jeez, what has gotten into you?"

"You didn't say Sania is pregnant," Edgar badgered on.

"I am telling you now. Sania's tummy is as big as a pumpkin. She is ready to pop anytime now."

"This is a game-changer," Edgar emphatically said, tapping the steering wheel a couple of times.

"What do you mean? You don't think he ran away now?" Arya asked, trying to understand Edgar's position.

"Not at all. I am now almost certain that Samir had an affair," Edgar said with conviction.

Arya stared on, gesturing with her hands for Edgar to explain.

"You know which season is most ripe for husbands to start cheating on their wives?" Edgar asked, with his eyes wide open.

"Go on; I know you have an answer," Arya said sarcastically.

"Yes, I do. The pregnancy season. Most husbands cheat when their wife is pregnant with a baby."

"I now see where you are getting your wisdom, the celebrity gossip magazines," Arya said dismissively.

"That doesn't mean it is not true. Check the VICAP, and

you will know that I am not blowing these stats out of my ass," Edgar said, bolstering his argument.

Every law enforcement official in the country knows about the VICAP. And, thanks to the countless law enforcement shows on TV, regular folks across the country have come to know about the program as well. VICAP stands for the Violent Criminal Apprehension Program. It was created by the FBI in 1985 to track crimes of a particular nature; sexual assault, kidnapping, missing persons, homicide, and serial killings. The program is now widely used by state and local law enforcement officials while investigating crimes that fit specific criteria. They use it to compare similar cases, find correlations and patterns, track across jurisdictions, and solve cold cases. The tool has become invaluable for identifying and tracking serial killers, where separate victims might not otherwise be connected as part of the same pattern.

When Edgar invoked VICAP, Arya knew he was on firm ground with his argument.

"Okay, you might have a point here," Arya said reluctantly. "For Sania's sake, I hope you are wrong here."

"Take a right here," Arya said, as they neared the exit for Norristown.

"Do they know that we are on our way now?" Edgar asked, switching to the right lane to make an exit.

"LT had a word with their sergeant; they should be expecting us." Arya referred to the detectives in the Norristown precinct, who were in charge of the Omar Raqqa missing person case.

IT WAS HALF-PAST one when Edgar and Arya walked into the Norristown precinct. The precinct was a little larger than theirs, but not as tidy.

Norristown is a borough in Montgomery County, about fifteen miles from Center City. During the height of its popularity, the Norristown area used to be the prime location for various industries – retail, banking, and the government center. After World War II, the region gradually lost its popularity to nearby towns and has declined ever since. However, one thing is on the rise – the crime rate. As per FBI crime data, Norristown has one of the highest crime rates in the state of Pennsylvania. Every cop in the city is aware of the notoriety, and they act differently when they encounter a suspect from the area.

Edgar was the first to notice the front desk officer walking back to his post and gestured to Arya. As they reached the officer's station, they both flashed a smile.

"We are from the Germantown precinct," Edgar started to introduce themselves but didn't go far as he was interrupted by the desk officer.

"Edgar James and Arya Martins?" the desk officer asked with an inviting smile.

They both nodded, expressing that the officer got their names right.

"I guess you are here to see Jimmy and Lyndsey." The desk officer referred to Jimmy Russel and Lyndsey Tanner, the detectives who worked the Omar Raqqa missing person case.

"You got it," Arya quickly confirmed.

"They are at Katie's," the desk officer flatly said.

"Katie's?" Edgar asked, not knowing what it meant.

"Katie's Diner," the desk officer clarified. He went on to explain that both Jimmy and Lyndsey are at the diner, having their lunch. "They are expecting you guys," he said.

The officer went on to give directions to the place; it was not that far, just a few blocks away from the precinct. Both Edgar and Arya exchanged pleasantries with the officer before heading out towards Katie's Diner.

———

WHEN EDGAR and Arya pulled into Katie's Diner, they didn't expect the parking lot to be packed. The restaurant was located in a strip mall right next to an Asian nail salon. As Edgar was pulling into a 'Salon Customers Only' parking spot, Arya pointed towards a Honda that was pulling out from a parking space that was right in front of Katie's Diner. Edgar put the car in reverse and backed about a hundred yards before pulling into the now open parking space.

As Edgar and Arya walked in through the wooden door, they were overwhelmed by the smell of tasty food. Arya could feel her stomach growl and felt glad that she had walked into the right place at the right time. If you got to describe the ambiance of Katie's Diner in a phrase, it would be 'Student Ghetto.' The hangout was basically a college sports bar. It overflowed with TVs that either played recorded or live sports. It had countless draft stations, several foosball tables, and banners of nearby universities that decorated the draft house. The place even had a 'Hump Day Party' banner displayed prominently on top of a make-shift podium. It was definitely a great hangout place for college kids.

"What the heck are Jimmy and Lyndsey doing in a frat house?" Arya said, just loud enough for Edgar to hear.

Edgar broke into a smile. "I guess they know how to party."

"There they are." Arya pointed her hand at a table that was next to the draft house.

Edgar looked at the direction Arya was pointing and found a man motioning his hand towards them.

Arya and Edgar walked up to the table, barely avoiding bumping into a college kid and spilling his beer.

"What a scene, huh," one of the men said, slightly chuckling.

"Got to admit this is different than I thought," Edgar replied, as they took the seats across from the Norristown detectives.

"Jimmy Russel," one of the Norristown detectives introduced himself by extending his hand to both Edgar and Arya.

"Lyndsey Tanner," the other Norristown detective followed Jimmy by introducing himself.

"You must be the Germantown detectives. Let me guess – you must be Edgar James, and you are Arya Martins." Jimmy pointed at Edgar and Arya as he said their names.

"Jeez, you must be Sherlock," Lyndsey said exaggeratedly, rolling his eyes and teasing him for pointing out the obvious. "What did you think? Edgar was a woman?" Lyndsey asked.

"You never know. Look at you, Lyndsey!" It was Jimmy's turn to take a jab at his partner for having a popular women's name. That started a round of back and forth between Jimmy and Lyndsey.

"Do you have to start this in front of the guests?" Lyndsey finally asked, shaking his head and expressing disappointment with Jimmy for starting this argument.

"I didn't, you did. Maybe you forgot because of your age," Jimmy countered.

"Oh, right! You are getting younger every day, and I am getting old," Lyndsey pushed back.

To Arya, they looked like an old couple bickering with each other, almost in a cute way.

Both Jimmy and Lyndsey looked like they were in their sixties. Both of them white, Jimmy had an old-man paunch, and Lyndsey looked fit for his age but had more grey hair. They both dressed in old-school detective suits, something the detectives would have worn in the Dragnet days. Arya would later learn that both of them joined the force at the same time and were a year out to get out with full pension. They had been partners for the previous thirty years, bursting doors and keeping the streets clean. With that kind of mileage between them, they are indeed an old couple who knows everything about each other.

The bickering lasted for another couple of minutes, and, when it finally stopped, Jimmy took out a case file in his hand and said, "I guess you are here for this."

"Omar Raqqa's case file," Jimmy said, almost butchering the man's last name. Jimmy leaned forward and extended the case file across the table.

Arya reached forward and accepted the case file from Jimmy.

"The case file looks pretty thin," Arya said, as she flipped it open.

"There is a reason for it," Lyndsey quickly chimed in.

"What do you mean?" Edgar was curious about the last statement.

"I mean, we don't even know if there was a crime committed here," Lyndsey said.

"You guys think Omar might have disappeared on his own?" Edgar asked, interpreting Lyndsey's answer.

Jimmy and Lyndsey shrugged. "Can't say either way definitively. We could not establish that he was kidnapped."

Arya and Edgar looked on as Lyndsey continued, "Also, there is this whole thing about the jurisdiction."

"Dubai?" Arya asked, remembering the conversation she had with Ashton, where he mentioned that Omar disappeared during a business trip there.

Lyndsey nodded.

"What about his family? What do they think?" Edgar asked.

"That is another thing. Raqqa's family is not here; they are in Saudi Arabia," Lyndsey started.

Jimmy jumped in, "At least that is what we think. We tried reaching out, but nada," Jimmy shook his head, expressing that they ran into a wall reaching them. "Who the hell wouldn't report or talk to the cops if your husband is missing?"

"You mean to say that Mrs. Raqqa never reported her husband was missing?"

"That is exactly what I am saying," Jimmy said emphatically.

At that moment, a waitress walked to their table to get their orders. The waitress must have been a college student from one of the nearby colleges; she looked young and had a beautiful smile.

"Darling, I will go for a round of usual." Jimmy gave a good-ole smile.

"Me too," Lyndsey joined in.

"Of course, dear." The waitress replied in a rather fond manner, implying Jimmy and Lyndsey were regulars at this joint.

"What about you, guys? Any drinks?" The waitress turned her attention towards Edgar and Arya.

"Do you have iced tea?" Edgar asked.

That question by Edgar got one of the wildest reactions he had ever seen. "Jeez, what are you, nine?" Jimmy laughed. "Get a proper drink, Jesus."

Edgar was slightly taken back, but he calmly said, "No, thank you. On the job, I will have a regular iced tea."

"I will have a Stella on the draft," Arya ordered her drink.

"16 or 24?" the waitress asked about the pint-size.

"Always 24."

The waitress and Arya exchanged a smile before the waitress walked away.

"That's my girl." Jimmy leaned forward to give a high-five to Arya.

"Iced tea, Jesus," Lyndsey expressed his disbelief.

Arya saw the opportunity to mock Edgar and joined in on the fun. Edgar took it sportingly, nodding and smiling.

The waitress returned back to the table with drinks and placed them on the table. "You guys ready to order?" she asked, opening a pocketbook.

Arya hadn't eaten a proper meal from the previous evening, and she was ready to hit the joint; the food smell was quite inviting. Arya and Edgar turned towards the old-timers for recommendations and went with them.

As the waitress left the table, Arya was engaged in a conversation with Jimmy about the history of this joint, and Edgar turned his attention towards Raqqa's file.

As she was hearing Jimmy, Arya glanced casually at Edgar and spotted a photo in his hand. She immediately reached out and pulled the photo from Edgar. Her eyes narrowed as she examined it closely. It was a picture of a man, taken by a closed-circuit camera, who was standing next to a shipyard container and had his hand on the container lock keypad.

"What?" Edgar asked. As Arya pulled the picture from Edgar before he got a good look, he was not sure what or who was on the photo.

Arya placed the photo on the table for everyone to see. "What is this?" she asked, shifting her gaze across the table at Jimmy and Lyndsey.

"This is the reason why we even started the investigation," Lyndsey said, shifting his eyes from the picture to Arya.

"Is this Raqqa?" Edgar asked. It was hard to make out the face of the man; it was dark, and his back was to the camera.

"No, we don't think so." Jimmy shook his head.

"What did you mean when you said this started the investigation?" Arya asked, trying to flush out details.

"Do you want me to explain?" Jimmy looked at Lyndsey, and Lyndsey nodded to express his agreement.

"I assume you guys know that Omar Raqqa sent out a resignation letter to his supervisor – Landon?" Jimmy's gaze landed squarely on Arya.

Arya nodded. "Yes, we do. I met with Ashton, Raqqa's replacement, and he filled me in with the details – Raqqa missing an important meeting in Dubai and his resignation letter to Landon."

"Did you read the resignation letter?" Lyndsey asked.

"Yes, it looked vanilla – nothing out of the ordinary."

Jimmy and Lyndsey nodded, expressing that was also their judgment on the resignation letter.

"But…. Ashton said something that didn't make sense. He said that Landon reached out to the authorities to start the investigation after receiving the resignation letter," Arya stated.

Jimmy shook his head rapidly. "He is wrong. That was not the reason."

Lyndsey continued, "Do you guys know Raqqa was leading a merger between two shipping companies?"

Arya and Edgar exchanged glances and shook their heads to express their lack of knowledge about the merger.

"At the time of the disappearance, he was overseeing a merger between two shipping companies – one based out of the Middle East and another here in the U.S."

Arya began to wonder how it was relevant to Landon filing the missing person complaint.

"As part of the merger, complete forensic auditing was conducted. In the audit, Aries Financials discovered someone used the special access code assigned to Raqqa to access this shipping container."

"How can you be sure that this was not Raqqa? It is so dark!" Edgar asked, wondering how the detectives decided it was not Raqqa on the picture.

"Good question, son," Jimmy said, pointing his index finger at Edgar. "Do you see the timestamp?"

"May 31st," Edgar read the timestamp on the bottom corner of the picture.

"Raqqa disappeared on May 27th in Dubai. Do you see the gap?" Jimmy asked.

"When did he send the resignation letter?" Edgar asked.

"June 1st," Lyndsey said quickly.

"I don't see a gap here. It seems Raqqa came back to the country sometime after May 27th, accessed the container on May 31st, and resigned on June 1st," Edgar connected the timeline.

"Very good, son," Jimmy beamed. "I wish my son is as smart as you," he said in almost a patronizing way.

Arya was examining the photo when the exchange was happening between Jimmy and Edgar. Her eyes raised when she realized that the man on the picture couldn't be Omar Raqqa. "This is not Raqqa," Arya declared, looking up from the photo.

"Are you guessing?" Edgar asked, turning his attention to Arya.

"No, I am certain." Arya placed the photo on the table and tapped the man shown on the picture. "This can't be Raqqa."

Edgar was shocked to hear Arya declare it with absolute conviction.

Jimmy exchanged glances at Lyndsey. "You are the smart one," he said with a grin, looking at Arya.

"Why don't you explain?" he asked, knowing Arya had cracked the code.

"Looking at the man standing right next to the container,

it is quite obvious that he is tall. I would say that he is close to six feet."

Jimmy nodded, inviting her to continue.

"From the employment records, we know that Raqqa is far from being tall. He is listed as only five feet and two inches."

"Bingo!" Jimmy flashed a grin. "Mark my words; this girl is going places."

The sudden flattery made Arya blush. "Not such a big deal," she muttered, trying to be humble.

"Let me say something to you straight. Don't ever do that." Jimmy looked straight at Arya. "Don't underplay your talent or achievements. If you do that, people will climb on your back and take credit for what you did."

Jimmy's words struck a chord with Arya. It echoed almost word-by-word with what her father once said. Arya nodded respectfully, taking Jimmy's words to heart.

Edgar's face beamed with pride, hearing flattering words about Arya, his partner, and true friend.

"The food is here," Jimmy announced, almost in a celebratory tone. "Hmm… It smells good," he continued, as the waitress gently placed the plates in front of each of them.

"Can I get anything else for y'all?" the waitress asked in a southern accent.

Jimmy lifted his almost empty beer glass. "Refill, dear."

"Of course, Jimmy." The waitress walked over to the bar counter and returned to their table with a replenished glass of beer.

Another two minutes elapsed before the waitress left the table. She was engaged in a lively conversation about her boyfriend with Jimmy and Lyndsey. When she finally left, Arya jumped right back into the conversation about Omar to find out everything the detectives knew about the case.

"I assume Landon filed the case because he realized

earlier what I just figured out," Arya asked, taking a bite of the diner's signature grilled sandwich.

"Yeah," Lyndsey replied. Jimmy could just nod as his mouth was stuffed with food.

"Were you able to figure out who this person is?" Arya asked, pointing at the surveillance picture of the man opening the shipping container.

"No. But whoever it was, we think he knew the place pretty well. Could be an insider." Lyndsey said.

"Insider?" Arya leaned forward, becoming more curious. "You mean he worked for the shipping company? What makes you say that?"

"Open the Marisomo section in the case file," Jimmy said, motioning his hand to gesture Arya to keep flipping.

"Marisomo?" Arya asked, keeping an eye on the file as she skipped through sections.

"Marisomo is a shipping corporation based out of Egypt or Yemen. I am not too sure." Lyndsey looked towards Jimmy for his input.

Jimmy shrugged and said, "I don't remember either; one of the countries from the Middle East."

When Arya landed on the section labeled Marisomo, a large brown-colored department issued envelope stared right back at her.

"Open it," Edgar opined, as Arya exchanged a quick glance at him.

Arya lifted the envelope from the case file and opened it with an elevated sense of anticipation. She was not sure what to expect to see in the envelope. Given it had changed the direction of Omar's investigation, she thought it had photos or documents revealing the identity of the mystery person.

She was half-right with her assumption. The envelope did contain a set of photos, but, as far as she could tell, it did not clearly show the mystery person's face. The images were all taken by the closed-circuit television (CCTV) cameras. The first photo showed a man wearing a hooded jacket exiting the shipping container. The pictures that followed captured the same man calmly walking towards the secured area's exit. In all the photos, he seemed to be looking down or looking away. His face was not visible in any of the pictures. As he exited, he appeared to be holding onto a rectangular-shaped case, possibly made of aluminum, which was not in his possession when he entered.

"He seemed to know where the cameras are," Edgar chimed.

"The kicker here is that some of the cameras in the secured area corridor is hidden," Jimmy added.

"So, he knew where the cameras were placed. Now I see why you classified him as an insider," Arya said, looking towards Jimmy and Lyndsey.

"One more thing here that would light you up. The Marisomo security team mentioned that the cameras were newly installed; it had been there only from March."

"So, he must still be employed there," Edgar opined.

"Might be or not," Lyndsey said and took a long swig of his beer.

Arya and Edgar looked keenly at Lyndsey for him to continue.

"There was an independent security firm that installed the cameras. They sub-contracted the job to a smaller firm, and one of their employees could be our guy," Lyndsey said and went back to his beer.

"When we looked into the firm, we got a kahuna-sized surprise."

Arya's eyes lit up.

"They never did the job. It seemed the whole paperwork was phony."

"Shit. This is some elaborate scheme." It was now Arya's turn to take a swig of her beer.

"Yeah, no kidding. We tried looking into the person who awarded the contract, and he is nowhere to be found."

"What?" Arya was surprised.

"He was a Yemeni national, and we found out that he had left the country."

"Why?"

"He just said that his wife had a baby, and he is going there to see her."

"And he never returned?" Arya asked, guessing that was the case.

"Bingo. He is gone."

"This smells." Edgar shook his head in disbelief.

"Nah, it stinks," Arya added, referring to the way this case has turned out.

It seemed the moment weighed the same way to both Edgar and Arya. They took a deep breath, leaned back on the chair, and stayed silent for a minute, processing what they had just learned.

"Okay, let me see if I got this straight," Arya started. "Raqqa was working on a merger involving Marisomo when he disappeared. A few days later, his supervisor, Landon, receives a resignation letter from Raqqa. A couple of days later, Landon finds out that Raqqa's code was used to access Marisomo's secured shipping warehouse."

Jimmy and Lyndsey nodded to signal their agreement with Arya so far.

"By looking at the surveillance pictures, it has become obvious that whoever accessed the secured shipping container was not Raqqa. It was someone else using Raqqa's code. Your investigation has also revealed that someone deliberately falsified orders to send the surveillance camera installation job to a non-existent company. Upon further digging, you guys found out that whoever awarded that contract is a foreign national, Yemeni, and he has now left the country for good."

"Damn, you nailed it," Jimmy said, lifting his beer.

"But why?" The picture of the mystery man carrying a rectangular aluminum case rushed back to her memory. "What was in that case? Marisomo should know what was missing from that container. It should be pretty easy; they should have an inventory of everything that was shipped." Arya blurted out the questions in a rapid fashion.

"Slow down, tiger." Jimmy gestured for Arya to be less loud. "We hit another dead-end there. Nothing was missing as per Marisomo's shipping records. Whatever was in that rectangular case was not legally shipped; it was smuggled."

Arya and Edgar's mouths dropped upon hearing that the case was smuggled.

"Were you or Marisomo able to find out more?"

"No. We all know that in that part of the world, anything goes for a price." Lyndsey flicked his thumb to gesture money.

"This case is getting interesting," Edgar sighed.

"This seems to be a well-coordinated plan. It seems Raqqa was kidnapped, possibly killed, to get to Marisomo's shipping container," Arya deduced the motive behind Raqqa's case.

"I would agree," Jimmy said.

"What else did you guys find?" Edgar asked.

"Not much, the investigation has gone cold. We are not the CIA to go poke our nose in Yemen or Dubai. We have no jurisdiction, or, for that matter, resources."

"What about his house? Did you find anything?"

"Nada. Raqqa's house was cleaned out; the place was clean as a whistle," Lyndsey added.

"That confirms our working theory," Arya said with conviction.

"The only personal belongings of Raqqa we have are what he had kept in his office. It was not much. A couple of photos of his family, gym bag and clothes, a membership card to a fitness center, and a rowing club. It is all in the evidence locker, and you can find pictures of it at the tail end of the file."

"Thanks," Arya nodded with a slight smile.

"Did you find anything from the fitness center or the rowing club?" Arya asked, hoping for something that could remotely help with the investigation.

"No. Raqqa seemed to be a regular in both places, but we didn't find anything." Jimmy shrugged his shoulders.

"Wow! I didn't expect this when we came here," Arya said, referring to what they had discovered. A highly planned and coordinated effort to disappear or most possibly murder Raqqa to access and retrieve the smuggled item from the shipping warehouse.

"Do you mind if we take the case file?" Edgar asked.

"It's all yours," Jimmy said, emptying his beer bottle with one last large gulp.

"You mean the case file?"

"No man, the case is yours," Jimmy grinned.

"You must be kidding, right?" Arya asked, feeling puzzled with this new development.

"Nope. I got my marching orders from my LT; Raqqa is now Germantown's case. Not ours," he said, making a gesture to express that they have washed their hands off the case.

"You know why? I mean, don't get me wrong; we are happy to merge our case with Raqqa. It might even be the right move, but I never thought you guys would give it away just like that," Arya said, snapping her fingers.

"Okay, I can give you the diplomatic bullshit answer about how we are happy to share information for the betterment of the case. But…." Jimmy paused and leaned forward to whisper, "We all know that is just bullshit." He then leaned back and said with a grin on his face, "Because I like you kiddos, I will let you in on the secret. This Raqqa case is a loser, and we have hit a dead-end here. We can't proceed any further unless we get the suits to help us out. With what just happened two days ago, helping a missing person case would be the last thing Feds would do."

"I guess transferring this would get this off your score-card," Arya asked, connecting the dots.

"Yup. When your LT called, my boss saw this as a perfect opportunity to get the case moved. In one move, he got brownie points for playing nice with you guys, and also had the loser case cleared off our dock."

"How naïve am I! All the while, I was thinking you guys were helping us out of your goodwill," Arya smiled broadly.

"That is also true," Jimmy grinned from ear-to-ear, pointing at Arya.

Their lunch lasted for another fifteen minutes, and, when it ended, Arya was not sure how exactly Raqqa's case was connected with Samir's disappearance. But her strong gut feeling was that both of the cases were related; if you crack open one, the other one will follow.

ARYA AND EDGAR'S drive back to their precinct involved lengthy conversations about both cases. It ranged from the facts they knew about Samir and Omar's employment in Aries Financials and to outright speculations if they were both kidnapped by the same person. In the end, they could not conclude if both the cases were connected, except that both men worked for Aries Financials and disappeared under mysterious circumstances within a few months.

When Edgar brought out their similarity in descent, Arya refuted it by saying that Omar is a Saudi national, and Samir is a Pakistani. Both are Muslims, but they are from different countries. In the end, they decided to table it as a possible similarity.

Arya also pointed out the difference in reaction to Omar and Samir's disappearance by their families. In Omar's case, they didn't file any report, and they basically moved back to Saudi Arabia. However, in Samir's case, Sania was the person who filed the complaint to start the investigation.

In the end, they were confident about two things.

First, they had to find out if Samir and Omar knew each

other when they worked in Aries Financials. And second, they were convinced that whatever package that was smuggled through Marisomo was the motive behind Omar's disappearance. They had to dig deeper to find out the mystery man's identity and what was in that package.

"I AM GOING to hit for a cup of joe; do you need me to grab you one?" Edgar asked as they walked into the Germantown precinct.

"You read my mind, partner," Arya beamed, as she playfully bumped him on his shoulders.

"Be careful, next you know what I would be reading," Edgar joked, referring to the reason why Arya hadn't settled in with anyone yet.

"You know who you sound like? My mom." Arya made a face, expressing how ridiculous Edgar sounded.

They zigzagged each other with their smarty comebacks for another minute or so before laughing it off like they usually do. Edgar then took a detour to the cafeteria, and Arya proceeded upstairs to the squad room.

Arya waved to a couple of detectives as she walked into the squad room.

"What case you got?" one of the detectives yelled.

"Missing person, why?" Arya asked.

"You seem to be clogging the fax machine. I had to haul a whole stack of papers from there for you," the detective complained.

"Really? How the fuck did you manage that?" Arya made a smug remark.

"Jeez. You and your mouth."

"Got to say; learned from the best." Arya pointed the finger at him, and they both chuckled.

As she made her way to the desk, Arya noticed a stack of papers piled up on her desk. She had requested a collection of faxes from various airlines that had flights from Philly to Los Angeles on September 10th.

Arya leaned back on her chair and rested her foot on the table as she started examining the faxes one by one. In the next ten minutes, she went over faxes sent by all the airlines – American, Delta, and United. As she examined them, her expression changed from curiosity to being baffled.

"What the heck are you reading?" Edgar asked, handing a cup of coffee to Arya.

"Proposal from my suitors," Arya made one of her wiseass remarks.

"How much do you have to pay for them to take you?" Edgar joined in on the wiseass game.

Arya reached over and punched him on the shoulder. "Asshole."

"Takes one to know one," he smiled, rubbing the spot Arya landed her punch.

"From the airlines," Arya said, raising the papers in her hand.

"PNRs?" Edgar asked. Airlines typically maintain a detailed passenger list called PNRs – Passenger Name Records. Not many people know about the extent of information that is being collected every time they fly. PNRs were not designed just to collect passenger information like their names, dates of birth, contact information, and if a passenger requested wheelchair assistance, but also information about their travel histories in the previous six months and details about the method of payment used.

"How the heck did you get that?" Edgar asked, expressing his surprise on the speed and ease by which Arya managed to get the airlines to divulge the PNRs. Typically, the airlines keep that information close to their vests. You need to obtain warrants for them to share PNRs with law enforcement.

"9/11. I said the records are needed for the investigation," Arya whispered, leaning closer to Edgar.

"Shit. That is wrong on so many levels," Edgar scowled.

"Come on, get over it. We are investigating a disappearance that happened on 9/11. So technically, I didn't lie." Arya shrugged her shoulders.

Edgar shook his head, expressing that he still couldn't believe that Arya pulled that crap.

"Do you want to just sit there and pout or help me with this?" Arya questioned, holding the stack of PNRs in her hand.

"What did you find?" Edgar asked.

"It was not what I found; it was what I didn't find," Arya gave a cryptic reply. "I scoured through the PNRs of all the airlines that had a flight from Philly to Los Angeles on the evening of September 10th, and I didn't find Samir's name on any of them."

"What time did his wife say his flight was?"

"7:10 in the evening. There was only one flight scheduled around that time to fly to Los Angeles, American. Samir Tariq is not listed as one of the passengers." Arya shook her head, gesturing that was a surprise.

"Hmm…," Edgar said thoughtfully after taking a long sip of his coffee. "Maybe we are looking at it the wrong way. What if he didn't travel direct, and he had a stopover?"

Arya gestured to indicate Edgar had a point. "Maybe Sania got it wrong. She mentioned that Samir had a direct flight. Maybe she got it confused."

With a renewed sense of optimism, Arya and Edgar divided the laborious work of going through the PNRs. There were 527 departures on September 10th from Philadelphia International Airport, and, out of it, close to 300 departures were in the afternoon. Based on the timeline provided by Sania, Samir was dropped off at the airport around 5:00 PM. Given that knowledge, they decided to check all flights that departed after 5:00 PM. That left them close to 165 flights to sift through to look for Samir's name on the PNRs.

"I wish the airlines had sent you a soft copy of the PNRs. This is way too much work," Edgar complained, as his wrist-watch reminded him that it was almost 7:00 PM.

"Me too. Who knows? Maybe, one day, we will truly be in the twenty-first century, and all this will be disseminated into a searchable digital format." As Arya was going through the PNRs, she started to describe an article she read on The New York Times, which talked about next-generation phones that would put the internet in everyone's pocket.

"Yeah, right. We will have robots cleaning our houses and doing our dishes," Edgar said sarcastically.

They both exchanged glances and started laughing at the absurdity of their discussion.

It was almost 7:30 when Edgar wrapped up his search. His face said it all; disappointment was written all over it.

Arya, without lifting her head, signaled that she had two more PNRs to go.

As Edgar waited, he started to stretch his legs to loosen up his tight hamstrings.

When Arya finished her last PNR, she slammed the desk in frustration. Edgar didn't have to ask how the search went; it was quite obvious. They both came up empty after hours of exhausting work.

Edgar and Arya exchanged a knowing glance; the words didn't have to be spoken out aloud. They both know what this means; Samir had lied about his flight to Los Angeles. He never left town on September 10th.

Edgar leaned forward, removing the pen from his mouth,

and asked, "You know what this means," in a manner that had 'Didn't I say so' written all over his face.

"I know," Arya heaved a deep sigh. The last thing she wanted to admit was that Edgar was right about Samir. Samir had clearly lied about his travel to Sania. Typically, when husbands do that, it means one thing – they are having an affair.

Edgar motioned his hand, like shooting a basketball, and made a sound like he swished it through a basket.

"You now owe me seats to the 76ers game when Shaq-Kobe comes to town," Edgar grinned.

Arya's father's firm is one of the major sponsors to the 76ers, and that comes with many privileges. A season pass to a couple of courtside seats was one of them. Arya knew Edgar's wife was a huge Lakers fan, as she grew up in Los Angeles as a kid, and, when their anniversary fell on June 15th, she knew the best gift she could get for them. The coveted tickets to Game 5 of NBA finals – Lakers vs. Sixers, and not just any tickets; courtside – right next to the Lakers bench. Edgar and Simone had the night of their life, as the Lakers beat the 76ers that night and won the NBA championship. They were there when the final buzzer sounded, and, in Simone's words, the moment was surreal, and she would never forget it in her life. Edgar described the night similarly to Simone, but for very different reasons. He had the best sex of his life that night.

"I know what you are aiming with those seats," Arya teased him.

"What can I say? I am just a married man," he grinned.

Both of them enjoyed the back-and-forth banter, and they broke into a silly laugh.

"What next, genius," Arya asked, bringing the conversation back to the case at hand. "This is turning out to be messier than I thought," Arya said, alluding to her initial gut about the case when she left Sania's house last night.

Edgar leaned back and closed his eyes like he was replaying all the known facts about the case in his mind.

"Follow the money," he said, opening his eyes.

"What? This is not Watergate!" Arya exclaimed. The phrase 'Follow the Money' became popular among the public after the movie *All the President's Men* released. In the film, the character Deep Throat advises Robert Redford to follow the money to crack open the Watergate break-in investigation.

"If that strategy worked for the President, it would certainly work for a cheater." Edgar paused to certainly add for dramatization. "If you are cheating on your wife and going to run away with your mistress, you will most certainly need to have a few things hidden. And the first thing the cheaters hide is money." Edgar raised from his chair and walked closer to Arya. "Having a mistress is not cheap; it is expensive."

"Wow! Is this something I should bring up to Simone?" Arya joked.

Edgar rolled his eyes and signaled, "Enough with the silliness."

Arya, getting the visible cue from Edgar, shifted her conversation back to the case. "Credit card transactions, bank statements, airline tickets, what else?"

"All his financials. From what we know, he resigned from his job three months back. How were his finances before and after leaving the job? How was he keeping up the lifestyle?" Edgar closed his eyes, thinking about the case. "You know what I don't get? How could his wife not know that he doesn't have a job? We now know that he lied about his job and didn't have a high-income job like he had claimed. He had a blue-collar job, and, with that, how the hell did he manage to stay in that pricey neighborhood?"

"All good questions that we don't have answers for yet." Arya nodded, gesturing her approval to Edgar's way of thinking.

"Money never lies! You either have it or not. If you do, it will always leave a trail." Edgar nodded his head, looking into Arya's eyes, gesturing his firm belief about his approach.

Arya nodded, signaling that she had bought into Edgar's argument.

"Okay, let's get going on this." Arya started breaking down the areas they wanted to dig deep into. Bank statements, credit card transactions, airline tickets, deposits made to their checking account after he resigned, the overall state of their financials….

Their discussion came to an abrupt stop when Arya's phone started to ring.

Arya shook her head and placed her hand on her forehead in disbelief that she forgot about her parents' anniversary dinner.

"Hey, Mom," Arya answered the call, still shaking her head.

"Uh-huh, can you hold for a moment." Arya closed the mouthpiece and looked at Edgar.

"Get out of here. I will start making some calls. It will take some time to get hold of Samir's financials." Edgar encouraged her to leave immediately so that she can make the anniversary dinner on time.

"You sure?" she mouthed without making a sound.

"Are you kidding me. Go and be with your family. I will get a few things organized, and we can touch base tomorrow." Edgar gestured towards the door.

"Mom, how can you think I forgot? I was just about to leave when you called."

Hearing Arya lying to her mom prompted a smile from Edgar.

"Shut up," Arya mouthed towards Edgar, drawing a bigger smile from Edgar.

"Mom, I am not going to be late. I will be there before anyone notices…." Arya continued to argue with her mom as she headed out for the night.

A FEW MILES from the Germantown precinct, a Toyota High-lander was parked in the southeast corner of Waverly Avenue and Eaton Street. The darkness enveloped the streets and inside the SUV. The engine was shut off, and the person inside the SUV sat in complete darkness. There was no music on, nor was anyone talking in the car. It was complete silence. There was only one thing that was lit inside, and that was the eyes of the driver. The driver was a young female, must be close to her late twenties or early thirties, and was no taller than five feet and two inches. Her eyes were hazel or brown, and her sclera was as white as fresh snow on the ground. Her eyes glistened when the lights of a passing car shined briefly upon her. She might have had tears welled up.

And one more thing, she was most definitely pregnant – her belly brushed against the steering wheel. It was Sania Tariq, sitting alone grimly, and her gaze was laser-focused on the house on the opposite side of the street. The house design seemed inspired by Tudor Revival architecture, with its half-timbering brickwork, steeply pitched roof and chimneys that shoot high from the roof.

The windows in the house, which seemed to be too many to count, remained firmly closed. There was no light in the house except the foyer, where a chandelier seemed to be on. Sania shifted her gaze from the house to her wristwatch to check on the time. It was almost eight o'clock.

She knew in her gut what she was doing was a bad idea. She was warned not to come to this house, not once, but repeatedly, by a person she trusts. She knew coming here could raise some uncomfortable questions and land him in a terrible place. However, here she was, waiting a few feet away from the house with the hope of seeing him. Just like an addict who could not resist a drink, Sania could not resist the urge to come here.

It had been three days since she last saw him, and her mind started to go crazy. *Did something happen to him too?*

As time painfully passed by, she couldn't wait any longer. She had a backup plan in her mind if someone other than him opens the door. Her mind battled if the plan would hold up under his wife's suspicious eyes, but she didn't care at this point. It was time to find out.

Sania stepped out of the vehicle and made her way gingerly towards the front door of the Tudor. She wavered for a moment as her fingers touched the ringer, but it didn't last long. She rang the bell once and waited. When no one opened, she rang twice. The seconds passed by, and there was no response. She stepped back from the porch to check if any of the lights were turned on, and all she saw was the lonely light shining from the foyer chandelier. She hung her head in disappointment; he was definitely not home.

With disappointment all over her face, she made her way back to her vehicle. It was time for her to get back home. Maybe he would call tonight and explain the reason for his no-show for the last three days. With that faint hope, she started the SUV and drove away to her house.

. . .

AS SHE DROVE AWAY, she didn't notice a silver-colored Honda parked about a hundred yards behind her Toyota. A man inside the car had a camera mounted with a telephoto lens, and he had just fired close to twenty shots. The photos captured Sania waiting inside the car, walking towards the house, ringing the bell, and walking back with her head hung in disappointment.

He leaned back in his seat and closed his eyes like he was searching for an answer. He was expecting Sania to know where the man of the house was, but now he was not sure. As he thought more, he became more convinced that something happened between the night of September 10th and early hours of September 11th.

His thoughts were hauled back to the present when his Nokia phone started to buzz.

"Carter," he announced his name on the phone.

"Where are you? I thought you ran away with the money." A woman's raised voice rung out loudly.

"Ma'am, it's good to know how highly you think of me," he sarcastically expressed his point.

"First, don't call me ma'am. It makes me sound old. Call me Julia Berg," she declared firmly.

"Ms. Berg, having met you, you would be the last person I would call old. You are one of the most beautiful people I have seen in my life."

"Are you hitting on me?" Julia asked in an 'I can't believe you just did that' tone.

"Ma'am...." Carter paused to correct himself. "Ms. Berg, it was just an innocent compliment from an elderly man. Nothing more, nothing less," he cleared the air.

"What else would I think? You have been a no-show from the moment you took the money."

Carter, with all the years of his service, has seen many people react the same way as Ms. Berg. It's not new to him. He let her rant for a couple of minutes until she was ready to listen to his side.

"Ms. Berg, what did I say when I took the job?" he asked flatly.

"I don't remember," Julia replied flippantly.

"I remember it very well. I flatly refused to take this job."

"So, what are you trying to say?" Julia argued.

"I am just trying to make a point. I accepted this job for one and one reason only – your father. We are having this conversation only because he intervened and asked me to take this job."

He paused for his point to land firmly.

"I also remember very well that I made it clear that I won't be checking in with you every day to give you updates. You will hear from me only when I have something concrete."

"Yeah, yeah, you said that. But that was before Eli disappeared. Now I am going nuts here." Julia started to choke up.

"I can't wait anymore." She paused, trying to rein in her emotions. "You know he hasn't come home in three days."

Carter remained silent, knowing that if he shared what he had learned about Eli Berg, it would end up upsetting her even further.

Julia, clearing her throat, said, "This whole thing is my mistake. I should have never listened to my friends and suspected him of cheating. Maybe he figured out that I hired you and got terribly upset."

"I am certain that was not the case. He has no clue about me," Carter confidently said.

"What then? I hired you, and a few days later, poof! Eli is gone." Julia directed her anger inwards and chided herself for suspecting Eli of cheating.

"Julia, you are a bit harsh on yourself." He deliberated for a moment on what to say next.

In the last week of him following Eli, he became confident of one thing. He was not sure if Eli was sleeping with Sania, but he was certain that Eli was in love with her. You could lie with your words and actions, but your eyes would never lie. During all of the years he had spent interrogating suspects, it was their eyes that separated the truth from the lies.

The pictures he took of Eli with Sania were mostly taken at the same place and at the same time. They always met at the same secluded spot by the Schuylkill River Trail and at eight o'clock. The only exception was the night of September 10th.

Carter knew that pictures by themselves could be explained away as circumstantial. Before going to Julia, he wanted to get a picture of them being intimate. However, the situation had changed in more ways than anticipated. After the night of September 10th, he hadn't seen Eli Berg; he seems to have disappeared into thin air. From September 12th, he started following Sania with the hope that she would lead him to Eli. How wrong did he turn out to be in his thinking? It was not just Eli who has gone missing; Sania's husband, Samir Tariq, had also disappeared. It seems both of them vanished on the same night.

To make matters more complicated, he now believes that Sania herself might be in the dark with their disappearances. She had been filing police reports to find her missing husband and religiously visiting the river trail like before to meet up with Eli. Carter was puzzled by the way things had turned out. He had never been this wrong in his long career as a cop and later as a PI. The case that started out to be a straightforward one, a wife suspecting her husband of cheating, had turned topsy-turvy.

"You still there?" Julia's voice jerked Carter back to the present.

Carter, in his heart, knew that the time had come for Julia to hear the truth. If he was in her position, he would want to know what he had learned.

"I think it is time for us to meet," Carter calmly said, lighting up a cigarette.

20

"Thanks, George," Edgar flashed a thumbs-up sign to the bellman as he brought the *Philadelphia Inquirer* newspaper to him.

The bellman tipped his hat, signaling his appreciation towards Edgar for being a policeman and standing on the front lines to protect the community.

This was one of the remarkable changes Edgar noticed in the way people treated him after 9/11. In the past, he had seen people showing reverence towards his line of work, but not at this magnitude. 9/11 has undoubtedly changed the perspective of many ordinary citizens towards the police and firefighters. When the first responders rushed towards the burning towers, being considered heroes was the last thing in their minds. They were not driven by glory or fame but by duty and sacrifice. They are now rightfully being celebrated as heroes of the community.

With the *Inquirer* in his hand, Edgar gave the room that he was standing in a 360-degree treatment. He was in an expansive waiting room of one of the high-rise buildings, near downtown, that housed ultra-luxury condos, which seemed to have sprung up recently along the river. In this building, the posh condos were one of the most sought-after properties for the ultra-rich, like ballers, investment bankers, celebrities, and people with deep pockets from other countries. Last year, when Arya mentioned that one of the luxury condos was sold for 7.2 million dollars, his head spun out of utter disbelief. When he later learned that some of these condos go unoccupied for months or even for a year, his first thought was that it went unsold because of the ridiculous sale prices. But how naïve he turned out to be when he learned that they were not only sold, but they were sold well above asking price to wealthy buyers from other countries. It seems these luxury condos attract considerable attention from foreign buyers because these transactions could be used to avoid paying taxes. He never understood how buying an ultra-luxury penthouse translates into tax write-offs, or, for that matter, how it was even legal.

No wonder Edgar didn't take up investment banking or become a CPA. If he did, he would be terrible at it. If not for Arya, he would have never known much about this or have come here.

Edgar took a seat in the cigar-colored chesterfield leather sofa that was unoccupied and flipped open the *Inquirer*. Like every other newspaper in the country, the entire front page had news about only one topic – the 9/11 Attacks and Investigation. The top section of the front page was focused on the investigation into the attacks, and the bottom part had coverage about the rescue and recovery effort in New York. Sadly, whoever was still trapped in those rubbles would be dead by then. The article discussed the hundreds of family members who were still holding on to their hope of finding their loved one who had gone missing on that fateful day. As Edgar read that article, his mind drifted onto Samir's case and how horrible Sania must be feeling at this time.

Hearing footsteps behind him, he turned to see if it was Arya, but it turned out to be someone else. He let out a deep sigh and turned his attention towards the top section of the newspaper. As he read the details about the investigation, his expression changed as he became deeply engrossed in the investigative elements. The article started with information about the hijackers: how many of them, how they entered the country, which part of the world they came from, how they entered the country, and where they stayed. The article then veered into sensitive information, like where the hijackers possibly trained to fly the aircraft and how they managed to hijack the plane. The article was very well-written and had more information about what went into the planning of these attacks than Edgar had expected a newspaper to have at this moment. Edgar wondered how strange it was that the paper had more information than him, a law enforcement officer. He hoped that he would learn more about the investigation when LT Cooper returns from the JTTF meeting today.

"Hey, you." Arya walked behind Edgar and tapped his shoulders.

Edgar jumped, hearing the words from Arya. "Jesus!"

Arya broke out into a burst of laughter. "Can't believe you got scared like a little girl."

George, the bellman, walked into the waiting room, hearing the noise.

"Hey George, can you believe what Edgar just did?" Arya turned towards the bellman.

Edgar made a gesture to express that it was not funny and started walking towards the exit.

"You got to admit it was a little bit funny," Arya bumped her shoulder into him playfully.

Edgar smiled, shaking his head, and gave in to Arya.

The playful banter lasted until George walked back with a couple of go-cups.

"Coffee for you," George handed a cup to Edgar and turned towards Arya, "Caramel macchiato for you, dear."

"George!" Arya leaned in and gave him a loving hug.

"You know you are spoiling her," Edgar commented with a good-humored intent.

"Don't listen to him. You are the best," Arya said, as she walked towards the front door.

"Be safe," George called out, as both Arya and Edgar exited the building.

21

"How did the anniversary dinner go?" Edgar asked as he started the car.

"Surprisingly, well." Arya went on for the next few minutes detailing the celebration in the luxurious Four Seasons Hotel. She explained her pleasant surprise to see her brother there; he had flown all the way from London just for the occasion.

"You know how much that meant for my dad," Arya said, arching both her eyebrows.

Edgar nodded to signal that he understood her implication. How could he not remember? Arya must have gone over her family dynamics so many times.

"The chosen one returns!" Arya mimicked her father's ecstatic reaction to seeing his son at the party. It seemed her brother had kept his visit as a surprise, and, as he had planned, it became the highlight of the party.

"Aren't you a little harsh here?" Edgar reminded Arya that it was her decision to not be at the helm of their father's empire, and not her parents'. They never showed favoritism towards her brother when choosing him to run their business alone.

Arya gestured with her hand to signal that she was just kidding and was not serious.

"How come you didn't come upstairs?" Arya asked, checking her face in the vanity mirror as she applied lip gloss.

"I didn't want to interrupt in case you got lucky last night," Edgar smiled in a teasing way.

Arya's love life seemed to be the go-to topic of conversation for Edgar and Simone since she broke up with her last boyfriend.

Arya gave him one of those looks that signaled him to knock it off.

"Okay, what did you find? You sounded giddy on the phone," Arya turned the attention to the case. Edgar had called Arya earlier in the morning to let her know that he would pick her up from her condo.

Edgar nodded to signal that he had some news about the case. "We had a breakthrough in the case."

The look on Arya's face changed immediately; she became enthusiastic and curious.

"After you left, I got a call that was patched through to me from a state trooper. He claimed that he saw our man, Samir Tariq, on the wee hours of the morning of September 11th."

"Where?" Arya hurriedly asked.

"On 95 South, near Linwood."

"Linwood? Isn't it near the border of Delaware?"

Edgar nodded. "Yes. He made a traffic stop because of broken taillights."

Arya looked up slightly like she was trying to remember something. "It doesn't add up. When I stopped by their house, Sania showed me Samir's car, a Toyota Camry, in the garage. I remember checking the car out, and, as far as I could recall, the taillights weren't broken."

"This is where it gets interesting. Samir wasn't driving his Camry; he was driving a rental – a white Ford Transit van."

Edgar paused to make his next statement sound more dramatic.

"Now hear this. Guess what was written on the side of the van? Aether Solutions."

"Aether?"

"I looked it up. Aether Solutions act as a one-stop-shop to businesses for installation, design, and maintenance of their electrical systems. They service mainly New York City."

The conversation with Ashton immediately flashed through in Arya's head. She remembered finding out from Ashton that Samir Tariq worked as a service technician and not as an investment broker in Aries Financials. At first, Samir lied about his position in Aries Financials, and then he hid his resignation. Sania seemed to have no knowledge of both fronts. It had become quite evident to Arya that Samir was duplicitous, but what she hadn't figured out is why.

"Did you hear what I just said?" Edgar asked, breaking the silence that befell between them.

"Yeah, yeah," Arya responded, getting her senses back to the present moment. "I was just thinking, why?"

"What do you mean?" Edgar asked, keeping an eye on the road.

"We now know for sure that Samir had been lying to Sania for a long time…," Arya began to lay out a laundry list of lies they had discovered so far. "…about his past work history, his position in Aries Financials, his resignation, his recent travel to Los Angeles, and his new employer."

"When you put it that way, it does sound like he is a pathological liar," Edgar concluded, adding his color about the psyche of Samir.

"But why? Was Samir ashamed of his true job? Did he lie to Sania to make himself look good?" Arya threw out questions which they both agreed that Sania would be the best person to have a definitive answer.

"This is going to break her heart," Arya sighed, feeling worse about exposing Samir's lies and shattering Sania's view of him.

"I know. But you are doing it for her own good." Edgar paused before adding, "Maybe she already suspected it. Based on my experience, wives always know when their husbands lie. This is especially so when the lies are this big."

Arya nodded, looking down, agreeing with Edgar.

"Also, I think that was not the end of Samir's lies." Edgar held his gaze squarely on Arya and said, "I think Samir did not work for Aether Solutions either."

Arya looked up at him in a way that demonstrated her state of mind – befuddled and utterly shocked. "What makes you say that?"

"The van."

"The van that trooper stopped?"

Edgar nodded. "I ran the van's plates that trooper gave me, and it was a rental."

"Okay. Maybe Samir rented it – maybe he was a sub-contractor who worked on a job for Aether." Arya alluded to the common practice where large companies, like Aether, hire sub-contractors to work on their behalf at a client location.

Edgar nodded, signaling that he was aware of that practice. "I know companies tend to demand the contractors to dress in their company's uniform and paint their vehicles with their logo. This, unfortunately, gives the clients the wrong impression that the contractors were indeed employees."

"Exactly. Aether might have done that here."

This type of exchange was one of the reasons why Arya loved working with Edgar. She doesn't have to mince her thoughts or sugarcoat her words around Edgar. He doesn't mind her challenging and poking holes in his theory about the case. This might sound like something that should be customary or typical, but, in reality, it was not, especially when it involves a female officer challenging a male officer.

They both decided that the best step would be to call Aether and confirm Samir's employment status. They presumed the answer would be negative as Samir drove a rental and not a company-issued van. However, they hoped that Aether Solutions maintained records about the contractors who worked on their behalf. That would help them paint a picture of Samir's employment and source of income after he resigned from Aries Financials.

"For now, let us assume Samir was a contractor, given the van was a rental. However, it doesn't explain why Samir rented the van from Enterprise," Edgar floated the question.

"Enterprise Rental?"

Edgar nodded.

"Okay, why is that odd? Don't most people rent from Enterprise?"

"Yes, but they don't spray-paint them," Edgar explained that companies like Hertz or Enterprise do not allow customers to spray-paint their vehicles.

"I didn't know that. Do you think Samir might not have known that?" Arya asked, thinking aloud why Samir might have painted the van.

"It is possible, but I doubt it, given he was not new to this line of work." Edgar alluded to Samir having worked as a maintenance technician in Aries Financials and other places before that.

Arya slightly nodded her head, signaling to Edgar that he had a valid point.

"On a different note, what else did the state trooper say? The state trooper might have been the last person who saw Samir before he disappeared," Arya switched the conversation to the traffic stop.

"You mean how Samir acted? Like his mental state?"

Arya nodded. "Yes."

"He said everything was normal. The stop went by the book. He gave him a warning for taillights and wrote him a ticket for driving without a license."

"Whoa, whoa!" Arya almost jumped from her seat. "What do you mean by driving without a license? He had one."

"I meant to say that he didn't have the license with him that night. The trooper said that Samir claimed that he must have accidentally left his license at his home."

"That doesn't make any sense. Samir was at the airport that evening, and we know that you can't fly without showing ID."

"You forget that he never intended to fly to LA that night." Edgar reminded her that they did not find Samir Tariq's name on the PNRs for any of the Philly flights for September 10th.

After Arya gestured that Edgar might be right, she shifted her gaze towards the highway where a cop was standing at the passenger side of a car, possibly issuing a ticket. That visual prompted Arya to think something totally out of the box.

"How did the trooper know it was Samir driving the van that night? What if it was not?" Arya raised both her eyebrows as she threw a curveball at Edgar.

Edgar was genuinely surprised by Arya's question. He had assumed Samir was driving the van; he never thought of this possibility. "Do you think he was carjacked?"

Arya shrugged her shoulders. "I don't know, maybe. I was just throwing it up as one more thing for us to think."

Arya and Edgar agreed that they should keep an open mind about Samir. They have evidence that he had lied to Sania about his job, but nothing definitive that he was unfaithful and had plans of disappearing.

"I think we need to get the trooper in with our sketch artist," Edgar said.

The trooper might not have seen Samir's license, but he saw the face of the driver. They both agreed that having the state trooper sit with the sketch artist was the right move. It should confirm if it was indeed Samir driving the van that night.

If it was not Samir driving the van, it would open a new can of worms, Arya thought to herself.

"Enterprise Rental might not be able to confirm if Samir was driving the van, but they should be able to confirm who rented it," Arya added.

"I know." Edgar smiled as the car came to a stop in front of Enterprise Rental.

22

"WHAT CAN I do for you, Detectives?" A young man behind the counter greeted Edgar and Arya.

"We are here about one of your rentals," Edgar announced.

"Sorry to hear that you had a bad experience. My name is Jeff, and I will have it taken care of," Jeff rambled on.

"Slow down, what did you say your name was...? Jeff?" Edgar asked as he raised his right hand to gesture Jeff to stop talking.

Something about the tone of Edgar's voice made Jeff stop cold and not utter another word until Edgar finished with his question.

"We are not here because we rented from here, genius." Edgar rolled his eyes. "We are here to inquire about a van that was rented from here."

"Oh!" That was the only word Jeff could squeak through his mouth.

Seeing Jeff's discomfort, Arya stepped in to ease Jeff's nervousness caused by Edgar's high-handed approach.

"Jeff, my name is Arya Martins." Arya smiled. "Can you look up and tell us who rented this van?" Arya went on to read the plate number of the van, which was stopped by the state trooper.

It was clear that Jeff was so much more at ease with Arya than Edgar. He began to breathe again.

"Let me look it up," Jeff said with a half-smile. Jeff's fingers danced over the keyboard effortlessly as he pulled up the rental record of the van.

"Got it," he announced. "It was rented about a week ago by a man named Samir Tariq."

Edgar and Arya exchanged glances that relayed that this outcome was expected by them.

Jeff raised one of his fingers to gesture that he found something more. "This van was reported as stolen."

Arya leaned towards the counter. "When was it reported?"

"Yesterday, September 13th. It was supposed to be returned on September 11th, but I guess it wasn't returned by this guy, Samir Tariq." Jeff just butchered Samir's last name, Tariq.

"Is that why you are here?" Jeff asked.

Arya ignored Jeff's question and asked, "Did you take Samir Tariq's ID when the van was rented?"

Arya wanted to confirm that it was indeed Samir who had rented the van.

"I assume so. I was not here, but let me check." Jeff went on to hit a couple more strokes on the keyboard to navigate further. "Here it is," he said, proceeding to turn the monitor towards Arya and Edgar.

The screen showed the license of the person who rented the van, and, without a doubt, it was Samir Tariq who rented the Ford Transit on September 4th, 2001.

"Did you guys call Samir before filing the complaint?"

Edgar asked. It would have been unusual to file a complaint without first calling the phone number.

It looked like Jeff's nervousness had evaded, and he was more at ease. After reading through the notes left on the system, Jeff answered, "It seems they tried to contact the guy, but it seemed to be disconnected or out of service."

"Do you have the phone number?" Arya asked.

When Jeff relayed the phone number, Arya and Edgar exchanged glances as they both didn't recognize the phone number. It was a different number than the one Sania had provided earlier.

"Did this help?" Jeff asked enthusiastically.

"It did. Thanks," Arya smiled, making Jeff feel better about himself.

As Arya and Edgar walked out of the Enterprise with the printouts of Samir's rental record, one more lie and deceit of Samir became known to them. Samir's second cell phone.

"You know what it means?" Edgar asked, referring to Samir's secret cell phone.

"I know," Arya sighed, feeling bad for Sania. A secret cell phone, more often than not, meant that the husband was having an affair.

Their conversation came to a halt when Edgar's phone started to ring.

Edgar answered the phone but didn't stay on the call for long. Whatever said on the call was brief.

"It was Ray," Edgar gestured towards the phone. Ray Irvin, a fellow detective in their squad, was inching towards his retirement and had a way of getting his paperwork done by taking advantage of young detectives in the squad, and Edgar was his favorite go-to guy because he can't seem to say no.

"What did he want now?" Arya sighed.

"It is not like that; he did a solid for me."

"What?" Arya couldn't believe that Ray did a solid for someone else.

Edgar started laughing. "Give him a break. You know you might like him if you give him a chance."

"No, thanks." Arya gestured to Edgar that he could keep Ray for himself.

"Now, I am actually curious. What did Ray do that qualified as a solid?" Arya arched her eyebrows, expressing her keen interest.

"Samir's financials."

"Don't tell me he ran the financials for our guy?" Arya asked, expressing disbelief.

Ray going out of the way to help Edgar was not the only reason for Arya's exaggerated expression. It was also the timeframe by which Ray was able to pull it off. It would typically take a week to work with agencies to run the financials, and Ray being able to do it in a day was a complete shocker.

Edgar nodded. "That is exactly what I am saying; he has them all nicely laid out for us."

Arya shook her head in disbelief. "Maybe you are right. I might have misjudged the man."

"Amen to that," Edgar jested. It was not common for Arya to admit that she misjudged someone. It was even rarer for her to admit Edgar was right in any of their disagreements.

ARYA AND EDGAR had decided earlier to stop by Sania's house to find more information from Sania about Samir's past. From their investigation so far, it had become apparent that Samir had been living a double life from the moment he had gotten married to Sania. However, Arya was not sure if Samir was cheating on Sania, in the traditional sense, with a woman.

Arya felt in her gut that there was something more significant in play than the run-of-the-mill philandering husband story. The scale of lying by Samir was astounding. He had lied about where he worked before Aries Financials, his position in Aries, his resignation from Aries, and his new business for Aether Solutions. Those lies were just the ones he had said regarding his work. Then you have the odd coincidences that occurred in Aries Financials at the time of his resignation, like Omar Raqqa's disappearance, the suicide of the other Samir Tariq, and the break-in to steal a package from Marisomo's secure facility. To add to the intrigue, Omar Raqqa's access codes were used during the break-in.

Was there some kind of connection between those odd

criminal coincidences and Samir's disappearance? Arya couldn't tell so far, but she was determined to find out. She was never a big fan of coincidences, happy or unfortunate.

Arya felt that there were too many blanks that they couldn't fill regarding Samir's past. However, they could turn to Sania to fill some of the blanks about his background. Arya wanted to start by learning about Samir's education, work history, and family history. Once the basic profile was created, Arya wanted to build Samir's profile by learning about his relationship with Sania. How did they meet? How did their relationship lead to marriage? Did they experience any marital issues in the past? And finally, did Sania ever suspect any abnormal behavior by Samir?

As Samir was a foreign national, Arya had earlier requested similar information from the State Department. Based on what they had learned during the investigation regarding Samir's lying, she was glad that she had reached out to the State Department. Arya desperately wanted to compare the accounts and see if there were discrepancies regarding Samir's background. Based on what she had learned so far in the investigation, she would bet that they would definitely find differences between both those two accounts. The places where the accounts differ would help paint the real Samir and not the one he chose to reveal. Arya, in her gut, knew that would break open the case.

"What exit did you say?" Edgar asked, trying to remember the exit for Sania's house.

"Change of plans. We are going to the precinct," Arya declared.

Edgar glanced towards Arya with a quizzical look.

"Samir's financials," Arya said, with her gaze squarely on Edgar. "You are right. Samir's financials would give us a better understanding of the true Samir. He has certainly been living a duplicitous life, and nothing would cast a light better than his financials."

"Also, his motives to lie," Edgar added. "If he was having an affair, we should be able to find that out. Affairs are usually expensive."

At every turn, Edgar seemed to be holding on his theory that Samir was having an affair. Arya, however, didn't think that was the reason for Samir to be missing.

"How far did you go on the financials?" Arya asked, switching the conversation back to the financials.

"I asked for the past year. I thought we can dig in deeper if we needed," Edgar said evenly.

Arya gestured that she agreed with Edgar. In her gut, she knew that Samir's activity during the last five months, starting from May, when Omar disappeared, would be the key to this whole case.

———

FOR THE PREVIOUS HOUR, Edgar and Arya had locked themselves in one of the interview rooms to sift through Samir's financials. In their experience, Interview Room One, on the far side of the cafeteria, was the place to hunker down if you wanted to be left alone. Being the furthest room from the cafeteria meant one thing; it was the room that was least frequented by detectives. Whenever they find themselves submerged in a mountain of documents, they always find themselves in that room.

Arya was pleasantly surprised by Ray's work; he was able to get more of Samir's financials in a short amount of time than expected. When Edgar informed her about Ray's help with Samir's financials, she thought that Ray would, at most, get Samir's bank statements and his credit report. She had never imagined that he would be able to get all of Samir's bank and credit card transactional data for the previous year. Having access to Samir's credit report is one thing, but having access to Samir's credit card transactions is a game-changer. With that level of detail, they would now be able to get a snapshot of Samir's everyday life. She was extremely curious to find out if Samir's lifestyle changed after he resigned from Aries Financials.

Arya made a mental note that she should thank Ray and put in a good word with the LT.

With the trove of data in front of them, they decided to take the 'divide and conquer' approach. Edgar took over documents related to Samir's bank, house, investments, business filings, and taxes. If Samir started a small business, he would have had to register with the state and file taxes for it.

On the other hand, Arya focused her analysis on Samir's credit card transactions. Arya knew the best way to find a person's secret would be to follow the trail of their credit card transactions. In this day and age, it was almost impossible to lead a portion of your life, even the one you want to hide, without ever using a credit card.

As she sat in the room analyzing the transactions, it reminded Arya of the case that she and Edgar had worked on last year – the Tracy Handler case. It was a case that started off as a missing person case and ended up as a double homicide. Tracy Handler was a young woman in her late twenties when she disappeared in the middle of the day. The tragedy was that the day of her disappearance was one of the happiest days in her life. She had just called her husband and left a voicemail about the most joyous news in her life. She was becoming a mom. Unfortunately, the news that brought her the most happiness also ended up being the reason for her murder.

Tracy was white, blonde, and had one of those photogenic looks that made the case apt for TV. The increased attention meant a lot of calls about possible Tracy sightings in the town. It also drove up community participation, and a lot of volunteers signed up to look for her. The search parties went for days, and it stretched all across the town, from woods to the malls. The non-stop press coverage also brought out a lot of crazies, who came up with falsehoods to get their face splashed on the camera. Even with all the attention, they couldn't find Tracy. With every passing day, the hope of cracking the case began to dwindle until they spotted an anomaly in the credit card transactions of Tracy's husband – Will Handler. Will had used his credit card to buy a gift VISA card that allows a person to add funds and use it as a debit card. Following the trail of transactions on that card, they discovered that Will had made purchases such as women's jewelry and watches after Tracy had disappeared. Digging deeper, they discovered that he was also using that card to make rental payments on a property. When Edgar and Arya visited the property, they were met by a young woman who happened to be Will's secretary. When Arya confronted the secretary, she sang like a canary. She provided evidence that implicated Will for murdering his wife, Tracy. Will Handler was eventually convicted by a jury and was sentenced to the death penalty for killing his wife and his unborn child. The justice was served, and Arya remembered, very well, how crucial the role of credit card transactions was; they got the ball rolling in the right direction.

The circumstances in Samir's case were different than Tracy's case, but she hoped that the trail of credit card transactions would give them a much-needed break.

"You could hide a credit card from your wife, but you could never hide them from the mighty credit bureaus," Edgar had earlier remarked.

After reviewing credit reports, it became apparent that

Samir was not the type who carried many credit cards, and he had only two. Arya began to rifle through the reports to look at the transactions on both of the cards, and she straightaway knew that something was fishy. One of the cards, a VISA, had transactions only from the beginning of May 2001, and the other card, a Mastercard, went back for years. The reason was staring right at Arya's face: VISA card opening date – May 2nd, 2001. That definitely piqued Arya's curiosity. As she dug deeper into the nature of transactions on both the cards, her jaw dropped in surprise.

All the transactions on the Mastercard seemed to be something you would expect from running a household – groceries, utility payments, insurance payments, wardrobe upkeep, and so on.….

However, the transactions on the VISA card painted a different picture. There were purchases related to travel – tickets for flights that zigzagged the country, rental car reservations in San Diego and Culver City, and foreign transactions in Kuala Lumpur. There were payments made to a rental apartment in Culver City, and to flight schools in Arizona and Florida. Finally, the last transactions on the card were related to van rental – reservations in Enterprise Rental and purchases in Home Depot, possibly for paint.

"How did a service technician, who was out of a job, manage to pay for all of this?" Arya wondered. When Arya checked the payments made on the cards, she noticed that only the minimum payment was made for May, June, and July. The payment for August was pending.

"Okay, that explains the 'how' part? He never paid those balances," Arya thought to herself. "But why?" Arya leaned back on her chair, looked upwards towards the ceiling, and closed her eyes as she contemplated the answer to the question, "Why did Samir make all these transactions?"

At the same time, across the table, Edgar was deeply

engrossed in parsing his stack of Samir's financials. He started off with the real estate, and it checked out. In essence, there were no other properties than the home in East Falls, and there were no credit checks for any rental properties. The investments came next. For a person pretending to be an investment banker, the investments seemed almost non-existent. It looked like he dabbled on investing in an S&P 500 index fund, which he liquidated by the end of August 2001. Taxes came next, and Samir seemed to have filed them on time. Edgar flipped through them to check for business disclosures, and he came up empty. The filed tax returns looked pretty straightforward; W2 from Aries Financials and no other income was declared. Samir also took the standard deduction every year, and there was no mention of any small business. A quick scan of the occupation section revealed that Samir was truthful; he declared himself as a Service Technician on those forms.

"How did he manage to live in that neighborhood?" Edgar wondered as he saw the income that was declared on the taxes. "Where did he get the money to buy that home?"

Edgar found the reason for that very question in the next set of documents – bank statements. Edgar noticed that Samir did banking in two different banks. This did not immediately raise concern for Edgar as many people in the country keep their money in multiple banks.

Edgar started off with the account that was opened in 1997. It was the year Samir got married to Sania, and they had bought their home the same year. There was an initial deposit of close to four hundred thousand dollars made when the account was opened.

Samir must have made a lot of money when he worked in Saudi Arabia, or he must be coming from a family of wealth to have had that kind of cash sitting in the bank, Edgar thought to himself.

Other than the initial deposit, everything else looked normal – monthly mortgage payments, payments to a Mastercard account, and so on....

Edgar quickly sifted through the document and didn't find any payments or debit card transactions that remotely reflected that Samir was having an affair. Edgar was slightly disappointed by it, but he reminded himself that there was one more bank account that needed to be analyzed.

Edgar was struck dumb when he analyzed the second account. The account was opened very recently in May 2001 in a regional bank named JNC. Just like the other account, there was an initial deposit, but it was much smaller - one hundred thousand dollars. But there was a difference in the way the initial deposit was made between both accounts. The initial deposit to the first bank was a cashier's check. The initial deposit to the second bank was a wire transfer from an account-based out of a Dubai bank. Edgar highlighted the difference and made a mental note to look into the account in the Dubai bank later.

Edgar sifted through the various transactions on the JNC Bank account, and he noticed a pattern emerging. The majority of transactions in the last four months were cash withdrawals. Most of them were quite small, in the range of hundreds of dollars, but there were some outliers, where withdrawals were in thousands of dollars. But none of them ever went over ten thousand dollars. Edgar had earlier learned in his training that any withdrawal over ten thousand dollars would automatically be flagged and added for authorities' purview. Looking at these transactions in Samir's account, Edgar wondered if that was an angle he had to consider. *Was Samir trying to hide these transactions? Why would anyone need to withdraw that kind of money in such a short period?*

As Edgar pondered over those questions, he became

more convinced that Samir had something to hide. What does a married man hide more than anything else? An affair. Who has a secret cellphone and a secret bank account? A person who was having an affair. He has a need to keep his phone calls and payments to his mistress a secret from his wife. As he thought about it more, Edgar started to like his gut feeling about the case a lot more. *Samir was having an affair, and it played a role in his disappearance. He probably ran away with his mistress, leaving his wife and unborn baby behind — a real lowlife.*

With that thought in mind, Edgar turned his attention to other miscellaneous transactions on the account. There were a few payments, less than fifty dollars each, made to the same credit card company.

Secret credit card, Edgar thought in his mind, speculating about the small payments.

In the sea of transactions, Edgar almost missed a small withdrawal of twenty-five dollars in May 2001. Upon closer inspection, he noticed that this particular withdrawal was different – it was a bank transfer, and the other withdrawals were for cash. Edgar peered further into the transaction and found out that the twenty-five dollars were drawn by JNC Bank as a setup fee for opening a safe deposit box in the bank.

The revelation about the safe deposit box definitely piqued Edgar's interest. As far as he could remember, Arya never mentioned Samir having a safe deposit box in the bank. It could be possible that Arya forgot to say that to him, or that Sania forgot to disclose it to Arya. Nowadays, many Americans have a safe deposit box where they store documents for safety reasons. However, in Samir's case, Edgar had the same initial gut feeling that he had before. Samir was keeping this safe deposit box as a secret from his wife. Secret cellphone, secret bank account, and now a secret safe deposit box. All roads were leading to the same place – Samir was living a secret life.

For the next thirty minutes, Edgar and Arya exchanged their discoveries with each other. Edgar went first with the information he had learned and his suspicions based on it, and then Arya followed.

As they did with every other case, they passed no judgment about each other's analyses or suspicions. They both listened to each other with the utmost respect and followed their usual practice – writing down each other's suspicions and their initial judgment about it on the whiteboard. They then followed up with poking each other's theories about the revealed information for the next twenty minutes.

"Let's go with what we have learned so far about Samir," Edgar started. "First – his job. Samir not only lied about his past job in Saudi Arabia but also about his position in Aries Financials with his wife, Sania."

Edgar gazed straight into Arya's eyes and continued, "Next, he lied about his resignation, or, in other words, he withheld his resignation news from Sania."

Arya looked straight at Edgar without saying a word.

"Next…." Edgar paused as he searched for Arya's notes on the table. "We then have him traveling all over the country. Los Angeles, San Francisco, Miami, Newark, Boston, and on and on.…"

Edgar shifted his eyes from Arya's notes to her. "Don't you think it is strange that he was paying rent for an apartment in Culver City?"

Arya nodded, agreeing with Edgar's sentiment.

"Wow! I almost missed it," Edgar exclaimed, staring at the statement. "The purchases in Kuala Lumpur."

"Why that one in particular?" Arya narrowed her eyes, trying to understand why Edgar was so excited about this transaction.

"How did he go there? We have his complete financials, and I don't see any payments for an overseas trip."

"Maybe he paid through different means."

"How? If he had another bank account or a secret credit card, we would know. We have all the accounts that were opened with his Social Security number. Unless...." Edgar paused with a 'eureka' expression on his face.

Arya restlessly gestured Edgar to keep going; his dramatic pause raised her curiosity.

"Unless he had a different Social Security Number which we didn't know of," Edgar delivered his revelation.

"Now, I think you have an active imagination. We know that Samir had multiple bank accounts, and one of them had a huge infusion of cash in May. Maybe he paid cash for the ticket," Arya provided an alternate theory.

"Maybe." Edgar sat back in his chair and thought for a moment. "We can verify it easily with his passport. Do you have that?"

Arya shook her head. "I checked with Sania, and it looked like Samir took it with him during his trip to Los Angeles on September 10th."

"Supposed trip to Los Angeles, which turned out to be a lie," Edgar corrected Arya.

Arya raised both her hands to gesture that she stood corrected.

"I have requested the State Department for records, and we should get them by tomorrow." Arya went on to share her request to the State Department about Samir's immigration record.

Edgar nodded approvingly. "That is a good move. State Department's records should have more information about Samir's past – his work in Saudi, as he came to the country on a work visa."

Arya, without acknowledging Edgar's compliment,

jumped onto the topic that has been troubling her mind. "Forget about how he went there. Why did he go to Kuala Lumpur? He was a service technician who resigned from his steady job and was working part-time." Arya arched one of her eyebrows slightly, "Why did he go there? What job did he have there?"

Edgar shrugged his shoulders. "It beats me."

"The whole thing is bizarre. A secret credit card and a secret bank account were opened in May, almost in the same timeframe he resigned from his job. He then went on to use those new accounts to pay for some bizarre things, such as air travel, rental property, and rental cars."

"Don't forget about the safe deposit box," Edgar interjected.

Arya nodded. "True. This whole thing smells fishy. Samir was definitely leading a secret life. But why?

"What was he hiding?" Edgar interjected.

Arya knew where Edgar was leaning. *The Affair.* Arya knew that was a very plausible theory. Still, she found certain coincidences that were not adding up with that theory.

"What about Omar Raqqa?" Arya asked. "He disappeared quite mysteriously."

"Coincidence," Edgar offered a simple explanation.

"What about the other Samir Tariq who committed suicide? What about the theft that happened in the Mari-somo facility? It all happened during the same timeframe as Samir resigning from Aries Financials. Are you going to saying all these were just a big fat coincidence?"

Arya sat back, leaving Edgar with silence as he pondered the gauntlet of coincidences.

"I can't explain. It could be a coincidence or some sort of an elaborate plot." Edgar paused as a thought flashed through his mind. "If it is an elaborate plot, what could it be?"

Arya shrugged her shoulders. "I have no clue."

A silence fell on the room for a long minute as they both searched their minds for possible motives. They both came up empty.

"I think the time has come for us to have an in-depth conversation with Sania," Edgar broached the topic that had also been making rounds in Arya's head.

"I think so too." Arya nodded her head, agreeing with Edgar.

When all was said and done, they both suspected Samir was living a duplicitous life. They both believed the timing of Samir's JNC account pointed to one thing; it's a cover to hide his transactions from Sania's eyes. With all that said, they both believed that Sania knew more than she had shared so far. It was time for them to make the trip to meet Sania with questions that might shatter her perception of her husband, Samir.

No wife is in total darkness to her husband's secrets. They always knew when the wheels were about to come off. With what Edgar had learned, the wheels were definitely coming off with Samir's story.

24

"You heard it right; it is Culver City," Edgar said. He shifted his eyes towards Arya and flashed a smile to signal that the conversation was going per their plan.

Arya nodded briefly, acknowledging Edgar, before turning her attention back to her own conversation on the phone with her friend from the State Department.

Edgar was on the phone with his mate from college, Greg Kelly, a detective with the LAPD. Upon sifting through Samir's financials, Edgar and Arya had decided that they needed to dig deeper into certain aspects of Samir's life. Samir's reasons for paying rent for an apartment in Culver City, his new bank account and bank locker, his travel internationally to Kuala Lumpur, his considerable uptick in domestic travel during the previous three months, his benefactor who wired the large payment from Dubai bank, and any links to Omar Raqqa and the Marisomo Corporation. There were so many questions that needed to be answered.

Edgar had turned to his college mate, Greg Kelly, an LAPD detective, to ask for a favor and find out about Culver

City. Similarly, Arya turned to her friend in the State Department to get access to Samir Tariq's records.

"You sure?" Arya said on the phone, sounding surprised.

"Thanks, man, I owe you one," Edgar smiled on the phone as he steered the car to turn left into Sania's neighborhood. "Call me the moment you find out about the apartment. Don't worry about the time."

Edgar paused for a moment as he listened to Greg on the other end of the phone before answering, "Simone is not in town; she has gone to meet up with her mother."

Greg must have cracked a joke, as Edgar's face lit up, and he broke into a big laugh. "You haven't changed a bit, Greg. Trust me, being home alone for a week is not the same as being a bachelor. When you finally get hitched, you will get it."

As Edgar and Greg continued with their banter, Arya wrapped up her call with her friend and was in a state of disbelief.

"Got to go, Greg. Just about to reach the wife's house. Call me the minute you find out about Culver," Edgar quickly wrapped his conversation with Greg as the car came to a stop in front of Sania's house.

"Greg is going to come through. He is close with a detective in Culver City PD, and he is going to hit him up with our request." Edgar flashed a smile, glancing at Arya. Edgar then went on to fill Arya about his conversation with Greg.

There was no reaction from Arya. She sat still, staring blankly at the road. It was almost like she didn't hear anything that was said by Edgar.

"What's wrong?" Edgar asked, reaching towards Arya's shoulders.

Feeling Edgar's hands, Arya slowly turned towards Edgar.

"What's wrong?" Edgar repeated his question, seeing the bewildered expression on Arya's face.

"Samir." Arya paused for a brief moment, adding to Edgar's curiosity. "State has no record of Samir ever going to Kuala Lumpur."

"What? We have his credit card activity," Edgar was trying to make sense of what he had just heard.

Arya shook her head. "Nothing on his passport."

"Maybe his credit card information was stolen…," Edgar thought aloud.

"I am not sure," Arya sounded doubtful. "It was not just that State did not have him visit Kuala Lumpur. They instead had him in Mexico during that same period."

"Hmm…. Do you think Samir's credit card was stolen in Mexico?" Edgar speculated.

"Possibly, but we have a problem with that theory. We have no transactions in his financials for Mexico. How did he go to Mexico, and how did he buy anything there?"

"Car and cash," Edgar provided an explanation.

"Cash. You know who drives all the way to Mexico in a car and does all their transactions in cash?" Arya's gaze squarely fell on Edgar.

"Someone who wants to hide what they were doing from the authorities," Edgar answered, coming to the same realization as Arya.

"Exactly. I think we just found out that Samir's secrecy might be bigger than hiding an affair from Sania."

"Jesus! Do you think he was into something illegal?"

"I think it is very much possible. Looking at what we have unearthed so far, I am not going to rule that out. Would you?" Arya eyed Edgar.

Edgar nodded, gesturing his agreement with Arya's assessment.

"One more thing – Samir Tariq's education."

"What about it?"

"In his application to enter the country, it was marked

that he has a Ph.D. degree in Chemical Engineering from Lahore University."

"Chemical? That is odd, given he was working as a service technician in Aries Financials."

"Yes, I thought the same," Arya nodded.

"I will give you that it is a peculiar choice, but Samir wouldn't be the first person to have worked in a field different from his degree."

"I know, I know," Arya mumbled, looking disturbed.

"What is it? Spit it out." Edgar could see Arya was clearly troubled.

"It seems Samir had applied for a visa before he got married to Sania, and he was rejected."

"When?"

"1993, 1994, 1995, and 1996."

"Four times?"

Arya nodded.

"Why was he rejected that many times?"

"My friend couldn't tell from the records."

"Wow! Four times. Got to give it to the guy; he was persistent," Edgar sighed.

"You know what? Samir might have married Sania for the wrong reasons."

"What do you mean?"

"Sania is a U.S. citizen, and marrying her would get Samir into the country. Given how persistent he was in the past, I wouldn't rule that out."

"Do you think Sania would have fallen for that?"

"Do you think it is a stretch? Look at what we know that she has fallen for – his previous job in Saudi, his position in Aries Financials, his resignation, and his new contracting job."

Edgar sighed deeply. "What do you suggest?"

"It is time to find out." Arya got out of the car and began to walk towards Sania's front door.

25

EDGAR STOOD on the edge of the front porch as Arya rang the front doorbell for the third time. Just like the other two times, this attempt turned out to be futile.

"I guess she is not home," Arya sighed, turning towards Edgar.

"Isn't that her car?" Edgar gestured with his hand towards the white Toyota Highlander, parked alongside the curb in front of Sania's house.

Arya gestured that Edgar was right. "I guess she must have gone out by a cab or with a friend."

Edgar shrugged. "Why don't you call her mobile?"

"Come on!" Arya threw her hand in disbelief. "Don't you think I would have called her if she had a mobile?"

"I would if I didn't know you for as long as I know you." Edgar smiled teasingly.

"Smartass." Arya punched playfully on Edgar's shoulders.

"Detectives, are you looking for Sania?" A loud voice broke through the silence of the night and reached the ears of Edgar and Arya.

They both turned around to find a large white man,

sporting a Philadelphia Eagles jersey, waving at them. He was standing near the front door of the house which stood opposite to Sania's house.

Arya exchanged a quick glance with Edgar before replying, "Yes, we are."

"She is not at home," the man yelled from across the street as he walked towards the road.

Arya and Edgar walked towards the man and met him near the edge of the street.

"Hi, I am Tom Halladay. I live across the street," he said as he extended his hand.

"I am Detective James, and this is Detective Martins, from the Germantown PD. Do you know where Ms. Tariq went?" Edgar said evenly, without shaking Tom's extended hand.

Tom, taking the cue from Edgar, lowered his extended hand. "Yes," he nodded.

"My wife took her to the hospital."

"Why? What happened?" Arya jumped in.

"My wife, Kate, went over to Sania's house this evening to check up on her husband's case, and, when they were talking, Sania started to experience severe cramps – contractions."

Hearing the news, Arya was flooded with a rush of happiness, and a smile dawned on her face.

"She is having a baby," Arya grinned as she tilted her head towards Edgar.

Edgar reacted with a smile, knowing how close Arya was with Sania in the past. "That is good news."

"Sania mentioned that you are her friend from college." Tom held his gaze on Arya and addressed her, "She had asked me to reach out to you tomorrow and let you know about her whereabouts."

"Where did they go?" Arya asked eagerly.

"Kindred Hospital. They left just over an hour back," Tom said, looking at his watch.

Arya and Edgar thanked Tom for the information he shared before walking towards their car.

As Arya reached the door, she paused. A thought rushed to her head. *If Sania had shared about their friendship in college with Tom and Kate Halladay, they might be close. Their insight might be useful in Samir's case.*

"Are you guys close with Samir and Sania?" Arya asked, walking towards Tom.

"We are friendly with each other, but I am not sure if I would call that as close," Tom explained.

"What do you think about them?" Arya asked, holding her gaze on him.

"What do you mean?" Tom's eyes narrowed.

"How long were you neighbors with them?"

"Little over three years."

"Three years – you should have some opinion about them." Arya leaned in.

In the meantime, Edgar walked back from his car and stood next to Arya.

"I mean, they don't cause any problems around the neighborhood." Tom searched for words. "To be honest, I really haven't spent that much time with Samir. You should talk to my wife, Kate; she is friendly with Sania."

Arya's eyes were fixed on Tom, and she could tell that Tom was holding back something.

"Thanks, we will. Does your wife have a mobile that we could reach?" Edgar asked.

"Yeah, she has one of the fancy ones. Blackberry." Tom grinned and went on to share Kate Halladay's contact number.

"Thanks. I heard they are pretty good." Edgar gave a half-smile and noted down her number in his pocketbook.

"I hope you find Samir soon. Poor Sania, she is devastated." Tom shook his head, gesturing his concern for Sania.

"Such a good person; she doesn't deserve to go through her first pregnancy under these circumstances."

Hearing Tom, Arya realized his words showed concern for Sania's feelings and did not reflect the same towards Samir's safety. *Tom was definitely holding something back.*

"Good person?" Arya gazed squarely at Tom as she stressed a phrase from Tom's earlier response.

Tom expressed his lack of understanding of Arya's question, "Sorry, I don't follow."

"You referred to Sania as a good person in the singular. Is there a reason why you didn't say the same about Samir?"

"I mean... Samir is a nice fellow," Tom said with a hesitation in his voice.

"Tom, if you know something, you should say it." Edgar leaned in.

"You know, I saw something. I don't know if that is even relevant here." Tom hesitated. "You know, I don't want to get Sam in trouble."

"Tom, Sam is already in trouble. He is missing. What you know might help us find him," Arya pushed him to look at it from a different angle.

Tom took a deep breath and said, "I hear you. I will tell you what I know, but please don't share this with Sania until it is substantiated. Poor girl, she has enough to worry already, and I don't want to cause an unnecessary rift in her family life."

Arya nodded. "You have my word; we won't share it unless it is warranted."

"Like a month back, I went to this sports bar with my friends from work to celebrate a lucrative deal."

Arya and Edgar gazed at Tom attentively as Tom continued with his account. "I don't smoke generally, but I get this urge to smoke whenever I drink. As I was drinking that day, I stepped out for a smoke. That was when I spotted

Sam going into this place late at night." Tom paused briefly and said the following with an added emphasis in his voice. "He was with a girl."

"Okay. Is it wrong to be with a girl?" Edgar asked, trying to understand the reason behind Tom's concern.

"It is wrong if you happened to spend a night with that girl." Tom arched one of his brows.

"You mean Samir was cheating on Sania?" Edgar asked rhetorically.

"How do you know that he spent the night and what was this place?" Arya followed up.

"The place was a low-end motel, and a couple of Benjamins did the trick with the desk clerk. He was happy to spill all the dirty details about Sam. It seemed Sam has been checking into this motel for over a week with that girl. I also learned that he was spending a solid four to five hours with her in that room. What else do you think was going on?"

Arya nodded, agreeing with Tom's inference. "Did you find out about the girl?"

"Nah, I told my wife, as she is better equipped to handle these situations."

"Your wife?" Edgar looked baffled about why he characterized his wife in that manner.

"I forgot to mention that my wife and I run a security firm, Dark Shadow. I manage the business side, and Kate is the brain behind the operational wing of the firm. The firm typically handles corporate background work and not cases of this nature. But spying is spying, right?" Tom grinned, feeling satisfied with his comment.

"Do you know if she was able to find out about the girl?"

Tom nodded. "Yeah, she mentioned her name was Nafisa...." He looked upwards, trying hard to remember her last name. "Sorry, I couldn't recollect her last name. It was one of those Middle Eastern names, tough to remember." He sighed.

"I understand," Edgar chimed in. "Do you recollect anything else about her? Was she working? Where she lived?"

"You know, Kate is very good at what she does. If she sets her mind on finding something, there's no stopping her. She is the best." Tom's face glowed as he complimented his wife.

This is so refreshing, Arya thought to herself. How many men take pride in their wives' work? And, among them, how many of them go around boasting about their wife? Very few, and Tom seemed to be one of them.

"I presume your wife was able to find about her," Edgar brought the focus back to his original question.

"Yes, she did. I remember Kate mentioning that Nafisa, whatever, worked out-of-state. Out of all places, she worked in New York City – the Big Apple."

"Anything else? Where she lived? Where she worked in New York?" Arya jumped in.

"I remember Kate mentioning that she lived somewhere close by. Sorry, I can't remember off the top of my head." Tom shrugged, expressing his inability to help further. "If you talk to Kate, I am sure she would be able to answer all your questions."

"Thanks, we will talk to her." Arya turned towards Edgar and gestured to find out if Edgar has any more questions for Tom. Edgar motioned back to express that he has something more to ask Tom.

Edgar closed his pocketbook and took a step towards Tom. "From where I stand, it feels like you and your wife have gone over and above for a neighbor. Do you guys act and care the same about the other families in this neighborhood?" Edgar swirled his forefinger to gesture the families in the neighborhood.

"Can you imagine if we did that? We would be considered

extremely kind by some people and seriously creepy by others at the same time," Tom laughed at his own joke. "Of course not; we both really like Sania."

After a boisterous moment, Tom's expression turned serious. "Sania was like an angel to us; she saved our son's life." Tom went on to explain about the moment that could have devasted their life, if not for Sania. Tom and Kate's only son, William Halladay, who was only seven years old at that time, was playing with a couple of his friends in their front yard. It was late in the evening, and the sun had just gone down. They were playing catch, and, when one of his friends kicked the ball, it bounced on the road and rolled towards the intersection. When William went to fetch the ball, a car from nowhere almost hit him, if not for Sania pushing William away from the vehicle. The driver of the car was probably distracted by his phone. He didn't even stop when Sania jumped in front of the car to push William away.

"Now you know why we are willing to go over and above for her. We owe her our happiness," Tom said, almost welling up as he replayed that near-tragic moment of their life.

Hearing that story brought a smile on Arya's face, and she felt proud of her friend.

"Thanks, Tom, for your time. We will head to Kindred to meet with…." Edgar's words came to an abrupt halt as they heard the sound of an approaching car.

"Kate is here," Tom announced, seeing a white Lexus coming to a stop in front of Sania's home.

Arya and Edgar turned around to find a blonde, dressed in a chic blue skirt and a matching top, get down from the Lexus. Kate Halladay looked very different from her husband, Tom. For one, Kate looked slim, fit, and attractive. She looked like someone who regularly worked out. Tom, on the other hand, looked like a person who never stepped into the gym.

He was built like an offensive lineman with his big belly but without the muscular upper body. Kate reached the back door of her Lexus and gently helped Sania get down from the SUV.

Upon seeing Arya approaching her, Sania smiled and took a couple of gingerly steps towards her.

"False contractions," Sania said, embracing Arya.

"I was just about to come over to Kindred," Arya explained that Tom had just told them about her going into labor and Kate rushing her to Kindred Hospital.

"I guess I troubled Kate for no reason." Sania flashed a brief smile and shrugged her shoulders.

"Come on, Sania, you could not trouble me even if you try." Kate reached out and hugged Sania.

"Oh! I should have introduced you guys first. Kate, this is Arya, my best friend from school, and …"

"She is Kate Halladay, your neighbor who you couldn't trouble even if you tried your best," Arya said with a smile, extending her hand towards Kate.

"That was funny for a cop." Kate took Arya's hand and smiled.

Arya then proceeded to introduce Edgar to Sania and Kate.

After a brief moment of pleasantries, Sania turned the attention towards her missing husband. "Arya, any news on Sam?"

Arya exchanged glances with Edgar before saying, "Yes, we are here to further discuss the case. Maybe we should take the discussion inside."

Kate interjected, "Good idea. It looks like it is going to rain any minute, and I don't want you to get drenched," she remarked, turning towards Sania. "I will prepare dinner and get it to you in an hour or so."

"You are a lifesaver, Kate," Sania said, embracing Kate.

Kate waved her byes and walked towards her residence with her husband.

As Sania unlocked the front door, Edgar stopped and made a gesture to express that he forgot something.

"I almost forgot; I have to make a call to LT to update about a different case. Arya, why don't you start without me, and I will catch up with you in a few minutes." Edgar excused himself and walked towards the curb.

As Arya followed Sania inside, she knew what Edgar was planning to do now. He was not going to call LT Cooper; instead, he was going to catch up with Kate and find out what she knows.

26

"So?" Sania's eyes were filled with curiosity as she searched for answers in Arya's eyes.

"We haven't found Sam yet, but we have made progress towards it," Arya opened with an optimistic note.

"What does it mean? Are you close?"

Arya didn't want to address her question with a 'Yes' or 'No' response. "Typically, in a missing person investigation, we start with the events leading up to the disappearance..."

Sania interrupted, "I thought I already told you about it – drive to the airport, flight to LA."

Arya nodded and answered in an even tone. "You are right. You provided us with excellent information that helped us kickstart the investigation."

"And? What did you find? Did you talk to Aries Financials?"

Arya nodded. "Yes."

Sania shifted her weight on the couch and leaned forward. "Arya, I have known you for a long time. I can tell when you are hesitating. Can you please give it to me straight?" Sania's eyes pleaded.

Arya took a deep sigh. "Sania, I don't know how to say it…. Aries Financials did not send Sam to LA."

Sania raised her eyebrows in surprise. "What do you mean? I remember dropping him in the airport, and he had a ticket out to LA that night."

"I know you dropped him at the airport. I don't know how to say it…." Arya struggled with words on how to phrase the situation without leaving Sania shocked.

"Arya, whatever you have to say, say it. I want to hear it," Sania said with a straight face.

"Okay. First, Aries Financials never sent Sam to LA on September 10th because Sam was not working for them at that time."

"What, they fired him?" Sania gestured disbelief.

Arya shook her head. "No. He resigned from Aries Financials in May, almost four months back."

"What do you mean? He was going to work every day. I packed lunches for him, and he left to work on the dot every day at 7:00 AM." Sania paused momentarily as she tried to digest the hard news. "What about all the trips in the last three months?"

"That was true. There are indications that Sam made trips across the country and even went on international trips."

"But for what?" Sania thought aloud.

"Do you know anything about Aether Solutions?"

Sania made a shrugging gesture. "Should I?"

"They are one of the big players in New York in the electrical systems market, and there is some indication that Sam might be working for them as a contractor."

"Did you say electrical? What would Sam do for them? He is a finance guy; you must have heard it wrong," Sania said with conviction.

Arya cringed, feeling the heavy burden of laying the hard truth on her friend. "Sorry to say, Sam lied to you about his position in Aries Financials. He was not in finance; instead, he worked as a service technician for them."

Sania's whole body shrunk upon hearing Sam's deceit.

Seeing Sania's sad expression, Arya crossed over to Sania's side on the couch and gave her a hug. "I am sorry, Sania."

"What does this mean?" Sania's eyes began to well up. "Why did he have to lie to me about his job?"

Arya remained silent, not knowing the answer that would console Sania.

"What about Omar Raqqa, his boss? Why did he lie? If Sam resigned four months back, why was he still meeting us?"

"Wait…." Hearing Omar was meeting with Sam till now surprised the heck out of Arya. "Did you say Omar met with Sam after the end of May?"

Sania nodded. "Of course, he was meeting him regularly even in August. Not just him, we even met as a family last month."

"Oh…," Arya gasped. "You met his wife?"

"Yeah. She was lovely; we enjoyed each other's company. We even went out shopping in the Prussia mall last month."

"So, let me get this straight. You met Omar and his wife after the end of May?"

"Didn't you hear me? Not just once, we met multiple times," Sania said in a raised voice. "Why are you asking? Did you talk to Omar? Did he say otherwise?"

"No, not that," Arya shook her head. "I was not able to reach him; do you have his home address?" Arya asked, wanting to check if the address matched with the one they got from the Norristown detectives.

"I don't remember off the top of my head, but I should be able to find out; Sam should have his information in his home phone book."

For the next few minutes, Sania searched for Sam's phone book in his study, which turned out to be futile. "Strange, I can't find it now. He usually keeps it here; he must have taken it with him."

Arya felt disappointed. "Do you know where Omar lives? Did you ever visit his place?"

Sania shook her head. "No, I did not. I know Sam did, but I never went to their place."

"I thought you might have, given you spent time with his wife."

Sania jumped as a new idea flooded her mind. "His wife. Why don't we just call her? I know Nafisa's number off the top of my head. She should be able to answer some of our questions."

Arya's whole body shuddered when she heard the name 'Nafisa.' Nafisa was the name of the woman who Tom saw with Sam in a motel, and he suspected Sam of having an affair with her.

"Did you say Omar's wife's name was Nafisa?" Arya asked, feeling shocked.

Sania stood baffled upon seeing Arya's expression. She slowly answered, "Yes. Nafisa Raqqa is Omar's wife."

"Coors or Sam Adams?" Edgar asked, holding the refriger-ator door open.

"Seriously! You don't have any local ones?" Arya frowned on Edgar's taste. "I can't believe you fell for the corporate beer."

"You are the last person who should pontificate. For God's sake, you have your donuts from Dunkin," Edgar made an exaggerated gesture.

"What's wrong with Dunkin? Don't you know that Dunkin's franchises are run by locals?" Arya sighed.

Edgar raised his hands and made an apology gesture. "I give up. Can we move on now?"

Arya chuckled. "We can after you hand me a Sam Adams. The name goes with our case."

"I feel sorry for your future husband," Edgar snickered, as he handed her a Sam Adams.

"Don't be. You know he would be getting all of this!" Arya placed her hands on her hips and made a sweeping gesture towards her body. They both started laughing at the absur-dity of their exchange.

They were sitting in the living room of Edgar's house and had a stack of pictures spread out in front of them. The photos were all taken by Kate Halladay when she had Samir followed in the last month.

Arya picked up a photo from the stack and looked at it closer. It was a photo of Samir and Nafisa entering a restaurant named Dar Marrakesh in Norristown. From the name of the restaurant, Arya presumed it is a Moroccan restaurant. Marrakesh is one of the major cities in Morocco, and it is located in the foothills of the snow-capped Atlas Mountains. The city is known for its bustling market, and it is one of the most vibrant cities in Africa. In high school, when Arya's friend visited Morocco for the summer, she showed her pictures of the famous Jemaa el-Fnaa square, Manera Gardens, and royal palaces to her. When her friend returned to New York, she didn't have any kind words about the city. She was furious about the town, as her favorite handbag was stolen by pickpocketers in the Jemma el-Fnaa square. And, to add to that, she was not a fan of the scorching heat and the sea of relatives she had to visit in her mother's country. Her biggest complaint was a lack of air conditioning in markets and other public places. Arya was shocked to learn that she didn't visit any of the historic palaces, tombs, and gardens of the city. Arya's friend committed the unbelievable sin of not visiting one of the most famous cities in the world, Casablanca. Arya remembered leaving her friend baffled when she asked her, "Did you visit the White House during your vacation?" Casablanca was originally named Casabranca, and it meant 'White House' in Portuguese. Arya was quite a history buff during her school years and was quite smitten with all these quirky facts.

"I know this place," Edgar said, referring to the Moroccan restaurant. "I went there once, maybe a year ago, with one of my college buddies. The food was amazing, especially their couscous, tagine, and mint tea. It was delicious."

"I think we need to pay a visit to this Moroccan restaurant," Arya said, holding her gaze on the pictures that were spread in front of her. "I count four, five, actually six pictures of them going to that place in the last month. It looks like the place they hung out the most." Arya shifted her gaze towards Edgar.

Edgar nodded. "Yes, it looks like they visited the motel only once," Edgar said, looking at the picture of Samir and Nafisa standing in the motel's parking lot.

"Definitely more than once," Arya corrected Edgar. "Remember Tom's conversation with the hotel clerk."

Edgar gestured in agreement. "Yeah, the one that kickstarted Kate spying on Samir."

"You know what I can't understand? Why is this guy pretending to be Omar Raqqa?" Arya asked, tapping on the picture that showed three people walking into a mosque – Nafisa, Samir, and Omar Raqqa. Omar and Samir were both dressed in white long sleeve thobe dresses, traditional attire for men in the Muslim world.

"Beats me," Edgar shrugged.

Arya picked up another photo from the stack. There were four people in the picture – Samir, Sania, Nafisa, and Omar Raqqa.

"This was taken when Omar, Nafisa, Samir, and Sania dined together in the Marrakesh restaurant." Arya handed the picture to Edgar. "Sania confirmed that Samir introduced this man as Omar Raqqa – his boss in Aries Financials."

"Strange, I don't get it." Edgar shook his head. "If Samir was cheating with Nafisa, why was he introducing her to Sania?"

"Is that your overwhelming concern?" Arya rolled her eyes in disbelief.

"The main question to be asked here is…; do Samir and this Omar guy have something to do with the disappearance of the real Omar Raqqa? If so, why?" Arya let the question hang for a moment.

Edgar silently thought about it for a moment when a thought flashed through his mind, making him jump. "Do you have the picture of the break-in in Marisomo?"

"Yes, I brought the Omar file home." Arya referred to Omar Raqqa's case file provided by the Norristown detectives – Jimmy Russel and Lyndsey Tanner. "Why?"

"Get it; I will tell you." Edgar gestured Arya to hurry up and get the file.

Arya flipped open a cardboard box that she brought from the precinct and pulled a black binder from it. "Here," Arya said, handing the Omar case file to Edgar.

Edgar hurriedly flipped through a couple of sections, and he paused when a large brown-colored envelope stared right at him. Edgar pulled a set of photos from the envelope that the closed-circuit cameras captured during the Marisomo break-in. It showed pictures of a mystery man dressed in a hooded jacket, leaving the secured section with a rectangular-shaped case, possibly made of aluminum. The man seemed to be highly knowledgeable about the cameras' placement, as he managed to keep his face hidden and not captured by the cameras during the break-in.

"What are you looking for?" Arya was curious, looking at Edgar's expression.

"Give me that photo," Edgar said hurriedly, gesturing towards the mosque photo.

Arya reached to her right and plucked the mosque photo from the pile and handed it to Edgar.

Edgar placed both the photos side by side.

"Jesus!" Edgar coiled back and covered his mouth to gesture his shock.

"What the fuck happened?" Arya frowned, gesturing her puzzlement.

"Look at both these pictures. Do you see any similarity?" Edgar wanted to see if Arya would come to the same conclusion as him.

Arya squinted, trying to focus on the picture. "Shit!" Arya's eyes widened in disbelief. "Unbelievable." In the mosque photo, Arya noticed that Omar had a large scar on the back of his hand, and a similar scar at the same spot could be seen on the man who broke into Marisomo.

"You know what it means: the fake Omar Raqqa was the man who broke into Marisomo," Edgar proclaimed.

Arya's eyes narrowed as she tried to make the next logical connection. "Does it mean Samir was involved in the break-in?" Arya let that question hang as they both searched for the answer.

"I don't know if we can say that yet," Edgar responded.

"Okay, let us see what we know for sure," Arya opened. "Samir worked in Aries Financials, and, for some unknown reasons, he lied about his position to Sania. Towards the end of May, the real Omar Raqqa, who happened to work in the same firm as Samir, disappeared during his business trip in the Middle East. At that time of his disappearance, he was working on the Marisomo merger and had access to their internal network."

Edgar's eyes narrowed, focusing on Arya's train of thought.

Arya, taking the visible cue from Edgar, continued. "A week after Omar Raqqa's disappearance, the fake Omar Raqqa broke into Marisomo's secured facility in Philly to steal a rectangular aluminum case, which was shipped from Pakistan." Arya deliberately paused to stress her following question. "Who could have possibly provided the access codes to fake Omar Raqqa?"

"Samir Tariq?" Edgar realized that Arya was alluding to Samir being the possible link between these events. "Wait a minute. Samir was not even in that real Omar Raqqa's group. How do you think he got access to it? He was just a service technician."

Arya closed her eyes like she was speculating the scenario in her mind. "Remember the guy who committed suicide? He had access to the records."

"Did I hear you right? Are you now speculating that your best friend's husband might have killed him to get his access codes and passed it onto Omar?" Edgar sighed reflectively. "That is some cold-blooded stuff. Do you think your friend would have married someone like that?"

Arya leaned back on the couch, with her arms crossed, and reflected about Edgar's question. "I don't know if Samir was the killer. Omar might have been the one who killed, but my gut tells me that Samir was somehow involved with this whole scheme. Look at the extent of all his lies. He seemed to have created an entirely different identity for himself. Why would he have done that?"

Edgar took a rather large slug of his beer, emptying the bottle. "I think you are right. This whole thing stinks. Samir might be or might not be a killer, but it definitely looks like he was involved somehow."

Arya fell silent, realizing how this revelation would devastate Sania.

"What do you think was in that case?" Edgar asked.

Arya's gaze shifted to the photo of Omar leaving the Marisomo facility with a rectangular aluminum case in his hand. "It must be something damn important to kill one or two people for it — if we presume that the real Omar Raqqa is also dead."

28

"WHAT ARE THESE PHOTOS?" Arya pointed to a photo that showed Samir talking to two people in front of a gas station.

"Culver City. Kate mentioned that Samir traveled to Los Angeles a few times in the last month, and during one of his visits, she had him tailed by one of her PI friends."

"I guess he didn't lie to Sania about going to Los Angeles. He just lied about the reason for his trip." Arya sighed, feeling sorry for Sania.

"I guess I was wrong about the reason for his trip. He didn't have a girl on the side in California; he traveled there to meet up with these two guys." Edgar pointed at another photo, which showed Samir walking into an apartment with the same two people.

"What is he doing?" Arya asked, looking at a different photo that showed Samir carrying a small TV into the apartment. "Is he gifting them a TV?"

"Guess where that picture was taken?" Edgar paused, fueling Arya's curiosity. "San Diego."

"What? What the hell was he doing in San Diego?" Arya

threw her hands to express her perplexity over Samir's behavior.

Edgar shrugged, gesturing that he was on the same boat as Arya. He had no clue, at least not yet. He was hoping his friend from Culver City would be able to find out something that would make Samir's behavior meaningful.

"Do you think there is a connection between Marisomo and what Samir was doing in Culver City?" Edgar asked, wondering about Samir's trips to California.

"I don't know; it would be a stretch to connect them. There is no Omar in any of these photos taken in Culver City or in San Diego," Arya answered.

Edgar stood up, stretching his hands towards the sky. "I think I need another beer. What about you?"

"When have I ever said no to beer?" Arya took a big slug and handed the empty bottle to Edgar.

As Edgar opened the refrigerator, a question popped in his mind that made him freeze.

Arya seeing, Edgar standing still next to the refrigerator, asked, "Are you going to get that beer or what?"

Edgar turned around and walked towards Arya without bringing beer from the refrigerator. He had an expression on his face that suggested that he was lost in his own thoughts and didn't hear Arya's previous remark.

"If stealing that package from Marisomo was the motive, why do you think Samir is still involved with Omar?" Edgar's gaze landed on Arya. "It had been more than three months since the break-in in Marisomo. Why are they still hanging out?"

"Do you think they got something else cooking?"

"I definitely think so," Edgar said with determination. "You know what bothers me...?" Edgar moved closer to the stack of photos. He tapped at a picture of Samir, Sania, Omar, and Nafisa walking out of the Moroccan restaurant.

"Why are they still pretending to be working together in Aries Financials?"

"What are you thinking?" Arya asked.

"It should be difficult for Samir to keep up this charade. Sooner or later, he would have to come clean about leaving Aries Financials. Why not do it earlier? Why keep this charade going?"

"Maybe he was waiting for Sania to have the baby before breaking the news," Arya offered an explanation.

Edgar tilted his head to the side and held his gaze at Arya. "Are you serious?"

Arya held up her hands. "I know.... I might be taking a charitable view on Samir's intentions."

"I would say you are making him altruistic. Looking at the facts in front of us, Samir was certainly not that." Edgar pointed at the photos of Samir and Nafisa together. "He cheated on his pregnant wife. I would say that makes him a lowlife in my book," Edgar expressed his disdain towards Samir.

Arya's eyes followed the many photos that showed Samir and Nafisa together. *Why the heck did Sania marry this immoral and dreadful person? She would have been so much better off if she had married Reza.*

"Maybe Omar found out about Samir and Nafisa shacking up and did something about it." Edgar's words jerked Arya back to the present.

Arya nodded slowly, agreeing with Edgar. That very same thought had entered Arya's mind earlier.

29

"WHAT CAN I DO FOR YOU?" A smiling face and an inviting voice of a woman greeted Edgar and Arya as they entered the premises of JNC Bank.

"We need to talk to the manager about a safe deposit box." Edgar flashed a smile towards the elderly lady.

"Sure. We can arrange that, but, unfortunately, you have to wait for a few months. All the safe-deposit boxes are taken as of now. But I can add you to the waiting list." She had one of those soothing voices and an inviting smile that makes everyone remember their grandmother.

"We are not here for opening a new one, but to find out about a particular safe deposit box." Arya flashed her detective shield to the elderly lady and introduced herself and Edgar as detectives from the Philadelphia PD.

"You are talking now above my pay grade. Let me see if I can get the manager for you." The elderly lady gestured for Edgar and Arya to wait as she went inside to one of the little offices to fetch the bank manager.

Arya and Edgar didn't have to wait long for the manager,

as the clerk came back with the manager, who introduced himself as Keith Robinson.

After a brief moment of introductions, Robinson gestured for the detectives to follow him to his office so that they could continue their discussion in private. The presence of two police officers in the bank caused a few heads to turn, and some of them stopped by to thank the detectives for their service. Edgar and Arya had never before seen that kind of admiration expressed by total strangers. It seems the way first responders selflessly acted after the 9/11 attacks have elevated them rightfully as heroes in the eyes of the countrymen.

"I was told that you are interested in a safe deposit box of a customer," Robinson said, as he gestured for Edgar and Arya to take a seat across the table from him.

"Yes, you heard right. We need to find out about the contents of a particular safe deposit box belonging to a customer named Samir Tariq," Arya replied.

"It was opened three months back," Edgar added.

Robinson nodded, gesturing his understanding of the request. "Sure, I can help with it. Can I see the warrant, please?" Robinson asked, extending his hand to receive the warrant.

Arya and Edgar exchanged a brief glance before Edgar responded. "The warrant is in progress, and we are hoping that you would let us take a quick look at the safe deposit box."

"I am sorry I can't do that." Robinson expressed that his hands were tied, and the bank's policy mandates him to reveal the contents only upon a judicial warrant.

Arya shifted her weight forward and leaned towards Robinson. "Robinson, can we trust you?"

"For what?" Robinson's eyes narrowed, feeling puzzled.

"What we are going to tell you concerns national security." Arya's gaze landed squarely on Robinson. "Can we count on you for not repeating what I am going to tell you?"

The sudden change in Arya's demeanor and voice added an element of mystery and increased Robinson's intrigue. Robinson knew Samir Tariq, but not as a friend or as a long-standing customer. He got to know about him because of Tariq's troublesome behavior last week. Robinson was called upon by a bank teller when Tariq's behavior towards the teller turned badgering, and he had to personally intervene to defuse the situation. The moment Robinson learned about the detectives' interest in Tariq's safe deposit box, his curiosity rose.

"Is it related to 9/11?" Robinson asked, shifting his glance between Edgar and Arya restlessly.

Arya stole a quick glance with Edgar, and both of them seemed to be taken aback with Robinson's question.

"Why would you say that?" Edgar jumped in.

Arya remained silent, and her eyes were focused on Robinson's body language. He seemed restless and shifty, like someone who was weighing something substantial in his head.

"Is it?" Robinson repeated his question, looking for an answer from the detectives.

"Before we say anything, we would like to know what made you ask us that question?" Edgar shifted the focus on learning the reason behind Robinson's question.

"Shit…, I knew there was something wrong with that asshole. I should have listened to my gut…." Robinson sounded frustrated and chided himself for not acting on his impulse.

"Okay…. Let us take it from the beginning. What made you connect Tariq with 9/11?" Edgar asked.

"Fuck, no! You are not even denying…; I am not going to

forgive myself," Robinson choked, feeling troubled with his perceived inaction.

Arya was taken aback with Robinson's behavior and began to wonder if Tariq being a Muslim man had anything to do with Robinson connecting Tariq to 9/11. She was aware of some incidents around her city and the country where racial epithets were being hurled against innocent Muslims. In some cases, their properties were being vandalized. She understood that the people were acting out of fear and wanted to show their outrage against the people who attacked their country. But they were wrong in directing their anger against innocent Muslims, who were just as American, and who felt equally outraged against the terrorists who attacked the country on 9/11. They loved the country like everybody else, and she couldn't imagine how they must feel to have their loyalty being suddenly questioned.

Arya wanted to question Robinson's motives, but, on second thought, she decided against it. At this stage, she knew it would be counterproductive and could make Robinson sound defensive.

"What makes you say that?" Arya gestured for Robinson to continue.

"Samir Tariq," Robinson said flatly.

"You know him?" Edgar asked.

Robinson shook his head. "I don't know him personally, but I know of him."

Arya gestured for Robinson to continue.

"I met him only once last week."

"And?" Edgar lead on.

Robinson sighed. "He was quite a character. I almost called you guys, the cops."

After a brief pause, Robinson asked. "I assume you guys

know that having a bank account is necessary for possessing a safe deposit box in a bank?"

Arya and Edgar nodded, gesturing their knowledge about the prerequisites of opening a safe deposit box.

"Tariq was here last week and caused quite a ruckus." Robinson paused and pointed at one of the teller windows. "She was badgered by Tariq."

"For what?"

"Tariq wanted to close his account and empty out his safe deposit box immediately, but unfortunately, the teller couldn't do either because of the upgrades." Robinson pointed to the hallway leading to the bank lockers and mentioned that the area was closed last week due to the upgrades. He went on to explain that security upgrades, like fingerprint readers, were being installed to modernize the facility's security infrastructure.

"Okay. How did Tariq react?" Edgar brought the focus back on to Tariq's behavior.

"Tariq flipped; he went batshit crazy and accused us of stealing his money." Robinson threw his hands in disbelief.

"I had to jump in and rescue the poor teller." Robinson shook his head, replaying the incident in his head. "He was causing quite a scene on the floor, and I had to smooth talk to bring him into my office." He gestured towards the chair Edgar was sitting on and said, "It took me five minutes to get him to sit on that chair. He was adamant about closing the account immediately."

"Did you close his bank account?" Arya knew that the financials they reviewed earlier could be a week off, and Samir might have closed his business with this bank.

"No, we couldn't." Robinson shrugged his shoulders. "Per bank policy, we couldn't close his account without emptying his safe deposit box. As the safe-deposit boxes were off-limits last week, we couldn't really close his account last week. Our hands were tied. My first solution was for Tariq to come back next week."

"I assume that was not acceptable to Tariq?" Edgar asked, connecting the possibility that Tariq wanted to close the bank account desperately because he wanted to disappear the following week.

Robinson nodded. "Exactly. It was a non-starter. He conveyed that he won't be available to come back next week as he would be going back to his country."

"Pakistan?" Arya asked, hearing Samir was planning to go back to his country.

"Yes. Tariq said he was from Pakistan," Robinson recounted his conversation with Samir from last week. Samir had expressed that he would be going back to Pakistan as he took a teaching job in a Lahore university.

"Teaching?"

"Yeah…. Tariq said that he was an engineer and wanted to make a difference for his people."

"Interesting. What happened?"

"So…, I came up with an alternate solution that seemed to satisfy Tariq." Robinson explained that his solution involved Samir signing the paperwork for closing the account and shipping the locker contents to a pre-specified address. This way, Samir wouldn't have to physically come to the bank next week to close his account.

"Did he do it?" Arya asked.

Robinson nodded. "Eventually, yes." He went on to explain that Tariq was initially reluctant with this solution, but his wife convinced him.

"His wife?" Arya was surprised to hear Sania knew about this bank account and didn't disclose it to her.

"Yes. She was here. I believe her name was…." Robinson's eyes drifted upwards like he was trying to remember her name.

"Sania Tariq," Edgar offered.

"Could be…. I am not sure." Robinson let his answer hang for a moment as his hands danced on the keyboard.

"You are right; her name is listed as Sania Tariq," Robinson said hesitantly.

"What is it?" Arya asked. She could clearly see that Robinson was holding something back. He looked unsure.

"Hmm…. I would have sworn that I heard Samir address his wife with a different name…, but I guess I was wrong," Robinson said weakly.

"I will be right back." Arya turned towards Edgar and gestured for him to continue his discussion with Robinson.

Instinctively, Edgar knew the reason behind Arya leaving the interview mid-way. *To confirm who accosted Samir to the bank – Sania or Nafisa?* From the look on Arya's face, he could tell that she believed the same as him. The person who accosted Samir to the bank was Nafisa. If it was Sania, Arya would have known about it. There was no reason for Sania to hide that fact from Arya.

As Arya exited the office, Edgar turned his attention back to Robinson. "Did they withdraw the funds in the account?"

"Yes, most of it. Per policy, they left a thousand dollars on their account and withdrew the rest of it."

"How? Did they wire funds to a different account?" Edgar was hoping for Samir to have wired the money, as it would invariably leave a money trail for him to follow up.

"Mostly yes," Robinson immediately said, like he remembered that from yesterday.

The word 'mostly' in Robinson's response caught Edgar's attention, and he went back to Robinson for an explanation.

Robinson proceeded to explain that Samir wired most of his money to a different bank, except for a couple of thousand dollars that he took as a cashier's check.

Upon hearing about the cashier's check, Edgar was

intrigued. Before he could ask his next question, he heard the sound of a door opening behind him. He turned around to find Arya entering the room with a folder given by Kate Halladay.

Arya landed a quizzical look on Edgar to find out if she could jump in with her line of questioning. Edgar nodded, expressing his consent for Arya to proceed with the photo ID.

Arya opened the folder and took out a photo that had a closeup shot of Samir and Nafisa dining in the Moroccan restaurant. "Robinson, can you identify the people in this photo?"

Robinson reached for his reading glasses on top of his desk and took a closer look at the photo. "Yes, of course. Samir Tariq and his wife, Sania Tariq."

"You sure, Robinson? If you need, take another good look at the girl's photo. Was she the woman who came to the bank with Samir?"

Robinson lifted his gaze from the photos to Arya's face and confidently said, "I might forget a person's name, but never their face. She was definitely the person who came to the bank with Samir."

Arya and Edgar exchanged glances, and they both understood the implications of this revelation. There was only one reason for Samir to introduce Nafisa as his wife and withdraw all the funds. *He might be planning to run away with her.*

Robinson was able to read the obvious from the detectives' expressions. "I guess she was not his wife."

Before Edgar could respond, Robinson continued. "I should have known."

Arya's eyes narrowed in interest and asked Robinson to explain.

Robinson slowly caressed his forehead as he let out a

deep breath. "I noticed that there was a little bit of tension when Samir requested a cashier's check."

"Cashier's check?" Arya asked, trying to place it.

Edgar quickly jumped in and filled Arya about his earlier discussion with Robinson about Samir's withdrawal of his account. After their brief exchange, Edgar turned his attention back at Robinson and gestured for him to continue.

"If I recall correctly, Sania…." Robinson paused and corrected himself from addressing the accompanying woman as Sania. "When Samir asked me to make a cashier's check for two thousand dollars, the woman objected. I could not follow what they were talking about, as they were engaged in a foreign language, but I could see that she was not happy with Samir. Even though most of their argument was in a foreign language, Samir did slip up and use English at certain times."

Robinson paused for a sip of water from the glass on his desk. He certainly seemed to be enjoying all the attention he was getting from the detectives.

"Where was I?" he asked rhetorically, before continuing, "Yeah, I remember – Samir spoke in English." His gaze lifted towards the ceiling like he recalled the words from memory. "I want Sania to be happy and have no trouble, even when I am gone."

"Those were his exact words?" Arya asked, almost in disbelief. Those words didn't look like something you would say about your wife to her replacement.

"I might have paraphrased a little bit, but that was the gist of it," Robinson said confidently. "At that time, I didn't think much of it. But now, it makes me wonder who would address the person in front of you in the third person, unless…." He let the sentence hang for a moment. "Unless he was not talking about the person in front of him."

"That was smart; you could have made an excellent detective," Edgar said, eliciting a proud smile from Robinson. Edgar didn't mind saying a few glowing words to stoke Robinson's ego because he needed him to continue to break the bank's protocol and share more information.

"Name of the bank and the account number?" Edgar asked, opening up his pocketbook to take notes.

"Let me check…," Robinson said as his hands danced on the keyboard. "LCI Bank and the account number is 389451902."

"LCI Bank, where is it located?"

Robinson held one of his fingers as he pushed a couple of keystrokes. "Lahore."

"He was going home," Arya thought to herself.

"Cashier's check?" Edgar asked, lifting his gaze from the pocketbook.

Robinson's fingers continued to dance on the keyboard as he pulled up the image of the cashier's check on the screen. "It seems it was made to Tangier Travels and…." He paused as he traversed to a different screen on his computer. "It seems the check was cleared on September 10th."

"I guess he purchased tickets for his escapades with his mistress," Robinson said with a mischievous smile.

"I hope it was worth it," Edgar smiled, encouraging Robinson's silly banter.

Arya was not surprised by Edgar's act of indulging Robinson. They had employed these acts of friendship and camaraderie when they wanted a subject to open up and divulge information readily.

"About the safe deposit box?" Edgar opened his request with a smile.

"I don't know…. I already broke a few rules here by disclosing Samir's financials with our bank." Robinson's voice trailed off.

"Robinson," Arya lowered her voice to almost a whisper.

"We shouldn't be telling you this." Arya glanced at Edgar.

Edgar, taking the cue from Arya, played along with Arya's ruse. "We can trust Robinson. He will keep it as a secret." Edgar, looking at Robinson, flashed a thumbs-up sign to express Robinson was on their side.

Robinson couldn't help himself from flashing a smile. He fell for their ploy hook, line, and sinker.

"You are right – it is related to the 9/11 investigation," Arya whispered.

"Oh, my God! I was right." Robinson's jaw hit the floor. "Was Samir involved?"

"That we can't tell. It is classified," Edgar said, finding a way to raise the stakes, and, at the same time, not disclose anything about it.

"Now you know why we have to look at the safe deposit box right away." Arya brought the focus back on the safe deposit box.

"Just a peek...." Robinson slowly rose from his chair. "You cannot take anything from the box," Robinson reiterated his concerns for opening the safe deposit box. "If my boss comes to know, I might lose my livelihood. It is a strict no-no in my line of work to open up someone's safe deposit box without their permission... or without a warrant."

"You can count on us." Edgar gestured towards Arya.

Robinson's eyes followed Edgar's hand and found Arya gesturing her agreement with Edgar's statement.

With that commitment, Robinson seemed satisfied. He gestured for the detectives to follow him as he walked out of the room.

EDGAR AND ARYA waited patiently as Robinson placed his right hand on the fingerprint reader which was installed on the wall next to the steel door.

"Permission Granted." The words flashed across a small screen, which was right next to the fingerprint reader.

"This was newly installed last week." Robinson gestured towards the fingerprint reader, eliciting a customary nod from the detectives.

The small screen refreshed and displayed a new set of instructions. "Enter your access code."

Robinson positioned his body in a way that would cover his finger movements to the detectives, who were standing right behind him before entering the access code.

Arya, seeing the extreme precautions taken by Robinson, rolled her eyes, and leaned closer to Edgar. "I feel like we are about to enter Fort Knox," she whispered, prompting a chuckle from Edgar.

Within a few seconds, a loud clicking sound filled the long corridor, announcing that the large steel door could now be safely opened.

"That is some state-of-the-art security for a consumer bank," Edgar said, looking at Robinson. "We don't even have that in the evidence room."

"What can I say…? The days have changed, and the customer demands that level of security nowadays." As they walked into the safe room containing the safe deposit boxes, Robinson explained that this type of security would soon become a standard across all the banks in the country.

"This way," Robinson pointed towards the north section of the safe room. Edgar and Arya followed Robinson and walked past several safe deposit boxes.

"I didn't imagine it to be this big," Arya said aloud, looking at the number of safe deposit boxes adorning the safe room.

"I get that response quite a few times," Robinson replied with a customary smile.

"Here it is...; 1190." Robinson pointed at a large ten by ten safe deposit box. "This one is Samir's."

"He had a big boy," Edgar whistled.

"Sure he did. That is the largest size we offer to customers in this branch."

Arya gestured for Robinson to open the safe deposit box. "Let's see what he has in there."

Robinson pulled his master key from his pocket and inserted it into the keyhole of the box. They all heard a slight click sound when Robinson turned the key counterclockwise and unlocked the box.

Robinson shifted his gaze towards the detectives and gestured to indicate that the box could now be opened.

"Thanks." Arya let her gaze hang for a moment on Robinson to express that he could now step out of the room.

"Sorry, I can't." Robinson explained that he had to stay in the room.

"We are not going to take anything," Edgar chimed in.

"I know, but still...." Robinson searched for a better way to tell the detectives that he had to stay in the room to ensure nothing was removed from the box.

Arya touched Robinson's shoulder. "We get it. Just like us, you have a job to do."

"Thanks for helping us with the investigation. We understand you are going out on a limb for us." Edgar smiled.

Robinson was a stickler for rules all his life. Usually, he would have never broken policy and allowed the detectives to look into a customer's account or a safe deposit box without a judicial warrant. However, Robinson knew that they were not living in normal times. 9/11 changed everything. If his small transgression with the policy helped with the 9/11 investigation, he was all for it.

Robinson gestured his appreciation for their understanding and stepped back for Arya to open the box.

As Arya slowly lifted the top of the silver-colored safe deposit box, Edgar moved next to her to get a better view of its contents. They were not sure what to expect, but, for sure, they didn't expect to find a pile of cash and multiple passports. There were three separate stacks of money, each was secured with a rubber band, and they all looked different.

"Different countries," Edgar said, as he took one of the stacks in his hand.

"Saudi Dinar." Arya gestured towards the stack in Edgar's hands, where the currency notes had the picture of the Saudi King Abdullah. She picked up another stack and said, "Egyptian Pound," and it had the image of the Sultan Hassan Mosque on the banknotes.

Edgar picked up another stack and lifted his gaze towards Arya with a quizzical look.

"Pakistan rupee," Arya said, pointing at the picture showing the Islamia College in Peshawar.

Edgar was stumped listening to Arya. "Are you making this up?"

"No, she is not," Robinson answered from the back. "I am quite surprised…, no, quite impressed, with your knowledge."

Arya could see that both of them were quite bewildered. "When I was a kid, I collected currencies from all over the world…. It was my hobby." She threw her hands.

"Only a rich trust fund kid would say that," Edgar made a snarky comment.

"At least I did something useful and not fuck it up," Arya said aloud with an attitude as she picked up a stack of passports that were tied with a rubber band.

A loud buzzing sound echoed in the room, capturing Arya and Edgar's attention.

"Sorry, this is from the front," Robinson said, reading the

message on his pager. "The armored services are at the location…."

"Please take care of it…. Trust us, we won't take anything from this box." Arya placed her hand on her heart, and her voice sounded sincere.

Robinson seemed satisfied with Arya's response and left the room to attend to armored services, leaving Arya and Edgar alone with the safe deposit box.

"Nice guy, bless his heart," Arya said, as she went back to the passport bundle.

The passport that was on top of the stack belonged to the United States. Arya removed the rubber band and flipped through the passports in her hand. The passports were all issued to different individuals by different countries – the United States, Morocco, Pakistan, Egypt, Saudi Arabia, and Yemen. But they all had one thing in common – a picture of Samir Tariq. He had different names, different looks – facial hair, hairstyle–, and sported various ethnic looks, but, unmistakably, the individual in all those passports was Samir Tariq.

"What the fuck?" Edgar's jaw fell to the floor.

Arya was equally baffled and stunned as Edgar. This was the last thing she expected to find in the safe deposit box.

Who is Samir Tariq? The same question dawned on Arya and Edgar's mind.

"What is that?" Edgar pointed towards a small rectangular brown envelope and reached into the box to pick it up. He reached into the envelope and pulled out a stack of photos. The photos looked like it was taken by a tourist visiting New York City. It was filled with pictures of various prominent landmarks - Empire State Building, Times Square, Penn Station, and several photos of Wall Street.

"It seemed he was fascinated with Wall Street," Edgar remarked, looking at the number of pictures taken there.

Arya tapped on one of the photos and said, "Nafisa."

"Yeah! That explains the fascination. She works there," Edgar remarked.

"Do you remember from the reports earlier if Aether Solutions had contract work in Wall Street?" Arya asked, connecting the dots.

"Yeah, I think you are right. I remember seeing something like that." Edgar closed his eyes for a moment as he tried to remember. "I think they had a contract with the New York Stock Exchange for HVAC maintenance."

"Hmm…. It now makes sense why Samir took a job with Aether." Edgar implied that working together would give Samir and Nafisa more opportunities to hang out without Omar and Sania's knowledge.

"What is this for?" Edgar gestured at the mini-DV cassette from the envelope. "Sex tape?"

Arya made a face, expressing her disgust with Edgar's implication. "Hopefully not."

"Are you still hopeful that there is some kind of an innocent explanation for Samir's disappearance?"

Arya shook her head. "No. I hope it is just an affair, and he ran away with Nafisa. But…." She let the sentence hang as her gaze shifted to the stack of passports and cash. "This doesn't look good. The whole thing doesn't make any sense to me."

"It makes sense if you think he was involved in something more sinister," Edgar touched on a topic that Arya was absolutely dreading.

Arya dropped the mini-DV cassette on the table and looked straight at Edgar. "What do you think?"

Edgar's gaze shifted towards the stack of passports, cash, and photos of New York City. "For your friend's sake, I hope that Samir was just a regular douchebag cheating on his pregnant wife."

30

WHEN ARYA LEFT THE BANK, she had more questions than answers.

Why did Samir have that many passports? How did he get them in the first place? It might be easy to forge passports and get them in movies, but Arya knew that was far from the reality on the ground. It was extremely hard to forge a passport, and one would need a skilled forger to do it. A skilled forger is hard to find; it is not like something you can advertise in a newspaper ad. You need to know the right places to visit and the right doors to knock on to find a forger. They live deep underground.

"You know what this means." Edgar's voice jolted Arya back to the present.

"We need to get a warrant." Arya turned her attention towards Edgar, who was behind the wheel.

"Yes, but before that, we need to bring LT up to speed."

Arya knew that they haven't updated LT Cooper with case updates. It was not intentional; they had planned to update him last evening, but LT was occupied with JTTF and was away from the station.

"I am concerned," Arya turned towards Edgar with a slight hesitation in her voice.

"For what?" Edgar narrowed his eyes in surprise.

"He might take the case from us and give it to the FBI or JTTF." Arya gestured her unhappiness with that prospect by stressing on the acronyms FBI and JTTF.

"Got to say, my suspicion antenna certainly spiked up when I saw the safe deposit box." Edgar referred to the multiple passports found in Samir's safe deposit box.

"Would you say the same if he was not a Muslim man?" Arya asked.

"Come on…," Edgar gestured his unhappiness with Arya's implication.

Arya gestured her apology by holding up her right hand. "Sorry, I didn't mean that. It is just…." Arya searched for the right word to express her feelings.

"I know. You are thinking about your friend." Edgar understood her state of mind.

"If our suspicion turns out to be remotely true, it will destroy Sania," Arya somberly said.

Edgar placed his right hand on her shoulder and gently patted her. "Do you want to look into it further before bringing it to LT?"

Arya shook her head. "No, that would be misconduct, especially after what we found in the safe deposit box. The stakes are too high."

Edgar slowly nodded.

Their conversation came to an abrupt halt as Edgar's phone rang loudly inside the car. Edgar looked at the caller ID briefly before answering the phone. "Hey Greg, hold on," he said, as he turned the car into the parking lot of a convenience store.

Arya gestured Edgar to put his phone on speaker, as she

was curious to know what Greg found out about Culver City.

Edgar mounted his phone on the dashboard and answered, "Hey Greg, I have you on speaker. Arya is with me."

"Hey Arya, how are you holding up dealing with this goofball?" Greg let out a big laugh, making fun of Edgar.

"What can I say! You can't pick your cards in poker; all you could do is work with them," Arya chuckled.

"True, except you picked him," Greg piled on Edgar.

The banter went on for another minute before the conversation turned serious.

"Okay, this is what I got so far about your guy – Samir Tariq," Greg started. "First, you are right about the apartment. He did rent a place on First and Jackson, a small four hundred square feet apartment, starting from mid-June."

"Is he there?" Arya jumped in, not able to resist her curiosity about the occupants of the place.

"Nah, no one."

"What?" Arya was surprised to hear that place was vacated. She had a glimmer of hope that Samir might be using that apartment as his love nest with Nafisa.

"It was vacated last month," Greg clarified.

"Was he staying there with a woman?" Arya asked, trying to find out if Nafisa ever stayed with Samir in that apartment.

"This is where it got interesting. According to the tenant next door, two young men stayed in the apartment, Khalid Al Mihdar and Nawaf Al Hazmi, and they mostly kept to themselves. When I showed Samir's picture, the neighbor didn't recognize him. And, to your other question, the two men did not have any girlfriends. None of the neighbors ever saw a girl coming to their place."

Arya and Edgar exchanged looks as Greg filled them with the description of the two men. They were both in their late twenties or early thirties, both sported a mustache and were Saudi nationals who just landed in the country. They spoke little English, and they had a thick accent. They were both religious as the neighbor heard them praying regularly in their apartment.

"The men from Kate Halladay's photos," Arya said aloud to Edgar, connecting the dots.

Edgar gestured that he agreed with Arya. It must be the two men whom Samir visited when he earlier traveled to Culver City.

"One more thing; it seems both the men worked in a convenience store that was part of a gas station." Greg paused as he flipped through the pages of his notebook. "Damn it! I missed writing down the name of the convenience store."

"Greg, did you find anything useful?" Edgar pulled Greg back to the meat of the conversation.

"Always, have I ever done anything that didn't turn out to be fruitful?" Greg tooted his own horn. "It seems both of them worked there for little over a month – late July/August – before they quit dramatically."

"What do you mean by dramatically?" Arya's eyes narrowed as she curiously asked that over the phone.

"It seemed both the men were quite boastful when they quit. They claimed that they were going to be famous very soon, and everyone in the country would know their faces shortly."

"Jesus! That is some serious attitude for a guy working in a convenience store."

"Tell me about it! I wish I could do that sometimes," Greg laughed.

"One more thing – I almost forgot; I showed the photo you had sent me earlier to the neighbor."

"Yeah, you told that before. The neighbor didn't recognize Samir," Edgar said with a resigned voice.

"That is true." Greg cleared his throat. "However, I forgot to tell you that he recognized the other guy in the picture."

"A guy? There was only his wife in the picture." Edgar was baffled.

"No, not that one. The one in LAX airport," Greg said, pointing Edgar to the photos that he had faxed last night.

"Kate's photos." Arya quickly flipped through Kate's folder and gestured Edgar to point out the photo that he had faxed.

"This one." Edgar tapped on a photo which showed Samir approaching a taxicab in the LAX airport.

Edgar and Arya's eyes narrowed as they studied the picture keenly. They exchanged looks, as they didn't see anyone else next to Samir.

Edgar turned his attention back at Greg. "Are you talking about the airport picture?"

"Yes, the taxicab one in LAX."

"The taxi driver?" All they could see was a faint outline of a man's face. They didn't recognize him.

"No, not the taxi driver. Look at the exit door."

Arya and Edgar's eyes shifted towards the right edge of the photo, which showed a man walking through the exit door.

"Shit!" Arya gasped in disbelief.

"Is that Omar?" Edgar squinted, trying to look closer at the man's face.

"Definitely. How the fuck did we miss that?" Arya gestured her frustration by placing her hand on her forehead.

"I guess you guys know the guy," Greg's voice came over the speakerphone.

"Yeah, we know of him." Edgar paused. A sudden thought rushed to his mind. They really didn't know the man; they didn't even have a name for him. Omar Raqqa, the name they got from Sania, had turned out to be a bogus one. Samir had provided a false name to Sania for her to believe that he was hanging out with his boss from Aries Financials. As it stood, all they had were questions with little to no answers. What is Omar Raqqa's real name? What did Samir and the fake Omar steal from Marisomo, and what were they planning to do with it? Is the fake Omar really married to Nafisa? Did the fake Omar know that Nafisa and Samir were having an affair? What was the connection between Samir, fake Omar, and the two Middle Eastern men? Where is everyone now? It looks like everyone had disappeared from the face of the earth – Nafisa, two Middle Eastern men, fake Omar, and Samir. All of them have vanished.

"Did the neighbor know the name of the man?" Arya pounced, sniffing that this might be the first clue to the identity of the mystery man.

"Yeah, his name is Omar Al…." Greg let the name hang for a moment as he turned the pages of his pocketbook. "Here it is… Omar Al-Farooq."

Arya and Edgar exchanged glances. There was a sense of excitement in the air. This could be the break they had hoped for.

"Omar Al-Farooq," Edgar whistled. "So, his real name is actually Omar."

"I guess he just switched his last name," Arya reflected.

"So, you guys know this man?" Greg asked, hearing the back-and-forth between Arya and Edgar.

"We know some details about him. But to be honest, we don't know what is true and what is fiction." Edgar sighed.

"I know the feeling." Greg signaled the emotion that every cop has, one time or the other. There comes the point in every case where the case turns into a maze. The only way forward is for the detectives to solve the riddle to crack open the case. Unfortunately, most people don't know that, and you can blame the TV shows for it. Every channel now has a cop show where the detective solves a case in less than an hour with the help of forensics from the crime scene – DNA, fiber, blood spatter, fingerprints, etc. In reality, the truth is far from fiction, and there are no magic fibers that solve a case. It usually takes a cop hitting the road, meticulously collecting leads, and using their imagination to see the forest from the trees to crack open a case. This case was certainly one of those cases where the trees were too small, and the forest was enormous.

"A real maze is what we have in front of us," Edgar echoed the sentiment.

"You said that the neighbor recognized Omar Al...." Arya struggled with Omar's last name and most certainly butchered it.

"Yeah, he certainly did," Greg said flatly.

"How did the neighbor know? Did Omar introduce himself?" Arya asked, focusing on Omar's identity.

"Kinda...." Greg paused, as a loud sound downed their voices.

"Where are you? It sounded like a truck," Edgar asked, as the rattling sound died down.

"Yeah, it was a truck. I just left a diner," Greg said as he opened the car door.

"Okay, where was I?" Greg asked rhetorically as he made himself comfortable on the driver's side of the car.

"You were saying that the neighbor never met this Omar...," Edgar recapped the point of their conversation before they went on a tangent.

"Yes, I remember. The neighbor never met the guy. This is his story. The neighbor is like in his fifties, is married, and has two kids. He has been living in this town for close to twenty years. He is an immigrant; he came to this country like twenty years back from Egypt. I checked his record, and it looks clean."

"Okay, looks like a decent fellow. What did he say?"

"Did I say he is religious? He prays five times a day and goes to a mosque down the street."

"Uh-huh, is that how he met Omar?" Arya jumped in, sounding eager to get to the point soon.

"Yeah. Like a couple of weeks back, the neighbor was at his neighborhood mosque for one of the prayer sessions. When he was getting ready to pray, he spotted Mihdar and Hazmi kneeling down, getting ready to pray. After the prayers, the neighbor decided to go over and greet those two young men. Just a casual neighborly thing to do. As he was approaching, he noticed that they were engaged in a spirited conversation with another fellow."

"Omar," Edgar guessed the obvious.

"Yeah. Mihdar introduced him as Omar Al-Farooq," Greg said evenly.

"What more did he say about Omar – his description?" Arya wanted to compare descriptions from Sania and Greg and see if they match.

"He said Omar was average height – around five feet seven inches –, broad shoulders, black hair, brown eyes, and respectful."

"Was he an American?"

"The neighbor assumed he was an immigrant, but he never asked his nationality. When I asked him to take a guess, he said that he could be a Saudi."

"Because of Mihdar and Hazmi?" Arya asked, presuming the neighbor guessed because of their nationality.

"Sorry, I didn't ask him," Greg quickly responded. "However, when I asked him if he knew what Omar did for a living, the neighbor said that Omar could be a soldier."

"Soldier!" Edgar and Arya exchanged looks, feeling puzzled with this development. "What makes him say that? Did Omar say that he was a vet?"

"No, Omar never said what he did. When I pressed the neighbor about it, he just said that it was his gut feeling with the way he talked and conducted himself. It seems the neighbor comes from an army family, and, growing up, he was surrounded by vets. He was just using that as a reference point to guess Omar's profession."

"Interesting." Arya made a mental note to check with the State Department for Omar's records. If he ever served in the military, the State Department would have it in their files when he applied for a visa.

"What did he say that he did?" Edgar asked, wondering how Omar introduced himself.

"It seems like the topic of Omar's profession never came up during their discussion. The neighbor said that their chat was cut short when Omar's phone buzzed, and he excused himself to go outside to take the call. The neighbor stayed in the mosque for another five minutes, doing small talk before he left to take care of his shop."

"Did he…?" Before Edgar could finish his question, Greg responded. "The neighbor never saw Omar after that run-in at the mosque. The only reason he even remembered meeting Omar was that it was the last time he recalled seeing Hazmi and Mihdar."

"What do you mean? They left with Omar?"

"He couldn't say that with certainty. He said that he knocked on their door the next day, and no one answered the door. After a week, he came to know from the landlord that Hazmi and Mihdar vacated their apartment."

"I guess Omar came to pick them up," Arya said, reflecting on what they just learned.

"The neighbor felt the same," Greg said quickly.

Edgar met Arya's gaze and nodded, gesturing his agreement with Arya's viewpoint.

"That's all I got, guys. Does it help?" Greg asked, turning on the engine of his car.

"Greg, this is good. Thanks, man, this helps." Edgar appreciated Greg for quickly jumping on this and helping them out.

"Yeah, Greg, this is awesome. This man – Omar – was a mystery for us till now, and we didn't even know his real name. And thanks to you, we not only have his name but a whole lot more."

"Anytime guys and give me a ring if …." Greg's response came to an abrupt halt when he heard Arya jump in with another question. "Greg, what were they talking about?"

"Who?" Greg asked, trying to place Arya's question.

"Omar and the two guys. You earlier mentioned that the neighbor had witnessed a spirited conversation between them when he approached them."

"Got it," Greg said as he understood the context of Arya's question. "Hold on." Greg pulled his notebook and flipped pages to the neighbor's section.

Arya and Edgar exchanged a look and patiently waited for Greg to respond.

"Here it is…. The neighbor said they heard them talking in Arabic, and they talked about a friend missing a flight."

"Friend?" Arya repeated, trying to make sure that she heard it right.

"Yeah. It seemed Omar was telling them that they have to go on a trip without their friend as he got the package for phase two."

"Phase two? What does that mean?"

"He didn't know. They never discussed it in front of him."

"Did he hear anything more about the package?" Edgar asked.

"Nah... They stopped talking when the neighbor got closer to them. He didn't hear anything more," Greg said quickly.

Hearing the word package from Greg triggered a profound thought inside Arya's head. "Marisomo," she whispered.

Edgar stopped his line of questioning midstream and shifted his gaze towards Arya.

"Marisomo. Omar must be talking about the package he stole from Marisomo." Arya reacted like she was hit with a sudden bolt of lightning. She was invigorated with this discovery. "What else could it be? We know that he stole a package from Marisomo. He must be talking about that."

"Maybe, maybe not. It could be something else that we are not aware of," Edgar threw an alternate viewpoint.

"Could be, but you know what I think of coincidences," Arya retorted.

"I think I am with Arya on this one," Greg jumped in. "A good cop would never believe in coincidences, especially without an explanation."

"Hallelujah!" Arya gestured a virtual high-five to Greg.

"All I am saying is that I would feel more comfortable if we had any other supporting evidence. Do we?" Edgar asked, shifting his glance from the phone to Arya.

An uncomfortable silence filled the air.

"Nothing from my end, guys," Greg said, breaking the silence.

"You said that they were talking in Arabic, right?" Arya turned her attention to Greg.

"Yeah. The neighbor said that him knowing Arabic was

the only reason he was able to make out their conversation. Otherwise, he would know zilch."

"Us too," Edgar stated the obvious.

Arya and Edgar queried a few more questions about the phone call that Omar received, but Greg was not able to add much to it. It looked like Omar didn't talk anything of value in front of the neighbor. After a few more questions, Arya and Edgar realized that they have got all they could get from Greg. The conversation came to a natural end. After a few pleasantries, they bid goodbye to Greg and thanked him again for his great work in Culver City.

Edgar exhaled a long sigh as he glanced at Arya. "This is crazy!"

Arya lifted her eyebrows and gestured the feeling was mutual.

"What does it all mean? Omar being involved with the same guys as Samir?" Edgar gave a quizzical look.

"You know what my gut tells me," Arya paused and met Edgar's gaze. "Samir and Omar knew each other. Samir knew the two Culver City Middle Easterners, and he got them a place to stay. From Greg, we now know that Omar met with the same two Culver City guys. You see, all of them are connected."

"Uh ah," Edgar listened keenly. "No contention so far. I was just saying that we cannot make the leap about the package."

"Hear me out." Arya leaned closer to Edgar. "We know for a fact now that Samir and Omar conspired together and stole a package from Marisomo."

Edgar nodded, gesturing his agreement.

"From Greg, we know that Omar mentioned that Hazmi and Midhar's friend would miss a trip with them. For a second, let us assume that friend he was referring to was

Samir." Arya stared into Edgar's eyes. "With that connection, everything else makes sense."

"Samir has the package from the Marisomo break-in. Omar has assigned Samir, or they have decided together, that Samir would cancel the trip with the Culver City men and take part in phase two." Arya summarized.

Edgar remained silent, contemplating the scenario in his head. "It is possible." He gestured that Arya's scenario was a realistic one. "Do you think Omar instructed Samir or they decided together?"

Arya thought for a moment. "You know what I think – there are no equals in these types of partnerships. I think Omar had the upper hand, and Samir was following his orders."

"What makes you say that?"

"Identity. Whose was protected?" Arya paused, giving Edgar to contemplate his response.

"Omar. Omar Al-Farooq. Look at the entire landscape – Aries Financials, Marisomo break-in, bank accounts, credit card transactions, flight bookings, and setting up an apartment for the Culver City men. Whose fingerprints are in all of this?"

"Samir Tariq."

"Exactly," Arya said with emphasis. "Whose name was protected?"

"Omar."

"We wouldn't have even known his identity if not for the lucky break of a neighbor, who was well-versed in Arabic, spotting them in the mosque."

"Jesus! You are right," Edgar arrived at the same place as Arya.

"What does it all mean? What is phase two?"

Arya shrugged her shoulders. "Beats me, no clue."

"Where is Samir now? Has he gone missing for phase two?"

"Not just Samir." Arya met Edgar's gaze. "We have a lot of people missing – Omar, Nafisa, Hamid, Midhar, and Samir."

An ominous and dark coincidence dawned on both Edgar and Arya. *All of them went missing around the same time, right before 9/11.*

31

EDGAR AND ARYA arrived at the precinct fifteen minutes past eleven o'clock in the morning. As they walked by the desk officer, Edgar and Arya motioned their hand to wave a casual greeting to him, as they do every day.

"Hey Jimmy," Edgar called out as he walked past the desk officer.

Jimmy held the receiver in his hand and seemed to be pre-occupied on the phone. At first, he didn't notice Edgar and Arya walking past him, and he didn't respond to them. It took a few seconds before it dawned on him that the voice that greeted him belong to Edgar.

"Hey, Edgar, Arya…." Jimmy raised his hands and called out their names loudly.

Edgar and Arya turned around and saw Jimmy calling after them loudly.

"What's up, Jimmy?" Edgar walked towards Jimmy. "So, you heard me at last. Your ears are not totally out…," Edgar laughed, poking fun at Jimmy for his delayed greeting.

Arya walked behind Edgar, and they neared Jimmy's desk.

"Yeah, very funny." Jimmy frowned or at least pretended

to glare at Edgar for pulling his leg. From the moment Jimmy turned sixty, he had become the butt of 'old man' jokes in the precinct. For people looking from outside, it might look distasteful and offensive. Jimmy didn't take it that way at all; he knew that it came from a good place. Jimmy Rollins had been working in the Germantown precinct for almost thirty-five years now. He has seen every officer in the precinct from their rookie years, and he is like a father figure to most of them. Jimmy didn't take any offense with the jokes; he thought they were almost endearing.

"I was just about to haul your ass back here. Where you guys been screwing around?" He shifted his gaze from Edgar to Arya.

"What is it, Jimmy? Do you need a refill for your Viagra?" Arya pushed Jimmy's shoulders playfully.

"Yeah, yeah, make fun. Wait till you get to my age and let us see how your libido works. You, young ones, would feel lucky if you get half of the action I get," Jimmy retorted back.

The banter continued for another couple of minutes before it winded down.

"Did LT ask you to page us?" Arya brought the conversation back to the phone call Jimmy mentioned.

Jimmy waved his hand. "Nah. LT is not here. He stopped by this morning, but it was very brief. He had to rush back for some meeting."

"Possibly JTTF," Arya guessed.

Jimmy motioned his head, gesturing his agreement. "I would say so."

"If not LT, what is it?"

"A young girl walked in thirty minutes back regarding her missing husband," Jimmy started.

"Sania Tariq?" Arya quickly asked as she turned her head towards the waiting room.

"She is not here," Jimmy motioned his hand to point

towards the interview room. "I asked her to wait in Interview Room Two."

"Thanks, Jimmy, will talk to her." As Arya and Edgar were about to head towards the stairs, they heard Jimmy's voice asking them to wait.

"It is not Sania Tariq that is waiting. Her name is Julia Berg," Jimmy said evenly.

Arya glanced towards Edgar as if to ask him if he knew any Julia Berg.

Edgar shrugged. "Never heard of that name."

"Me neither." Arya turned her attention towards Jimmy. "Why did you want to call us? Did she ask for us?"

Jimmy slowly shook his head. "No. She was here to file a complaint about her missing husband – Eli Berg."

"Eli Berg?" Arya repeated the name slowly. She then closed her eyes for a moment as if she was trying to place the name.

"Never heard of him too." She shrugged her shoulders and turned towards Edgar to see him concur with her.

"Let me make it easy for you, guys. I asked her about you two, and she doesn't know either of you," Jimmy started. "The reason I called is that I know you would like to talk to her about her case," Jimmy said cryptically.

"Us? Why?" Edgar looked surprised and curious at the same time.

"She mentioned that her husband left home on the night before 9/11 and hasn't seen him since then."

"Night before 9/11," Arya repeated as if she was trying to confirm that she heard that right.

"Yes. Just like your friend's husband." Jimmy nodded.

Arya's interest was certainly stoked now. "Did she say that her husband was a friend of Samir Tariq?"

Jimmy shook his head. "No, she did not."

Arya was bewildered. She thought Jimmy wanted to call them because there was a connection between both the cases.

Jimmy shifted his gaze from Arya to Edgar and brought it back towards Arya. "However, she said that her husband was having an affair, and he left her house that night to meet up with his mistress."

Jimmy paused for a moment as if he knew that would make his next statement more dramatic.

"Guess who her husband was having an affair with?" Jimmy's gaze squarely landed on Arya.

Arya drew a blank; she had no clue. She stole a glance towards Edgar, and he looked even more bewildered.

"Who?" Arya asked, feeling lost.

"Sania Tariq, your friend," Jimmy declared, leaving Arya and Edgar stunned.

Interview Room Two

THERE WAS no front wall to the interview room, only a mirrored wall. The interview room must have been painted at the beginning of the last decade, as the interior walls were exposed with peeled paint. The room was painted with a dark shade of grey, and it looked slightly bigger than it actually was, possibly due to the mirrored wall. There was a table in the middle of the room, with chairs on either side of it. One chair was on one side of the table and two chairs on the other side. They were all made of aluminum.

Julia Berg sat on the side of the table that had only one chair, and the two chairs placed on the other side of the table were empty. She was shown to the interview room by the desk officer when she walked into the precinct almost twenty minutes before. She nervously drummed her fingers on the table, feeling nervous and antsy. She took a big gulp from the can of Coke in front of her. It was her second can of

Coke in the last twenty minutes, and it was not helping her nerves. She desperately needed a smoke.

Like every other interview room in a police precinct across the country, this one was brightly lit. There is a reason why the interview rooms were all lighted up bright and vivid. It is for the mirrored wall. The mirrored wall actually serves as a one-way mirror. The one-way mirror is made up of a glass that is coated with a thin transparent layer of aluminum. This makes the mirror reflective and transparent at the same time, reflective at the brightly lit end and transparent at the darker end. This is the reason why the suspects are always placed in a brightly lit interview room, and the cops stand back and observe their behavior from the darker room.

Julia lifted her gaze from the binder in front of her and stared at the mirrored wall. She has seen enough Law and Order shows on TV to know that it was a see-through wall. She started to wonder if Arya Martins was on the other end of the mirrored wall. Julia had earlier learned from Carter, her Private Investigator, that the lead detective on Samir Tariq's case was Detective Arya Martins. Detective Martins is also Sania Tariq's close friend.

Walking into the precinct, Julia understood that it would take overwhelming proof to convince Detective Martins to believe in her side of the story. Julia's gaze shifted to the blue binder on the table, and she knew it in her heart that she had convincing evidence with her. Carter had come through with the evidence of Eli's transgressions, not just the present but also the past.

Julia's inner thoughts were interrupted when she heard the door. Her gaze lifted from the binder in front of her and landed on the door across the room. A man and a woman walked into the room. Julia, without thinking, rose from the chair as their gaze fell on her.

Arya gave a customary smile and introduced herself as Detective Martins before gesturing towards Edgar and introduced him.

"Julia Berg." Julia extended her hand to Arya first and then did the same with Edgar. Julia had a nervous smile on her face as they exchanged introductions.

"Please," Arya gestured towards the chair for Julia to take a seat.

"Do you need something to eat or drink?" Edgar offered.

"No. Thanks for asking," Julia replied politely.

"I guess you know why I am here," Julia nervously looked at both the detectives.

"To be honest, not much." Arya exchanged a brief look with Edgar before continuing, "We were told that you walked into the precinct asking to see us."

Arya decided not to reveal that the desk officer had already shared the information about her suspicion of Sania having an affair with her husband. Arya wanted to hear from Julia firsthand and read her face. Not for a second, Arya believed that Sania would be the kind of a person to sneak around and have an affair with someone's husband. Her bias was with Sania, and she suspected that Julia was somehow involved with Samir. Julia was possibly trying to distract the investigation with this 'affair' story. On the other hand, Edgar was not sure about Arya's theory. He thought Arya's interpretation was little farfetched and probably biased due to her history with Sania.

"Oh! I thought…," Julia hesitated with words. "The desk officer would have mentioned my missing husband."

"We didn't have much of a chance to catch up with Jimmy Rollins – the desk officer. He was on a call," Arya said, before turning the attention back to Julia's husband. "About your missing husband…."

"Eli Berg," Julia filled in the name.

"Eli Berg," Arya repeated the name as she noted it down.

"When did he go missing?" Edgar asked.

"September 10th," Julia said.

Arya lifted her eyes from the notebook and gazed at Julia. "Did you say September 10th?"

"Yes."

"When did you file the case?" Edgar asked.

"I haven't reported him missing." Julia's words drifted towards the end.

It was Edgar who jumped in with the next question. "Was there a reason why you didn't report him as missing for five days?"

"Because I know he was not missing," Julia replied curtly.

Julia's reply was confounding, and it baffled both the detectives.

"What do you mean?" Arya asked. "I thought you said your husband is missing."

"Yes. In the beginning, I thought Eli ran away...." She cleared her throat and continued, "But now, I think he is missing."

"Ran away?" Edgar asked. "With whom?"

Julia shifted her gaze from Edgar to Arya and said, "With her friend, Sania."

33

"Wait…. Are you saying that your husband, Eli Berg, has been having an affair with Sania Tariq?" Arya asked.

"I am not just claiming; I know it for sure." Julia's voice rang with an air of certainty. Her face carried an expression of anger and defiance, which is synonymous with a person who believes that they have truth on their side.

Julia flipped open the blue binder in front of her and raggedly pulled a few photos from it.

"Here…." She dropped the photos across the table, facing the detectives for them to take a look.

Arya and Edgar were taken aback by the sudden outburst by Julia. Both of them leaned in to take a closer look at the photos.

Edgar picked up one of the photos in his hand, and he intently studied it. There were two people in the picture sitting on a bench, probably in a park, having an intense discussion. In his mind, there was no shred of doubt that the woman appearing in the photo was Sania. He picked up another photo that was laid on the table, and it showed the same two people embracing each other in a hug, near a parking lot.

Edgar exchanged a glance at Arya, who seemed to be lost in her own world. Arya's eyes were glued to the photo on her hand, but her mind was clearly somewhere else.

Edgar cleared his throat rather loudly, which pulled Arya back from a distant world to reality. Edgar gestured with his eyes to ask for Arya's opinion, but Arya remained still. She had a blank stare, like someone who has seen a ghost.

"Are you alright?" Edgar whispered, leaning closer to Arya.

"I don't think so," Julia replied, leaving Edgar stunned.

"What did you say?" Edgar asked, shifting his gaze towards Julia. He seemed quite surprised by Julia's response to his question towards Arya.

"I said she is not okay," Julia gestured towards Arya.

Edgar was flabbergasted with Julia's response, and he turned towards Arya, looking for her response. "Arya?" he said with a hesitant voice.

For a moment, it looked like a dark cloud just lifted from Arya's mind. Arya lunged forward and pulled the blue binder closer to her. She hurriedly flipped open the binder and ruffled through the photos in it.

"What is it?" Edgar asked. He was utterly taken aback by Arya's reaction. Arya seemed to be acting irrational as she ruffled through the pages in the binder.

Arya picked up multiple photos from the binder, and it all confirmed what she didn't fathom a moment ago.

"How is this possible?" Arya whispered. "Why did she lie?"

"Who lied?" Edgar shook Arya's shoulders to break her from a spell.

"I will tell you who lied," Julia's voice rang confidently.

"What?" Edgar turned towards Julia.

"Sania. Sania Tariq lied to her," Julia said, leaning back on her chair.

Edgar was astounded by Julia's audacity, but Arya's silence revealed that there was truth to Julia's words.

Arya flipped open her phone and dialed Sania's home phone number. The phone kept ringing, but no one answered.

"Who are you calling?" Edgar asked.

Arya hit the redial button, and the incessant phone rings were heard. There seemed to be no one on the other end of the call.

"Arya…." Edgar began to ask his question again before Julia's voice interrupted him.

"She is calling her friend, Sania."

As Sania's voice came on the voicemail, prompting to leave a message, Julia jumped in. "She won't answer."

Arya turned towards Julia to find her shaking her head.

"How do you know that Sania won't answer the phone?" Arya asked, shifting her gaze squarely at Julia.

"Because she is not at home," Julia said, shifting her glance from Arya to Edgar and then back to Arya. "She hasn't been home from the morning or…," Julia hesitated and shrugged her shoulders, "or maybe from late last night."

"How do you know?" Edgar asked, staring at Julia.

"I had her watched by my Private Investigator," Julia answered curtly.

"PI! Who?" Arya asked.

"Y'all know him. He is one of you." Julia paused for a moment and said, "Carter."

"Raymond Carter?" Edgar asked, wondering if Julia was referring to a name well-known in the Philly police force.

"Yes." Julia nodded.

Raymond Carter was a name that was well known in the department. He was a no-nonsense detective who served out of the Center City precinct, and he went by the nickname of 'Tugger' in the force – like the baseball player. Tug McGraw (Tugger) was one of most loved pitchers in Philly history, and he was well known for his ability to close out games in the toughest of situations. Who could ever forget his contribution to Philly's run in the 1980 World Series title? Even today, you could see his name emblazoned upon the back of t-shirts and jerseys; he is a fan favorite. Similar to McGraw, 'Tugger' Carter was known to close out cases, and almost all of them translated into convictions. He not only closed his cases but helped with other detectives' cases, making him beloved in the force – just like 'Tugger.'

It had been a few years since Tugger had retired from the force, but his name still carried a lot of weight in the department. Once Edgar and Arya realized that Tugger was involved in the case, they knew that they needed to change their approach towards Julia.

"Was this from Tugger?" Edgar gestured towards the photos.

"Who?" Julia looked confused.

"I mean Carter," Edgar corrected himself and provided Tugger's real name.

"Yeah. Carter was the one who gave me all this stuff." Julia pointed at the photos.

Edgar shifted in his seat and tried to poke a bit into Julia's theory. "Julia, to be honest with you, these photos don't show much." He picked one of the photos on the table where Eli Berg's hands were rubbing on Sania's shoulders. "I can see that they were friendly, but affair -" He let that sentence hang for a moment before adding, "-seems like a stretch."

Julia held her gaze on Edgar as she leaned back on the chair. "You think I am imagining?"

Edgar hesitated, "I am sure you know your husband better…"

Julia interrupted Edgar as she turned towards Arya and asked, "What do you think?"

Arya's gaze was still on one of the photos where Eli Berg was seen walking back with Sania.

Edgar was expecting Arya to join him by probing Julia, and her silence surprised him.

"Arya?" Edgar gently called her name, trying to pull her back from her dazed state.

"She is telling the truth," Arya said, surprising Edgar.

Arya turned the photo towards Edgar and pointed her finger at Eli Berg. "I know him. This is Reza Tariq – Sania's ex-boyfriend."

34

Edgar was taken aback by Arya's revelation. He was expecting a reason for Arya's dazed state, but he didn't fathom the surprise would be of this magnitude.

"This changes the equation," Edgar summarized, clearing his throat.

"No kidding," Julia quipped.

"How long did you know this?" Arya turned her attention towards Julia.

"Jesus!" Julia exclaimed, throwing her hands. "You think I would have lived with him if I had known earlier? He not only cheated with another woman, but he also lied about his religion. He is a fraudster," Julia said with disgust in her voice.

"I guess you didn't know for long," Edgar remarked.

"Yes. I came to know last night," Julia answered.

"Carter?" Edgar asked, trying to confirm the source.

Julia nodded.

"You said that Sania was not at home. How did you know that?" Arya brought the focus back to the conversation they had earlier.

"I said Carter was watching her," Julia flippantly replied.

"Was?" Edgar narrowed his eyes.

"Yes. Carter was watching Sania till last night. But she disappeared this morning."

"What do you mean by disappeared?" Arya asked.

"She is not at home. Her car is in the driveway, but no one is answering her door."

A sudden thought flashed through Arya's mind. "Oh, God! She is having a baby."

"No. She is not. At least not yet." Julia shook her head; her voice, eyes, and expressions were all soaking in disgust towards Sania.

"How do you know?" Arya jumped in.

"Carter checked the hospital, and she was not there."

Their interview was interrupted by the incessant sound of Julia's cellphone.

Julia fumbled through her Coach purse and pulled out the cellphone.

Edgar and Arya looked on as Julia flipped open the phone and answered the call.

Julia's eyes shifted to Arya as she slowly brought down the phone. "Carter."

"Put him on speaker," Arya quickly replied.

There was a spring in Arya's voice as she leaned forward and started the conversation. "Carter, this is Arya Martins, and I also have Edgar James in the room. We are…"

Carter, in his deep baritone voice, interrupted, "I know you guys. How is Jimmy doing? Still giving out tickets like candy on Halloween day?"

"Nah. Jimmy is doing desk duty; the roads are safe now," Arya replied, evoking a chuckle from Carter.

"Jimmy, he is alright. He is a good man; say 'hello' from me."

"Sure, will do." Arya gave a customary quick reply as she was eager to jump back on the meat of the case.

"Okay, Detectives; I know you wanted to talk about the case."

"We have a lot of questions," Edgar jumped in.

"I can't say that I will have a lot of answers, but let me tell you something...." Carter stopped talking, and an uncomfortable silence filled the room.

"Carter, we can't hear you. You still on?" Arya spoke on the phone.

"Yeah, yeah... I don't like what I see right now," Carter gave a cryptic reply.

Arya and Edgar exchanged a curious glance at each other.

"What do you mean? Where are you?" Edgar asked.

"I assume you all know that I have been tailing Sania the last few days," Carter started.

"Yeah, Julia filled us in with the details." Arya shifted her glance towards Julia. "We have the pictures with us and ..."

"Then, you will know that Dar Marrakesh was the last place I saw Reza enter before he disappeared."

"Marrakesh?" From the investigation, Arya knew that Marrakesh was the Moroccan restaurant that Samir, Sania, Omar, and Nafisa met. She did not realize that Reza also frequented that restaurant.

"Yes, the Moroccan restaurant in Norristown."

"Yeah, we know the place. But we didn't know Reza also frequented that place."

"I can't say that he frequented but... that was the last place I saw him enter before he disappeared."

"When was it?" Edgar wanted to get the timeline.

"The night of September 10th."

Arya and Edgar exchanged glances. It was the same night Samir disappeared.

"Was anyone with him when he entered the restaurant?"

"I would say so. Samir and Sania."

Carter just threw a surprise that Arya and Edgar didn't see coming.

"Samir and Sania both met with Reza?" Arya blurted out the question.

"Yes, I would say so." Carter hesitated with his response.

Both Edgar and Arya noted the hesitation in Carter's response.

Arya leaned closer to the phone. "Carter, I heard the hesitation in your voice…."

Carter interrupted to clarify his position. "I know. Your question got me thinking. Let me back up. I was following Reza, not Sania before Reza disappeared. On the night of September 10th, I got a call from Julia that Reza was leaving their home late at night, and she was certain that he was going to hook up with Sania. She wanted to get a photo… how do I put it… in a rather intimate manner for her to believe that he was cheating on her."

Arya looked up to notice that Julia was nodding, gesturing her confirmation to Carter's explanation.

"I had followed Reza before, and I have always seen him meeting Sania alone. Most of the time, he met Sania on Kelly Drive. However, on the night of September 10th, I saw him drive in the opposite direction."

"Towards Norristown," Edgar jumped in.

"Yeah, he drove to that side of the town. At first, I thought he was going to shack up with Sania in some kind of a motel, but he surprised me by walking into a closed restaurant."

"What do you mean by closed?" Arya zeroed in on Carter's description.

"I must agree with Cooper. You are special! You jumped onto the point faster than anyone I have seen," Carter praised Arya, making her feel uncomfortable.

"What can I say? I am learning from the best." Arya,

feeling uncomfortable, did what she does best, passing the praise to a different person.

"Yeah. Cooper is good," Carter concurred, before jumping back to the topic of conversation. "The night when Reza walked into the restaurant, the board outside had a 'Closed' sign."

"Closed? How did he walk in then?" Edgar asked.

"I said closed, but not locked. I guess it was not locked because Reza walked right in."

"Was Sania and Samir there?"

"Not when Reza walked in. I was expecting Reza to go to a motel, not a restaurant. So, I waited outside." Carter paused for a moment before he continued, "I waited for like thirty minutes before I saw some activity."

"Reza walked out with Sania?" Edgar asked.

"No. I never saw Reza after that."

"What do you mean?" Arya asked. Carter had earlier mentioned that he saw some activity, and she assumed it was caused by Reza.

"I saw a van drive off…."

"Reza?"

"I thought it was Samir."

Arya arched her eyebrows in surprise. "What do you mean?"

"Okay, here is the story. It was late at night, and I hadn't slept in days, so I kind of dozed off. Not proud of it, but shit happens. When I woke up, I saw a man driving away in a Ford van. He was wearing black overalls; different clothes than Reza. I have seen Sania's husband, Samir, before. The height matched, and, because he was wearing different clothes than Reza, I assumed it was Samir."

Arya and Edgar exchanged glances. From their investigation, they had learned that Samir was ticketed on the night of September 10th, driving a Ford Transit van.

"Was it a white Ford Transit van?" Edgar asked, trying to connect with the information they had learned earlier.

"It was definitely a white van, and it was Ford. I remember seeing a Ford logo on the back. But can't vouch about the model. It could be a Transit. Why are you asking?" Carter replied.

Edgar went on to fill in the details about the traffic stop on the night of September 10th.

"Interesting. Do you have a sketch? It pained me that I couldn't positively identify who drove out of the restaurant. The sketch could give insight into that," Carter added.

"The patrol officer who stopped the van was supposed to fax us the sketch this morning. We were out all day, so I am not sure if we got it. Let me check if the fax came through earlier."

Edgar excused himself from the discussion so that he could check on the fax.

"Carter, what happened after the Ford van left?" Arya brought the focus back to Carter's account of events.

"I decided not to follow the Ford, and I waited." Carter continued on, "After ten minutes or so, I saw Sania walk out alone. This was when things went crazy…." Carter paused to add more drama to his narration, like a prosecutor in front of a jury, before he continued, "She walked straight towards Reza's car, Acura, parked outside. I thought she was going to wait for him, but she didn't. She just drove away like she owned that car."

The conversation was interrupted as the door opened, and Edgar walked into the interview room.

Arya turned towards Edgar, and, as she was about to ask about the fax, Edgar jumped in. "Ray is checking on it; he will stop by with details." As Edgar sat in his chair, he asked, "What did I miss?"

Arya gave a quick rundown – Sania leaving the restaurant in Reza's car.

"Alone?" Edgar wanted to clarify.

"Yeah, alone," Carter confirmed. "I was debating with myself if I should wait for Reza or follow her. Because she was driving Reza's car, I became curious and decided to follow her."

"Sania then drove all the way to Reza's front door. I followed her. She just parked outside, got out, and walked towards the cross-section of First and Emory Street."

"What happened then?"

"She hailed a taxi to her home."

"To her home?"

"Yes. I followed that taxi straight to Sania's home in East Falls."

"Jesus!" Edgar exclaimed. "Sania knew that Samir never got on that airplane!"

Arya looked at Edgar, still reeling from surprise. "She lied, but why?"

Arya couldn't believe that her friend Sania would lie to her face. Carter's account of the evening of September 10th contradicts everything that Sania had mentioned earlier. Sania not only knew that Samir didn't fly to Los Angeles that night, but she was with him till the wee hours of the night. But why? Why did she lie to Arya? What was she getting out of it?

"What happened then?" Edgar picked up the trail.

"I saw her walking into her home late that night and didn't see her coming out till the next day."

There was an uncomfortable silence as Arya and Edgar were waiting for Carter to fill in on the details.

"The next time I saw her go out, she walked into the Germantown police precinct."

"What?" Arya exclaimed in surprise.

"Yup. I saw her talking to you in the coffee shop."

"So, you didn't see Reza after that?"

"Reza or Samir. I haven't seen both of them after the night of September 10th," Carter declared.

Arya let out a deep breath. *Interesting.*

"So… both Samir and Reza disappeared on the same night…," Edgar said aloud.

"Not just the same night… they were seen at the same place on the night they disappeared," Carter added. Samir was spotted driving away from the Dar Marrakesh restaurant in a Ford van, and Reza was last seen entering that restaurant the very same night.

"Hmm…. Did you circle back to the Moroccan restaurant?" Arya brought the focus back to the last place Samir and Reza were seen.

"Not that night. I was parked all night in front of Sania's house," Carter answered. "I was still reeling from surprise. Never in a million years, I expected all of them dining in the same restaurant."

Arya nodded, understanding Carter's predicament; she had to admit that would have been a surprise for anyone.

"I realized something was not right when I came to know that Sania had filed a case about her missing husband. It was about the same time Julia called me."

Julia nodded. "I told him that Reza never came home."

"That is when a bolt of lightning went off in my head. What is the probability of anyone's husband and her secret lover going missing on the same night?" Carter asked rhetorically.

"Almost never." Edgar slightly shook his head.

"Bingo. Never in my career have I ever seen a case like that. Husband and her lover, both gone, poof!" Carter said dramatically.

"We can't be sure that Reza was her lover," Arya slowly said.

Edgar looked up. "Seriously?"

"One more thing," Carter interrupted. "I have been watching Sania closely from September 11th, and I have noticed her behave strangely."

"Strangely? What do you mean?" Arya pulled herself closer to the phone and was clearly intrigued by Carter's characterization of Sania's behavior.

"When I called Sania using Reza's phone, she answered by addressing the caller as Sam." Carter emphasized the name Sam in his deep voice.

"Sam?" Edgar asked rhetorically, feeling surprised.

"Yes. Sania did. It threw me off for a moment, and I began to wonder if I made a mistake." Carter went on to describe what he did next. "For a moment, I thought I made a mistake. I disconnected the call to check if I had the right phone."

"Reza's phone?" Edgar asked to confirm.

"Yes."

"Wait. How did you have Reza's phone in the first place?" Arya narrowed her eyes.

"Julia gave it to me," Carter answered.

As the detectives' gaze in the room shifted towards Julia, she answered with a steady voice. "Reza left in a hurry after he got the call from Sania on September 10th. When he left, he forgot his cellphone."

The implication was quite clear to everyone in the room.

"I thought Reza's phone would be useful as part of my investigation, and I got it from Julia," Carter filled in the rest.

"Was it useful?" Arya turned the focus back onto Carter's investigation of Reza's disappearance.

"This is where it got strange. I initially thought Sania was confused, given the circumstances."

Arya and Edgar nodded, gesturing that similar thoughts entered their minds.

"Did you call her back?" Edgar wanted to move this along.

"Yes. Sania still addressed the caller as Sam."

"I guess Sania could have acted that way out of shock. I remember talking to her, and she was in a dazed state," Arya imagined Sania's state of mind.

"I would have agreed with you if not for what she did next," Carter replied curtly.

Carter's cryptic reply piqued Edgar and Arya's interests.

Carter, after a few seconds of pause, continued. "After the second phone call, I saw Sania storm out of her house in her car."

"Where did she go?" Edgar asked.

"Kelly Drive." Carter emphasized the name of the place in his deep voice.

"Kelly Drive?" Edgar whistled in surprise.

"Exactly. The place where Sania frequently met Reza earlier," Carter added.

"Jesus! That is strange." Edgar took a deep sigh. "Let me get this straight — When Sania got a call from Reza's phone, she addressed the caller as Sam. Right after your second call, she stormed out of her house to see Reza in her regular meeting place."

"Yes." Carter signaled that Edgar had it right.

"That is strange." Edgar shifted his glance towards Arya, who seemed to be curiously silent.

"Just not that…." Carter was ready to throw another surprise. "Yesterday, she drove all the way to Julia and Eli's home and knocked on their front door."

"What should we call him? Eli or Reza?" Edgar shifted his glance from Arya to Julia.

"Does it matter? I don't care what you call him. He is a fraudster, and she is a whore," Julia fumed, shaking her head in disgust.

Arya stared at her with the same disgust. If Reza and Sania were having an affair, Reza should be the person Julia should blame. He was the one who took the vow with her, but, still, Julia was blaming Sania. Arya couldn't believe it; she thought it was time that wives assign the blame where it rightfully belongs; husband.

"Okay. Let us ratchet down a bit. Whatever Sania was doing, she definitely lied to you," Carter said.

Arya nodded, closing her eyes. That was something that she couldn't refute. Sania definitely lied about Samir leaving for Los Angeles that night, and she also hid the fact that she was in touch with Reza.

"I have to talk to Sania," Arya declared, opening her eyes. "There should be a good reason why she hid these facts."

"I agree. But we have a problem in our hands. Sania has been missing from last night. She is not at home, or at the hospital, or any other place she frequents. She seems to have vanished, just like the men in her life."

A sudden thought flashed across Arya's mind. "What about Marrakesh? Did you check back with the restaurant? Maybe the people working in the restaurant know something and can point us in the right direction."

"No such luck. I am standing in front of the restaurant, and no one is there. The place is locked."

"What do you mean?" Arya couldn't believe any restaurant would be closed at this time of the day.

"The place is not closed but locked. Get this, I checked with the store next door, and the store owner said that this restaurant has remained closed after that night."

"The place never opened after September 10th?" Edgar asked, wanting to confirm the timeline.

"Yes. No one has come or gone. It looks like whoever was running the place has been gone since Tuesday."

Their conversation was interrupted by a loud knock, and Edgar turned around to find a young policeman opening the door.

There is a protocol that the interview room is off-limits and should not be disturbed unless it is absolutely relevant to the interview.

Edgar stood up and walked across the room. As he

reached the young policeman at the door, he slightly rocked his head to gesture the reason for the interruption.

The young policeman was holding onto a file in his right hand, and he extended that handout. "This fax just came through, and Ray asked me to get this to you."

"Thank you," Edgar said as he reached out to get the folder from the policeman.

The young policeman gave an awkward smile before leaving the room.

Edgar, as he approached the table, was curious about the contents of the folder. Edgar flicked open the envelope to find a sketch that was drawn following the directions provided by the patrol officer who stopped a man on the early morning hours of September 11th driving towards Delaware on a highway.

As Edgar's eyes focused closer on the sketch, his feet stopped moving. He stood still. He couldn't believe what he was looking at. The sketch had an uncanny resemblance to someone's face he had just seen. It was Eli Berg, Julia's husband.

36

"THIS CHANGES THE EQUATION," Carter declared after Edgar shared the details about the sketch. "If it was Eli, then I never saw ..."

"Samir," Arya concluded. "In that case, Sania did not lie about Samir. She did not meet him in the restaurant. So, she told the truth." A sense of relief dawned on Arya, knowing her friend didn't blatantly lie to her.

"Except the part about sleeping with her ex-boyfriend." Julia made her presence felt.

"We don't know that," Arya frowned, directing her piercing gaze towards Julia. "Let us not assume Sania cheated; we don't have any conclusive proof. All we can say from these pictures is that Sania met Reza or Eli or whatever he called himself now." She pointed at the pictures spread across the table.

"Not once, but many times. Also, Eli lied about his identity," Julia pointed out.

"That was Eli's fault and not Sania's. Let us put the blame where it belongs." Arya was sick of always seeing a woman getting blamed for a man's fault. The tone of Arya's response stopped the back-and-forth between Julia and her.

"Okay. Julia, do you share joint accounts with Eli — credit cards and bank accounts?" Edgar asked, turning the attention back to the case.

"Yes." Julia nodded. "And I checked — no funds were drawn from our bank account, and there were no transactions on the credit card."

"That was the first thing I asked Julia to check," Carter announced on the phone.

"Interesting." Arya narrowed her eyes. "No transactions. Is it possible that Eli had an account that you didn't know about?"

"I would have said no if you had asked a week back, but now, I don't know." Julia shrugged her shoulders.

Their conversation was interrupted as the intercom speaker in the interview room came to life.

"Call for Detective Arya Martins; report back; inter-department call about a BOLO."

The intercom speakers are used inside the precinct to page police officers when they are outside the squad room but are believed to be inside the precinct premises.

Arya and Edgar immediately recognized the nature of the call. They placed a BOLO (Be on the Lookout) alert earlier for a missing white Ford Transit van, which Samir had rented before his disappearance. Based on their investigation, they learned that Samir had rented this van almost a week ago from Enterprise Rental in Philadelphia and missed his date to return the van. Based on their discussion with the state trooper, they also learned the van was stopped on a freeway leading to Delaware on the night of September 10th. During the traffic stop, the state trooper shared that he remembered seeing the 'Aether Solutions' company name and logo on the side of the van. Arya and

Edgar had assumed that it was Samir who was driving the van that night, but that theory came tumbling down when the state trooper sketch positively identified the driver of the white Ford Transit van as Eli Berg – Julia Berg's husband.

Arya turned towards Edgar. "Must be the BOLO on the Ford Transit."

"Is it Eli?" Julia stood up.

Edgar gestured for Julia to sit as Arya hurried towards the door to take the call.

"What does it mean - BOLO? They found Eli?" Julia asked, gesturing towards the door that Arya had just exited.

"No, no." Edgar shook his head. "We can't say that." Edgar went on to explain to Julia about the nature of BOLO alert, and they had to wait for Arya to get back before drawing any conclusions.

Before Julia could ask her follow-up question, they were abruptly interrupted by a buzzing sound emanating from Julia's cellphone.

Julia reached across the table to retrieve her cellphone. "Jason Elam," she read the name from the caller ID. "He is the business manager who I had reached out to earlier."

"Business manager?" Edgar was not sure what that meant.

"He manages all our finances — personal, business…. To put it plainly, he is our money guy."

Edgar quickly nodded before asking, "Is it about your bank activity?"

Earlier, Julia had mentioned that she reached out to her manager to check for any withdrawals or transactions by her husband, Eli Berg.

"Could be…. I didn't share all the details about my suspicions on Eli — like he has gone AWOL. But I did tell him that I have some suspicions on Eli and wanted him to keep an eye out," Julia explained.

"Carter, we need to disconnect. Julia had to take this call,"

Edgar announced on the phone before disconnecting the call with Carter.

"Talk," Edgar mouthed at Julia, as he placed the call from the bank manager on the speakerphone.

"Julia Berg," Julia answered the call in a normal-pitched tone, like how she would have answered any other day.

"Mrs. Berg, this is Jason Elam," Jason opened the conversation. "I am calling regarding the conversation we had earlier."

Julia shifted her glance towards Edgar and slightly nodded. The implication was quite clear; the call was related to Eli Berg.

"Jason, what happened? Did Eli make any withdrawals?"

"No, he didn't."

Edgar was deflated. For a moment, he thought that the call would lead him to Eli Berg.

"I don't understand. You mentioned it was regarding our conversation earlier — about Eli," Julia pressed on.

"Yes, you are right — it is about Mr. Berg."

Edgar lifted his gaze back towards Julia with anticipation.

"Mr. Berg called me," Elam calmly said.

"He called you, called you — like on the phone?" Julia was taken aback to hear that her husband called Elam.

"Yes, he did — like fifteen minutes back."

"Elam, my name is Detective Edgar James." Edgar jumped on the call and introduced himself as a detective in the Philadelphia Police Department. He further explained that Julia Berg was with him in the Germantown precinct.

"Is everything alright, Mrs. Berg? Do you need a lawyer?" Elam addressed Julia like a man whose foremost responsibility was to protect his client.

"I am fine, Jason. Thanks," Julia's voice came on the phone. "I am here because of Eli; he has gone missing."

"Missing!" Elam exclaimed.

"Yes. After the night of September 10th, he hasn't come home. No one has spoken to him until now," Julia explained. "When I came to see you, I should have told you...."

"No need... I am sure you have your reasons, Mrs. Berg," Elam replied. "What do you need me to do now?"

"Detective James has been handling the case, and I need you to answer any questions he has for you." Julia lifted her gaze from the phone towards Edgar.

"Sure, definitely," Elam retorted. "What do you need to know, Detective?"

"What did Eli Berg say when he called?" Edgar leaned closer to the phone and addressed Elam.

"He said that he was in an accident, and he is calling from a hospital."

"Accident? What happened?" Julia jumped in before Edgar could ask.

"Mrs. Berg, I believe he is okay," Elam reassured Julia that Eli sounded not like he was impaired or seriously wounded. "He didn't mention how he got into an accident, but he sounded okay to me."

"Where did he call from?" Edgar turned the focus to Eli's location.

"Bay Memorial Hospital."

"Near Delaware?" Edgar asked. Edgar remembered that Bay Memorial was the name of the hospital he visited last year. Edgar's friend had a terrible accident on his way to Delaware, and the paramedics had taken him to this hospital, which was located on the border of Delaware and Pennsylvania.

"Yes, I believe so," Elam confirmed. "He mentioned that he lost his wallet in an accident, and he didn't have access to his insurance information."

"So... he called for insurance details?" Edgar was

surprised. Of all the reasons in the world, Edgar never imagined this would be the reason for the call.

"Yes. I did fax a copy of Mr. Berg's driving license and his insurance information to the hospital."

Edgar shook his head. *Unbelievable.*

"What else?" Edgar wanted to hear more about Eli's conversation with Elam.

"Not much. Mr. Berg didn't ask for anything else."

"No money?" Julia asked.

"No," Elam replied quickly. "That was the strange part...." Elam paused, making the moment more dramatic. "When I asked him if he needed help — you know because he lost his wallet and I thought he would need assistance to get back to the city — he didn't take upon my request. He said that he is good."

"Did he explain further?"

"No. He didn't." Elam revealed that it was the end of their conversation. "After I hung up, I remembered Mrs. Berg asking me to keep an eye out.... So, I called."

After a few more follow up questions to Elam, Edgar was convinced that he was not going to learn anything more from Elam. Edgar proceeded to give his direct number to Elam, asking him to give a call if he heard again from Eli.

Elam noted down Edgar's number and assured him that he would do the needful.

Elam hung up after a quick exchange with Julia in which he expressed his concern about Eli's situation. During the exchange, Julia had asked Elam not to share about Eli's situation with her dad, as she would like to be the person to break the news to him. Elam readily agreed.

"Accident," Julia muttered. "Do you think I had it all wrong about Eli?"

Edgar ran his fingers through his hair and closed his eyes as if he was in deep thought.

"It is too soon to tell." Edgar opened his eyes and stared right at Julia. "There are too many things that don't add up."

As Julia looked on intently, Edgar continued. "Now we know that on the night of September 10th, your husband was driving Samir's van. If we assumed that he was telling the truth to Elam, still, it does not explain why he was driving Samir's van and why he was out of anyone's reach till now."

"He could have called me from the hospital," Julia relayed her thoughts loudly.

"True." Edgar nodded. "Any husband would call his wife in this situation, but Eli didn't."

Edgar gestured towards the phone. "I should call the hospital to find out if he is still there."

Edgar lifted his cellphone and dialed the number that Elam had given for the hospital. As the phone started ringing, Julia looked on anxiously.

"Hi. This is Detective Edgar James with the Philadelphia PD," Edgar introduced himself on the phone. "I am calling concerning a person who was admitted recently...."

"Hang on. Let me transfer you to the department who can help you with it," the person on the other end of the line answered.

After a minute of waiting, a voice came on the line. "This is Lisa. What can I do for you?"

Edgar again introduced himself and went on to explain the reason behind his call.

"Do you have a warrant?" Lisa asked.

"No," Edgar replied.

"Sorry, Detective. Patient's treatment is part of HIPAA, and we can't disclose it to the authorities without a warrant."

"I know the patient was treated in your hospital after the accident, and I am not asking about the type of treatment. All I want to know is if the patient is still in the hospital," Edgar explained.

"Sorry, Detective. The patient's admission is protected by HIPAA. My hands are tied without a warrant."

As Edgar shook his head in frustration, his gaze fell on Julia, and a sudden thought flashed on his mind. *Julia should be the person talking on the phone, not him. The hospital would be more inclined to divulge information to the wife rather than to a cop.*

Edgar chided himself for not thinking about it earlier, and he turned his attention back to the phone. "Lisa, I understand your position. However, I don't think I explained the situation clearly." Edgar went on to explain that Eli Berg's wife, Julia Berg, was next to him and had filed a case for her missing husband.

"See...? Our interest in Eli Berg is because he was reported missing. If you can confirm that he is in your hospital, you will make someone here very happy."

"Yes, that is true." Julia jumped on the phone and explained how grateful and relieved she would feel if Lisa could confirm that Eli was alive and was in the hospital.

Julia's emotional plea made a difference as Lisa agreed to look up the files and confirm Eli's admission status.

"Hang on," Lisa said as her fingers danced on the keyboard. "The computer has been acting slow all day... this might take a minute."

"Sure. Thanks, Lisa," Julia said.

As they waited, Julia and Edgar's gaze met, and Edgar flashed a thumbs-up sign to gesture that Julia had been handling the phone well.

Julia smiled and flashed the same gesture back at Edgar.

It almost took a minute before Lisa's voice came back on the line. "I have it here. Eli Berg, a brown male, age 31, was admitted to the hospital on September 11th at 3:17 AM."

"Yes, that is him, Eli Berg – my husband. What happened?" Julia said.

"Hmm… the case file says that your husband was in an accident. The paramedics responded to a 911 call on the early hours of September 11th and brought him to the hospital for treatment. Oh, Jesus!" Lisa exclaimed.

"What happened?" Julia said worriedly.

"It looks like it was a terrible accident. Your husband lost consciousness and didn't regain it till today. He was admitted as John Doe, and it looks like it was changed to Eli Berg today."

"Is he still there? Which room?"

"That is strange."

"What?"

"It looks like he was released from our care, overriding doctor's consent."

"What does it mean? Overriding?"

"It seems that the attending physician advised that your husband remains in care for a few more days, but your husband insisted on getting discharged today."

"So, he is not in the hospital now?"

"Yes. It looks like Berg left the facility less than an hour ago with his…." Lisa stopped her sentence abruptly, as if she was surprised by what she was reading in the discharge summary.

"With whom?" Julia asked.

"With you," Lisa said, leaving everyone on the call stunned. "The discharge summary states that the patient was advised against the discharge, but the patient, along with his wife, insisted on being released immediately."

"There has to be some kind of a mistake. I am Eli's wife, and I had no clue that he was even in the hospital. How did this happen?"

"I am not sure; I was not there," Lisa clarified her position. "I would assume that your husband must have identified that person as his wife."

"Why would he do that…" Julia's words trailed off as a thought stormed into her mind. *Sania.*

Edgar must have read her mind as he muttered, "Sania must have been in the hospital."

"Were there any calls made by Eli Berg after he became conscious?" Edgar asked.

"I am not sure if I can say that," Lisa hesitated.

"Please, Lisa, my husband hasn't come home yet. This might give us a clue," Julia pleaded.

"Alright, but please don't tell anyone that I disclosed this information." Lisa punched a few more strokes on the keyboard before coming back on the call. "It looks like a call was placed from his room this morning. Do you have a pen? I have the number with me," Lisa asked.

"Yes, go on," Edgar replied.

As Edgar was jotting down the phone number, Julia could tell that he had also recognized the number. It was Sania's home phone number.

Julia's face reddened in anger, as she now knew that her suspicion was indeed correct. Her husband was having an affair with Sania. The accident might have slowed down their plan, but it didn't change it. They were running away from their past lives.

Edgar held up his hand to gesture Julia to hold her off from shouting slurs directed towards Sania. Edgar didn't want the discussion with Lisa to change course, as he still had a few more questions.

"Thanks, Lisa. This helps," Edgar said. "What is the condition of Eli Berg — I mean with his mobility. Was he in a wheelchair, or was he mobile?"

"Let me look it up." Lisa punched a few more strokes. "It looks like Mr. Berg was mobile, but in a limited capacity. I guess that he can walk, but slowly. He can't run or move fast."

"Did anyone else visit him during his stay in the hospital?"

"Sorry, it doesn't say anything of that nature. We don't collect that kind of information."

"Do you have tapes that would have captured him leaving the facility?"

"Sure. There are cameras at the front entrance of the hospital… but I am sure you need a warrant if our security department had to hand over those tapes."

"I understand," Edgar replied. "Can you think of anyone else who can help us identify the person?"

"Probably the nurse and attending physician. But I was not there, and there is no way for me to confirm," Lisa said.

Edgar realized that he got all the information that he could get from Lisa. He thanked her for her help and gave her his direct number in case she found something that could be useful for the case, before disconnecting the call.

Julia simmered with anger. "I knew it all along. Here I am feeling worried about his safety, and, in the meantime, he is out prancing with his …."

Julia's outburst was interrupted abruptly as the interview room door opened, and Arya entered through it.

Julia turned towards Arya. "Guess what? We found out what happened to Eli."

"I know. He was in an accident," Arya said, as she approached the table.

FOR THE NEXT FIVE MINUTES, Edgar shared the details that Lisa shared about Eli Berg's hospital stay.

Arya, upon hearing the details about the hospital discharge, asked, "Do you think it was Sania who visited the hospital?"

"Who else?" Julia fumed.

Edgar raised his hand as if to tell her to control herself. "We can't say that for sure, but who else could it be?" Edgar asked, staring at Arya.

Edgar could tell that Arya was wrestling with something on her mind. Working all these years with her, he could tell when Arya had something cooking in her head.

"What are you thinking?" Edgar asked, holding his gaze directly at Arya. "How did you know that Eli was in an accident?"

"The call was from a state trooper. He had spotted the Ford Transit van and recognized the plates from the BOLO."

"Where was it?"

"Near the Delaware border."

"That fits with what we heard from the hospital. I guess Eli had an accident near the border, and they must have towed the Ford Transit van."

"No," Arya said. "He did not have an accident driving the Ford Transit van, and the state trooper did not spot the van in the impound lot."

"What?" Edgar was confused. "Walking into the room, you already knew that Eli Berg was in an accident."

"Yes. I knew, but not from the state trooper," Arya said evenly. "The state trooper spotted the van somewhere in the woods and, guess what, it was not damaged — the van was not in an accident."

Edgar leaned in, and Arya could tell that his curiosity was heightened.

"The state trooper did a visible inspection... the van was locked, and there was no one inside the van."

"If not from the state trooper, how did you know about Eli being in an accident?" Edgar asked curiously.

"After I finished the call with the state trooper, I did a

search on accidents around that area for the night of September 10th...."

"You should have gotten a hit for the early morning hours of September 11th," Edgar interrupted Arya as he connected the dots.

Arya pointed her index finger at Edgar. "Bingo!"

"I got a hit about an accident that said the victim was transported to the Bay Memorial Hospital from the scene of the accident. When I pulled the record, I found out that the victim had no ID, no wallet, or anything that could identify the victim. That was a bust, and I thought the 911 record might help me with the identification. When I looked it up, I was surprised to see that the person who placed the 911 call didn't identify herself."

"It was a calculated guess on my part that Eli Berg was John Doe."

Edgar nodded. "Good one."

"Who do you think reported the accident? Sania?" Edgar asked.

Arya thought for a moment and said, "I don't think so. We knew from Carter that Sania went directly to her home from the restaurant after Eli drove off with the van. Carter also mentioned that Sania never left her home that night. With this information, I would say that the anonymous caller being Sania is highly improbable."

Edgar nodded, gesturing his agreement with Arya's analysis.

"We all just missed something important here." Arya stood up from the chair. "The van. Eli was not driving the van when he met with the accident." Arya tapped her index finger on the table. "If this was the scene of the accident, the van was spotted near Midlex Reserve — which must be as far away as Joe's Coffee." Arya pointed in the direction of Joe's

THE HUNT FOR TRUTH

Coffee, which was at least five hundred feet away from the Germantown precinct.

"They are walkable, but it was not like they were next to each other," Arya concluded.

"Did you say Midlex Reserve?" Julia asked.

"Yes. Why do you ask?" Arya asked.

Julia didn't have to reply; the expressions on her face gestured her response. Julia knew the place.

"What is it, Julia? I can tell that you recognize the place."

Julia nodded. "I know where Eli is. Our family owns a property near the Midlex Reserve, and he must have gone there that night."

"Does he have…"

Edgar's question was interrupted by Julia as she answered, "Yes, Eli has the keys to the property. He goes there sometimes to hunt."

37

It took close to forty-five minutes on the 202 South highway before Edgar saw the exit sign to take 1 West.

"We are approaching the border," Edgar remarked, glancing towards Arya.

"We should be hitting the exit to Stoneridge Valley shortly," Arya remarked, glancing at the navigation map on the police cruiser.

The moment Julia mentioned that they have a family property close to the place where Samir's Ford Transit van was spotted, Edgar and Arya made their decision. They would be heading up straight to Bergs' Stoneridge property. The coincidence was striking — Eli being ticketed driving Samir's van, Samir's van being spotted close to the Stoneridge property, and Eli getting into an accident less than a mile away from the Stoneridge property. All the signs pointed to a logical conclusion that Eli must have visited the Stoneridge property on the night of September 10th.

However, the answer to the following questions still eluded them —

Why did Eli Berg drive Samir's van on the night of September 10th?

Why did Eli abandon the van in the woods next to the Stoneridge property?

Why was Eli walking back in the darkness of the night before getting into an accident?

Did Eli leave with Sania from the hospital? If they are together, where are they now — Stoneridge property?

AS THEY WRESTLED with these questions, Edgar turned towards the core question that started this case. *Where is Samir?*

He then proceeded to raise the following questions —

Did Samir ever leave Philly on September 10th?

Is it possible that Samir met up with Eli and Sania in the restaurant?

If not, how did Eli not only know about Samir's van but also get access to it?

ARYA HAD no answers for Edgar, but she had more questions of her own.

Were Omar and Nafisa somehow involved in Samir's disappearance?

What about all the other things that came up during the investigation — Marisomo break-in, Samir's secret trips across the country, Samir's secret bank accounts, Samir's relationship with Omar and Nafisa; Did any of those things have anything to do with Samir's disappearance?

DURING THE DRIVE, Edgar and Arya threw out different theories to their questions, trying to connect all the dots. But in the end, they were no closer to the answer compared to forty-five minutes ago. They could not see the forest from the trees. Samir's lies, Samir's secret trips, Samir's secret bank accounts, Marisomo break-in, Omar, Nafisa, Culver City, Samir's van, Samir missing his flight on September 10th, Sania and Eli's relationship, Eli driving Samir's van. They were not able to connect the dots that could tie everything together and solve the mystery. Arya felt that they were close — if they could only find that one missing thing that would crack open the whole case. They both agreed that one thing could be finding Eli Berg and finding out why he was driving Samir's van on the night of September 10th.

WITH THAT HOPE, they took the exit to Stoneridge Valley.

38

"IT SHOULD BE SOMEPLACE HERE," Arya remarked, as Edgar took a right on the Brandy Creek road.

"Can you call him?" Edgar asked, referring to the state trooper who spotted Samir's van.

Soon after the detectives decided that they would be driving to Berg's family property in Stoneridge, they called the state trooper. They asked him not to impound the abandoned van. Instead, they asked him to wait as they were on their way to the scene.

"No signal," Arya said, holding up her cellphone. She had wanted to avoid radioing him on the official channel, as it could lead to jurisdictional issues. The Germantown detectives had no business inspecting a possible crime scene that far out from their jurisdiction. They could follow the procedure and involve the right people, but that would take time. And that is something they couldn't afford. Arya had a hunch that Eli might be on his way to retrieve the van from the Stoneridge property.

"Slow down," Arya said, holding her hand to make a

gesture. Arya could see a winding road to her right, which seemed to be taking them to the woods.

"It should be that road," Arya said, glancing towards Edgar. "Do you want to…."

Arya abruptly stopped her question when Edgar interrupted. "That should be it… Berg's Stoneridge property." Edgar pointed towards a driveway to his left. The driveway seemed to be obscured from the road by a rather large rock wall; ancient, but well-maintained.

"What do you think we should do? Berg's property or to the van? Left, or right?" Edgar asked.

Arya's first impulse was to check the property and then swing by the van. The van was not going anywhere; the state trooper was holding guard.

"Left — the property." Arya pointed towards the driveway.

"You sure? You were quite confident that Eli would be coming here to get the van," Edgar asked.

"The van is not going anywhere." Arya shrugged. "If Eli had gone to the van, the state trooper would be holding him till we get there. I had asked him to hold anyone who came to get the van."

"That is good." Edgar nodded. "Let us check out the property then…," Edgar said, as he turned left and drove towards the driveway.

They noticed a 'Private Property – Do Not Trespass' sign as they neared the driveway.

"Not for us," Arya smiled. "We are the fucking cops."

Edgar shook his head. "Not because we are cops — we have owner's consent, remember?" He flashed a smile.

"Whatever. Both works for me," Arya waved her hand dismissively as she got down from the car.

The trees along the driveway seemed to have created an

archway, a tree tunnel, drowning out the already fading evening light.

Arya stood still by the entry gate. She seemed to be lost in thoughts as her gaze peered through the driveway.

"Is the gate locked?" Edgar got down from the car and walked to her.

Following her gaze, Edgar noticed a house that loomed large at the end of the long driveway. The house was an enormous brick building, which looked surprisingly beaten down.

"I didn't expect this," Edgar said, standing next to Arya. "The place looks like a haunted house."

"Haunted and abandoned," Arya added. "Look at the driveway; we can't drive... the tires would be flat in seconds."

"Why are the Bergs holding this property? Obviously, they don't need it. They should fix this place up and sell it. Look at the size of the property; I bet they can get a good price on it," Edgar remarked.

Arya glanced towards Edgar. "Didn't know that you are taking up real estate courses on the side."

"Wiseass." Edgar playfully pushed her, prompting a smile on Arya's face.

"I thought the gates would be locked," Arya said, noticing no locks on the gate.

"Maybe Eli is here... with Sania," Edgar wondered out aloud.

"I don't see any cars," Arya remarked as they entered the driveway.

"I bet there is a garage," Edgar made a point that Arya agreed with.

They both turned on their flashlights and slowly walked on the driveway. Just as they expected, the driveway was uneven and rocky. It took them less than a minute to get to the front door. They both felt uncomfortable; it felt like they were on a hike without wearing the right shoes.

"It is locked," Arya said, after checking the front door.

Edgar did a quick search for a ringer, and, failing to spot it, he knocked on the door a couple of times.

There was no answer.

Arya followed him and knocked a little harder on the door.

There was no answer.

"I guess there is no one," Edgar said. "Maybe we are wrong. Eli didn't drive up here."

Arya pointed to Edgar's left and gestured for him to check the windows on his side. Taking the cue, Edgar proceeded to his left to check for any signs that Eli or someone else was on the property. Arya did the same, moving to her right.

For the next five minutes, both of them surveyed the property and came up empty. There seemed to be no signs of life.

"I wish Julia had the keys to the property handy," Edgar said.

Julia had earlier mentioned that she didn't hold on to the keys to the Stoneridge property as she didn't find the property to her liking. In fact, during the summer, she finally convinced her father to sell the Stoneridge property. Eli Berg was then tasked by her father to make the property presentable to attract buyers. That was the only reason why Eli even had keys to the property.

"Okay, what is our plan?" Edgar asked as they both stood facing the front side of the house. "It is getting dark; we should probably find the state trooper."

"You are probably right." Arya agreed with Edgar, and they both started walking towards the car.

At that moment, a sudden thought flashed across Arya's

mind. *Why hasn't the trooper called? Maybe we are still out of the signal range.*

Arya flipped open the phone to find two signal bars on her cellphone.

"What?" Edgar asked, feeling curious at Arya's sudden change of expression.

"I was just wondering why the state trooper hasn't called. I thought maybe we don't have a signal, but we do." She motioned her phone towards Edgar.

"Maybe he doesn't." Edgar shrugged. "Anyway, we should find out soon. Let us get out of here."

As Edgar approached the car, he realized that Arya had stopped walking beside him. He turned around to find her staring back at the house.

"What is it, Arya?" Edgar asked, walking back to her.

"Did you notice the second-floor windows?" There were three double-hung twelve-over-twelve windows on the second floor, and Arya was pointing towards the middle one.

"No, why?" Edgar was confounded with Arya's question.

"Do you notice any difference between the three windows?"

Edgar narrowed his eyes as he tried to focus his eyes on the window. It was getting dark, and it was getting harder to spot the difference.

"It looks identical to me." Edgar glanced towards Arya.

"Jesus! I am not asking you to look at the architecture; look at the curtains."

Edgar focused his eyes back at the house and was now able to spot the difference. The two corner windows seemed to be closed with a curtain, but not the middle one.

"Are you talking about the middle one?" Edgar asked as the curtain was partially drawn.

Arya glanced towards Edgar. "Did you notice them when we walked in?"

Edgar shook his head, wondering where Arya was going with this discussion.

"I did. I could swear that the middle one was also closed." Arya's voice echoed the firmness in her belief.

Edgar glanced back towards the curtain. "That would be weird. Are you saying what I think you are saying?"

Arya nodded, gesturing that she now believes that someone was watching them from the top floor.

"Who do you think? Eli?"

Arya sighed. "I am not sure…."

Arya was interrupted by a sudden sound that erupted from behind. It was the sound of the police dispatcher asking them to respond.

Edgar motioned his hand to gesture that he would take the dispatch call. As Edgar walked towards the car, Arya turned her attention back to the window.

"Car 54," Edgar responded to the dispatcher.

"Shooting reported. Officer hit near Stoneridge and Waverly. All units respond. Suspect considered armed and dangerous."

"This is Car 54 responding. We are near the Stoneridge property. Where is the shooting?"

The dispatcher came back on. "State trooper was hit near…."

That was all Edgar heard before he noticed the approaching white Ford Transit van. It was driving right towards him at a very high speed.

"Arya!" Edgar called out as he dropped the radio and pulled the gun that was holstered on his hip.

Edgar realized that he hardly had any time left before the van would slam into him, jumped to his left, and fired a couple of bullets at the van.

Hearing Edgar's high-pitched yelling, Arya turned around to catch a glimpse of the van approaching the vehicle.

Most people, when they are confronted with a 'flight or fight' dangerous situation, end up choosing the 'flight' option. Evolution had taught us to pick the 'flight' option as that maximizes the survival rate. However, cops are different – they choose the 'fight' option. They are trained to go against the basic instinct.

In one action, Arya pulled her Glock 22 and sprayed an array of bullets at the van's driver. Arya's position gave her a perfect angle to aim for the driver's head as the van came to a standstill slamming into the parked police cruiser. The van driver did not anticipate that another officer was standing at a 180-degree angle, making him a sitting duck for a sideways shot.

The driver was completely blindsided and had no chance of escaping an array of bullets fired by Arya. One of the shots hit him on his hand, making him lose control of the van, and before he had time to react, another bullet grazed his right shoulder and hit him on the side of his neck. The blood started to ooze out of his neck as the third fateful bullet exploded on his right temple. The Glock 22 is one excellent firearm that carries superior firepower. In essence, it combines the power of a .45 caliber weapon with the flexibility of a .99 caliber gun. The driver had no chance of surviving the shootout. He was deader than a doornail.

"You okay?" Arya shouted towards Edgar, who was getting up from the ditch.

"Yeah…." Edgar flashed a thumbs-up sign and yelled, "I think he is dead."

"You bet your ass; he is cooked." Arya walked towards the van.

The blaring sounds from the van's horn were going off as the driver collapsed on the steering wheel.

"Jesus," Edgar said, as he stood next to Arya.

There was blood everywhere, and the driver's brain matter was scattered all over the seats.

"That was one hell of a shot." Edgar punched Arya's shoulders.

"We should have police cars rolling in any minute," Edgar said, as Arya walked towards the driver's side.

"Let us take a look at what was left of his face."

Edgar drew his weapon and nodded towards Arya as a gesture that he was ready to act.

Arya gently pulled the driver's head from the steering wheel so that they could see the assailant's face. Her eyes widened in shock, and there was an audible gasp from Edgar as they recognized the assailant.

It was Omar Al-Farooq, who pretended to be Omar Raqqa.

"Omar was after the van; why?" Edgar wondered aloud.

"Samir must have had something that was of value to Omar…," Arya thought for a moment and replied.

"What should be…." Edgar was abruptly interrupted as a bullet hit the van, barely missing Arya to the right.

The training kicked in; Arya and Edgar dived to their sides and took cover as the sprayed bullets ricocheted everywhere.

Edgar and Arya glanced at each other from their position.

"Who is shooting?"

"Whoever it is… they are not that good," Edgar said, as the bullets seemed to be fired at random.

"It is coming from the house," Arya said, pointing towards the second-floor windows. "Second-floor middle window."

"It is a woman… looks like Nafisa." Edgar peeked, trying to spot the shooter.

"We should attack the premises. I think she might be holding Sania and Eli."

Just as they were about to break out of their positions,

they heard a loud 'thud' sound. It sounded as if something fell out of the sky.

Arya and Edgar rushed from their positions and hurried towards the house, with their guns raised and ready to shoot. Arya signaled for Edgar to cover her side as they moved towards the front yard. Edgar, taking the cue from Arya, covered the side in case there was a third shooter.

As they neared the house, they could now clearly see that there were two bodies sprawled across the front yard. Arya signaled to Edgar – who was to her left – towards the bodies at the front of the house.

Just as they approached the bodies, they saw a movement in the middle window.

Edgar and Arya pointed their weapons towards that direction, ready to shoot. Arya was the first to make out the figure and recognize the person standing in the window. It was a woman. She had blood dripping from her face and was yelling loudly. *Reza*!

The woman in the window was Sania.

39

"SANIA," Edgar gasped.

"Sania, are you alright?" Arya yelled, holding her gaze at the window.

"Reza...," Sania repeated the name as she motioned her hand to point downwards.

Sania was pointing towards the motionless bodies on the ground. The implication was quite clear. One of the people who fell to the floor was Reza Tariq, also known as Eli Berg.

"Is anyone else up there with you?" Arya yelled, holding her gaze at Sania.

Sania stood still and didn't respond, as if she didn't hear Arya's question.

Edgar cautiously moved towards the bodies, still holding his weapon in a position to readily fire. There were two bodies on the ground that were separated by a few feet – a male and a female.

"Sania?" Arya yelled, a little louder.

Sania shifted her gaze towards Arya, but, still, she didn't respond.

"Sania, is anyone up there? Is it safe?"

This time Sania nodded.

A small smile, almost from relief, escaped from Arya's face. "Thank God," she muttered under her breath.

At that moment, Sania's eyes widened, and her expressions switched from sorrow to hope. "Reza…," she called.

Arya followed Sania's gaze to catch Eli's body wriggling on the ground, almost like a worm.

"Eli, can you hear me?" Edgar crouched next to Eli.

When Eli tried to speak, all he could do was to cough up blood.

"Don't move," Arya said. "Can you breathe?"

Eli nodded.

"Good. Don't move – you might have fractured a lot of bones. It is better not to move. Help is on the way," Edgar said.

Hearing a moaning sound, Arya shifted her attention towards the woman lying on the ground.

"Nafisa," Sania mouthed, pointing towards the woman's body on the ground.

Arya cautiously moved towards Nafisa with her firearm squarely pointed at her. She was ready to shoot if Nafisa took any offensive action.

"Nafisa? Can you hear me?" Arya asked, standing above Nafisa.

Nafisa coughed. Similarly to Eli, she was spitting blood.

"I am a detective with the Philly PD. I have a gun trained on you. If you make any sudden moves, I might have to shoot you. Do you understand?" Arya said firmly.

Nafisa moaned, coughing up blood.

"Shoot her!" Sania cried with anger. "She is the devil. Shoot her, Arya," Sania yelled, urging Arya to kill Nafisa.

Arya understood the raw emotions of Sania and could empathize with her. However, there was no way she could follow through with Sania's intentions. She is a cop, and that's not how they roll —shooting unarmed suspects.

"Is anyone else with you?"

Arya exchanged a quick glance with Edgar and motioned her head to the left, gesturing him to check the perimeter.

Nafisa mumbled as if she was trying to say something.

Arya cautiously moved closer to her, with her gun trained on Nafisa. "Is anyone?"

Nafisa muffled, coughing up more blood.

As Arya moved closer to Nafisa, she could now tell the severity of Nafisa's wounds. Nafisa certainly seemed to have gotten the worst of the fall when compared with Eli. Nafisa was lying amid a pool of blood; she was bleeding profusely.

"Nafisa," Arya called out, seeing Nafisa's eyes close. It looked like she was going in and out, barely being able to keep her eyes open.

Nafisa muttered something that sounded garbled.

Arya crouched down, next to Nafisa. It was quite apparent that Nafisa was now in no position to attack or harm anyone. She could barely keep herself conscious. Arya could sense that time was running out for Nafisa. If Nafisa didn't get medical attention immediately, she could be gone forever. There was a side of Arya, as Sania's friend, that wanted to let Nafisa die. But the other side of Arya, a cop, wanted Nafisa to be alive. There were a lot of questions that need to be answered, and, with Omar Al-Farooq being dead, she knew Nafisa could be the key to get those answers.

Arya motioned her hand to signal Edgar. "Radio in for medical. If we don't get assistance soon, Nafisa is toast."

Edgar, who was attending Eli, understood immediately that time is of the essence. He gently placed Eli's head on the ground and asked, "You okay?"

Eli nodded to gesture that he was fine. Edgar smiled,

knowing Eli was fine and hurried towards the cruiser to radio in for assistance.

"Why are you helping her? She should die," Sania said, as she approached Arya.

Upon hearing Sania's voice, Arya turned around and rushed towards Sania. Arya didn't know that she was emotional until she realized tears were rolling down her face. She quickly wiped them down with her right hand; she was not comfortable with showing that side of her – the emotional side – even with her friend, Sania.

"Are you okay?" Arya asked, gazing straight into Sania's eyes.

Sania nodded before turning towards Nafisa. "Why are you helping her? She should die."

40

SOME PEOPLE DESERVE TO DIE.

That was the overwhelming feeling in Sania's heart when she saw Nafisa being attended by the first responders. She glared at Arya, radioing her emotions, her true feelings. *Stop them from saving Nafisa; she deserved to die. Monsters deserve to die, and Nafisa was undoubtedly a monster.*

"Can you follow my index finger?" a woman's voice sounded, breaking the swirling thoughts in Sania's head.

Sania tilted her head to face one of the first responders who had a smile on her face and was holding up her index finger.

Sania nodded. "Yes."

The first responder followed up by motioning her hand from her right to her left, slowly. Sania knows this drill. She had a concussion when she was in college, and she knew exactly what the first responder was trying to do. The part she couldn't understand was why the first responder was checking her for head injuries. It was Reza, not her, who fell from the top floor. The moment Reza entered her thoughts, Sania couldn't resist herself from turning her head to catch a glimpse of Reza. Reza was sitting to her right and was getting attended by a couple of first responders.

"I shouldn't say this, but he looks okay." The first responder understood the feelings circling Sania and tried to reassure her. "Your husband should be okay; his injuries don't look too serious."

"Oh, no! He is not my husband," Sania responded, shifting her gaze back at the first responder. "He is my boyfriend."

The first responder was taken aback by Sania's response, and she was not sure how to respond. She looked confused.

Sania, sensing how her response sounded, smiled awkwardly and said, "It didn't come off right. What I meant was — he is my ex-boyfriend."

"Does he know that he is your ex?" the first responder asked, seeing the way Reza was looking at Sania.

Sania, hearing the first responder's observation, shifted her glance towards Reza. Their eyes locked for a moment. There was no denying what was on Reza's mind. He wanted to go back in time.

"You okay?" Arya's voice brought Sania back from the past, and she turned towards the voice to spot Arya walking towards her.

"Is she dead?" Sania asked, gesturing towards Nafisa.

Arya shook her head. "She is going to live."

"Damn it, Arya," Sania expressed her frustration and anger. "She deserved to die. She is a terrorist."

The word 'terrorist' froze the first responder who was treating Sania. The images of the plane crashing into the towers played in the first responder's head.

"Do you mean 9/11?" Arya asked, searching Sania's face.

Sania hesitated with her words. "I meant... I don't know. I don't know if they were involved in 9/11, but...." She paused, sensing the gravity of the words that she was about to say next. "I know they are all terrorists."

"Sania, who are you talking about? Omar and Nafisa?" Arya asked, resting her hands on Sania's shoulders.

An uncomfortable silence fell between them as Sania fought back the tears.

"Sania," Arya leaned towards Sania and embraced her.

Sania slowly lifted her gaze towards Arya. "All of them," she said, as tears rolled down her cheeks.

The insinuation of Sania's words stoked suspicions that had been circling in Arya's head. The investigation over the last few days into Samir's disappearance had exposed his secret life. It shined a light into his dark associations – Omar, Nafisa, and suspicious people in Culver City.

"Samir?" Arya's gaze was firmly on Sania.

Sania, with tears on her eyes, slowly nodded.

"When did you know about Samir?" Arya asked, holding her gaze at Sania. The tension in the air was palpable.

The first responder stepped back, sensing the gravity of the situation.

The wall holding Sania's emotions cracked, and she began to weep uncontrollably.

"Sania, this is important. Do you know where Samir is?" Arya held Sania's shoulders and lifted her gaze.

Sania was visibly shaking as she tried to hold back her tears. "I am not …"

"What?" Arya stared at Sania.

Sania shifted her gaze from Arya to Reza.

"Reza," Arya muttered as she began to walk towards Reza. She knew that time was of the essence. If Samir were still out there, the country might still be in danger.

"Arya, you can't believe how glad I am to see you by our side." Reza stretched his hands wide to hug Arya.

Arya stopped short and glared at Reza. "Where is he?"

Reza was taken aback by Arya's lack of warmth towards him, her college friend. "Arya…"

Reza's response was interrupted as loud sirens erupted.

Both Reza and Arya turned towards the blaring sirens and noticed a stream of cars approaching their location. The vehicles were not black and whites; instead, they were all black SUVs.

"Holy shit." Arya recognized that she doesn't have much time. "Reza, where is he? We don't have much time; tell me."

"What do you mean?" Reza was confounded. "Are we in danger?" Reza asked, looking at the SUVs screeching to a halt near them. "Who are they?"

"They are the FBI or CIA. Who the hell knows! They must have found out, and they must be here to take you guys in." Arya rushed her words. "Where is he?"

"Take us in? Where? Why?" Reza looked scared.

"To find out what you know," Arya said as she shifted her glance towards the SUVs and back at Reza. "Where is he?"

"Who?" Reza looked confused and scared.

"Samir," Arya blurted out, almost in disbelief that Reza even asked her that question.

"Please step back."

Arya looked up towards the heavy sounding voice and found a couple of men dressed in black suits approaching her.

"Who are you?" Arya asked, holding her ground.

Hearing Edgar's voice, Arya shifted her glance towards her right to find Edgar in the same boat as her. He was surrounded by suits.

The man standing in front of Arya, who looked professional and well-groomed, reached to his left jacket pocket and flashed his badge.

No surprises. As Arya expected, the badge had the familiar three letters. FBI.

"FBI Special Agent in charge, Damien Taylor." The agent introduced himself in a manner that exuded authority.

"This is a Philly PD investigation," Arya tried to hold onto their control of the investigation.

"Ma'am," Agent Taylor started before he got interrupted by Arya.

"Don't ma'am me." Arya never liked being called a 'ma'am.' That word rubs her the wrong way. "You can address me as Detective Martins."

Agent Taylor let out a deep sigh. "Okay, Detective Martins, let me spell it out for you. You are not in charge, nor the Philly PD." He paused for a moment before squarely holding his gaze at Arya. "I am in charge. Got it?"

Arya remained silent. She knew that she had no cards to play. The FBI obviously knew what she had found out during her investigation. This was a national security issue, and the FBI trumps Philly PD any day on terrorism investigations, especially given what happened on September 11th.

Arya shifted her gaze towards Edgar and nodded, gesturing him to do the same as her. She knew fighting the turf war was not going to work out.

As an agent reached out to handcuff Nafisa, she kicked him hard with her legs. "Don't touch me, you, Kafir." She yelled loudly before reaching for the rectangle pendant on her necklet.

"Stop her," Agent Taylor yelled, as Nafisa opened the pendant and brought it close to her mouth.

As she was about to put the pendant in her mouth, a female agent reached in and plucked the pendant hard, pulling it away from Nafisa.

"Kafir, you will all die," Nafisa yelled.

The female agent turned her gaze towards Agent Taylor after inspecting the pendant closely. "Cyanide."

"Cuff her. I want four eyes on her at all times; load her in the box," Agent Taylor said, calmly walking towards Nafisa. "We know who you are, Nafisa. Get comfy; you are going to spend a long time with us and be prepared to sing like a canary."

"Never." Nafisa glared at Agent Taylor. "I want a lawyer."

"Lawyer. Can you believe this asshole?" Agent Taylor scoffed. He turned towards Arya before shifting his glance back at Nafisa. "To the place you are going…." He paused as he leaned closer to Nafisa. "You better worship your lord."

"Take her away from my sight," he yelled, prompting the agents to cuff and escort her to one of the black parked SUVs.

Agent Taylor turned towards another agent to his side and declared, "I want this freaking building to be searched, top to bottom."

"Already on it. We have agents in the building," the agent replied.

Agent Taylor tapped the agent's shoulder and proceeded towards Arya. "I want all the materials related to your investigation on my desk by sunrise."

Arya nodded. It was pretty clear who was in command of the situation.

Agent Taylor, feeling satisfied with Arya's compliance, gestured his appreciation. "Good. I will put in a word with your supervisor."

"No need," Arya countered, drawing a glare from Agent Taylor.

"I don't need any favors." Arya gazed straight at Agent Taylor. "I just need you to know that Sania did nothing wrong."

"How do you know that?" Agent Taylor glared. "Do you know that she visited Saudi Arabia?"

Arya stuttered. "I don't…"

"Do you know her father was killed by a kafir?"

Arya shook her head.

Agent Taylor walked up to Arya. "I guess you don't know a lot about your friend."

Arya lifted her gaze at Agent Taylor. "I know her enough to know that she could do no harm to any human being."

"I hope you are right," Agent Taylor replied, walking towards Sania.

As Agent Taylor escorted Sania towards the parked SUV, she turned towards Arya and mouthed loudly, "I am not a terrorist."

For a moment, Arya was lost. She knew in her heart that her friend couldn't be a terrorist, even though she hid the facts about Samir and his disappearance.

"I know," Arya replied. "Just tell the agents what you know," Arya yelled out a last piece of advice as Sania was helped into the backside of Agent Taylor's black SUV.

41

Arya stormed into LT Cooper's office, racing past the detectives in the squad room who were yelling congratulatory messages. The detectives had heard about the news of the terrorists' arrests, and, quite expectedly, they were excited about it.

"Where did they take them?" Arya asked in a raised voice, marching into LT Cooper's office.

Arya must have shouted as silence fell on the squad room, and all eyes in it descended on LT Cooper's office.

LT Cooper, who was on the phone, obviously didn't like Arya's tone. He glared at her for a moment before turning his attention to the phone. "Sorry about the commotion, Chief."

Arya couldn't believe she almost yelled at her LT when he was on the phone with the Chief. She shook her head in displeasure as she chastised herself in her mind for acting in an unprofessional manner. Of all the people in the world, LT Cooper doesn't deserve to be yelled at. He is a consummate professional and a fair boss.

"Yes, I will be talking to both of them," LT Cooper

responded to the Chief on the phone. "Consider it to be handled."

There was no doubt in Arya's mind that LT and Chief were talking about her and Edgar. Obviously, it was about the showdown at Stoneridge, which resulted in the death of Omar and arrests of Nafisa, Sania, and Eli by the FBI.

As LT was having the conversation with the Chief, Arya stood by LT's front door and made a hand gesture towards Edgar, signaling him to come to LT's office.

"Sorry, Chief, I should have kept you in the loop," LT addressed the Chief on the phone.

Listening to the conversation, it was quite obvious that LT was taking heat from the Chief. It was evident that the Chief was not pleased to be kept out of the loop in the investigation that had links to the 9/11 terrorists.

"Yes. That is true. One of the detectives knew Sania Tariq beforehand," LT started before getting interrupted by the Chief on the phone. The Chief was chastising him so loud that Arya could hear his voice clearly.

Arya was immediately washed away with feelings of sadness. This was all her fault. The moment she realized the possible terrorism angle, she should have brought LT in the loop. There were too many red flags — bank accounts linked to the Middle East, multiple forged passports, Saudi associates in Culver City, and on and on. There were plenty of opportunities for her to realize that this case was bigger than a routine missing person case. Her past relationship with Sania had clouded her judgment, and she didn't follow the procedure that she was supposed to follow.

"What is going on?" Edgar whispered, walking into LT's office.

Arya raised her right index finger near her mouth, signaling Edgar to bring his voice down.

"Chief," Arya whispered, gesturing towards the phone.

"Understood. I am sorry for not keeping you in the loop, Chief," LT apologized.

Edgar exchanged a glance with Arya, inquiring if she could make out the Chief's end of the conversation.

Arya shook her head before leaning towards him. "Chief seems to be unhappy with you," she whispered.

"Me?" Edgar looked stunned. "But why?"

"Chief seems to think that you kept the chain of command in the dark and made the decision to visit Stoneridge."

Edgar's face turned pale, and he looked perplexed. "Why would they think that?"

"Shhh!" Arya shushed him, using a hand gesture.

"Yes. I will be there at 9:30 PM today." LT Cooper paused as he listened to the Chief on the other end of the line. "I will have the files with me and will give you a complete account."

It was another three minutes before LT hung up the phone with the Chief.

"LT…." Arya stopped her apology mid-sentence upon looking at LT's raised hand.

LT used a hand gesture and pointed at the blinds near the door. "Close it."

As Edgar was closing the blinds, Arya fixed her gaze at LT and apologized. "Sorry, LT."

LT got up from his chair and walked straight up to Arya. They stood so close that they could hear the other person's breath.

"LT," as Arya began, LT Cooper took a couple of steps to his left and stopped next to Edgar.

"Edgar James," LT repeated Edgar's name and locked his gaze at Edgar.

"Sorry, LT," Edgar apologized.

LT walked back towards his chair and sat perched on the edge of the table.

"Arya, Edgar." He shifted his glance from Arya to Edgar and back to Arya. "Why are you sorry?"

"We should have kept you in the loop," Arya said.

LT remained silent for a long twenty seconds before he turned his gaze towards Edgar. "What about you?"

"No excuses. Given the past week's events, it was inexcusable that we didn't bring it to your attention sooner. I am sorry." Edgar sounded sincere.

"It was my fault. Edgar wanted to bring you in, but I thought we should wait a little longer," Arya said, trying to deflect blame from her partner.

"That's not true, LT. As a team, we decided we needed to get something concrete about the Middle East links before bringing it to you. To be honest, we thought we didn't have enough."

LT gestured with his hand for both of them to stop talking. "What did you just say? You guys didn't have enough."

LT reached down to the table and brought a file to his hand. Arya and Edgar recognized the file immediately; it was their case file.

LT Cooper took out a photo from the file and pinned it in the center of the whiteboard.

"Do you recognize this photo?" LT Cooper asked.

Arya and Edgar both recognized it immediately. It was a photo taken in Culver City of two Middle Eastern men talking to Omar.

They both nodded, and Arya jumped first to chime in. "It was from Culver City. A few months back, Samir Tariq traveled to Culver City to meet with these two guys and then traveled with them to San Diego."

"Then?" LT Cooper gestured for Arya to continue.

"It seemed Samir rented an apartment for them in both the cities and even paid the rent using his secret bank account."

"What about this?" LT Cooper pinned another photo on the whiteboard. It was a picture of Omar, Nafisa, Samir, and Sania eating in the Dar Marrakesh restaurant.

"LT, can you tell us where you are going with this?" Arya was getting frustrated with the classroom style of questioning.

"Just answer me," LT Cooper firmly said, tapping his index finger on the group photo.

"It was taken in the Dar Marrakesh restaurant, a Moroccan restaurant frequented by Omar and Samir. Omar, Samir, Sania, and Nafisa – Omar's wife – all having dinner in the restaurant."

LT Cooper nodded and proceeded to reach across the table to retrieve another folder.

"LT, we knew all that. What are you getting at?" Arya asked.

LT raised his hand to gesture Arya to wait. He proceeded to take two more photos, passport-sized, from the folder and pinned them on the whiteboard.

"What about these?" LT Cooper eyed Arya and Edgar.

Arya and Edgar both moved closer to the whiteboard so that they could get a better look at the photos.

"These are the same two guys from Culver City," Arya and Edgar said at the same time.

"Khalid Al-Midhar and Nawaf Al-Hazmi," LT Cooper said, as he tapped each of the photos when he said their name aloud.

"Who are they? How do you have those pictures? This is not from our case file."

"These two pictures came from the top guys. FBI, CIA…. I don't know. All I know is by tomorrow morning, everyone in the country would know them."

"CIA?" Edgar asked. "What did they do?"

"Oh, no!" Arya exclaimed as a sudden thought dawned on

her head. All of a sudden, she turned pale and had difficulty breathing. "I can't believe this!" she muttered under her breath.

"What? What am I missing?" Edgar asked.

"Do you want to tell him, or should I?" LT asked, glancing towards Arya.

"Hijackers," Arya mumbled, reaching the table to get a grip.

"What?" Edgar was not able to make out Arya's words.

"The fucking hijackers!" Arya yelled.

"What the hell?" Edgar shifted his glance towards LT, and the expression on LT's face confirmed the improbable.

"I just can't believe we had pictures of these hijackers all these days." Arya raised her hand to her head. "How reliable is the information?" Arya turned towards LT.

"Very. The CIA and FBI just released pictures of all 19 hijackers, and these two were among them. We have them on tape clearing the airport security and…." LT paused like he was weighing on the enormity of his next statement. "As we speak, these pictures are being distributed to all the JTTFs in the country. And, in the next few days, the hijackers' faces would be plastered in every newspaper."

"This is what they meant when they said they are going to be famous." Edgar connected the dots in his mind. He remembered the earlier comments made by the Culver City men when they quit their jobs in the gas station.

"What about Omar and Sa…" Arya struggled to even say Samir's name in this context.

"Samir?" Edgar completed Arya's question.

"I managed to have a word with Agent Taylor in the last thirty minutes. And," He shifted his gaze towards Arya and added, "Agent Taylor believes that they are all somehow involved with the 9/11 attacks."

"No! What do you mean by all? Sania, Samir, and Eli?"

Arya was losing her mind as she struggled to even imagine that her good friends from the past could be involved in the attacks.

"I don't know. The investigation has just started. Agent Taylor believes that Sania and Eli know more than what they have disclosed."

"What about Samir?" Arya asked.

"You didn't know?" LT said, holding his gaze at Arya. "Samir is dead!"

42

"Oh, God! Please don't tell me that he was one of the hijackers!" Arya's head was spinning as she fathomed that possibility.

"Why don't you take a seat?" LT Cooper put his hand over Arya's shoulders and guided her to one of the chairs in his office.

"No. Samir Tariq was not one of the hijackers." LT Cooper sat next to Arya and patted on her shoulders.

"Then... how do you know?" Edgar jumped in. "We never found his body."

"You guys didn't. But the FBI did." LT Cooper shifted his glance towards Edgar.

"How? Where?" Arya blurted out her questions in a rapid fashion.

Before LT could respond, there was a knock on the door. LT shifted his gaze towards it to find a Uni standing on the other side of the glass door.

LT stood up from his chair and motioned with his hands for the Uni to open the door.

"LT, there's a call from a reporter to the switchboard, and

he is asking to talk to you," the Uni respectfully said. "It is regarding the shootout in Stoneridge."

"Who is the reporter?"

The Uni proceeded to reveal the name of the reporter and the newspaper where he was employed. LT immediately recognized the reporter; he is widely respected in the police community for a series of articles he has written in the past, showcasing the life of a cop in a dangerous world.

"Patch it through," LT said, raising from his chair.

"LT, it seems your phone is unreachable." The Uni signaled towards LT's desk phone.

Edgar noticed the phone was off the cradle, and he leaned forward to place it back correctly.

"Thanks, Edgar," LT said before turning towards the Uni. "We good now?"

The Uni nodded. "Thanks, LT, we will have the call patched through," he said before closing the door.

"Where were we?" LT turned towards Arya.

"Samir's body," Arya brought the focus back to where they left the conversation.

"Yes. Samir Tariq was definitely not one of the hijackers, but he was definitely on the wrong side of the law."

Edgar and Arya nodded. Based on their investigation, they suspected that that would be the case. There were too many red flags.

"Whatever I am going to say stays in this room," LT firmly said, eyeing both Arya and Edgar.

There was something in LT's tone that raised the temperature of the room. Arya and Edgar felt it deeply in their bones as they nodded.

"Omar Al-Farooq was being tracked and watched."

"By whom?" Arya rhetorically asked, even though she knew who that could be.

"FBI? Agent Taylor?" Edgar asked pointedly.

"CIA," LT Cooper said slowly, stressing each syllable.

"CIA!" Edgar exclaimed. "When?"

"Should be before the attacks," Arya uttered, peering into LT's eyes as if to draw confirmation from him.

"Yes. What I was told is that Omar was considered a person of interest by the CIA."

"How the hell was he not picked up?"

"Remember, I said CIA and not FBI. CIA has no jurisdiction to arrest people inside the country."

"Shit. They should have told the FBI or us," Edgar said with anger.

"They could. But we don't know how much intelligence the CIA had on Omar. What I was told was that he slipped into the country using forged passports."

"JTTF?"

"Yes. We will learn more in the months to come. Intelligence is flowing."

"It should have…. Earlier."

"Should have, would have, must have. We all know that Monday morning quarterbacking is easy and cheap. Hindsight is always 20/20. Instead of finger-pointing, we all need to do one thing now. Put all our focus and energy into stopping another attack."

"Another attack?"

"Yes. CIA and FBI have intelligence that strongly indicates that follow up attacks were planned."

"Jesus." Edgar sank in his seat.

The phone in LT Cooper's office started to ring loudly, drawing everyone's attention.

"Must be the reporter," LT remarked as he went around the desk to get the phone.

"Jim," LT answered the call by addressing the reporter by his first name, showing his familiarity and relationship with the hard-hitting reporter.

"I guess congratulations are in the order," Jim Devine, the reporter, answered.

"Thanks, thanks." LT smiled. "How did you know? Not many people know about the promotion."

"Promotion," Arya and Edgar whispered almost simultaneously. This was the first they had heard anything about LT being promoted.

"Had lunch with my wife, and she knows that we are friends."

"I must have guessed it. You married well – the Chief's sister."

The back-and-forth conversations between LT Cooper and the reporter drew a blank face from Arya and Edgar. They both were completely in the dark. They had no idea about the promotion.

"It looks like LT is getting promoted," Edgar whispered, leaning closer to Arya.

"This is the first I have heard of it," Arya whispered.

"Okay, Jim. I know that you didn't call me at this time of the day and wait fifteen minutes on the line to just wish me." LT stopped smiling. "What is this really about?"

"Calling about Stoneridge." Jim proceeded to drop a bomb. "My source is telling me that it was related to 9/11."

"Where did you hear that?" LT blurted out grimly.

Arya and Edgar noticed the sudden change in LT's demeanor. He became serious and highly concerned.

"Who is the source?" LT looked disturbed.

"Come on, Coop, you know I can't tell you that. All I can say is that the source is highly reliable, and I trust the source."

"Jesus! Look, Jim, I can't confirm or deny. But…." LT let out a deep sigh. "I can't emphasize this enough. This is literally a matter of national security, and I implore you not to print this story."

"National security. What the hell is going on?" Edgar whispered.

Arya responded with a shrug to signal that she was equally in the dark.

"Coop – I am hearing that one of the people who was shot had links to the hijackers."

"Hijackers? Who told you that?"

"Come on, Coop, I can't divulge my sources. I am hearing that Feds have identified all the hijackers, and their pictures are being circulated to all the authorities. Are you saying that is not true?"

"Okay, Jim, I am going to play it straight with you. But this is strictly off the record."

"Off the record, it is," Jim confirmed that he understood.

"Your source is right. One of the people who got shot in Stoneridge might have ties to 9/11."

"Might?" Jim pushed.

"This is too early in the investigation. There are a lot of moving parts and a lot of agencies. All I can say is that there is a strong indication that the link could be true."

"Okay, I can live with that. What about your two detectives? I heard they were the ones who tracked them down."

"That is true. Arya Martins and Edgar James, two detectives from my precinct, were involved in the incident."

Arya and Edgar looked surprised, hearing their names being mentioned in the call with the reporter.

"I heard one person died, and two people were arrested by the FBI."

"Jesus, Jim. Who the hell is your source?" LT Cooper asked, feeling upset.

"Someone well connected," Jim said with a half-smile.

"Jim – if you believe what you are saying, you know how sensitive this whole situation is. There is a massive inter-agency investigation going on, and you can't print anything that would tip off these monsters."

The emotional answer cut through to Jim Devine. He remained silent for the next thirty seconds, evaluating what he should do.

"Twenty-four hours, Coop. I can hold off for another twenty-four hours."

"Jim, seriously? Twenty-four hours won't be enough." LT shifted the receiver from his right hand to his left. "I can't stress the criticality! What you are printing could tip off the people we are trying to catch."

"Coop, if I don't print this, someone else would. The cat's out of the bag." With that as the parting remark, Devine hung up on LT Cooper.

"TWENTY-FOUR HOURS!" Agent Taylor bellowed; his voice was filled with frustration. "That is not much."

"I know, Damien." Cooper nodded in agreement. "I had to pull all the stops to get the story delayed by twenty-four hours. The reporter was hell-bent on going forward with it."

"Damn it, Mike. This is going to blow up," Agent Taylor fumed. "Who is the reporter? Do I know him?"

"You might have crossed paths with him. His name is Jim Devine; he is with...."

"I know Devine," Agent Taylor interrupted. "Does he know that I am in charge?"

"No. I don't think so...." LT Cooper hesitated as he replayed the conversation in his head. "I am certain that I did not disclose any operational details."

"Good, good," Agent Taylor retorted. "Let me call Jim; he owes me one."

"That is good. Does Devine owe you big enough for him to kill or delay this story?"

For the first time, Agent Taylor let out a small smile. "Does saving one's daughter buy you a big enough favor?"

"Jesus!" LT Cooper exclaimed. "When did that happen? I am tight with the guy, and he never said anything."

"It is a long story, Mike. It happened almost ten years back when Jim was working in DC."

"What the hell happened?"

"Some other day, Mike. We don't have much time; let me call Jim before he gives the story to his editor," Agent Taylor explained.

LT nodded, gesturing his agreement with Agent Taylor's assessment.

Guessing the conversation was about to end, Arya stepped in front of LT's vision and mouthed, "Sania."

LT shook his head, gesturing that he can't get in the middle of a federal investigation.

"Please," Arya held her hands together, in front of her chest, as if she was pleading her case.

"Got to go, Mike." Agent Taylor was about to conclude the call when LT Cooper raised Arya's plea.

"Damien, one more thing," LT Cooper started.

"What, Mike?"

Hearing the hesitation in Cooper's voice, Agent Taylor asked, "Is it about those two?"

Cooper was not surprised that Taylor was able to accurately determine the cause of his hesitation. "Yeah…." He stretched the word.

"They are," Agent Taylor caught himself from disclosing and asked, "Is someone with you?"

Arya shook her head, hoping that LT would not reveal her presence. She felt sure that Agent Taylor would not say anything further if he found out that she and Edgar were in the room.

LT Cooper took a deep breath and told the truth. "I have those two detectives, Edgar James and Arya Martins, in the room with me."

Agent Taylor's tone shifted immediately. "Am I on speaker?"

Before Cooper could respond, Agent Taylor jumped in. "Never mind; I know you wouldn't do that without telling me upfront."

LT Cooper felt good hearing Agent Taylor's vote of confidence.

"Why don't you put me on speaker, Mike," Agent Taylor added.

"Taylor, you are on speaker," LT Cooper said, as he lowered his receiver back to the cradle and pressed the keys to place Agent Taylor on the speakerphone.

"Detectives, let me start by saying that you guys did a good job on the field today." Agent Taylor sounded like a man who was in charge.

"Thanks," Edgar replied to the compliment.

Arya's silence was immediately noticed by both LT and Agent Taylor. As LT gazed directly at Arya, she replied back. "Agent Taylor, where is Sania?"

"Straight to the point, Detective Martins. I like it when people act that way. Tariq and Berg both are in our custody."

"Agent Taylor, I know for a fact that they never made it back to your field office."

"I know. You talked to your friend, Agent Callahan," Agent Taylor remarked, surprising Arya.

"How did you know that? You are not even from the Philly field office."

"That is my job, Detective. And I am good at it," Agent Taylor oozed confidence.

"Firstly, I did not say that they were in the local field office. If you heard me right, all I said was that they are in custody."

"Where?"

"In a classified location."

"You are making a mistake. Sania is not a terrorist," Arya said, hearing Agent Taylor's response. Hearing that Sania was taken to a classified location meant only one thing; the FBI believes that Sania was involved in the attacks.

There was a long pause on the other end of the line, before Agent Taylor said in an even tone, "I know."

The words from Agent Taylor sparked hope in Arya's eyes. "You know. That is good. Why is she still in custody?"

"There is a lot about this case that you don't know."

"Can you…?" Before Arya could complete her question, Agent Taylor interrupted her.

"Detective, I don't have much time to talk on the phone. We are in the middle of the biggest national security situation that this country has seen in quite some time."

Arya could feel that she was about to get shut down, and she couldn't think of anything that she could say to change the direction of the conversation. She felt desperate.

"I asked LT Cooper to put me on the speakerphone because I personally wanted to thank you both for your work. But now the time has come for me to go," Agent Taylor said, as he checked the time on his watch.

"Wait, wait… Agent Taylor," Arya blurted out. "I know both of them, Eli Berg and Sania Tariq. I can get them to tell me everything they know."

"Detective, who said that they are not talking, and we needed help?"

That was the last card Arya had to play, and she was now left with nothing.

44

"Arya." Edgar gently placed his right hand on Arya's shoulders.

Arya, who sat crouched on her seat, lifted her gaze towards Edgar. "I will be fine." She took a deep sigh and ran her hand over her face to collect herself.

"Agent Taylor did say that Sania is not a...." Edgar stopped himself as he looked around the squad room. The room was mostly deserted, and Edgar continued with the conversation after feeling sure that no one could overhear him. "Sania is not suspected of terrorism."

"I know." Arya let out a deep breath. "That is good, but...." She hesitated.

"What?" Edgar leaned in.

"I still have a lot of questions. What happened to Samir? Where did he die? How did he die? If not during the attack, who killed him?"

The question hung in the air for a few seconds before Edgar responded. "Does it matter?"

Edgar's response seemed to have caught Arya off-guard; she was not expecting that reaction from Edgar.

"Hear me out." Edgar pulled his chair closer to Arya and continued. "We now know Omar and those Culver City guys were involved in the 9/11 attacks."

Arya's gaze was firmly on Edgar as she listened to Edgar.

"Samir and Omar were in cohorts for a long time. We also know that Samir definitely met with Culver City guys before Omar met them."

"Oh, shit!" Arya jumped up.

"What the hell happened?" Edgar was surprised by Arya's sudden reaction.

"I know about the next attack."

"What?" Edgar raised his brows in surprise.

"The theft. Marisomo theft. It is all connected."

"You think…?" Edgar was trying to process what Arya meant.

"Yes. I think Omar smuggled some kind of chemical…."

"Chemical?"

"Chemical that could be used to cause mass casualties."

"Biological?" Edgar asked. "Like the ones Saddam used in the Middle East?"

Arya nodded.

"What makes you think it is biological?"

"The aluminum case in the Marisomo theft. What could fit in that case that could cause mass casualty? Also, remember the masks they had bought?"

Edgar quickly pulled Samir's case file and skipped over to the financials. "Yes, you are right. They did not use the masks during the theft, but Samir bought masks and suits that could be used as a defense during the attacks."

Arya shook her head. "I can't believe that Sania was married to a terrorist."

Edgar jumped up from the seat. "I think we need to get this to LT. I don't think…."

"FBI knows. Agent Taylor knows."

"What? How can you be sure of that?"

"I think that is why they are holding Sania and Eli. They are trying to figure out where Samir could have hidden that aluminum case."

"You are right." Edgar collapsed back in his chair.

At that moment, a sudden thought appeared in Arya's mind. "Oh, my God!" Arya exclaimed so loudly that made a few heads turn towards their direction.

Arya raised her hand to gesture that everything is alright.

"What the hell happened?" Edgar asked.

"I think I know where the case is," Arya declared, as she raised her phone and flipped it open.

"Where?" Edgar looked baffled. "What are you checking on the phone?"

"Photos," Arya said, as she opened the gallery folder on her camera phone.

"What photos?" Edgar asked as he leaned in closer to Arya.

Arya quickly swiped through pictures without even looking at them. To Edgar, it appeared as though Arya knew precisely the photo she was looking for.

Edgar looked on silently as he didn't want to interrupt Arya.

The wait was not that long as Arya landed on the picture that she wanted to examine.

"Oh, God. I am correct," Arya said, staring at the picture she took in the JNC bank.

The picture showed the contents of Samir's locker box, which he had opened in the JNC bank just before the Marisomo theft.

"Do you see it?" Arya asked, tilting the phone towards Edgar.

Edgar narrowed his eyes and took a closer look at the photo. The photo showed the locker box's contents –

multiple passports, cash, drawings, maps, scribbled notes, and a key.

When his eyes landed on the key, Edgar paused and lifted his gaze towards Arya.

Arya nodded. "Key is the answer to our question."

"Do you think that is a key to a...?"

Arya interrupted Edgar and finished his thought. "Key to a storage location."

"How can you say that? It could be a spare key to his car, house, or any number of things." Edgar played devil's advocate, challenging Arya's hypothesis. They realized early on as partners that the best way to eliminate each other's blind spots in an investigation is to rigorously challenge each other's theory about the case. They both strongly believed that this increased the odds of success considerably and made them a strong team.

"Do you have a safe deposit box in a bank?" Arya asked.

"You know I do." Edgar crossed his hands across his chest.

"What do you have in it?" Arya asked, ignoring the defensive posture of Edgar.

Edgar's gaze drifted upwards as he tried to recall. "Passports, birth certificates, marriage certificate, and some of Simone's jewelry."

"I rest my case," Arya said, crossing her hands across the chest.

"What! What did you prove?" Edgar furrowed his brows, trying to imagine what he had missed in Arya's argument.

"Oh, man! You must have missed your coffee; you are really slow today." Arya shook her head. "The items in your safe deposit box. You don't have anything that is not valuable. I don't know anyone who keeps spare keys to their car or house in their bank locker. That is one dumb argument."

"So, you think...?" Edgar settled down on his chair.

"I don't think; I am sure about the key. Look at the safe

deposit box contents – forged passports, cash of different countries, NYC pictures... Don't you see it is all connected?"

"To the 9/11 attacks?"

Arya let out a deep breath. "Based on what we just heard in there," She paused, motioning her hand towards the LT's door. "This might not be over. Samir and Omar might be in on the follow-up attack."

"Jesus!" Edgar exclaimed. "Phase Two that Omar discussed with the Culver City hijackers. The aluminum case... Biological attack. It all makes sense now."

Arya nodded. "I think that is a good possibility with what we know about the case and Marisomo. Samir and Omar both worked in Aries Financials to get access to Marisomo. And," Arya paused to clear her throat. "And from our investigation, we know that Omar and Samir orchestrated the break-in to steal the aluminum case."

"The purchases in Samir's card – masks, suits, rental vans...."

"Damn it!" Arya jumped.

"What?" Edgar was flabbergasted with Arya's sudden outburst.

"I know the target of the follow-up attack." Arya declared with a firm voice, gazing directly at dumbfounded Edgar.

45

"WHAT? WHERE?" Edgar got up from his chair like he was shot out of a cannon.

Arya, without answering Edgar, pulled her phone out and scoured through the pictures of Samir's safe deposit box.

"What are you doing?" Edgar asked, still feeling confounded with the events that transpired at the last minute.

"Damn it! I can't believe this!" Arya chastised herself quite loudly.

"What the hell is going on?" Edgar asked, visibly confused with Arya's reaction.

"Look at the photos and the map." Arya handed the phone to him.

Edgar grabbed the phone from Arya, wondering what he missed earlier. The first thought that came to Edgar's mind was that these photos were taken by a tourist visiting New York City. United Nations Headquarters, Penn Station, Madison Square Garden, Wall Street, New York Stock Exchange, and Times Square were prominently featured. A few other photos looked like close-up photos of ductwork.

Edgar ignored the ductwork photos and went back to landmark photos taken in New York City. When they first looked at the pictures in the JNC bank, they didn't suspect Samir to be involved in the 9/11 attacks. Having learned about Samir's involvement in the attacks, these photos paint a different picture.

"Manhattan," Edgar said, as he lifted his gaze towards Arya. "But where?" Edgar referenced the many landmarks – possible targets that were surveilled by Samir.

"I have an idea," Arya said, as she pointed at the photos of ductwork.

Edgar narrowed his eyes as he studied it carefully. "It looks like pictures of ductwork, vents, and..."

"I think it is a refrigerant line or some part of the HVAC unit," Arya interrupted.

Edgar lifted his eyes from the phone and looked at Arya. "I would agree with you. This looks like parts of the HVAC system."

Edgar placed the phone on the table and asked, "We already knew that Samir was a maintenance technician. What has this got to..."

Edgar stopped his sentence mid-way as a sudden thought erupted in his mind. "Holy mother of God! HVAC system!" Edgar shuddered as the consequences of his thought reverberated in his mind. "The case; I agree with you now. The aluminum case Samir and Omar stole should have had a chemical agent. They must be thinking of using the HVAC system as a dispersion system for a biological attack."

Hearing Edgar arriving at the same conclusion as Arya, she felt reassured with her analysis of the situation. "I think the same."

"But where?" Edgar glanced at Arya's phone as he said, "There are too many targets. How could we narrow it down?" Edgar let out a deep breath as he ran his fingers through his hair.

Arya leaned across the table to pick up the phone. Edgar lifted his gaze on her as she calmly scrolled through photos on her phone.

"What are you doing?" Edgar asked, feeling puzzled.

"I am about to show you the target of their phase two attack," Arya said flatly.

"What?" Edgar shot up from his chair, feeling astounded.

"New York Stock Exchange," Arya said emphatically, holding the phone across Edgar's face. The historic Stock Exchange floor was front and center in the photo.

"Jesus!" Edgar said, staring at the photo. "Why do you think..." Edgar stopped his question mid-way as he knew the answer to his question. "Nafisa," he whispered.

Arya nodded, signaling her agreement with Edgar. "Nafisa worked in the New York Stock Exchange. There had to be a reason why she worked there."

Edgar nodded as more parts of the puzzle started to fit in. "Aether Solutions. New York Stock Exchange is one of their clients."

"Yes. That should be the reason why Samir took a contractor job with them. It gives him insider access to their HVAC system."

"This must be the reason why Samir didn't join the Culver City men as hijackers. He was chosen to carry out phase two of the 9/11 attacks. A biological attack on the heart of the American business empire – New York Stock Exchange."

"But... Samir is dead, along with Omar and Nafisa," Edgar said, implying that the threat of phase 2 attacks had been thwarted. "We should be safe."

Arya lifted her head for a moment as she tried to further analyze the situation.

"We can't say that." Arya's voice was sharp, and her eyes were searing with focus.

Edgar narrowed his eyes as he tried to fathom the reason behind Arya's statement. "Why? All of them are dead. Who is going to carry out the attacks?"

"Edgar…." Arya stepped in, and her eyes looked straight into Edgar's eyes. "Samir Tariq was married to my best friend, and she didn't know that he was a terrorist. He was a sleeper. So does Nafisa and Omar. They were part of a sleeper cell."

Edgar's eyes sparked with clarity as he understood what Arya was trying to imply. "We don't know if there are more sleeper agents in the country."

Arya nodded. "Exactly. If I had to place a bet — I would bet that there are other sleeper cells in the country."

"Jesus! We need to warn LT; the FBI; the CIA," Edgar screamed as he stormed towards LT's office.

"Edgar, Edgar," Arya called after him as Edgar hurried towards LT's office.

The detectives, who were still in the squad room, turned towards the commotion in the squad room. They had no clue why Edgar was sprinting towards LT's office. They stood there confused, calling out Edgar's name.

Upon rushing to LT's office, Edgar found the lights were turned off in LT's office, and he seemed to have left for the day.

"This is what I was trying to tell you," Arya said as she approached Edgar. "He is gone for the day. He has a meeting with the Chief."

"With the Chief? How do you know that?"

"I heard him talking to the Chief earlier." Arya went on to fill Edgar about LT's heated conversation with the Chief.

"Jesus. He is in trouble because of us. What the hell is wrong with the Chief? We almost identified the terrorists."

"Almost is the keyword here." Arya stressed the word 'almost.' "Anyway, I think it will be okay. The shootout in the Stoneridge worked out in the end."

"What should we do? Call LT?"

Arya didn't answer Edgar's rhetorical question, and she proceeded by pulling her phone from her waist and called LT.

"What the hell is going on?" Ray and a couple of other detectives approached Arya and Edgar.

Arya and Edgar both responded similarly by raising their hands to signal the detectives to remain silent.

Arya threw in a couple of expletives as the call to LT went to voicemail.

Arya disconnected the call without leaving a voicemail and redialed LT's cellphone. "For God's sake, pick up."

After the second ring, the call went to voicemail. It appeared LT was purposely sending the call to voicemail.

"Please, God," Arya mouthed as she tried LT's phone again.

The third time was the lucky charm, as LT answered the call.

"LT, this is Arya," Arya answered, as LT Cooper answered the phone.

"I know. I am in a meeting with Chief; can this wait?" LT answered in a rushed voice.

"No. This can't wait," Arya responded flatly.

LT was taken aback by Arya's abrupt response. "Excuse me. What's so urgent that it can't wait?"

"LT," Arya took a deep breath before she responded. "New York is going to be hit with a biological attack."

46

FOR THE NEXT FEW MINUTES, Arya and Edgar filled in LT and the Chief about their investigation and analysis of the current situation. The safe-deposit box, photos of prominent New York landmarks, Marisomo break-in, Nafisa's job in New York Stock Exchange, Aether Solutions, Samir's rental van that was spray-painted with Aether Solutions' logo, and finally conversations about Phase Two of the attacks in Culver City.

There was a collective gasp from LT, and the Chief as Arya and Edgar finished their analysis about the investigation.

"This is…." The Chief searched for the words, "If you guys turn out to be correct, this is monumental. This is huge."

LT signaled his agreement by concurring with the Chief before turning his attention towards Arya and Edgar. "Who else knows about this?"

"No one. We just finished our analysis, and we called you right away," Arya answered.

"Good, good. You did the right thing," LT acknowledged.

"Give us a minute," LT said, before placing Arya and Edgar on hold.

A minute turned into three minutes, and an uncomfortable silence ensued between Edgar and Arya.

"What is going on? Why are we on mute for so long?" Edgar asked, breaking the silence.

Arya shrugged. "I am not sure. I did not expect this reaction."

Before Arya could complete her response, the silence on the phone line shattered as LT's voice came on the line. "Chief and I just spoke to Agent Taylor and filled him on the details you shared."

Arya and Edgar exchanged glances as Arya mouthed, "I should have guessed this."

"Arya, I gave your number to Agent Taylor, and your phone should be ringing any minute. I want you and Edgar to work with Agent Taylor…"

As LT was speaking, Arya noticed her cellphone started ringing. "Agent Taylor is calling," Arya interrupted LT on the call.

"Go ahead, answer. Keep me in the loop every step of the way." LT gave his parting thoughts as he disconnected the call.

Arya and Edgar hurried into one of the empty interview rooms before Arya answered the call by placing it on speaker. "Agent Taylor, you are on speaker, and I have Detective James in the room."

Agent Taylor ignored any pleasantries and jumped right into the crux of the issue. "Cooper filled me in with the details. Where are we with the keys?"

"It was in JNC Bank's safe deposit box. Samir rented it around the time of Marisomo break-in."

"Did you guys call…?" Agent Taylor hesitated as if he was trying to remember the name of the bank manager.

"Not yet. We haven't called Robinson." Arya explained that they wanted to check in with LT about their analysis before taking any action.

"Got it. I must have called right after you hung up with Cooper." Agent Taylor conjectured the sequence of events.

"I have Robinson's cellphone number with me and ..." Agent Taylor interrupted Arya before she could finish her thought about calling Robinson.

"Go ahead, Detective. I can stay on hold."

"I know what Robinson would ask of us before he hands over the contents of the safe deposit box."

"Warrant?" Agent Taylor guessed.

Arya nodded. "Yes."

"We don't need one. We are dealing with an imminent threat to the nation and national security trumps in this situation."

Edgar lifted her gaze towards Arya as she parted a small smile. "Desperate times warrant desperate measures," she mouthed.

Edgar couldn't agree more. If any situation could be deemed as DEFCON 1, this was undoubtedly one of them. A biological attack in the heart of New York City would leave the city crippled and the country terrified.

"HELLO, Detective. Thanks for calling me back," Robinson, manager of JNC Bank, said, as he answered Arya's call.

Arya furrowed her brows in surprise. "Did you call me?" Arya asked in a tone that signaled surprise.

"Yes. I called earlier in the day and left you a message, just before 11:00 in the morning," Robinson explained.

Arya flipped her phone to check if she had any unread messages. As Arya had suspected, she had none. Even though the day was as crazy as it could be, she was pretty sure that she didn't miss a call from Robinson.

"That is strange. I just checked my phone, and I don't see any messages from…"

Before Arya could complete her thought, Robinson interrupted. "Sorry, Detective. I meant to say that I called your main precinct number. You know," he cleared his throat before continuing, "It seems I lost your business card. When I wanted to call you this morning, I kept looking for your card, but…"

Arya interrupted. "That's okay. What did you want to tell me?" Arya asked, eager to know the reason behind Robinson's call to her. She hoped that Robinson has some new information about Samir's case.

"I guess you didn't get the message I left with the other officer," Robinson started. "It was related to Samir Tariq's safe deposit box."

Arya's hope piqued, and then a moment later, it came crashing down upon hearing that bank had mailed the contents of the safe deposit box in the morning.

Arya and Edgar gasped almost at the same time.

"Are you saying it was shipped to Pakistan?" Edgar asked, remembering the conversation they had with Robinson in the bank.

"Unfortunately, yes," Robinson answered with a slight disappointment in his voice.

"Jesus!" Edgar let out a deep sigh. "Did we not tell you that it was related to 9/11, and we are going to get a warrant?"

For a long ten seconds, Robinson remained silent. When he finally answered, Robinson's tone changed. He sounded professional, and his words became more measured.

"Detectives, the bank followed procedure. There had been

no judicial warrant issued for the bank to hold Mr. Tariq's safe deposit box."

"Jesus." Edgar shook his head as he glanced at Arya. "He is covering his ass."

Arya nodded, signaling her agreement with Edgar. Robinson's intent was quite evident; he was trying to protect his job and the reputation of the bank.

"Robinson," Arya interrupted Robinson's long-winded answer. "We are not accusing you of anything. Can you..."

Agent Taylor, who was hearing the conversation between the detectives and Robinson, interjected. "Detectives?"

Arya, hearing Agent Taylor's voice on her phone, placed Robinson on hold and answered Agent Taylor's call.

Agent Taylor informed the detectives that he heard their conversation with Robinson, and he had an idea. "If the bank had shipped the contents just this morning, the package should still be within U.S. borders. Instead of quibbling with Robinson, ask him for the shipping details. FBI should be able to interrupt the package," Agent Taylor directed the detectives.

Arya and Edgar exchanged glances, and both of them reacted in the same way – upset and angry. They didn't like being chastised by a Fed, who had no idea what they do every day to keep the streets safe. They would have shown their middle finger to the FBI under any other circumstances, but not today. 9/11 changed everything. All that matters was to catch the terrorists before they attacked the country again.

"Got it," Arya reluctantly answered before turning her attention towards Robinson's call.

After initial apprehension, Robinson proceeded to reveal the shipping information to the detectives.

"I shouldn't have disclosed these details without the warrant," Robinson said hesitantly.

"We know, and we really appreciate your cooperation. The country thanks you." Edgar assured Robinson that his actions were crucial to the investigation, and it would not come back and bite him in the ass.

"Thank you, Detective, I am the sole breadwinner, and I don't want to lose my job for doing the right thing," Robinson explained his predicament. He also apologized for not holding onto the contents of the safe deposit box.

Edgar empathized with Robinson. "We understand your position. You didn't have any legal warrant to place a hold request in the system."

"Yes, yes," Robinson said hurriedly. "You are right. I couldn't do it. However, I told my staff not to ship the contents before checking with me, but it seems they forgot. I am so sorry."

"We understand." Edgar felt sorry for the guy; it was quite apparent that Robinson felt bad about what had transpired.

"Thanks, Robinson, we got to go. We will reach out to you if we need anything more." Arya jumped in and prudently brought the call to an end.

"Agent Taylor," Arya called, turning her attention back to Agent Taylor's call.

There was no reply from Agent Taylor.

"Agent Taylor," Arya called again to no avail.

Arya raised the phone to check if the call got disconnected, and it was not.

The silence lasted another five seconds before Agent Taylor's voice came on the line.

"Hang on," Agent Taylor said in a voice that sounded flippant.

Arya and Edgar shook their head in unison as they both thought the same thing. *What a prick.*

It was another three minutes before Agent Taylor came back on the line.

"Detectives, this is addressed. I have agents tracking the package, and it looks like it hasn't cleared the Customs facility in the airport."

How does U.S. Customs at the airport get involved with mail packages? Edgar wondered in his head. "I thought Customs officers at the airport check only the baggages that travelers bring into the country." Edgar feebly spat out his inner doubts, invoking an 'Are you serious' expression on Arya's face.

"Detective James, what did you say? I couldn't hear you." Agent Taylor's voice came on the line.

To Edgar, seeing Arya's expression, it became evident that his question should not be repeated aloud, especially in front of officers from another agency.

As Edgar thought of a response to Agent Taylor, Arya jumped in to save Edgar's face. "Edgar was checking if we should head out to the Philly airport to meet with the Customs officers."

Edgar let out a sigh and mouthed a 'thank you' directed towards Arya.

"That won't be necessary. The field agents are on the way to the airport." Agent Taylor paused as he heard a distinctive sound that indicated another incoming call.

"Detectives, I got to go. I need to attend a different call."

"Agent Taylor, what should we do?" Arya blurted out, realizing Agent Taylor was about to hang up any minute.

"Nothing. Stay put. Your work is done with the case," Agent Taylor said bluntly, as he hung up on Arya and Edgar.

47

Before Arya could get another word out of her mouth, Agent Taylor had hung up on them.

"Can you believe this?" Arya fumed. She couldn't believe that Agent Taylor was cutting them off the case.

"Suits. What I heard about them from Ray is right; they are arrogant pricks." Edgar shook his head and joined in with Arya at FBI bashing.

"This is our case." Arya shot up straight from her chair, fuming. "We worked our tail off to get it this far. And now," Arya punched her hands forcefully on the table. "He just cuts us off, just like that," Arya said, snapping her fingers.

"Unbelievable," Edgar said, shaking his head. "What can we do? Customs, airport, USPS – all federal jurisdiction. Maybe we should call LT and run our options by him."

At that moment, a lightbulb went off in Arya's head.

"How the fuck did we miss this?" Arya yelled, evoking an expression of shock in Edgar's face.

"Unbelievable. I can't believe we didn't think of this." Arya chided herself.

"Okay, you got to spell it out for me. I have no idea what

the hell you are talking about," Edgar said, gazing straight at Arya.

"The key we found in Samir's safe deposit box. I am confident that the key is not going to open any storage location that has the package."

"You mean the chemical or biological agents?" Edgar asked, trying to ensure that he understood it correctly.

Arya nodded, signaling her agreement. "Yes. The key is not going to lead them to the package that was stolen from Marisomo."

Edgar raised his brows, signaling his surprise with the conviction shown in Arya's voice. "How are you sure?"

"What do we know about the timeline?" Arya shifted her gaze squarely at Edgar.

"What timeline? Theft or ..." Before Edgar could finish his question, Arya interrupted.

"Samir's activities on the evening of September 10th," Arya said flatly, standing so close to Edgar that he could feel her breath.

"Sania dropped Samir in the airport around 5:30 in the evening. Instead of walking into the airport, Samir waited for Sania to leave the parking lot and left the airport in his rental van."

Arya nodded as she said, "He must have parked the rental van in the airport."

"The next place Samir was confirmed to be spotted was in the Moroccan restaurant, Dar Marrakesh."

Arya raised her hand to raise an objection to Edgar's point. "Remember, Carter was not sure that he spotted Samir in the restaurant. All we can assume for sure is that rental van drove away from the restaurant."

Edgar nodded, signaling his agreement. "Okay. Eli was then spotted driving the rental van near Delaware before disappearing."

"Yes. Now we know that Eli didn't intentionally disappear. He got into an accident," Arya added.

"The horrific 9/11 attacks happened and then..."

"Sania reported Samir to be missing to the police."

"Yes. We know all of that, and how does that explain your theory about the key?" Edgar asked, looking perplexed.

"From our investigation and the information shared by the FBI, we now know for a certainty that Samir was involved with the 9/11 hijackers, and Omar – possible leader of the sleeper cell."

Edgar nodded, agreeing with Arya's conclusions.

"We have also learned that Samir, who was possibly the twentieth hijacker, didn't participate directly on the attacks because he was selected to carry out Phase Two of the 9/11 attacks," Arya said somberly. Arya's mind was still not able to register that her best friend was married to a terrorist who was responsible for the unfathomable attack on her country.

Edgar gestured that he agreed with Arya's assessment so far. However, he expressed that he was still perplexed with Arya's theory about the key.

"This is where the theory falls apart about the connection between the key and the Marisomo package."

Edgar was now intrigued; his eyes were fixed on Arya, and he was gobbling up every word that came out of Arya's mouth.

"Do we agree that the Marisomo package should be connected with Phase Two of the 9/11 attacks?" Arya asked, looking straight into Edgar's eyes.

"Without a doubt. There is no other reasonable explanation for the elaborate theft." Edgar signaled his agreement.

"I think we can reasonably assume that Samir was planning to attack the New York Stock Exchange right after the 9/11 attacks."

Edgar nodded. "Yes. Samir took the HVAC technician job

with NYSE, and, given what we know, that is an excellent assumption."

Arya was expecting Edgar would agree with her assessment. "In that case, Samir should have already had the package."

It took a minute for Edgar to realize the truth in Arya's analysis. Samir had signed off with Robinson to ship the contents of the safe deposit box to his hometown in Pakistan. There is no way that the key had anything to do with the Marisomo package.

"Oh, my God!" Edgar exclaimed. "You are so right. Samir should have had the package in his possession for carrying out a biological attack."

Arya nodded. "Exactly."

A lightbulb just went off on Edgar's head. "If Samir had to carry out the attacks on the morning of 9/11, Samir should have had the package close to him."

Arya nodded. "Bingo."

Edgar cracked a half-smile, but it didn't last long when a thought dawned on him. "Jesus! The van. That is why Omar shadowed Sania; he wanted to find the van. It must be in the van."

"I thought the same, but not anymore," Arya said, shaking her head slowly. "FBI took custody of the van and the Stoneridge house. If the package was anywhere near, they would have found it out by now."

"Agent Taylor wouldn't be searching for it now," Edgar finished Arya's thoughts.

"Exactly. I think Omar and then Agent Taylor both thought the package was in the van, and I am sure they were surprised when they found out they were wrong."

"That explains it," Edgar said, as he thought about the events that led to Sania and Eli's kidnapping. "Where do you think it is, if not in the van?"

"I don't know." Arya took a deep breath. "I don't know. It should have been stored someplace that Samir frequented and could access at that time of the night."

Arya and Edgar began to brainstorm — where else could Samir have stored the package? Arya was sure that Sania nor Eli knew about the location, and, if they did, they would have shared it by now with Agent Taylor. Edgar agreed with Arya's hypothesis; it didn't make any sense for Arya or Eli to hold on to that information.

For the next few minutes, they combed over Samir's financials to see if they missed any storage location payments. Zilch; they came up empty. There were no payments made from Samir's accounts to any of the storage locations.

"Damn it." Edgar slammed his fist on the table, feeling frustrated.

Arya raised her gaze towards Edgar as he fumed. "The answer has got to be here. We are missing something."

"I have an idea," Arya said, starting to punch keys on her phone.

"Who are you dialing?" Edgar asked, wondering if she was calling LT.

"Kate Halladay," Arya said, as a familiar ringing sound came on the line.

Edgar slumped on his chair, next to Arya, and stared at the phone. He felt and looked exhausted.

After four unsuccessful rings, Kate's upbeat voice came on the line. Unfortunately, it was a voicemail greeting that asked the caller to leave a voicemail.

Arya left a short message asking Kate Halladay to call back when she gets the message. Arya also left her mobile phone number in the message in case Kate had misplaced Arya's business card.

"Do you think it is strange that the Halladays did not call us all day?"

"What do you mean?" Arya asked, wondering where Edgar was going with his question.

"From what we know, Sania and Kate were friends, and they seemed to be in touch daily…"

Edgar didn't have to complete his thought; Arya understood where exactly Edgar was going with this discussion. Why hadn't Kate called to inquire about Sania? Sania had been gone almost the entire day.

"I think it is time for us to pay a visit; I have a bad feeling." A strong sense of worry dawned on Arya, fearing Omar or Nafisa might have hurt the Halladays.

"Before we go all the way… let us call the husband," Edgar said as he shifted his body forward to reach for the phone.

Similar to the call to Kate, the call to Tom went to voicemail.

"Let me try again," Edgar said as he dialed Tom's number. No response.

After three more attempts, Edgar gave up.

Arya, taking the cue from Edgar, redialed Kate's number. No luck, same result.

At this point, both Edgar and Arya came to the same conclusion. Something terrible must have happened to the Halladays. They had two options at their disposal. They could either drive to the Halladays' residence to check on them or work with the dispatcher to get a nearby police cruiser to do a quick wellness check. After a quick deliberation, they decided to go with the dispatcher route. It was the fastest and the best option available on the table. A police cruiser was just three minutes away from the Halladays' residence.

Just after they asked the dispatcher to send a cruiser out

to check up on Halladays, the prickly silence in the room dissipated as Edgar's phone erupted with a familiar sound.

"Tom Halladay," Edgar revealed, lifting his gaze from the phone and stared at Arya.

Arya motioned her hands and gestured Edgar to answer the phone.

"Mr. Halladay," Edgar answered the phone, hoping that it was Tom who made the call.

"Hello, Detective James. How are you?" Tom Halladay's voice was even, and there was no hint of being under duress.

"Not too shabby. You okay?"

"Yes, I am okay." Tom paused for a moment before he continued. "Sorry, Detective; I missed your call. I got to admit that I was surprised and alarmed at the same time, seeing you called me four times in the last fifteen minutes."

"Are you at home?"

"No, I am at the gym. Why?"

"Anyone at your home? Your wife?"

"No. Kate's mom's health took a sudden bad turn, and she drove last night to Connecticut to pay her a visit." Tom hesitated for a brief moment before asking, "Detective, what is with all these questions? Anything I should be worried about?"

"No, no," Edgar said, switching his tone to sound more casual. "Detective Martins had been trying to reach your wife today, and as she was not reachable, we thought we could reach her through you."

Tom signaled his understanding behind the call. "Unfortunately, my wife is in the hospital now, and the cellphone reception in the hospital is quite horrendous."

"Oh! That explains it," Edgar replied curtly.

"You know, I can ask her to call Detective Martins in the morn…." Tom stopped and yelled an expletive. His voice sounded like he was in pain.

At that moment, Edgar and Arya both got worried if Tom Halladay was attacked.

"Tom, what happened? Are you okay?" Edgar hurled a set of questions, hoping Tom was not in danger.

"Jesus. My back, it hurts. I must have pulled a muscle doing my row today." Tom winced in pain.

"In the gym?"

"Nah. I was at the river this morning. I love rowing my boat when it is calm," Tom said, like a man who loved rowing. "Do you row, Detective?"

"Not in a very long time. I tried once, but I didn't fall in love with it, like you," Edgar answered with a smile.

At that moment, a thought flashed in Arya's mind. *She remembered Sania mentioning that Samir was in love with rowing, and he used to disappear for hours.*

Arya shot up from her chair and reached for the phone. "Mr. Halladay, did you ever row with Samir?"

"Yes. Maybe a couple of times, and please call me Tom." Tom smiled.

"Where did you row?"

"With Samir?" Tom asked.

"Yes, yes," Arya replied hurriedly.

"Schuylkill River," Tom answered quickly.

"Did Samir use any lockers?"

"Yes, he used the lockers in Kelly Drive."

Arya and Edgar exchanged a glance. Edgar could sense where Arya was going with her line of questioning. The sense of anticipation was rising for both of them.

"In fact, if I remember it correctly, Samir had one of those exclusive lockers."

"Exclusive lockers? What are they?" Arya and Edgar both had no idea what that term means in this context.

"It is one of those lockers that was assigned to him exclusively, and no one else could use it. He doesn't have to empty out the locker after a row, and he can store things overnight. Trust me, it is convenient if you row quite often as Samir," Tom explained.

Tom had no idea how relevant and monumental the information he shared. In fact, it will end up as the critical information that ends up thwarting a biological attack on the country.

IT WAS forty-five minutes past nine, and the traffic on the roads leading to Kelly Drive from Germantown was light. Edgar took advantage of the ideal driving conditions and stepped on the gas from the get-go. With the skies lit up with the dazzling lights and blaring sirens, they gained time to reach the rowing office on Kelly Drive.

"Yes. Samir was serious about rowing. He owned a trailer to transport his sculler to and from the Schuylkill River." Arya was on the phone, filling LT in about their new findings.

LT Cooper had just left the diner, where he had a working dinner with the Chief. He was on his way to his house.

"Does Agent Taylor know?"

"No. Not yet. I called you first," Arya said, as Edgar made a sharp turn to take an exit into Kelly Drive.

"Who else is with you guys?" LT's mind raced about the next steps.

"Just us. Edgar and I," Arya said flatly.

"Jesus. That is not good. What happens if someone else is already there? You guys should have gone with backup."

It was clear from LT's voice that he was not happy that Arya and Edgar were acting like cowboys and not following protocol.

"It was just a hunch. We didn't want to cause a hoopla if the hunch was wrong."

"Did I just hear you say hoopla?" LT raised his voice, signaling his displeasure with Arya. "We are in the middle of the biggest national security crisis that this country has seen since World War 2. Nothing is hoopla if there is a one percent chance that we can stop the next attack or kill the terrorists."

"Got it, LT. We are sorry," Arya said, in a lowered voice.

"Okay. How far are you out?"

"Maybe five more minutes for us to reach the rowing office?"

"Did you call to check if anyone is even working at that time?"

"We didn't, but Tom Halladay informed us that the lockers were accessible 24/7. There is a separate gate to get to the lockers."

"Tom Halladay?" LT asked, trying to place the name.

"Samir and Sania's neighbor. His wife was the one who works in the security business, who…" Arya was interrupted by LT Cooper before she completed her thought.

"Yes. I remember now," LT said, clearing his throat.

"Tom gave us the security code to enter the premises, and he also shared Samir's locker number."

"Jesus Christ. Why the heck he didn't do that before?" LT asked, wondering out aloud why Tom waited till now to share information about Samir's locker.

"We didn't ask." Arya hesitated before continuing, "We

thought Samir was missing and didn't suspect him to be involved in the attacks."

"Did Halladay share the combination for Samir's locker?"

"No. He doesn't know that."

"That is what I thought. What is your plan to get Samir's locker opened? I hope you were not planning to shoot your way in."

"Of course not, LT." Arya couldn't believe LT thought that they would have thought of such a dumb plan. "Tom Halladay mentioned that there is an intercom or a remote phone on the premises that would connect us with the supervisor."

"Got it. You were planning to invoke the 9/11 attacks and get the supervisor to open the locker."

"Pretty much it. If the supervisor didn't budge, our presence would at least secure the locker until we get a warrant to get the locker opened."

"Okay, good."

An uncomfortable silence filled the line for thirty-odd seconds before LT's deep voice came back on. "Okay, this is what I want you to do." LT started with an authoritative tone. "I want you and Edgar to clear the perimeter of the rowing office, but I don't want you to go inside."

As Arya raised her voice to express her displeasure about LT's directive, LT cut her off. "Arya, listen; I want you and Edgar to follow my instructions. No going inside, am I clear?"

LT's voice was so loud that Edgar could hear him clearly.

"Loud and clear. We won't go inside," Arya said with a gloomy voice. "Can I at least ask why? Because if we go in and call the supervisor, we could get the ball rolling before the brass descends on the location."

"Because you might be right about the follow-up attack. There is enough verifiable intelligence now to confirm that a biological attack in New York City was planned by Al-Qaeda to take place after the planes hit the towers."

"Oh, my God. We are right," Arya exclaimed in shock.

"Yes. That is why I am asking you not to go anywhere near the lockers. What if you are right, and the biological agents were stored in those lockers. We have no idea if it is Sarin or Anthrax. Both you and Edgar are neither trained nor equipped to secure and safely handle those biological agents. You might even accidentally set it off."

Arya had heard enough to know LT was right. She was nodding her head as LT finished his thought. "You are right, LT. We will secure the perimeter."

"Good, good. I will call Agent Taylor and get a team out there that handles biological agents."

"We are almost rolling in. Anything else, LT?"

"Call in your backup before you step out of your vehicle. I am serious." Those were the last words from LT before he disconnected the call.

49

THE CRUISER CAME to a stop in front of a T-junction. On the right, they could hear the Schuylkill River breathe, and on the left, there was a narrow meandering road.

"The office must be on the left," Arya said, gesturing to the narrow road by pointing her left hand towards it.

"You sure? I remember Tom mentioning the rowing office was by the river." Edgar flipped the lights from low beam to high beam to get a better view of the place. "Maybe, we shot by it." Edgar raised his suspicion.

"I don't think so. I was watching the road like a hawk, and I didn't see any office," Arya said confidently.

Edgar glanced towards the meandering road on his left and said, "You want to check it out?"

Arya nodded. "We are already here. Let us…"

Before Arya could complete her sentence, a muffled sound shattered the silence and stopped her mid-sentence.

"What the hell was that? Is it a gunshot?" Arya asked, replaying the muffled sound in her head.

Edgar's first instinct was to turn towards the direction of the sound, and his gaze shifted towards the narrow meandering road. For the next five seconds, he replayed the muffled sound in his head, and he became certain about the source of the sound.

"Gunshot," he mouthed to himself before plucking the radio off its hook. "This is Car 54. Do you read?"

"Loud and clear, Car 54. Proceed," The dispatcher announced.

"Shots fired in Kelly Drive. Calling for backup," Edgar said, glancing towards Arya and mouthed silently. "Sounded like it was fired with a silencer."

Arya nodded, agreeing with Edgar's assessment when the dispatcher's voice came back on the radio. "Officer, are you or your partner under fire?"

"Negative. We are not. We were in the vicinity when we heard the shots."

"Backup is on the way. Proceed with caution, and the backup's ETA is six minutes."

"Do you hear it?" Arya whispered, staring right past Edgar into the narrow road.

"Not exactly. What is it?" Edgar asked, placing the radio in its place.

"It sounded like an engine." Arya pointed towards the narrow road.

The sound was getting more pronounced as time progressed.

"It looks like we are going to have some company soon," Edgar said, pulling his gun from the holster.

Arya soon did the same and asked Edgar to cut out the lights.

"We have to assume that whoever fired the gun is here for Samir's locker." Arya expressed her opinion, and, to which, Edgar signaled his agreement.

Edgar backed the cruiser by the bend and cut the lights off. They hoped that it would give them an advantage in spotting the approaching vehicle and, in the meantime, making it difficult for them to be spotted.

Both Arya and Edgar, without blinking, stared at the narrow road, with their Glocks drawn and ready to shoot.

With every second, the sound of the approaching car began to rise, and at the same time, Edgar and Arya's heart began to pound a little louder.

Within a few seconds, as they anticipated, the narrow road shifted from complete darkness to be filled with light from an approaching vehicle.

At first glance, the oncoming vehicle looked like a truck or an SUV — the position of headlights led them to believe it was not a sedan. It was traveling at a steady pace, but not too fast.

"Can you make out the number of people in the car?" Edgar asked. However, his eyes never shifted towards Arya from the approaching vehicle.

"I can't tell. We have to assume that it is a two-member team, given what we know about how this cell operated."

Edgar nodded in agreement. Their earlier analysis revealed a pattern that showed cell members operating as a two-member team whenever they carry out tasks related to their operation. At first, it seemed weird to see them working in pairs, like how cops did. Later they learned that the pairing was done intentionally to prevent breaches in their operation.

As the vehicle neared the T-junction, it slowed down to make a hard-right turn. This allowed Arya to make out the vehicle type. It was a mid-size truck, and it looked like it was painted white.

Edgar's plan was to wait for the vehicle until it gets to the junction and surprise them by lighting up the sky with lights and sirens. If the vehicle refused to stop or take evasive action, they would have the position to crash their cruiser into the truck. Arya, however, was not a hundred percent behind this plan. She would rather shoot at the truck's tires and jump on them with their weapons drawn. Edgar didn't want to shoot at the truck without knowing for certain that people in the truck were terrorists. All they heard was a muffled sound, which they presumed was a gunshot. Edgar's argument was, what if they were wrong, and the muffled sound didn't come from a gunshot. As they didn't have much time to debate the pros and cons, they decided to go with Edgar's approach as a starting point. They decided to calibrate the plan and switch to a more aggressive tactic if they became certain that terrorists were in the truck.

Just as they planned, they took action as the truck neared the junction. The familiar police lightbars lit up the sky, and the blaring sirens shredded the silence of the dark night. A message was blasted over the loudspeakers for the driver to stop the truck. But the truck didn't stop, and instead, bullets started to fly towards the cruiser. The truck driver must be using some kind of a semi-automatic weapon as the bullets pelted the cruiser at a rapid pace. Edgar and Arya dove from the car as the rapid-fire shattered the windshields and the driver-side windows.

Edgar took cover behind a tree trunk and returned fire at the truck. In the meantime, Arya ran towards the truck and fired two shots from her Glock. Each shot successfully hit a back tire, making the truck lose its balance and swerve into a ditch.

Just as soon as the truck crashed into the ditch, two men, who appeared Middle Eastern, climbed out of the truck and began to run away from the detectives using gunfire as a shield. Edgar and Arya were severely undermanned in terms of gunfire. Their Glocks were no match to the Kalashnikova, the AK 47s, in the terrorists' hands. The bullets were flying from the Kalashnikova at a rapid pace, leaving Edgar and Arya with no choice other than to take cover.

"Jesus!" Edgar exclaimed. "How the heck did they get that gun?"

Arya, who was behind a tree trunk, quickly peeked. "Shit. They are getting away; we need to stop them."

Just as the words from Arya came out, there was a sudden burst of sirens.

"The cavalry is here," Edgar said, giving out a relieved smile.

For the next minute, the place was filled with heavy gunfire. The cavalry matched the Kalashnikova with the fine American made Colt M4 Carbine automatic guns and returned fire. The stage was set — it was two terrorists against twenty well-trained officers; the fight didn't last long. By the time anyone could count to ten, two bodies fell on the ground, and the gunfire came to an end.

A commanding officer motioned his hand to signal two of his men to perform a visual inspection of the terrorists' condition. The two men, dressed in full protective gear, cautiously approached the fallen terrorists, just like how they were trained to act in these situations. The bodies of terrorists were close to each other, not separated by more than ten feet, and, with one look, it became quite apparent that both of them were dead as a doornail. Their bodies looked like a cardboard box that got stuck in a shredder; the body parts were half-shredded and looked severely damaged. Their bodies were soaked with blood. The 5.56 mm gas-operated rotating bolt bullets traveling at the speed of two thousand nine hundred feet-per-second did what it was designed to do – Kill. There is a reason why Colt M4 Carbine is a preferred weapon for U.S. Armed Forces; it is the deadliest assault weapon designed by mankind.

"Detectives." The commanding officer of the unit addressed Edgar and Arya as they approached the officer.

"Commander Miller," Edgar addressed the officer. "Who called in the SWAT team?"

Edgar and Arya didn't expect the SWAT team to come to their rescue when they radioed in for help. They expected Philly PD to come alone.

"I am sure you were happy to see my face for a change." Commander Miller gave a half-smile as he shifted his glance from Edgar to Arya.

"Come on, Miller, seriously!" Arya rolled her eyes in disbelief. Miller and Arya had a little bit of history between them. They dated a year back, and, to Miller's dismay, it didn't last long. When Miller thought their relationship was getting to the next level, Arya called it off without giving a reason. Since then, Miller has been trying to get back together with her without much luck.

"Good try, Miller," Edgar jabbed him.

"What can I say? I thought saving you guys from a couple of rotten terrorists would get me in the good books, but…"

"Miller, stop it," Arya scowled. Arya's tone and body language made it very clear – this was not the time or the place for these jokes.

"Okay," Miller sighed, raising his hands. "We are in the operational wing of the JTTF, and we were called in by…" Commander Miller was interrupted by Arya before he could finish.

"By the FBI. Agent Taylor." Arya put two-and-two together.

Miller nodded. "Yes. But not just the FBI, it was also the Chief."

Arya nodded, signaling she understood the reason for the Chief calling in on the SWAT. LT Cooper must have briefed both Agent Taylor and the Chief right after they hung up the call with him.

"Did you find anything on the men?" Arya gestured her hand towards the fallen terrorists.

"If you are asking about the case containing the biological weapon, I would say not yet."

Miller's answer surprised both Edgar and Arya. They didn't expect Miller to have been briefed about their assessment of the situation.

Before the detectives could ask, Miller responded. "Agent Taylor had instructed us to neutralize the terrorists and secure the vehicle by any means," Miller gestured towards the truck.

As Arya took a step towards the truck, Miller reached out and grabbed her hand. "No one is authorized to go near the truck. We have clear instructions to secure the truck and wait for the containment team."

Everyone on the force knew the containment team's expertise – securing and handling chemical and biological weapons.

In the next five minutes, the containment team arrived on the scene along with Agent Taylor.

Edgar and Arya had to act as bystanders as the containment team approached the vehicle in their fully protected hazmat suit.

Agent Taylor stood a few feet away from the detectives, monitoring the situation closely. If he was tensed, he didn't show it. He looked cool as a cucumber and didn't show any emotions on his face.

"Agent Taylor," Arya said, as she approached Taylor.

"Detectives, I must say you both have surprised me. This is some serious work," Agent Taylor said, signaling his genuine appreciation towards both Edgar and Arya.

Edgar and Arya both gave a customary nod and a half-open smile. "Thanks," they both said in unison.

At that moment, a voice rang out from the agent close to the truck, which caught everyone's attention. "We got something."

As everyone's eyes shifted towards the truck, a man wearing a hazmat suit emerged from the truck, holding an aluminum container.

50

Three Weeks Later
October 6, 2001

IT HAD BEEN close to four weeks since the horrific attacks
were carried out in the heart of America. By all estimates,
more than three thousand lives – mothers, daughters,
fathers, sons - were feared dead on that fateful day –
September 11, 2001. None of those innocents, when they left
their home – kissing their loved ones –, had any idea that
would be the last time they would get to see them, embrace
them, and kiss them. They did not deserve to die. It was a
meaningless attack, perpetrated by evil people for their own
twisted reasons in their minds. There is no way God would
allow those barbarians to enter heaven for killing three thousand innocent lives.

The only event in recent history comparable to the 9/11
attacks was when the Japanese attacked Pearl Harbor. That
attack fundamentally changed the nation's mindset; it woke

up a sleeping giant to confront the evil in the world. That attack made it clear to the American people that oceans cannot protect them, and the only way to be safe is to defeat evil. Just like the Pearl Harbor attacks, the 9/11 attacks had a similar impact on the American psyche. The morning after 9/11, every American knew it in their hearts that oceans could no longer protect them from evil. The evil had to be confronted and defeated. That is the only way to be safe.

The nation was shocked by 9/11, but their spirits were not shaken.

Every American till their death would remember when President George W. Bush stood atop of the World Trade Center and addressed the American people. He chose simple words to address the nation and send a powerful message to the terrorists camped halfway around the world in Afghanistan.

"I can hear you; the rest of the world can hear you, and the people who knocked these buildings down will hear all of us soon."

- President George W. Bush

IT WAS a powerful message that the nation needed to hear. Not only the workers, who were clearing the rubbles of the World Trade Center, cheered this simple message from the President, but the entire nation cheered. It is exactly the message the grieving nation wanted to hear from their Commander-in-Chief – direct and straightforward –; we are going to get those bastards who attacked us.

The days after the 9/11 attacks, the nation came to know the faces of the evil men who used airplanes as missiles and crashed them into the World Trade Center and Pentagon. If not for the heroes of Flight 93, the terrorists would have used that aircraft as a missile and attacked the U.S. Capitol or the White House. The nation owes the passengers of Flight 93 an enormous gratitude for preventing those attacks. They were heroes.

As the news started to sprinkle out about Al-Qaeda, Osama Bin Laden, and the terrorist camps being operated out of Afghanistan, certain information was kept out of the public domain. Only a few people knew how close the nation came to experience another attack – a biological attack. A biological attack in New York City would have been catastrophic and could have left the country paralyzed for decades. A very few people knew about the details of that attack. Detectives Arya Martins and Edgar James were part of that very elite circle who knew the top-secret information.

WITH GREAT KNOWLEDGE comes great restrictions. The day after nightfall blitz in Kelly Drive, Arya Martins and Edgar James were commanded to come to the Chief's office at 8:00 AM in the morning with all the files related to the Samir Tariq investigation. When they reached the Chief's office, they were greeted by not just the Chief and LT Cooper, but three more men. Arya and Edgar recognized one of the men – Agent Taylor –, but they had never seen the faces of the other two men. They both looked to be in their late forties or early fifties, and they carried an air of authority in their demeanor.

The customary pleasantries were brief between the Chief, LT Cooper, and the detectives. The previous night's encounter was weighing heavy in everyone's mind. The detectives carried an expression that clearly signaled that they were not sure why they were commanded to the Chief's office with Samir Tariq's files.

"Detectives." Agent Taylor gave a curt smile as he shook both their hands. "Good work yesterday." The appreciation, like the smile, was brief.

As Arya's glance shifted towards the two men standing next to the Chief, Agent Taylor proceeded by introducing both of them to the detectives.

"Agent Tennyson – Operations Division at the CIA, and Officer Dawson from the GAO division of the NSA," Agent Taylor introduced.

Arya and Edgar were both equally stunned to hear the identities of two men. *NSA and CIA. Why are they here? What do they want from us?* These were some of the thoughts that flashed through their mind as the two agents shook their hands.

"GAO?" Neither Edgar nor Arya had ever heard of that term. Like everyone in the country, they have heard of the big hitters – CIA and NSA –, but not GAO.

"Global Access Operations," Officer Dawson elaborated. The GAO division is responsible for 'Collection Overseas' – monitoring a large proportion of the world's transmitted civilian phone, fax, email, and other forms of communications. They primarily monitor and collect information on non-U.S. citizens, entities, corporations, or organizations. If they need to monitor U.S. citizens abroad, they need special authorization from the U.S. Attorney General. If the U.S. citizens or organizations reside in the United States, they need authorization from the Foreign Intelligence Surveillance Court – FISA.

"Did you get the files?" Agent Tennyson asked.

Arya glanced towards LT Cooper, who nodded –

signaling Arya his approval before she handed out the file she had with her.

"This is everything?" Agent Tennyson asked, glancing at the case file that seemed light.

"Yes," Arya replied. "That is Samir Tariq's case file."

"How about Omar Al-Farooq?" Officer Dawson jumped into the conversation.

"We didn't open a separate file on Omar Al-Farooq. Any information we learned about him was a byproduct of Samir's Tariq's investigation. So…"

"You merged both files?" Officer Dawson completed the sentence in a manner that sounded almost like a question.

"Yes and no. We didn't have to merge any files as we didn't open a new file for Omar Al-Farooq."

"How about the file on Omar Raqqa from Aries Financials?" Agent Tennyson asked, surprising Edgar and Arya. They didn't expect both these officers to know about the other Omar Raqqa so soon.

"How did you know?" Arya asked, shifting her glance from Agent Tennyson to LT Cooper and then back at Agent Tennyson.

"Your LT didn't have to tell us. We have been tracking Omar Al-Farooq for some time now. We suspected he might have played a role in Omar Raqqa's mysterious disappearance."

"Then how the hell did he manage to pull this off?" Edgar blurted out, showing his anger with the situation. "Shouldn't you have stopped it?"

The outburst from Edgar turned everyone's heads towards him. Everyone – Arya, the Chief, and LT Cooper – had the same thought in their mind, and they were glad Edgar asked.

Agent Tennyson and Officer Dawson exchanged a brief glance before Officer Dawson approached Edgar. "This case is more complicated than you think. Most of the hijackers didn't even know what the plan was. We are not even sure when and how much Omar Al-Farooq knew."

"Trust me when I say this; we feel the same outrage as everyone here or around the country. Don't think for a moment that we didn't warn about the attacks. Unfortunately, no one believed that this can happen in our soil. Why would they? This was unprecedented."

"So, you guys saw this coming?" Arya asked, holding on to the agent's statement.

"Sorry, Detectives; that is all we could say," Agent Tennyson said firmly. "All this is classified." The agent swerved his glance towards everyone in the room. "Do you get it?"

"Yes," the Chief said.

"Not just what we discussed here, but also…." Agent Tennyson tapped on Samir's file in his hand, "Everything on this file is classified."

Everyone in the room nodded, signaling their understanding.

"Good. We are all on the same page."

"Anything else?" Agent Tennyson asked.

"Where is Sania?" Arya asked, shifting her glance from Agent Tennyson to Agent Taylor.

"She is safe." Agent Taylor looked directly into Arya's eyes, "That is all you need to know. Everything else is classified."

"You must be fucking kidding me," Arya blurted out. "That is all I need to know. Unbelievable!" She threw her hands wide in frustration. "When you guys were doing God knows what, Edgar and I have been chasing every single lead…"

"Arya," LT Cooper's voice reverberated loudly. "Cut it out. This is not the place or time." He paused to correct himself.

"In my opinion, it is never a time or a place to question each other's intentions without evidence. Like us, I am sure these agents were busting their ass every day trying to save Americans. Unfortunately, we hear only their failures. We never hear about the countless times they stopped these jihadis from blowing up Americans."

Arya, along with everyone else in the room, was taken aback by the emotional outburst from LT Cooper.

The Chief cleared his throat and said, "Well said." He shifted his gaze from LT Cooper to the detectives and emphasized the message, "We are all in the same team."

"Sorry, Chief, that was not my intent," Arya tried to explain. "I just want to know if Sania is safe. Sania is my…"

Agent Taylor stepped in. "Your friend. We know that." He shifted his gaze towards the other two federal agents in the room and said, "I think we have some wiggle room without compromising classified information."

Agent Tennyson and Officer Dawson both nodded, signaling Agent Taylor to proceed.

Agent Taylor turned towards Arya and said, "Sania Tariq is safe. She is currently under the custody of the federal government. I can't say where or by which division of the federal government."

"What do you mean by custody? She is not a terrorist. I am sure she had no clue about Samir's…"

"Detective Martins, hold on." Agent Taylor raised his hand to gesture Arya to hold on to her questions. "You might have misunderstood. She is not being held because we are suspecting that she is a terrorist."

"Why then? Why can't…." Arya stopped herself as she realized the reason for Sania's detention. "You are holding her for information."

It was now Agent Tennyson's turn to step in. "Sania had been married to Samir Tariq for well over three years. Even though she didn't really know the man behind the name Samir Tariq, she still knew a lot of information about her husband. She has traveled with Samir to many countries, including Saudi Arabia and Pakistan, stayed in different houses and hotels, and visited many of his so-called friends and relatives. The Feds believe that she knew a lot more than what she can fathom."

Arya let out a deep sigh; this was a lot to take in. All of a sudden, in the fight against the terrorists, Sania Tariq has become extremely valuable. She might have a small piece of information that could be immensely valuable for locating, hunting, and killing the terrorists.

"Is she under threat from terrorists? Did you guys hear any chatter?" Arya asked, looking at Agent Taylor.

"What do you think?" Agent Taylor asked rhetorically. "She has stayed with him in Pakistan and Saudi Arabia. In one instance, we believe she actually met…." Agent Taylor stopped himself from saying the name. "I can't say any more. It is classified. You have to know how vital she is going to be in our war against the terrorists. Any information she provides is going to go a long way. She is an extremely valuable asset to us."

Nothing needs to be said more about Sania's safety. CIA, NSA, FBI, and any other agency would go to tremendous length to safeguard Sania. All of a sudden, Sania has become one of the key assets in the fight against Al-Qaeda.

"Who killed Samir Tariq? How did he die?" Arya asked, eliciting glances between Agent Taylor, Agent Tennyson, and Officer Dawson. The question caused an uncomfortable silence in the room, and it lasted until Agent Taylor decided to break the silence.

"Detectives," Agent Taylor shifted his gaze towards Edgar and Arya, "What do you think happened? I am sure you have a theory."

Edgar exchanged glances with Arya before saying, "Initially, we thought Omar might have killed Samir because of an affair between Samir and Nafisa."

Agent Taylor half-smiled, crossing his hands across his chest and gestured for Edgar to continue.

"Later, when we realized Samir and Omar were terrorists, the affair killing didn't make much sense. We now don't even think they had an affair. They must have been meeting to plot their plan to..." Before Edgar could complete his sentence, Arya bluntly interrupted.

"Sania or Eli must have killed Samir." Arya's response caused all the eyes in the room to land on her.

"Interesting." Agent Taylor raised his brows. "Do you agree with your partner?" Agent Taylor asked, shifting his gaze towards Edgar.

Edgar nodded.

"Let us hear more, Detectives," Agent Taylor motioned his hand for the detectives to continue.

Edgar exchanged a quick glance with Arya before continuing, "We believe that the Dar Marrakesh restaurant was used as a front by Omar's sleeper cell to plan their operation. On the evening of September 10th, after Sania dropped Samir in the airport, we believe he took the Ford Transit rental and drove to that restaurant."

Edgar paused to see if there were any objections and when he found none from Agent Taylor, he continued. "Sania and Eli must have met Samir in the restaurant, and something happened there, which led to..."

Arya interrupted Edgar's account and said, "Sania killed Samir in the restaurant."

Edgar was surprised by the tone of Arya's voice; she sounded confident.

"What makes you say that?" Agent Taylor asked, turning towards Arya. "Why not Eli?"

"It couldn't have been Eli. From our investigation, we know Sania was already in the restaurant by the time Eli went there that night."

Edgar nodded, connecting the dots from what they learned earlier from Carter.

"Sania must have suspected Samir and must have followed him to the restaurant." Arya became more confident with her assessment. "Tell me, am I correct?" Sania looked squarely at Agent Taylor.

Agent Taylor turned towards LT Cooper and nodded. "You are right, Cooper. She is going to go places."

LT Cooper smiled, beaming inside with pride.

"Detective Martins, you are right. Samir did go to the Dar Marrakesh restaurant that night to tape a suicide video that could be used as propaganda for recruitment in their jihadi world. When he was taping..."

"Sania walked in," Arya completed the sentence.

Agent Taylor nodded. "Sania realized the true colors of Samir. She then confronted Samir about his intentions and pleaded with him to forgo his evil plan to attack the United States. However, Sania's effort turned futile, and the situation got out of hand. Sania ended up shooting Samir to stop him from carrying out the attack."

"Sania is a fucking hero!" Arya's eyes were beaming with pride. "If not for her, we might have had a biological attack in New York City."

Agent Taylor nodded. "I would say so."

"Why did Sania report Samir to be missing?" Edgar jumped in with a question that was troubling him.

"Good question; I did ask her about it." Agent Taylor cleared his throat and continued, "After Sania shot Samir, she called Eli Berg for help. Eli came up with a plan to dispose of Samir's body in Stoneridge woods, and he asked her to report Samir as missing to avoid any suspicions on her."

"Why? I don't get this. Sania is a hero; she stopped an attack on the country. She could have shown the video and turned over all the evidence she had on him. Why didn't she do that? She would have got a medal."

"Because of her child," Arya connected the dots. "Sania didn't want her child to shoulder the enormous pain of knowing her father was a terrorist who killed thousands of people. That is an unbearable scar for a child to carry. She put her child's happiness over a freaking medal."

Agent Taylor didn't have to say anything to confirm it; the expression on his face confirmed it. Arya was right.

"What about Eli Berg?" Edgar asked.

"He is under investigation?" Agent Taylor responded.

"Investigation? Why?"

Agent Taylor raised his right hand to gesture Arya to stop. "I don't want to get into a discussion here. I am sure you know that his real name is not Eli Berg."

"Would you have done the same if his earlier name was not a Muslim name?"

"Please, don't even imply that I am a racist." Agent Taylor glared.

"Sorry, Agent Taylor." Arya raised her hands to signal her apology. "I shouldn't have said that. What I was trying to point out is Eli's effort in this whole episode. If Eli had any terrorist links, why would he have helped Sania to stop this attack?"

"To be exact, Sania killed Samir before Eli got there. We also know the history between Eli and Sania. We know he has feelings for her."

"So, are you saying Eli is a terrorist who gave up on attacking the United States because of his love for Sania?" Arya threw her hands up as she couldn't believe the floated theory.

"Not at all. We are not saying that." Agent Taylor took a

deep breath and stared squarely at Arya. "Look, you might be right. I do agree with you that Eli might have had different reasons for changing his identity. But we can't just assume that is the case. It needs to be investigated thoroughly. The stakes are too high, and we can't take any chances here."

Arya nodded, now seeing Agent Taylor's position.

"What should we tell Mrs. Berg?" Edgar asked. "She already filed a missing person report."

"Nothing. Tell her that you are still looking, and the case is active," Agent Taylor said, before adding, "If Eli Berg is innocent, it is probably better for him not to get back to his past life now."

"Not just for his benefit, but also for his wife," LT Cooper added, implying both of them could end up being targets.

Arya and Edgar nodded in agreement.

"You both have done a tremendous job." The Chief approached the detectives. "If not for the two of you, we might have had a biological attack on our country. You both should be proud of yourself." Arya and Edgar both replied in unison, "Thanks, Chief. We just did what everyone else on the force does every day. Protect and Serve."

"Damn right. You said it better than I could have said it." The Chief smiled proudly. "What do you guys say?" The Chief glanced towards the federal agents in the office.

Everyone nodded, agreeing with the Chief's words.

Agent Taylor realized Arya's unique position in this situation, approached Arya, and looked squarely at her. "Detective, your contribution here won't be forgotten by me. Trust me, when I say it, you will hear from me in the future. You will know about your friend."

THAT WAS the last conversation Arya had with Agent Taylor. The next time she would hear from him was three weeks later. It was in the form of a mail.

After a long evening at work, which had become a routine to law enforcement officers across the country, she came home to find a brown envelope slipped under her front door. There was no address written on the envelope, nor was there any sender's name on it. It just had two words scribed boldly in the center of the envelope – AS PROMISED.

Arya's heart raced when she read those words. She immediately realized who it was from – Agent Taylor – and what the envelope might hold – information about Sania.

As her heart was beating wildly with anticipation, Arya hurriedly opened the envelope to find a single 8 x 10 photo in the envelope. There was nothing else in the envelope. When her eyes landed on the picture, a smile spread across her face. The photo showed a close-up shot of a beautiful human being — who looked so small and, at the same time, large enough to fill her heart with joy. The baby appeared to be smiling and sleeping at the same time. No one had to tell Arya whose baby was in the photo. She knew.

At the top left corner and bottom right corner of the photo, Arya noticed two sets of numbers: 35.28, -110.93. They were printed so small that Arya needed a magnifying lens to read them clearly. For a moment, she couldn't make out what the numbers were meant to be.

Arya knew the numbers had to be of significance for it to be printed on the photo. Arya pondered the meaning long and hard. *What does 35.28 and -110.93 mean?*

Arya's eyes lit up as a sudden thought dawned on her. She hurried to her office room, flipped open her laptop, and visited a mapping software that she believed could provide an answer about those random numbers.

She squinted her eyes to read the numbers and typed into

the search box on the mapping software. When the search yielded a location, she knew what she should do next.

IN THE NEXT FIFTEEN MINUTES, she made two calls; one to her partner – Edgar James – and the other to her boss – LT Cooper. She didn't tell them where she was going, nor did they ask. All she had to say was she found out where to go to get some answers, and they understood what it meant.

It was late in the evening; it was that time of the day when the sky paints itself with a rich spectrum of colors. As the time straddled between daylight and darkness, Arya stared at the sky and soaked herself in the beauty of nature. All of a sudden, everything looked beautiful.

Arya then threw her bag into the backseat and got into her car. As the engine roared, she reached across the dashboard and keyed in the destination location on the navigation system.

Leupp, Arizona.

As the music came on, the car sped past the city towards the wilderness of the west.

ACKNOWLEDGMENTS

As always, I have many people to thank for helping me bring this book to all of you.

Special thanks to my patient editor Jason, whose keen eyes made this book so much stronger. To the fantastic publishing team at Nava Waves – thanks for all the behind-the-scenes work that made the publishing experience enjoyable and seamless. I was lucky to have some excellent proofreaders and beta readers who provided valuable feedback that helped shape the novel. It has been an immense pleasure to work with everyone at Nava Waves, and I look forward to our long partnership.

Nothing is possible without my family. Without their unwavering support, I wouldn't have become a writer. The heart of my family is my wife, Indu, and my son, Akash. They have listened patiently to my ideas, even during vacations, while I worked out the plot and themes of the novel. As my first readers, they have kept me on the right path more times than I can count. Thank You for the endless love and encouragement.

To my readers, Thank You for choosing my book and giving the gift of your time. There are no words to express my deepest gratitude, and I sincerely hope you enjoyed the book. Thanks for reading.

ABOUT THE AUTHOR

Sury Patru Viswam spent twenty years advising Fortune 10 companies before retiring to pursue his true passion – writing fiction.

His debut novel, The Destiny: Embrace the Unknown, was released in February 2019 and became an international bestseller. The Hunt for Truth is his second novel.

Sury earned his master's degree in computer science from Wright State University, Ohio, and now lives in Plano, Texas, with his family. When not writing, Sury enjoys reading, traveling, and exploring life.

Find out more about Sury by visiting www. surypatruviswam.com.

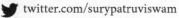 facebook.com/authorsurypatruviswam
twitter.com/surypatruviswam
instagram.com/surypatruviswam

ALSO BY SURY PATRU VISWAM

The Destiny